KUNG FU PANDA

4 KUNG FU-TASTIC TALES!

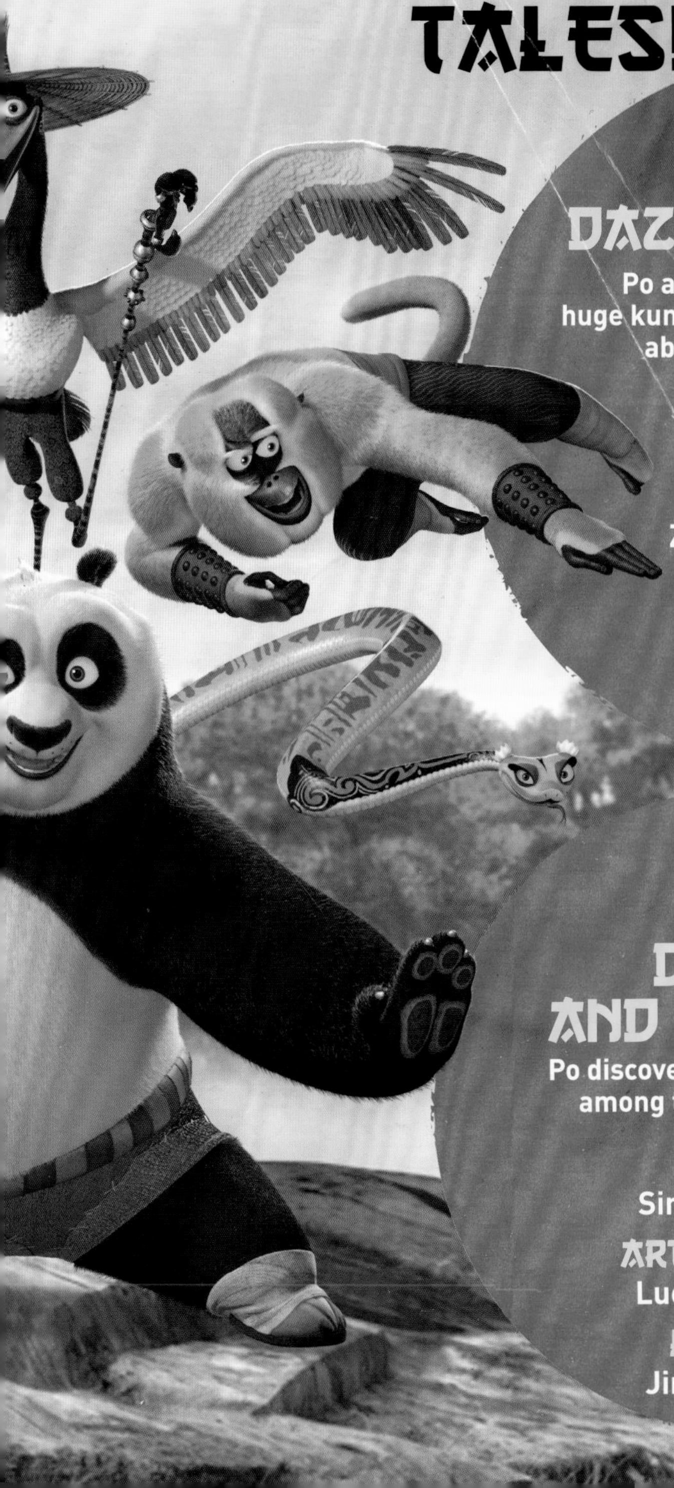

PAGE 57

DAZE OF THUNDER

Po and his friends must face a huge kung fu master gorilla who knows about elemental sorcery...

WRITER
Simon Furman

ARTIST
Zak Simmonds-Hurn

COLORS
Tracy Bailey

LETTERS
Jim Campbell

PAGE 82

DIVIDE AND CONQUER

Po discovers a possible traitor among the Furious Five...

WRITER
Simon Furman

ART & COLORS
Lucas Ferreyra

LETTERS
Jim Campbell

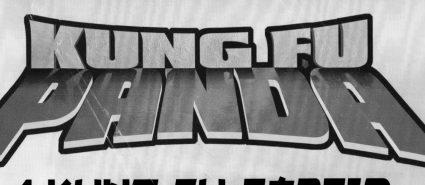

WELCOME TO THE VALLEY OF PEACE! IF YOU HAVE ANY TROUBLE, YOU MIGHT WANT TO ASK THESE GUYS FOR A BIT OF KUNG FU HELP!

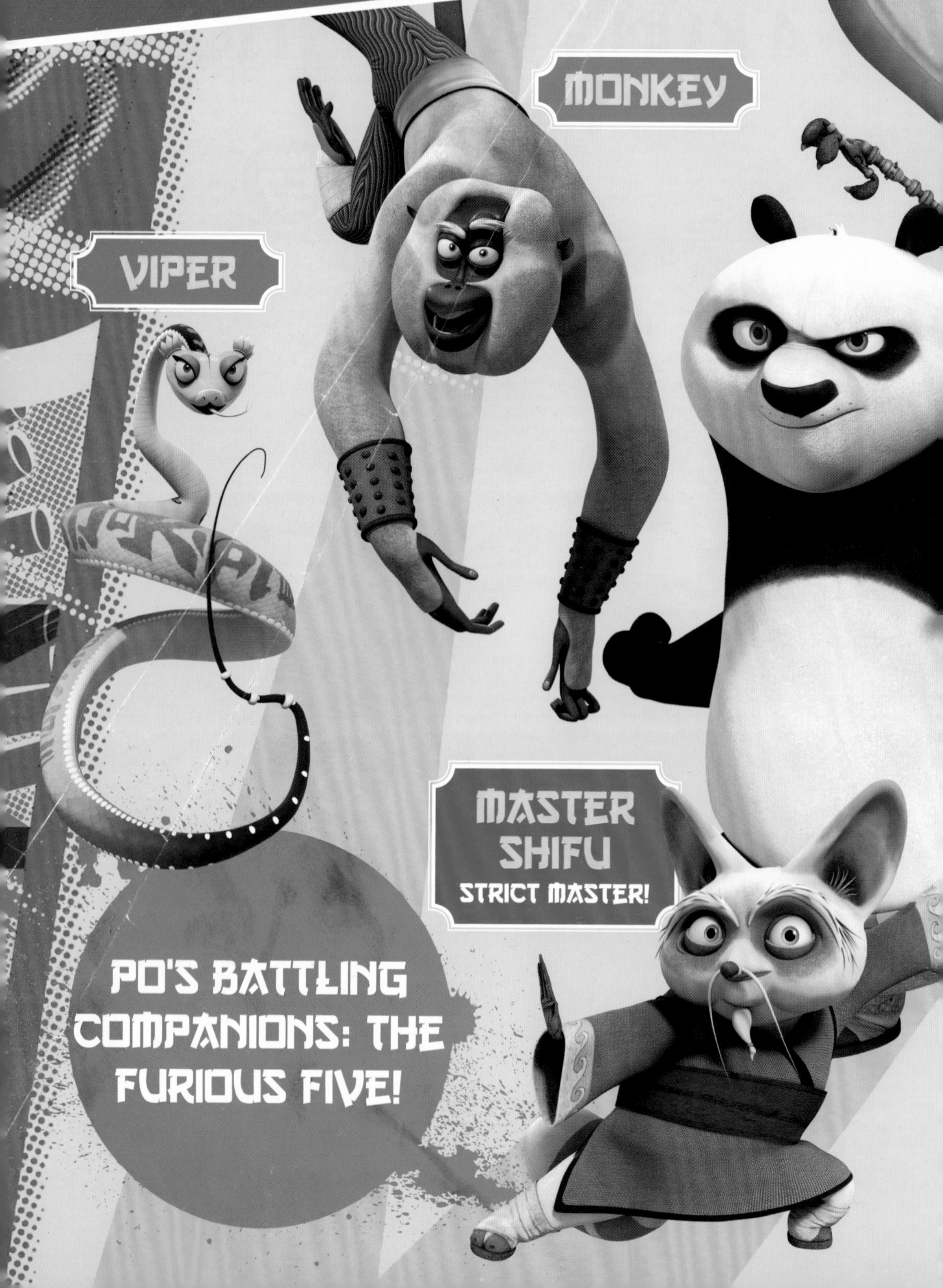
MONKEY
VIPER
MASTER SHIFU
STRICT MASTER!
PO'S BATTLING COMPANIONS: THE FURIOUS FIVE!

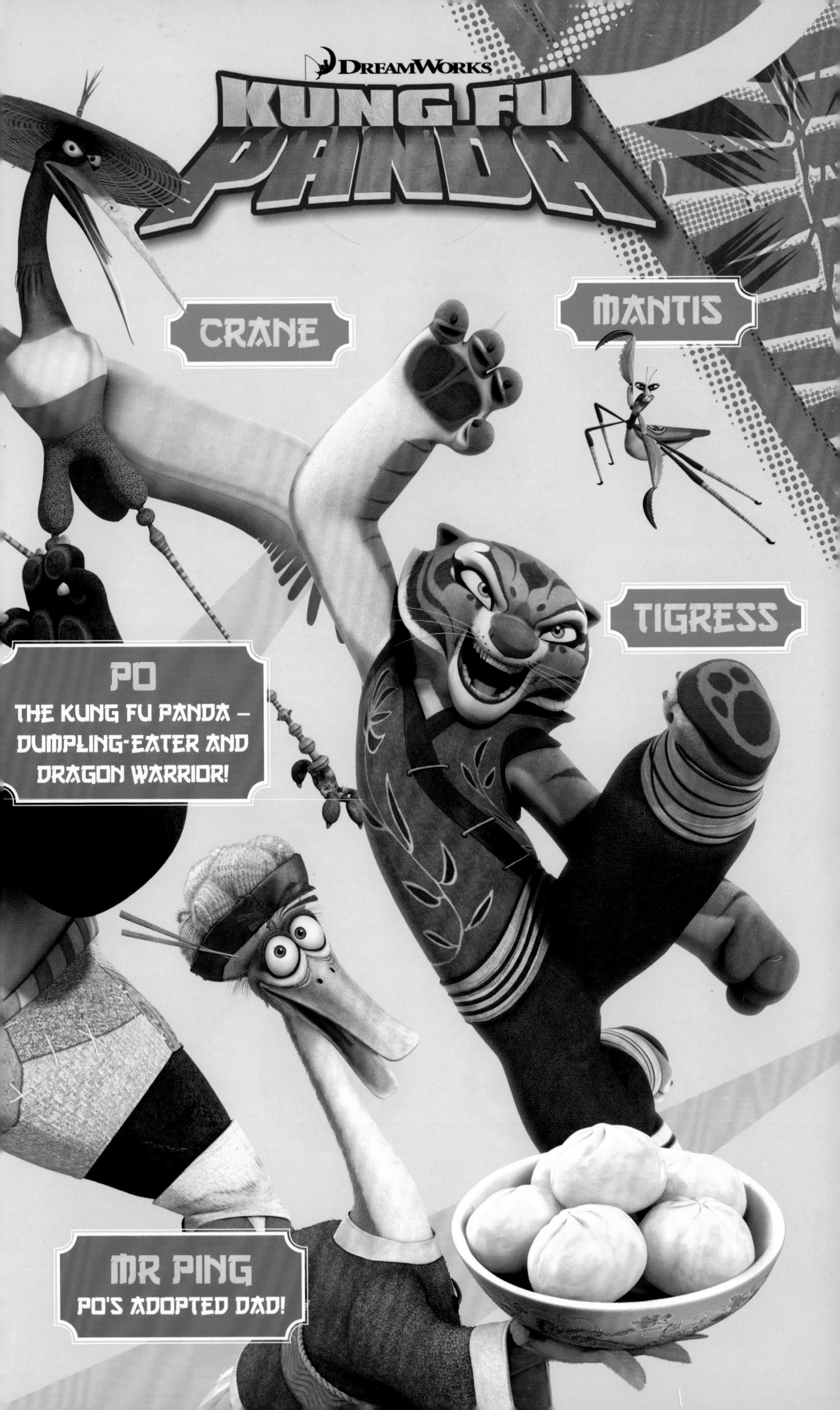
DREAMWORKS
KUNG FU PANDA
CRANE
MANTIS
TIGRESS
PO
THE KUNG FU PANDA – DUMPLING-EATER AND DRAGON WARRIOR!
MR PING
PO'S ADOPTED DAD!

WAKE ME UP BEFORE YOU PO-PO

CHAPTER 1

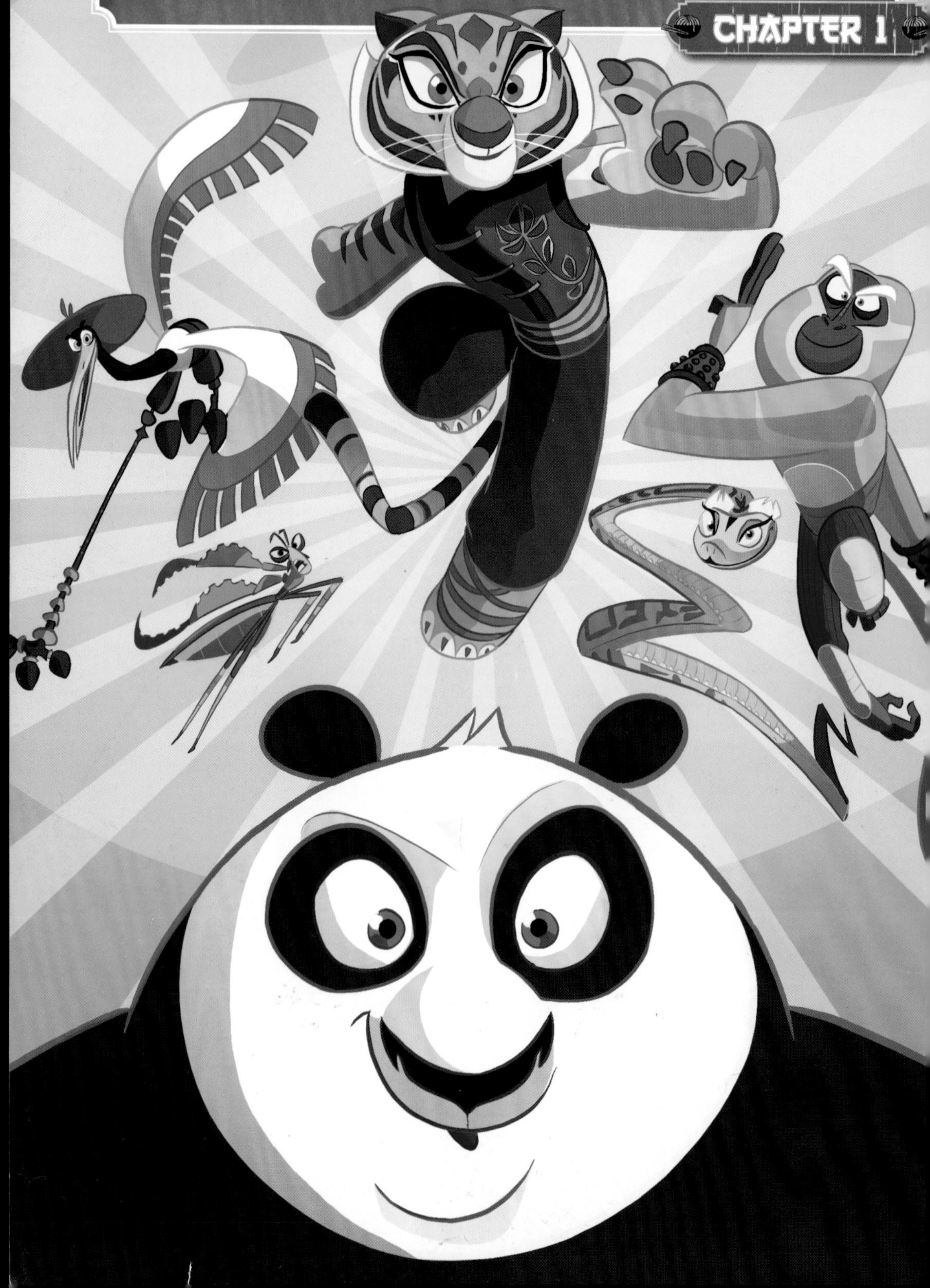

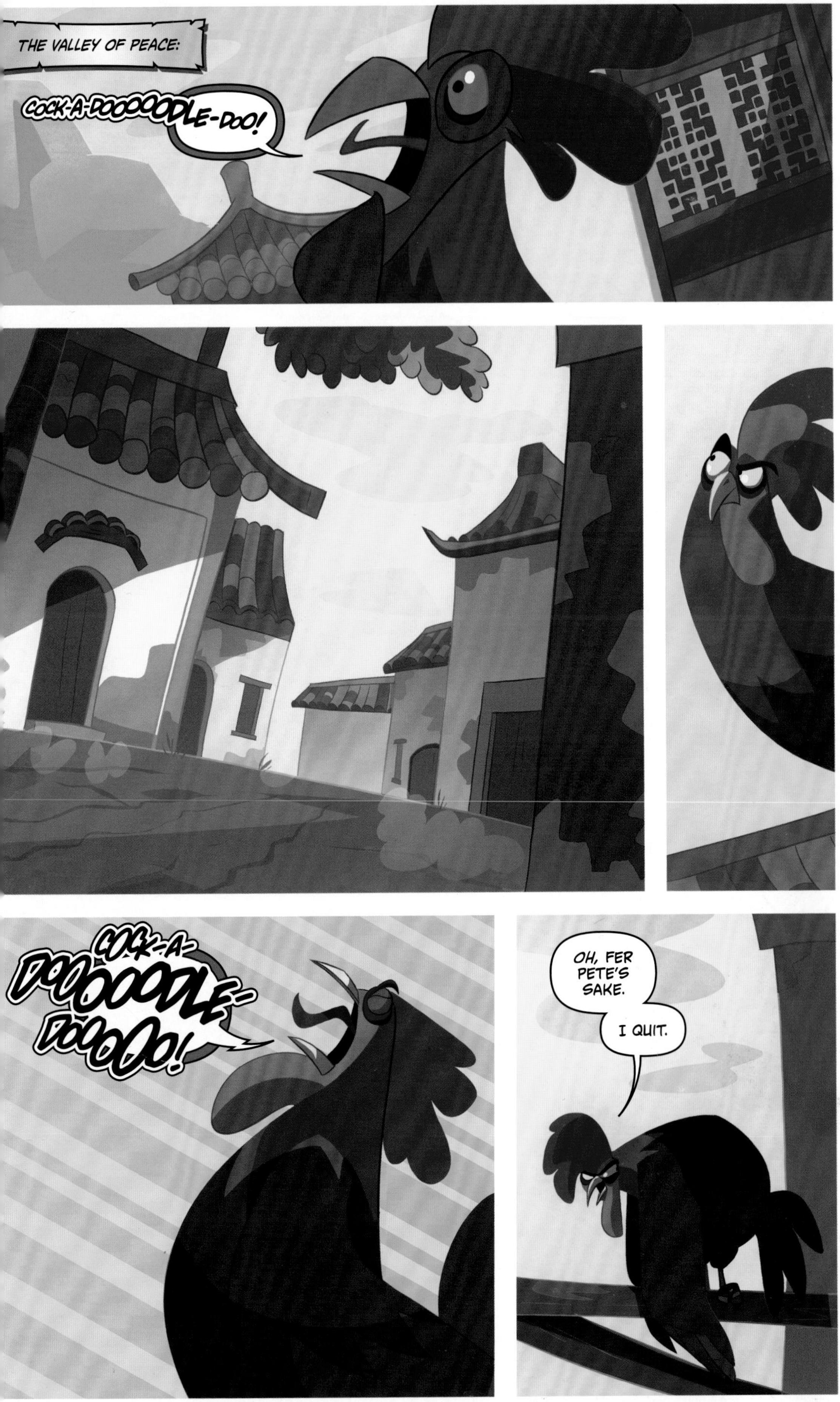
THE VALLEY OF PEACE:
COCK-A-DOOOOOODLE-DOO!
COCK-A-DOOOOODLE-DOOOOO!
OH, FER PETE'S SAKE.
I QUIT.

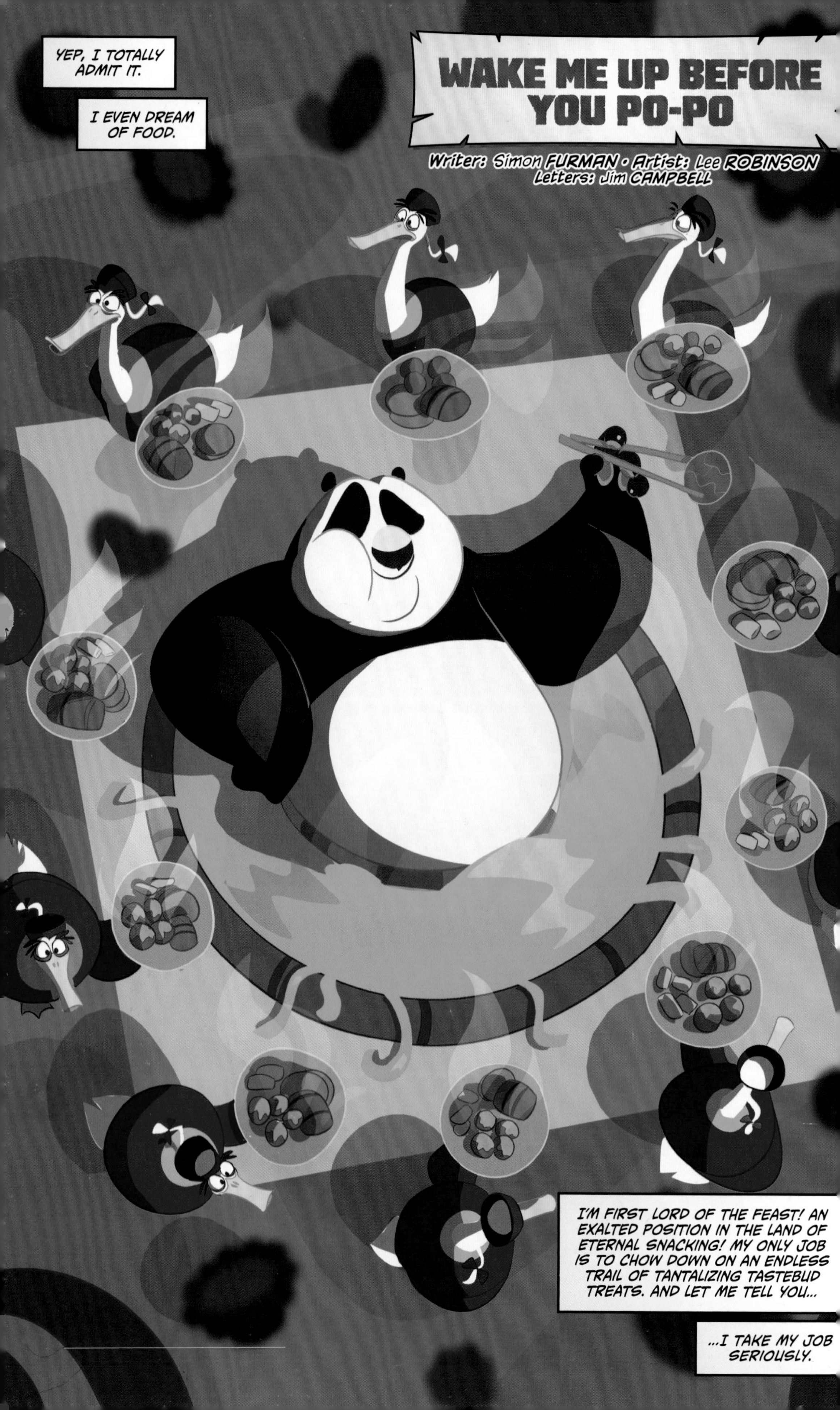

YEP, I TOTALLY ADMIT IT.
I EVEN DREAM OF FOOD.
WAKE ME UP BEFORE YOU PO-PO
Writer: Simon FURMAN • Artist: Lee ROBINSON
Letters: Jim CAMPBELL
I'M FIRST LORD OF THE FEAST! AN EXALTED POSITION IN THE LAND OF ETERNAL SNACKING! MY ONLY JOB IS TO CHOW DOWN ON AN ENDLESS TRAIL OF TANTALIZING TASTEBUD TREATS. AND LET ME TELL YOU...
...I TAKE MY JOB SERIOUSLY.

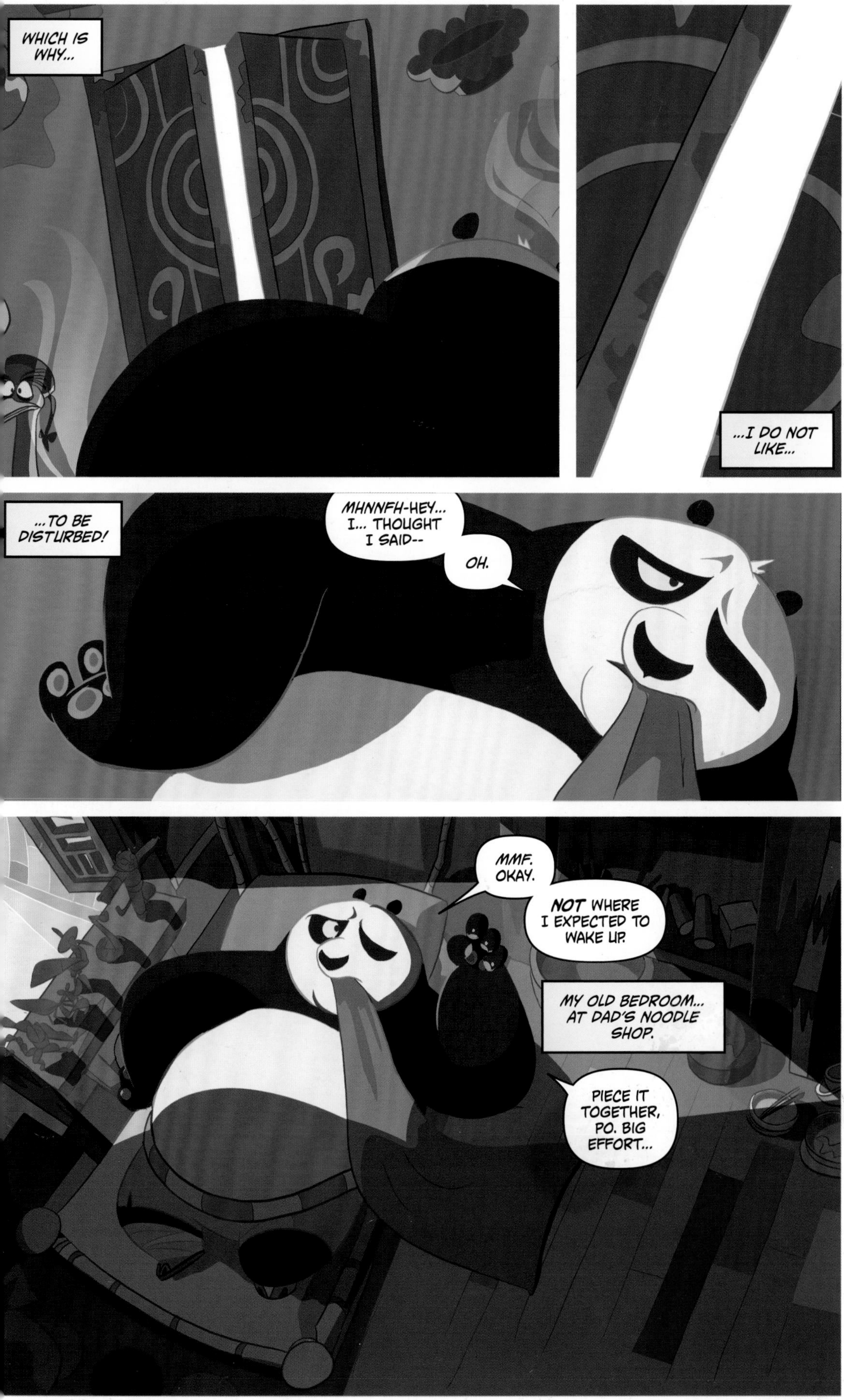

WHICH IS WHY...
...I DO NOT LIKE...
...TO BE DISTURBED!
MHNNFH-HEY... I... THOUGHT I SAID--
OH.
MMF. OKAY.
NOT WHERE I EXPECTED TO WAKE UP.
MY OLD BEDROOM... AT DAD'S NOODLE SHOP.
PIECE IT TOGETHER, PO. BIG EFFORT...

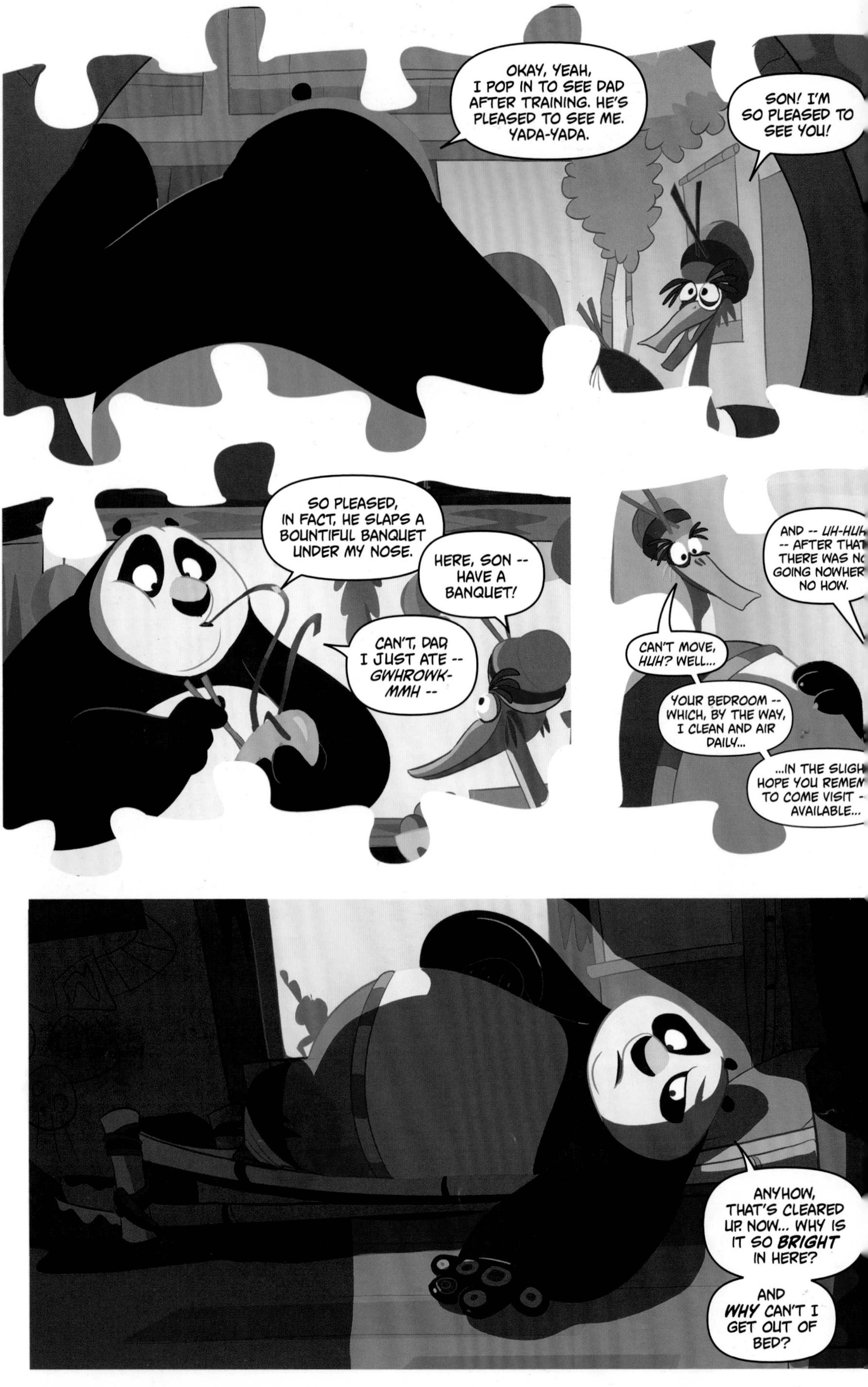
OKAY, YEAH, I POP IN TO SEE DAD AFTER TRAINING. HE'S PLEASED TO SEE ME. YADA-YADA.
SON! I'M SO PLEASED TO SEE YOU!
SO PLEASED, IN FACT, HE SLAPS A BOUNTIFUL BANQUET UNDER MY NOSE.
HERE, SON -- HAVE A BANQUET!
CAN'T, DAD. I JUST ATE -- GWHROWK-MMH --
AND -- UH-HUH -- AFTER THAT THERE WAS NO GOING NOWHERE NO HOW.
CAN'T MOVE, HUH? WELL...
YOUR BEDROOM -- WHICH, BY THE WAY, I CLEAN AND AIR DAILY...
...IN THE SLIGH HOPE YOU REMEM TO COME VISIT - AVAILABLE...
ANYHOW, THAT'S CLEARED UP. NOW... WHY IS IT SO BRIGHT IN HERE?
AND WHY CAN'T I GET OUT OF BED?

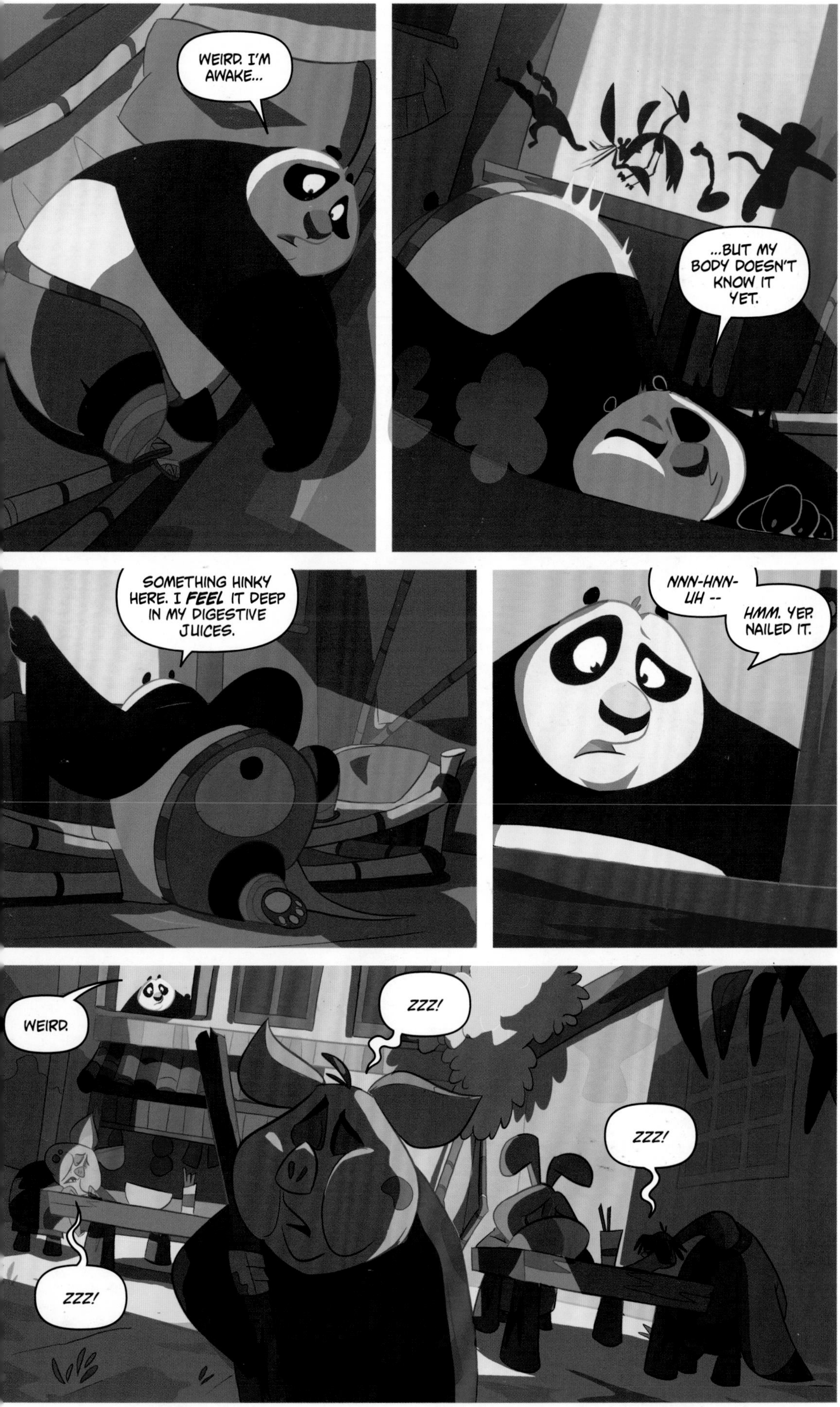
WEIRD. I'M AWAKE...
...BUT MY BODY DOESN'T KNOW IT YET.
SOMETHING HINKY HERE. I FEEL IT DEEP IN MY DIGESTIVE JUICES.
NNN-HNN-UH --
HMM. YEP. NAILED IT.
WEIRD.
ZZZ!
ZZZ!
ZZZ!

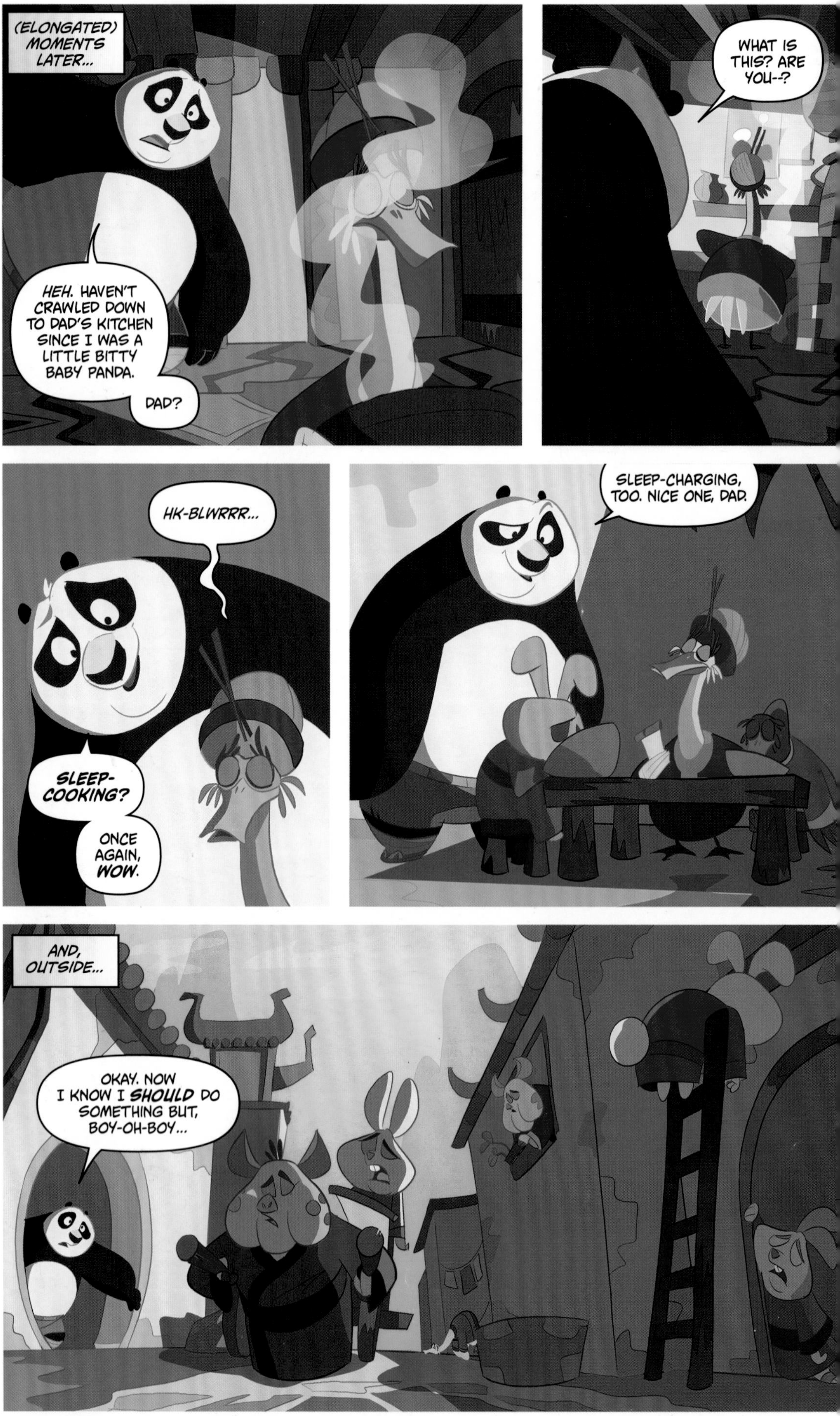
(ELONGATED) MOMENTS LATER...
HEH. HAVEN'T CRAWLED DOWN TO DAD'S KITCHEN SINCE I WAS A LITTLE BITTY BABY PANDA.
DAD?
WHAT IS THIS? ARE YOU--?
HK-BLWRRR...
SLEEP-COOKING?
ONCE AGAIN, WOW.
SLEEP-CHARGING, TOO. NICE ONE, DAD.
AND, OUTSIDE...
OKAY. NOW I KNOW I SHOULD DO SOMETHING BUT, BOY-OH-BOY...

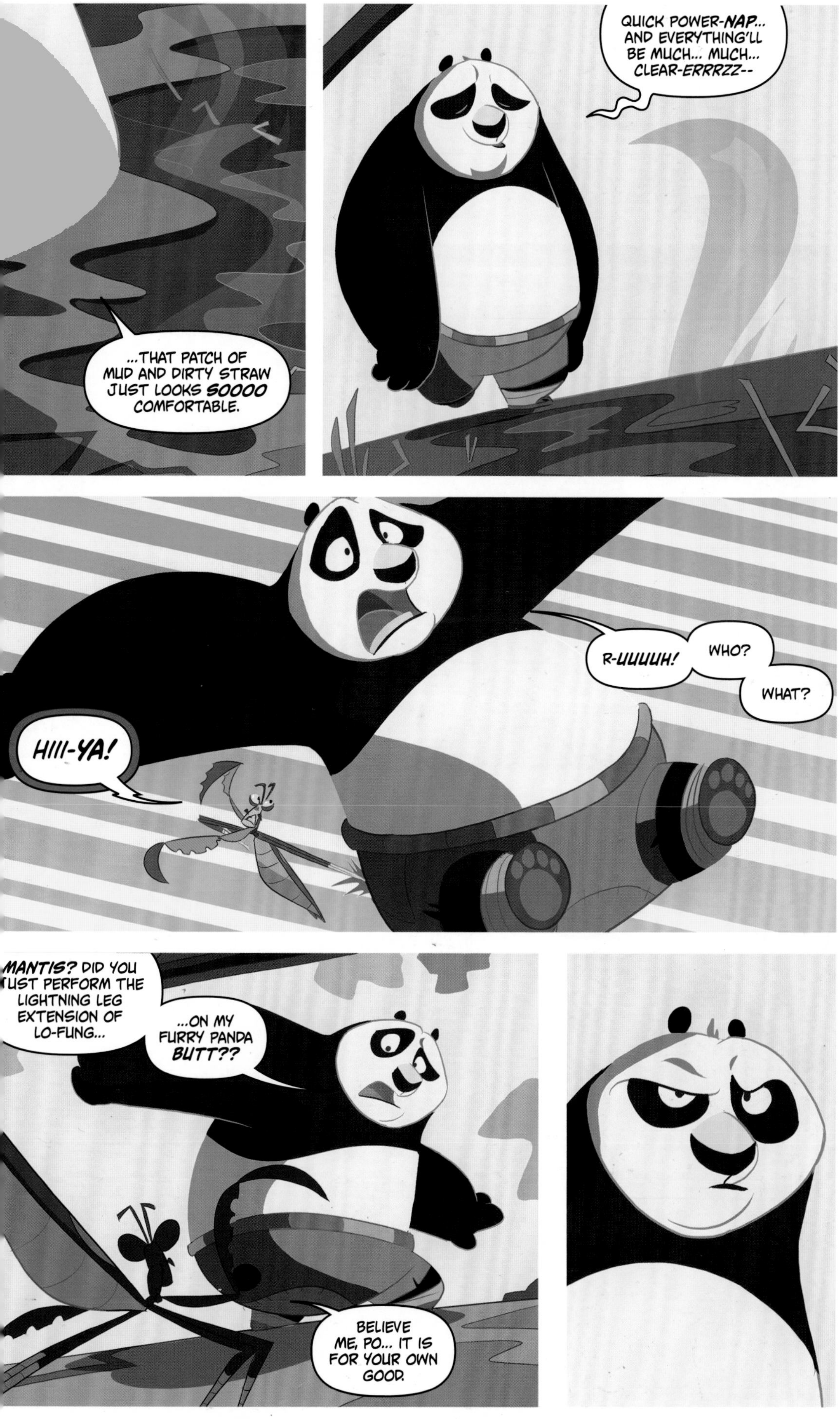
...THAT PATCH OF MUD AND DIRTY STRAW JUST LOOKS SOOOO COMFORTABLE.
QUICK POWER-NAP... AND EVERYTHING'LL BE MUCH... MUCH... CLEAR-ERRRZZ--
HIII-YA!
R-UUUUH!
WHO?
WHAT?
MANTIS? DID YOU JUST PERFORM THE LIGHTNING LEG EXTENSION OF LO-FUNG...
...ON MY FURRY PANDA BUTT??
BELIEVE ME, PO... IT IS FOR YOUR OWN GOOD.

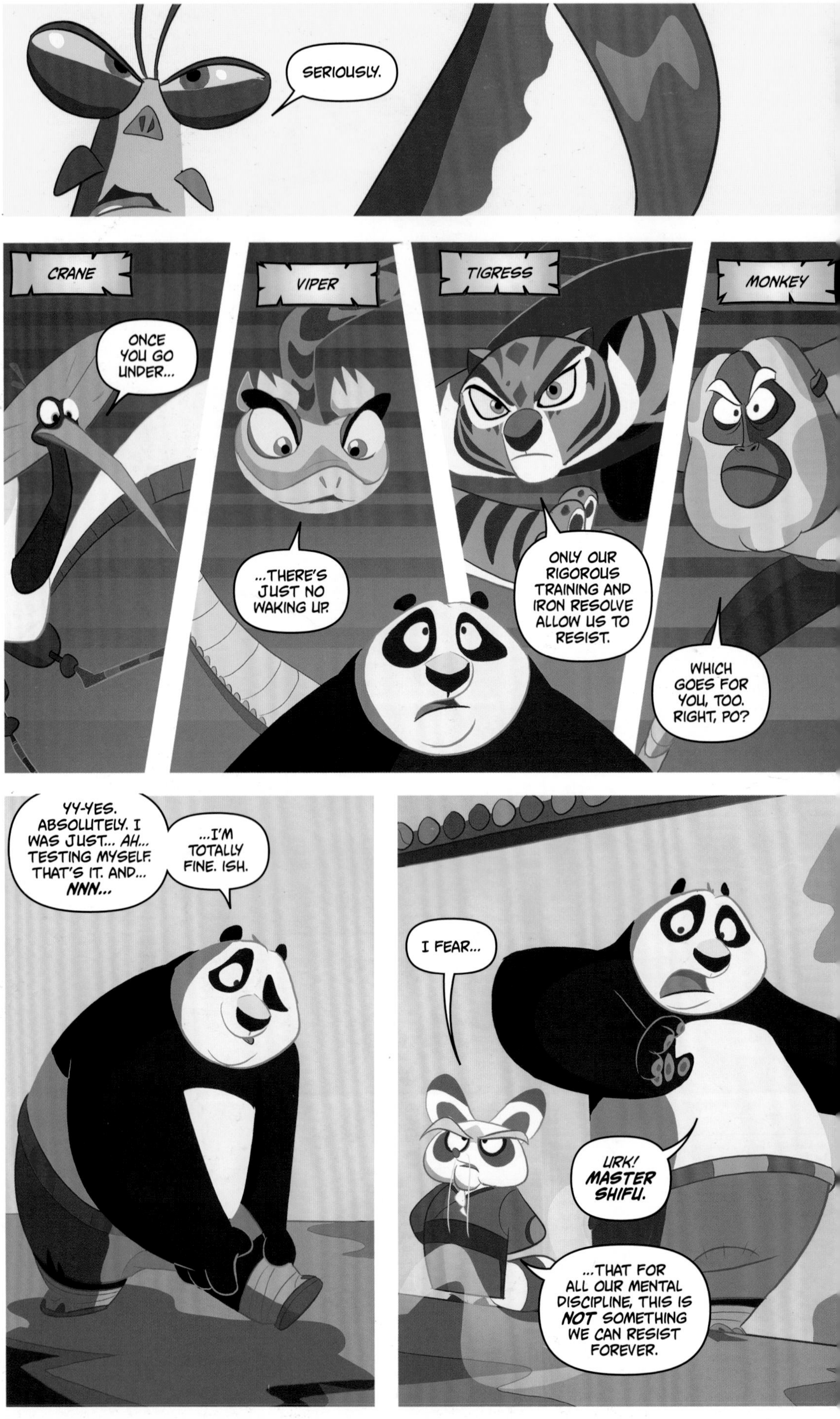
SERIOUSLY.
CRANE
ONCE YOU GO UNDER...
VIPER
...THERE'S JUST NO WAKING UP.
TIGRESS
ONLY OUR RIGOROUS TRAINING AND IRON RESOLVE ALLOW US TO RESIST.
MONKEY
WHICH GOES FOR YOU, TOO. RIGHT, PO?
YY-YES. ABSOLUTELY. I WAS JUST... AH... TESTING MYSELF. THAT'S IT. AND... NNN...
...I'M TOTALLY FINE. ISH.
I FEAR...
URK! MASTER SHIFU.
...THAT FOR ALL OUR MENTAL DISCIPLINE, THIS IS NOT SOMETHING WE CAN RESIST FOREVER.

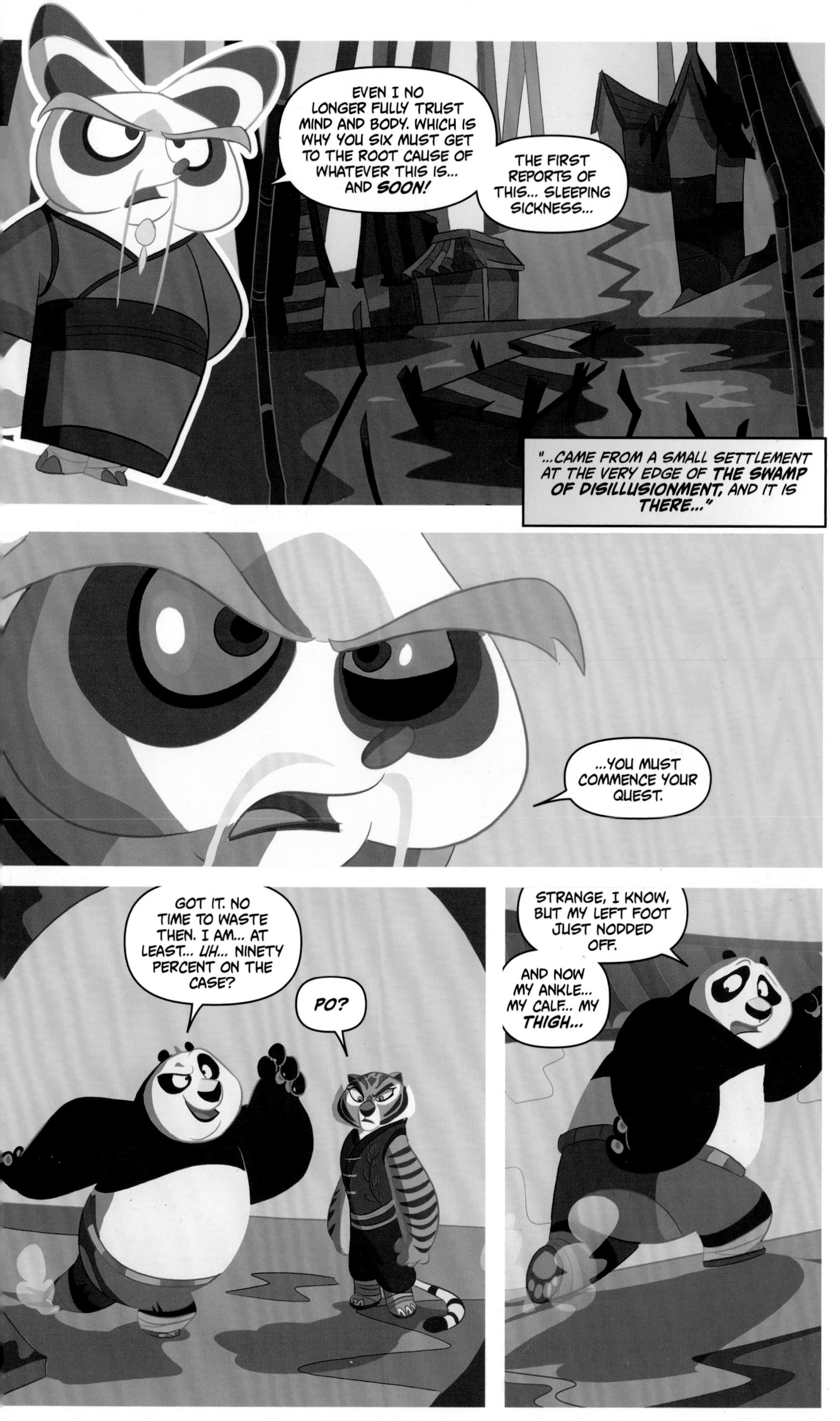
EVEN I NO LONGER FULLY TRUST MIND AND BODY. WHICH IS WHY YOU SIX MUST GET TO THE ROOT CAUSE OF WHATEVER THIS IS... AND SOON!
THE FIRST REPORTS OF THIS... SLEEPING SICKNESS...
"...CAME FROM A SMALL SETTLEMENT AT THE VERY EDGE OF THE SWAMP OF DISILLUSIONMENT, AND IT IS THERE..."
...YOU MUST COMMENCE YOUR QUEST.
GOT IT. NO TIME TO WASTE THEN. I AM... AT LEAST... UH... NINETY PERCENT ON THE CASE?
PO?
STRANGE, I KNOW, BUT MY LEFT FOOT JUST NODDED OFF.
AND NOW MY ANKLE... MY CALF... MY THIGH...

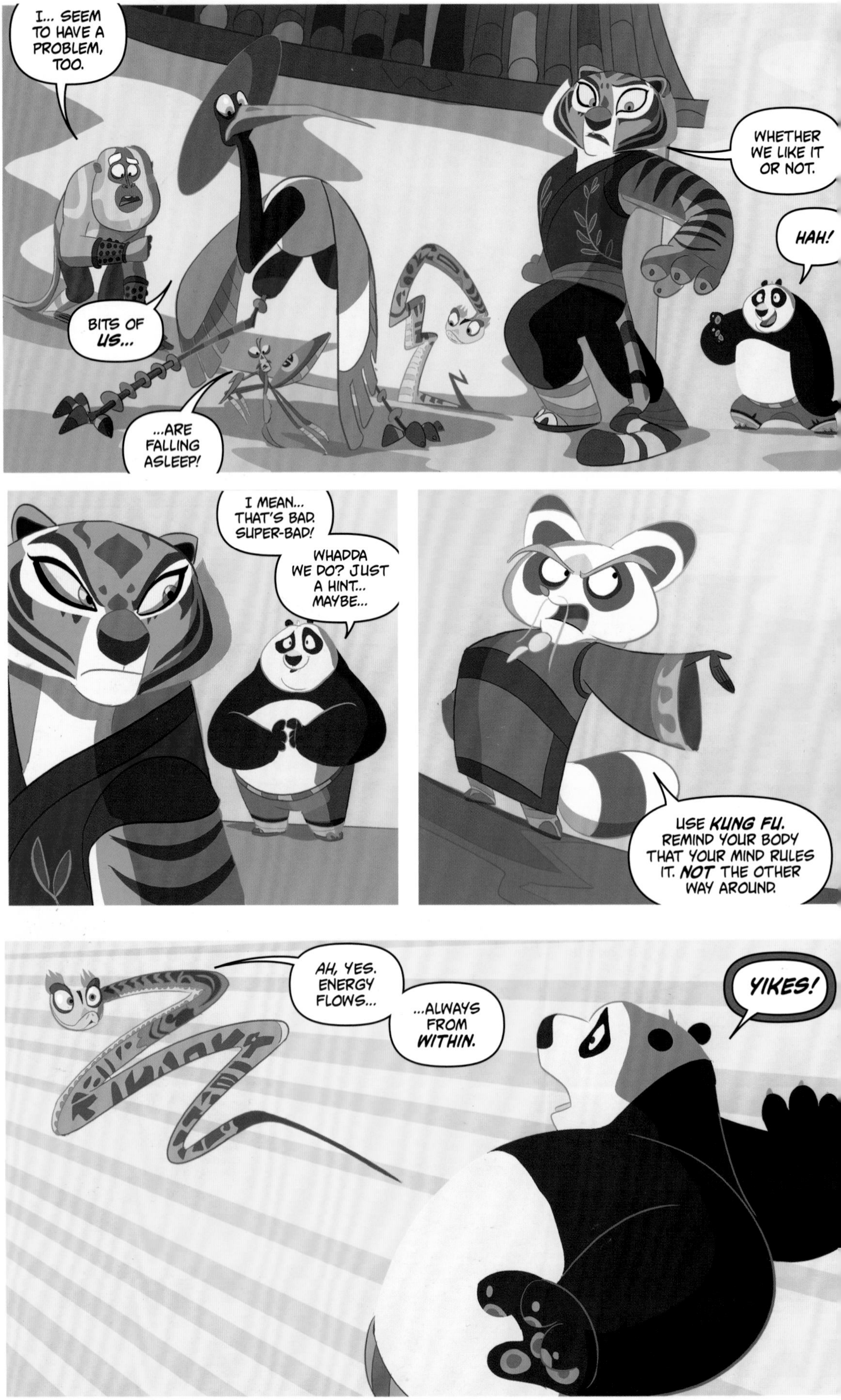
I... SEEM TO HAVE A PROBLEM, TOO.
BITS OF **US...**
...ARE FALLING ASLEEP!
WHETHER WE LIKE IT OR NOT.
HAH!
I MEAN... THAT'S BAD. SUPER-BAD!
WHADDA WE DO? JUST A HINT... MAYBE...
USE ***KUNG FU.*** REMIND YOUR BODY THAT YOUR MIND RULES IT. ***NOT*** THE OTHER WAY AROUND.
AH, YES. ENERGY FLOWS...
...ALWAYS FROM ***WITHIN.***
YIKES!

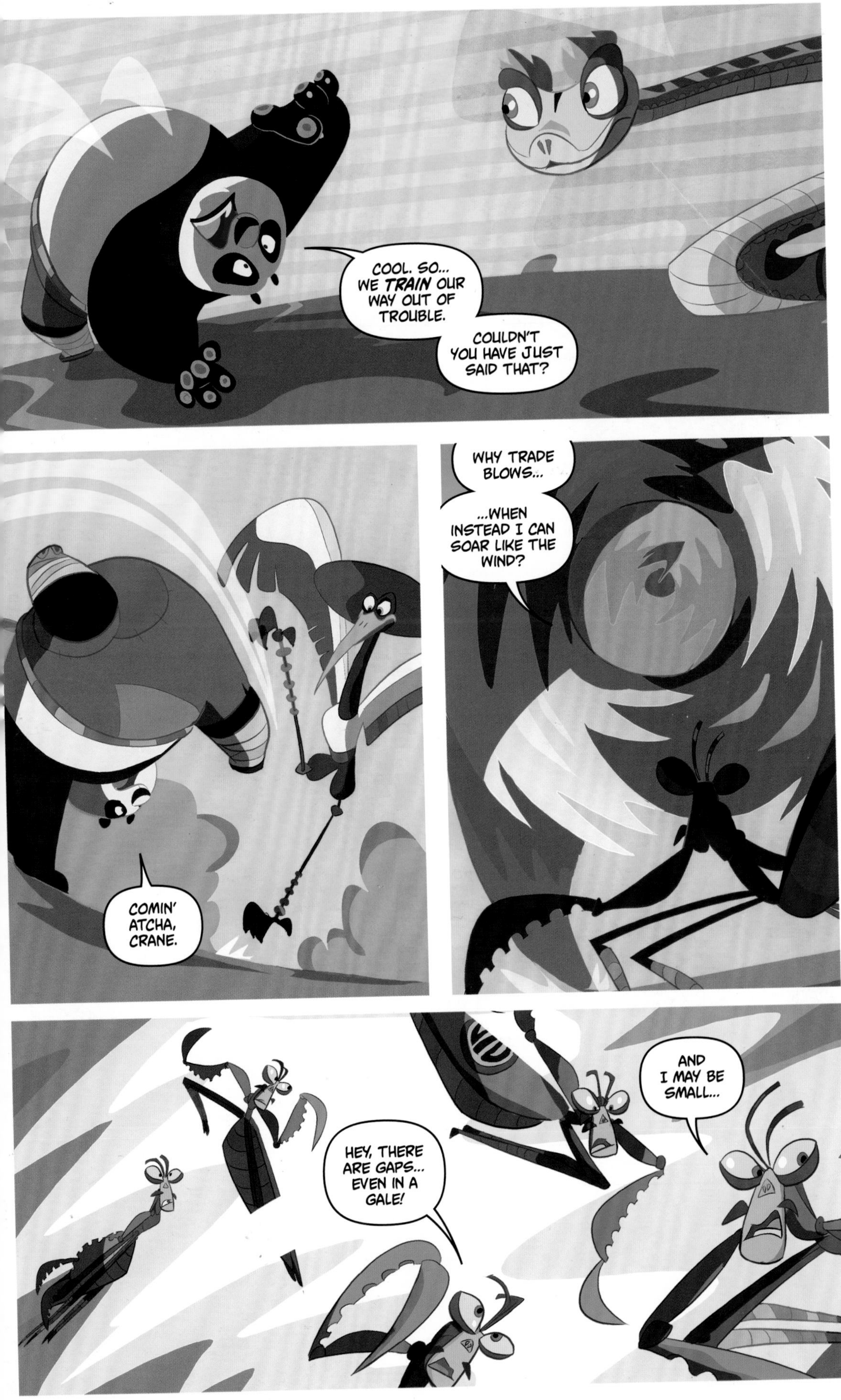

COOL. SO... WE *TRAIN* OUR WAY OUT OF TROUBLE.
COULDN'T YOU HAVE JUST SAID THAT?
COMIN' ATCHA, CRANE.
WHY TRADE BLOWS...
...WHEN INSTEAD I CAN SOAR LIKE THE WIND?
HEY, THERE ARE GAPS... EVEN IN A GALE!
AND I MAY BE SMALL...

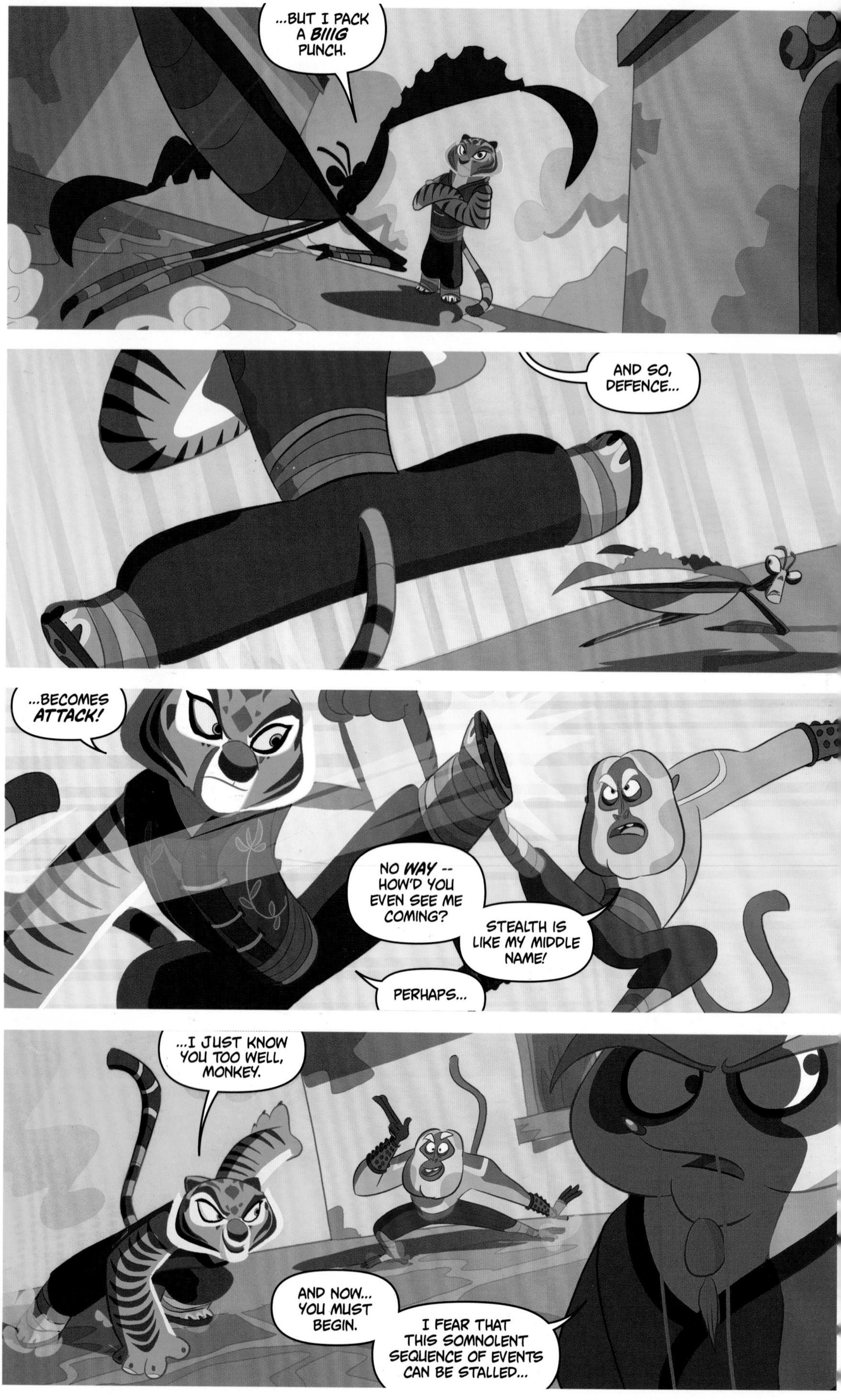
...BUT I PACK A BIIIG PUNCH.
AND SO, DEFENCE...
...BECOMES ATTACK!
NO WAY -- HOW'D YOU EVEN SEE ME COMING?
STEALTH IS LIKE MY MIDDLE NAME!
PERHAPS...
...I JUST KNOW YOU TOO WELL, MONKEY.
AND NOW... YOU MUST BEGIN.
I FEAR THAT THIS SOMNOLENT SEQUENCE OF EVENTS CAN BE STALLED...

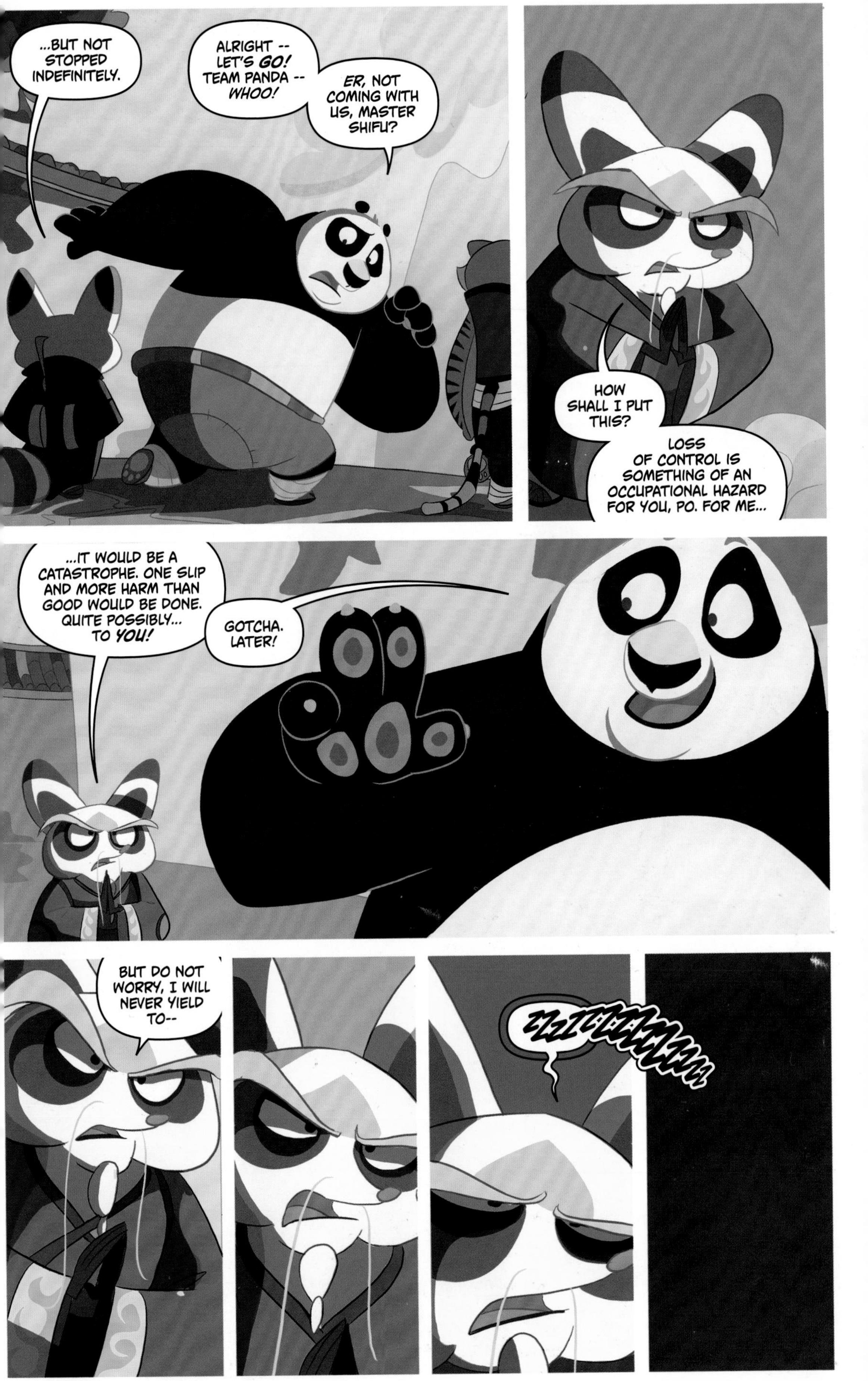
...BUT NOT STOPPED INDEFINITELY.
ALRIGHT -- LET'S GO! TEAM PANDA -- WHOO!
ER, NOT COMING WITH US, MASTER SHIFU?
HOW SHALL I PUT THIS?
LOSS OF CONTROL IS SOMETHING OF AN OCCUPATIONAL HAZARD FOR YOU, PO. FOR ME...
...IT WOULD BE A CATASTROPHE. ONE SLIP AND MORE HARM THAN GOOD WOULD BE DONE. QUITE POSSIBLY... TO YOU!
GOTCHA. LATER!
BUT DO NOT WORRY, I WILL NEVER YIELD TO--
ZZZZZZZZZZZZZZZZ

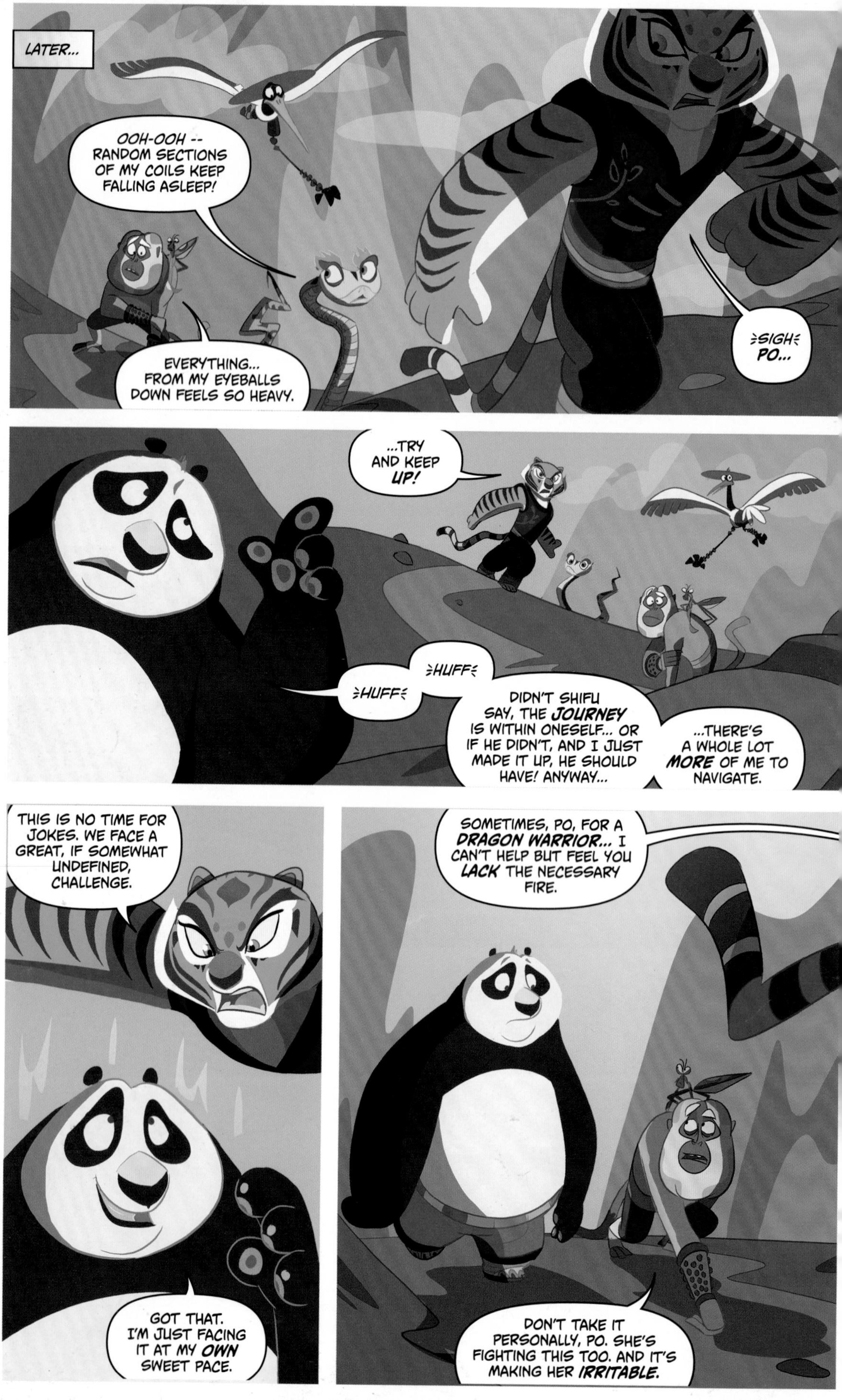
LATER...
OOH-OOH -- RANDOM SECTIONS OF MY COILS KEEP FALLING ASLEEP!
EVERYTHING... FROM MY EYEBALLS DOWN FEELS SO HEAVY.
SIGH PO...
...TRY AND KEEP UP!
HUFF
HUFF
DIDN'T SHIFU SAY, THE JOURNEY IS WITHIN ONESELF... OR IF HE DIDN'T, AND I JUST MADE IT UP, HE SHOULD HAVE! ANYWAY...
...THERE'S A WHOLE LOT MORE OF ME TO NAVIGATE.
THIS IS NO TIME FOR JOKES. WE FACE A GREAT, IF SOMEWHAT UNDEFINED, CHALLENGE.
GOT THAT. I'M JUST FACING IT AT MY OWN SWEET PACE.
SOMETIMES, PO, FOR A DRAGON WARRIOR... I CAN'T HELP BUT FEEL YOU LACK THE NECESSARY FIRE.
DON'T TAKE IT PERSONALLY, PO. SHE'S FIGHTING THIS TOO. AND IT'S MAKING HER IRRITABLE.

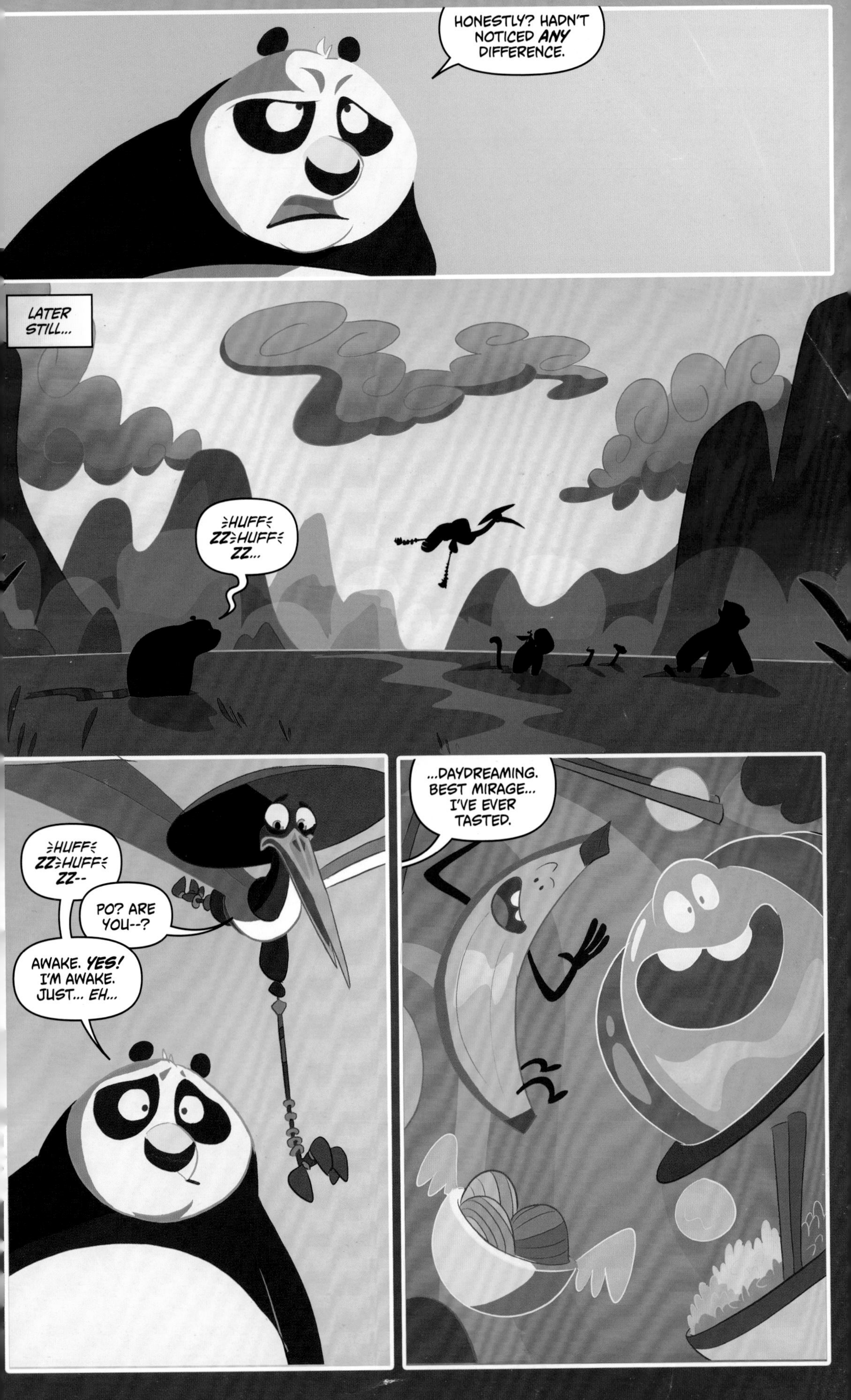
HONESTLY? HADN'T NOTICED ANY DIFFERENCE.
LATER STILL...
HUFF ZZ HUFF ZZ...
HUFF ZZ HUFF ZZ--
PO? ARE YOU--?
AWAKE. YES! I'M AWAKE. JUST... EH...
...DAYDREAMING. BEST MIRAGE... I'VE EVER TASTED.

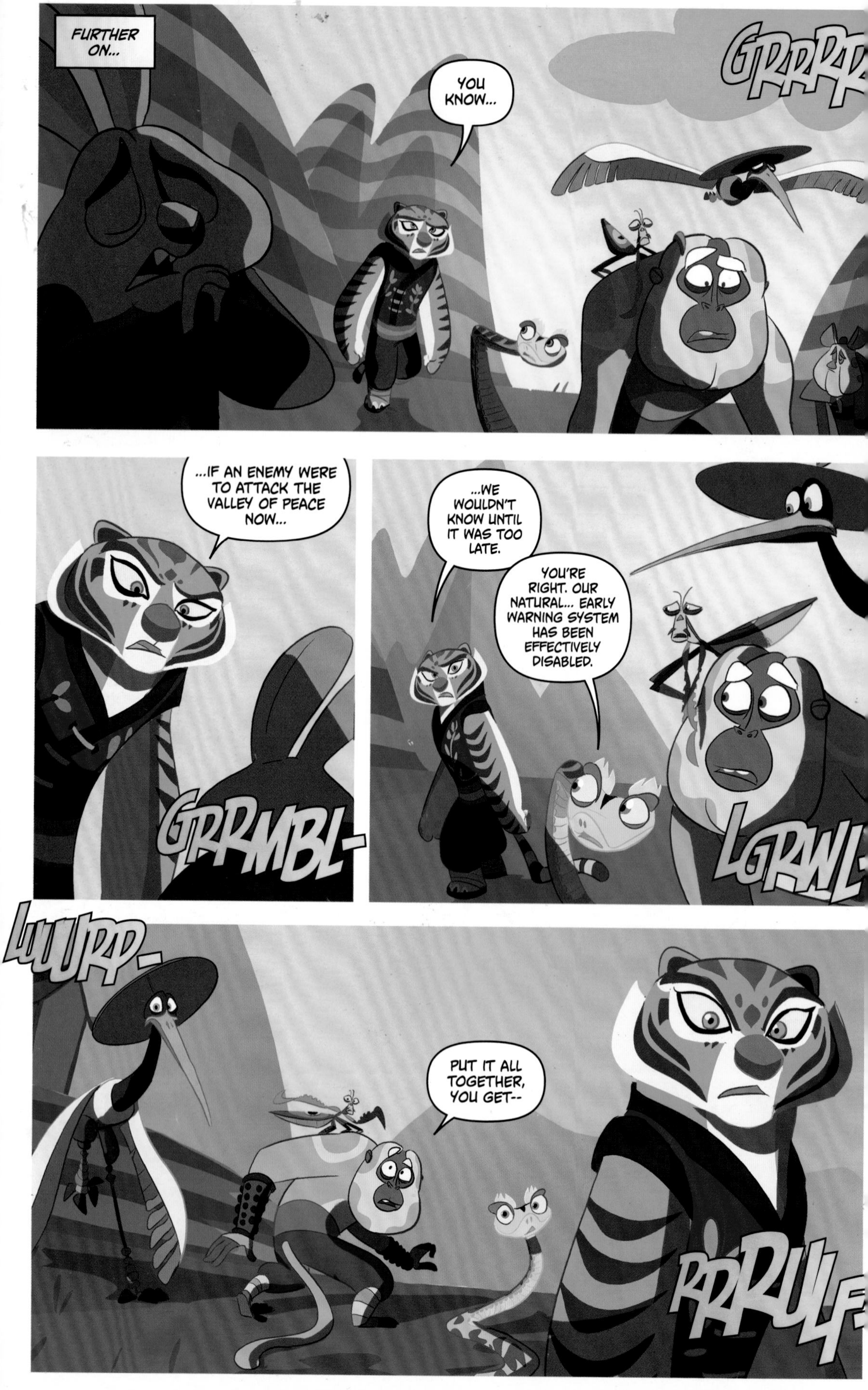
FURTHER ON...
YOU KNOW...
GRRRRR
...IF AN ENEMY WERE TO ATTACK THE VALLEY OF PEACE NOW...
GRRMBL-
...WE WOULDN'T KNOW UNTIL IT WAS TOO LATE.
YOU'RE RIGHT. OUR NATURAL... EARLY WARNING SYSTEM HAS BEEN EFFECTIVELY DISABLED.
LGRWL-
LUUURP-
PUT IT ALL TOGETHER, YOU GET--
RRRULF-

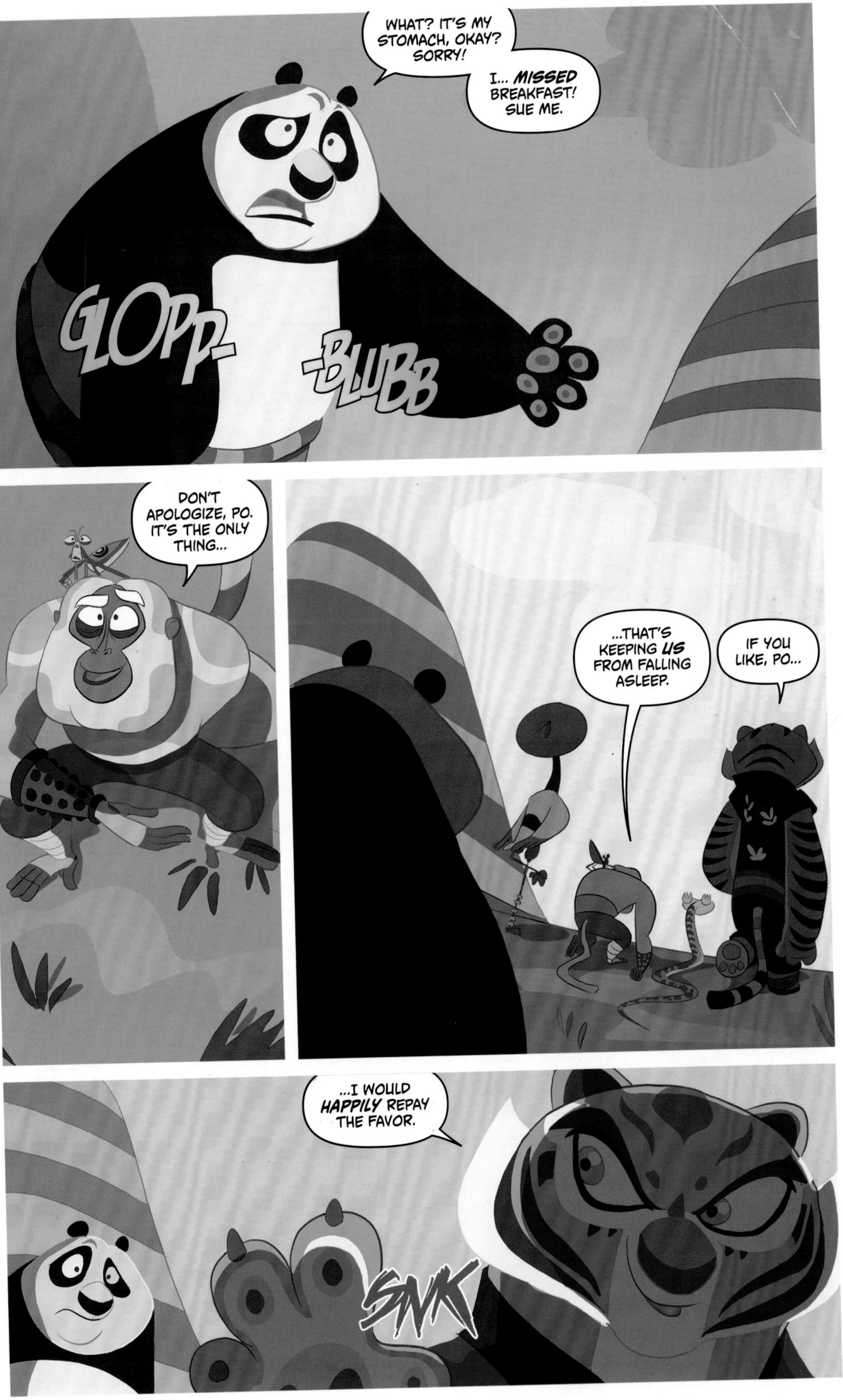
WHAT? IT'S MY STOMACH, OKAY? SORRY!
I... MISSED BREAKFAST! SUE ME.
GLOPP-
-BLUBB
DON'T APOLOGIZE, PO. IT'S THE ONLY THING...
...THAT'S KEEPING US FROM FALLING ASLEEP.
IF YOU LIKE, PO...
...I WOULD HAPPILY REPAY THE FAVOR.
SNK

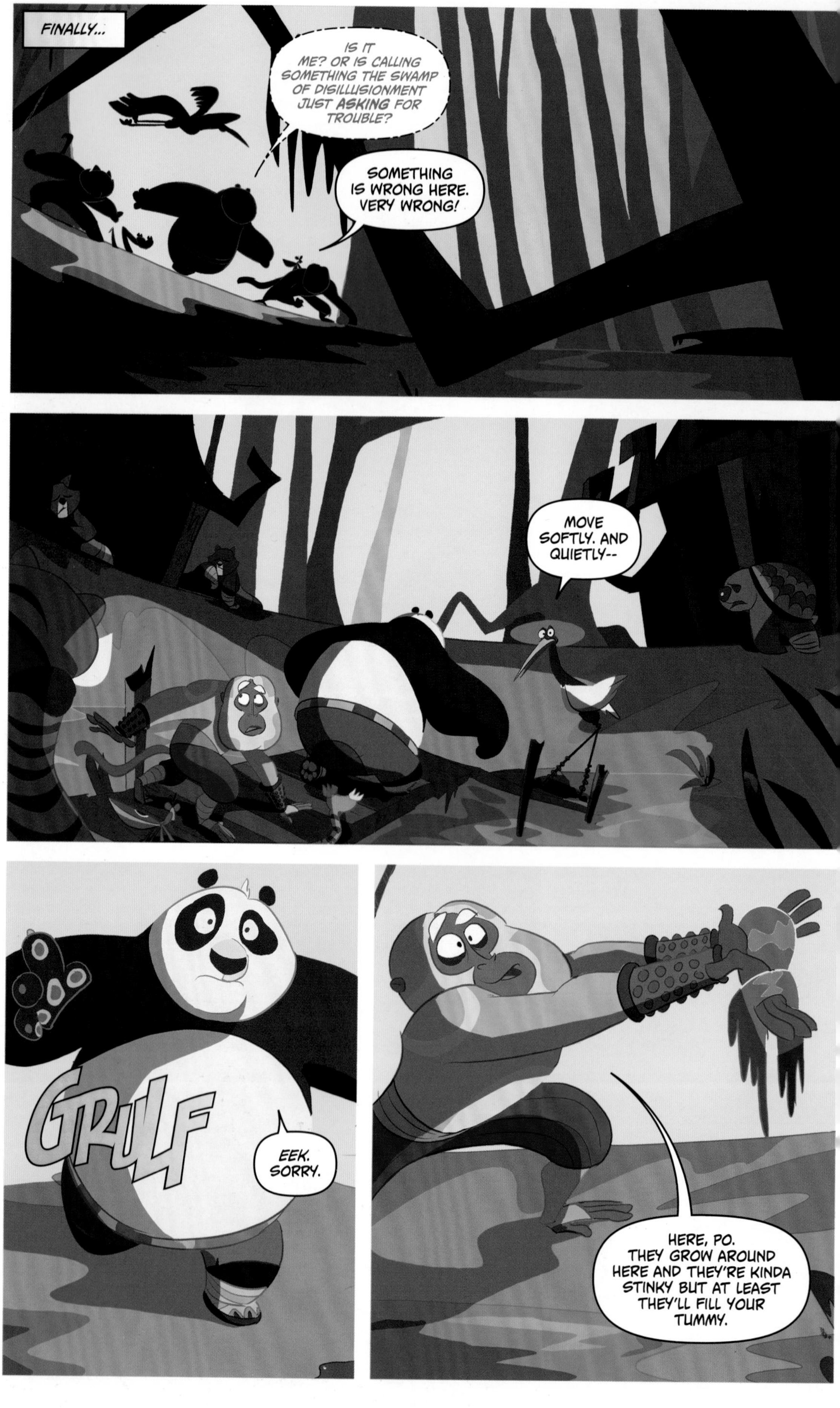
FINALLY...
IS IT ME? OR IS CALLING SOMETHING THE SWAMP OF DISILLUSIONMENT JUST ASKING FOR TROUBLE?
SOMETHING IS WRONG HERE. VERY WRONG!
MOVE SOFTLY. AND QUIETLY--
GRUMF
EEK. SORRY.
HERE, PO. THEY GROW AROUND HERE AND THEY'RE KINDA STINKY BUT AT LEAST THEY'LL FILL YOUR TUMMY.

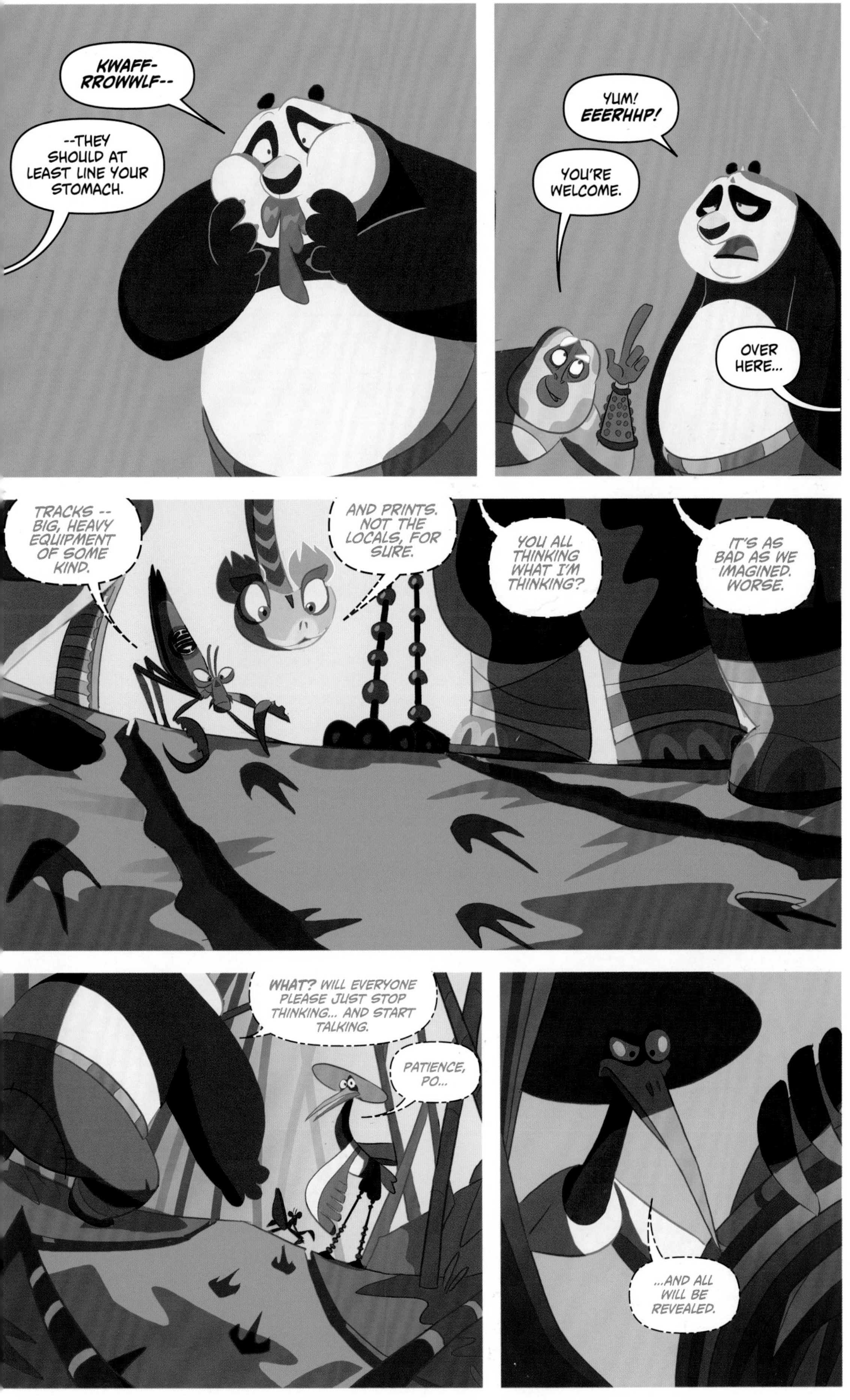
KWAFF-
RROWWLF--
--THEY SHOULD AT LEAST LINE YOUR STOMACH.
YUM! EEERHHP!
YOU'RE WELCOME.
OVER HERE...
TRACKS -- BIG, HEAVY EQUIPMENT OF SOME KIND.
AND PRINTS. NOT THE LOCALS, FOR SURE.
YOU ALL THINKING WHAT I'M THINKING?
IT'S AS BAD AS WE IMAGINED. WORSE.
WHAT? WILL EVERYONE PLEASE JUST STOP THINKING... AND START TALKING.
PATIENCE, PO...
...AND ALL WILL BE REVEALED.

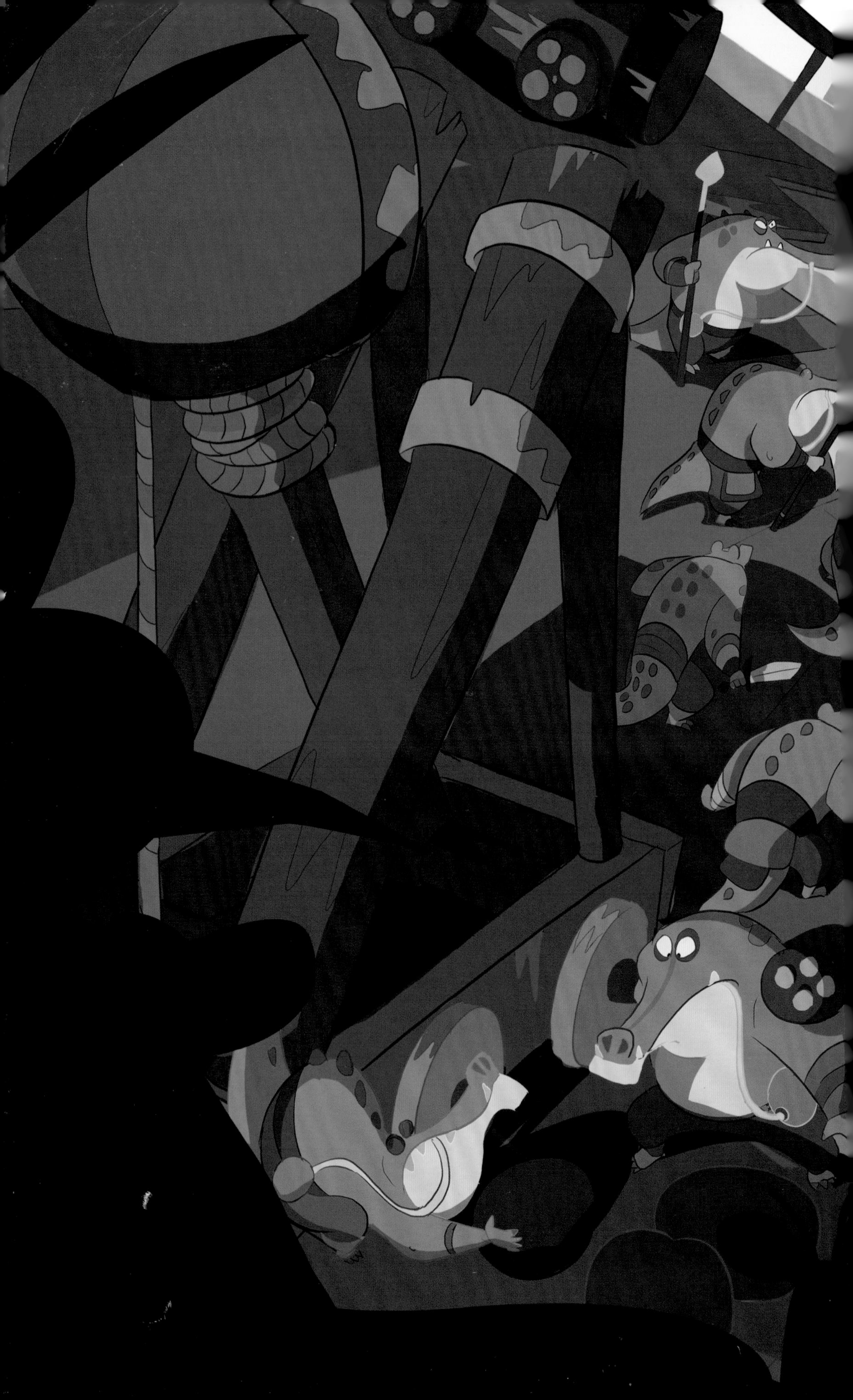

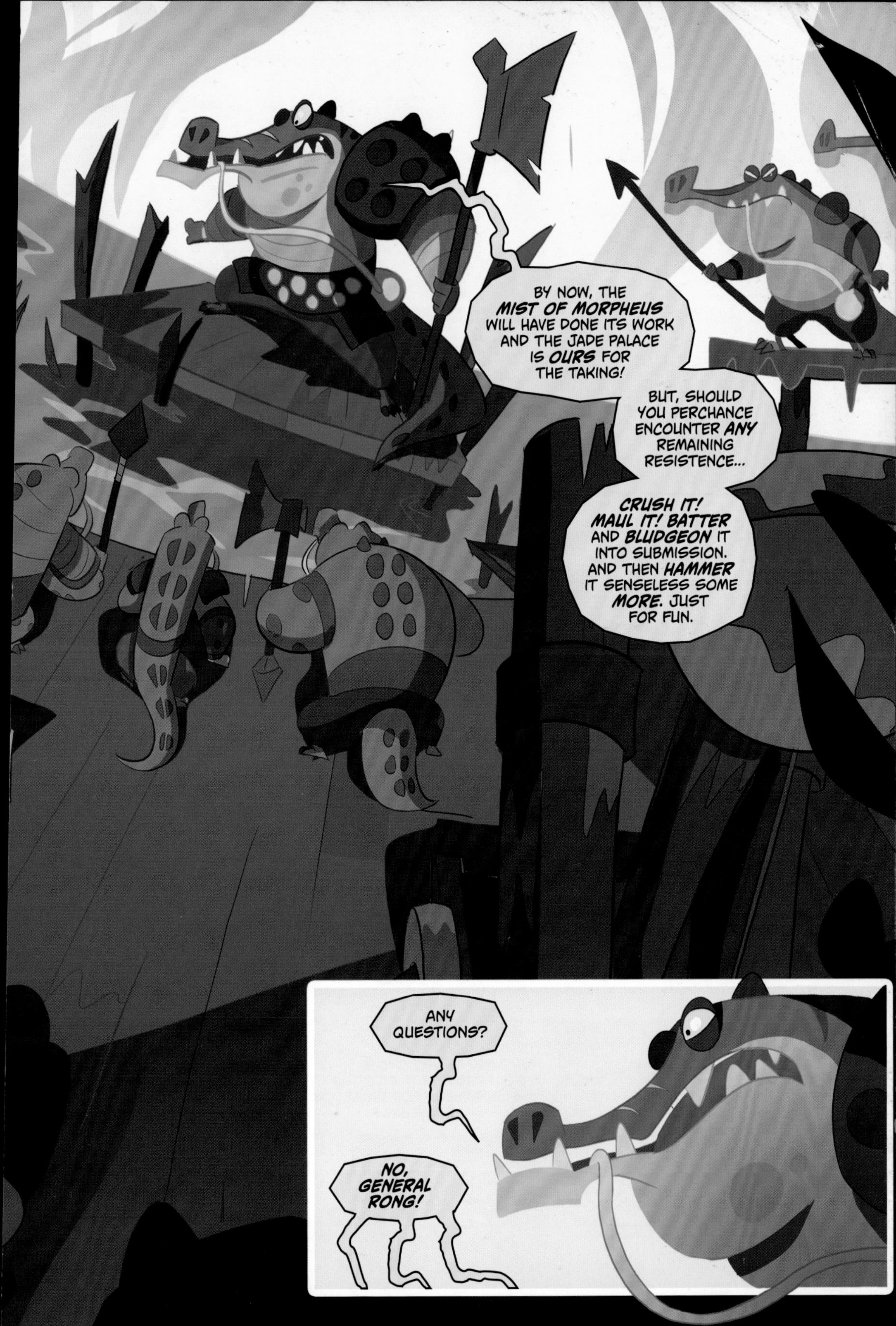
BY NOW, THE MIST OF MORPHEUS WILL HAVE DONE ITS WORK AND THE JADE PALACE IS OURS FOR THE TAKING!
BUT, SHOULD YOU PERCHANCE ENCOUNTER ANY REMAINING RESISTENCE...
CRUSH IT! MAUL IT! BATTER AND BLUDGEON IT INTO SUBMISSION. AND THEN HAMMER IT SENSELESS SOME MORE. JUST FOR FUN.
ANY QUESTIONS?
NO, GENERAL RONG!

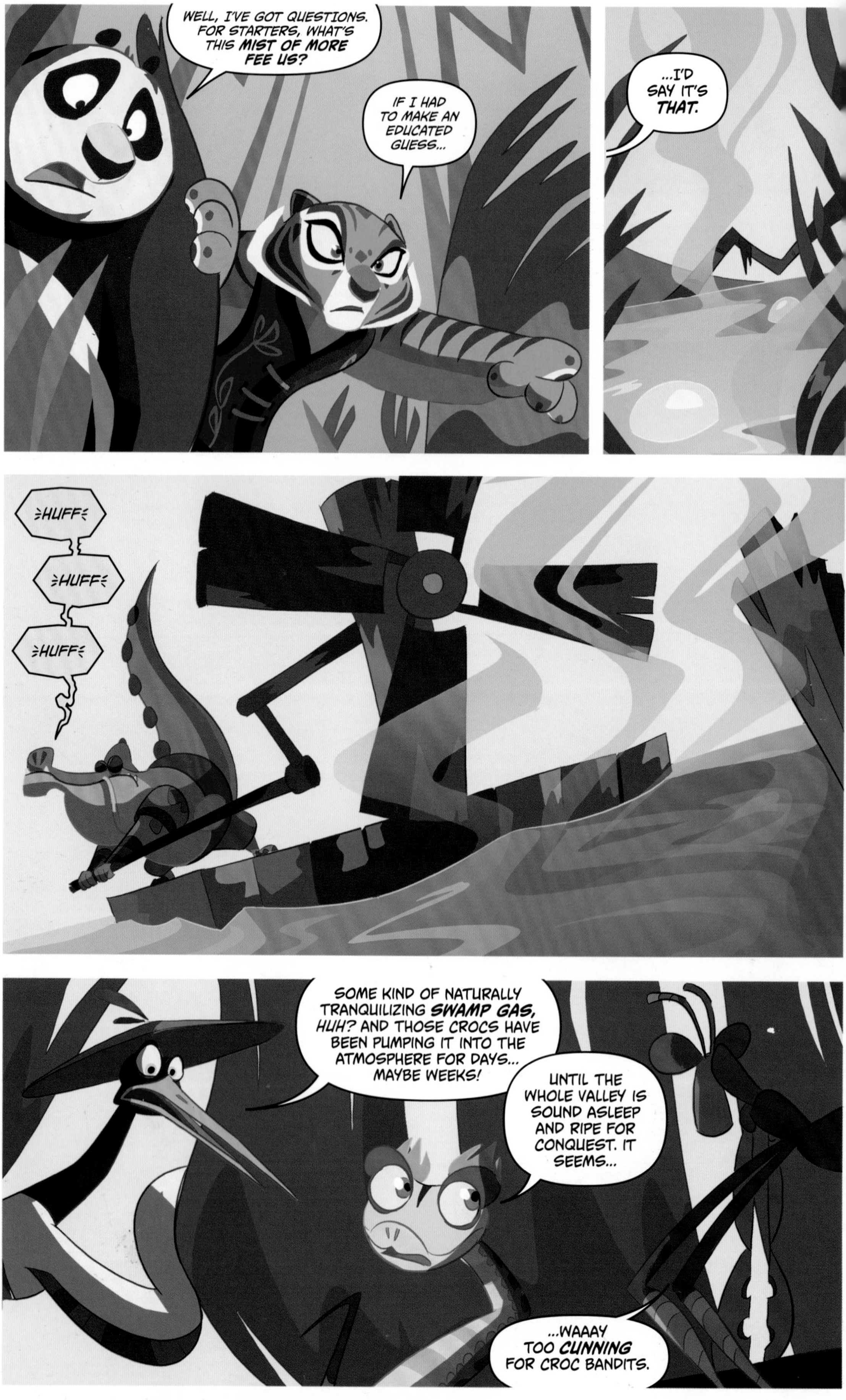
WELL, I'VE GOT QUESTIONS. FOR STARTERS, WHAT'S THIS MIST OF MORE FEE US?
IF I HAD TO MAKE AN EDUCATED GUESS...
...I'D SAY IT'S THAT.
HUFF
HUFF
HUFF
SOME KIND OF NATURALLY TRANQUILIZING SWAMP GAS, HUH? AND THOSE CROCS HAVE BEEN PUMPING IT INTO THE ATMOSPHERE FOR DAYS... MAYBE WEEKS!
UNTIL THE WHOLE VALLEY IS SOUND ASLEEP AND RIPE FOR CONQUEST. IT SEEMS...
...WAAAY TOO CUNNING FOR CROC BANDITS.

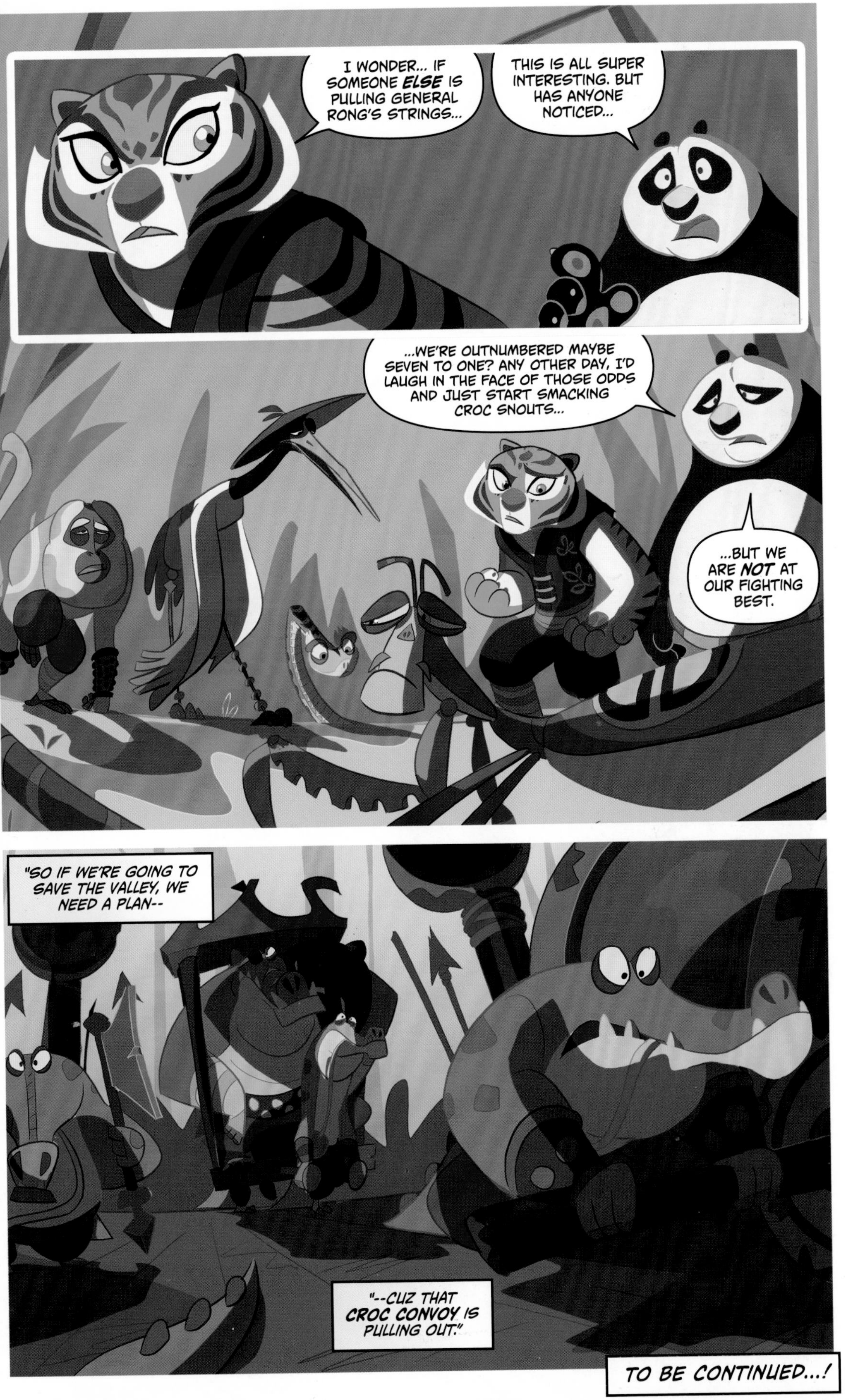
I WONDER... IF SOMEONE *ELSE* IS PULLING GENERAL RONG'S STRINGS...
THIS IS ALL SUPER INTERESTING. BUT HAS ANYONE NOTICED...
...WE'RE OUTNUMBERED MAYBE SEVEN TO ONE? ANY OTHER DAY, I'D LAUGH IN THE FACE OF THOSE ODDS AND JUST START SMACKING CROC SNOUTS...
...BUT WE ARE *NOT* AT OUR FIGHTING BEST.
"SO IF WE'RE GOING TO SAVE THE VALLEY, WE NEED A PLAN--
"--CUZ THAT *CROC CONVOY* IS PULLING OUT."
TO BE CONTINUED...!

WAKE ME UP BEFORE YOU PO-PO

CHAPTER 2

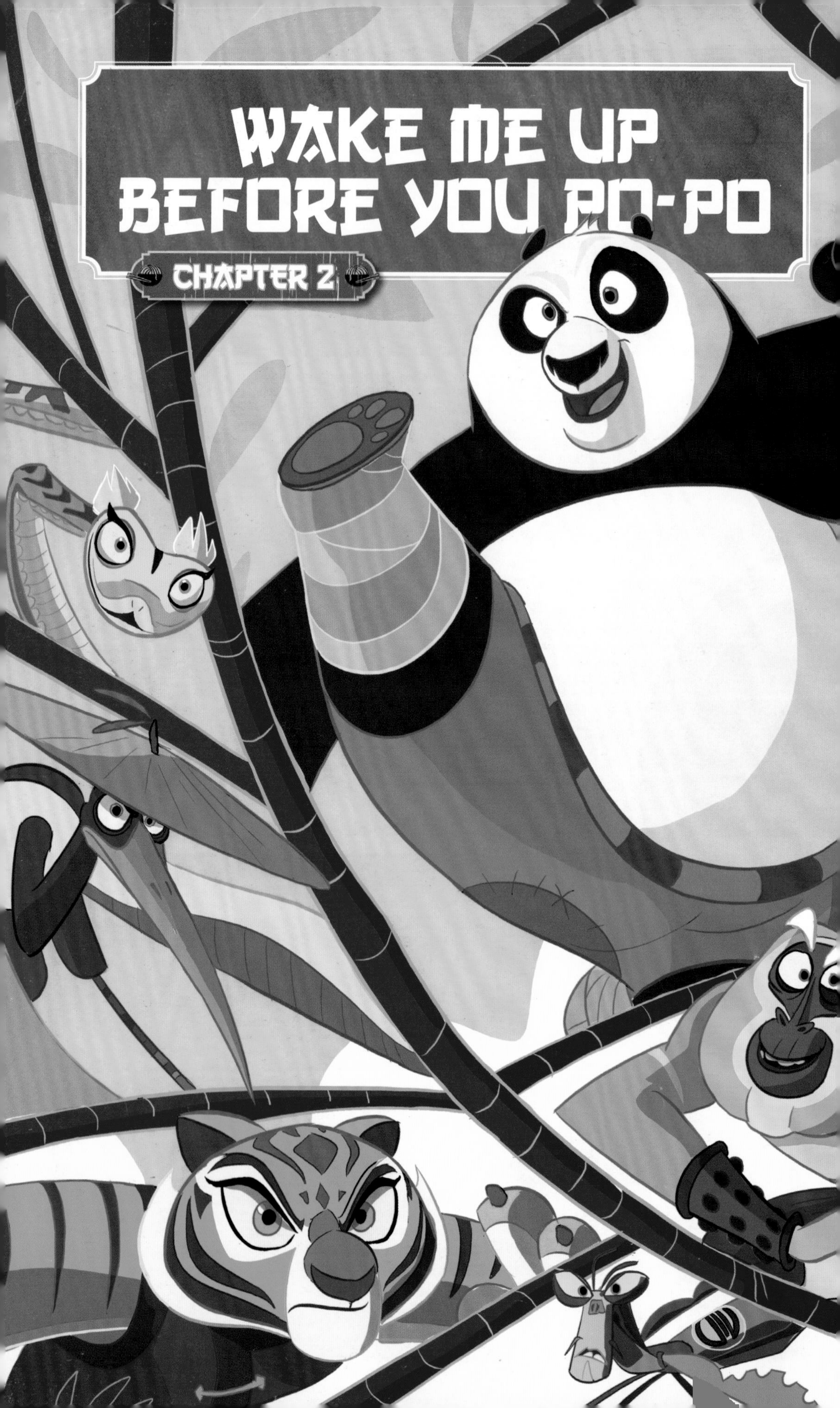

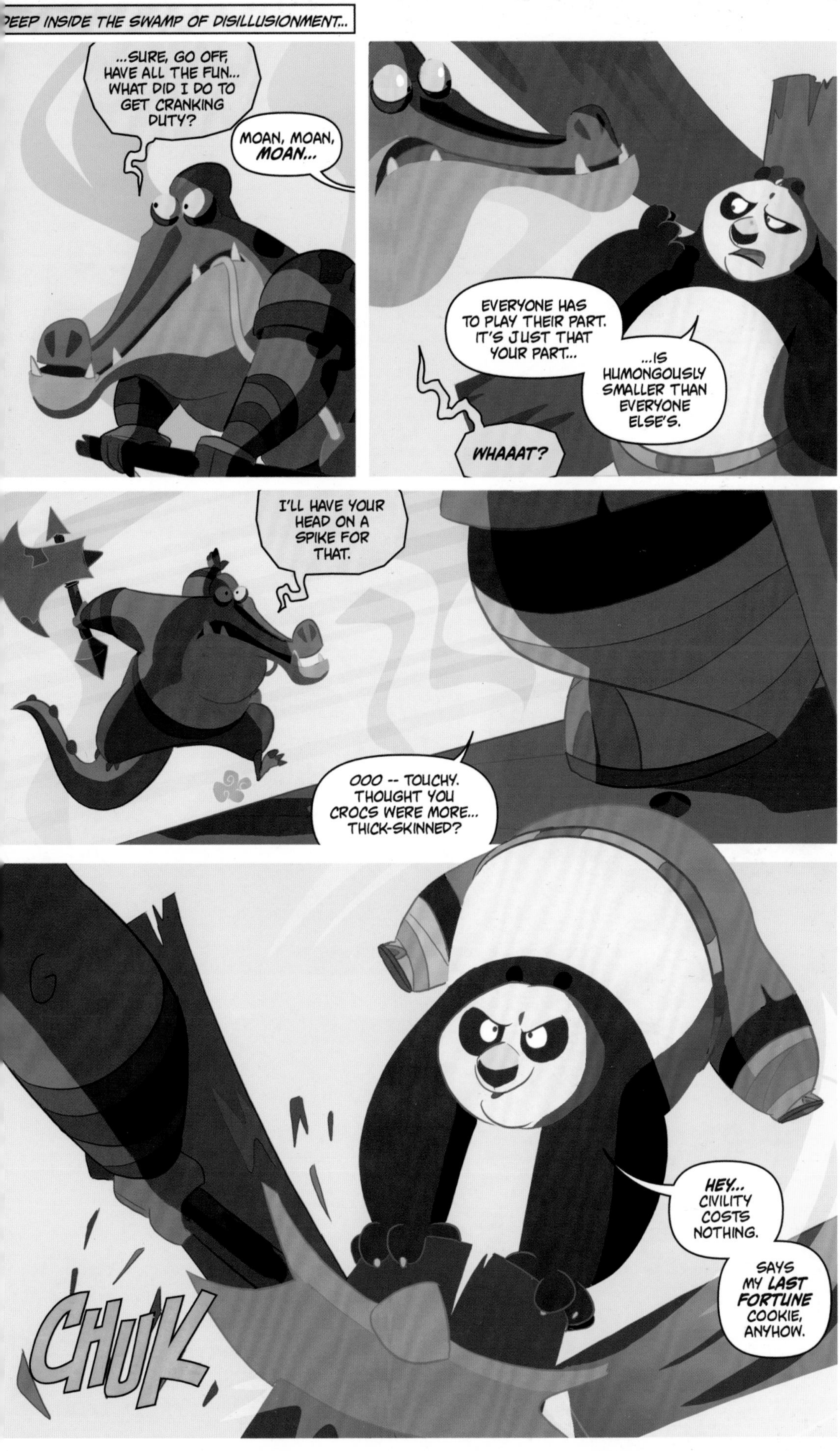
DEEP INSIDE THE SWAMP OF DISILLUSIONMENT...
...SURE, GO OFF, HAVE ALL THE FUN... WHAT DID I DO TO GET CRANKING DUTY?
MOAN, MOAN, MOAN...
EVERYONE HAS TO PLAY THEIR PART. IT'S JUST THAT YOUR PART...
...IS HUMONGOUSLY SMALLER THAN EVERYONE ELSE'S.
WHAAAT?
I'LL HAVE YOUR HEAD ON A SPIKE FOR THAT.
OOO -- TOUCHY. THOUGHT YOU CROCS WERE MORE... THICK-SKINNED?
CHUK
HEY... CIVILITY COSTS NOTHING.
SAYS MY LAST FORTUNE COOKIE, ANYHOW.

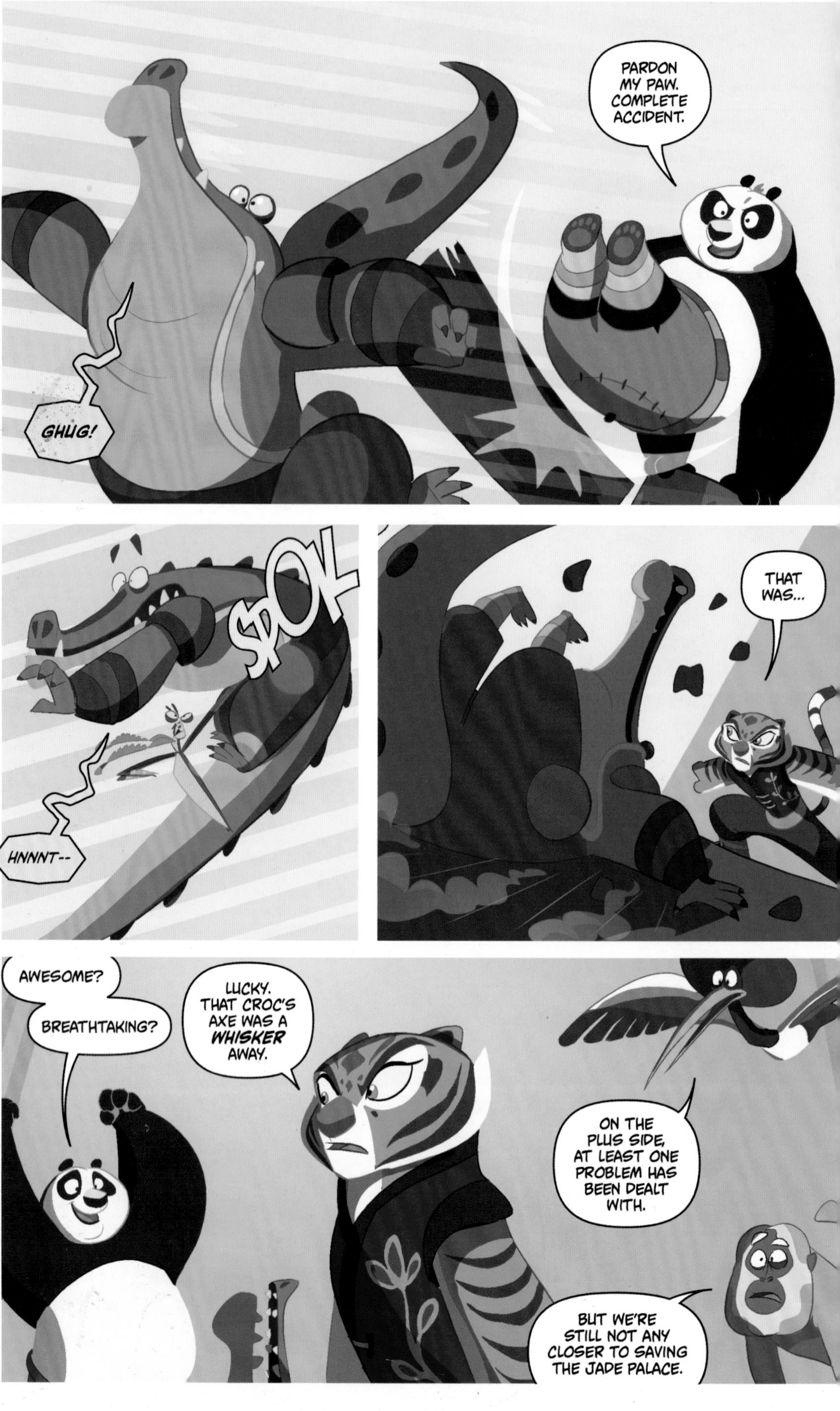
PARDON MY PAW. COMPLETE ACCIDENT.
GHUG!
SPOK
HNNNT--
THAT WAS...
AWESOME?
BREATHTAKING?
LUCKY. THAT CROC'S AXE WAS A ***WHISKER*** AWAY.
ON THE PLUS SIDE, AT LEAST ONE PROBLEM HAS BEEN DEALT WITH.
BUT WE'RE STILL NOT ANY CLOSER TO SAVING THE JADE PALACE.

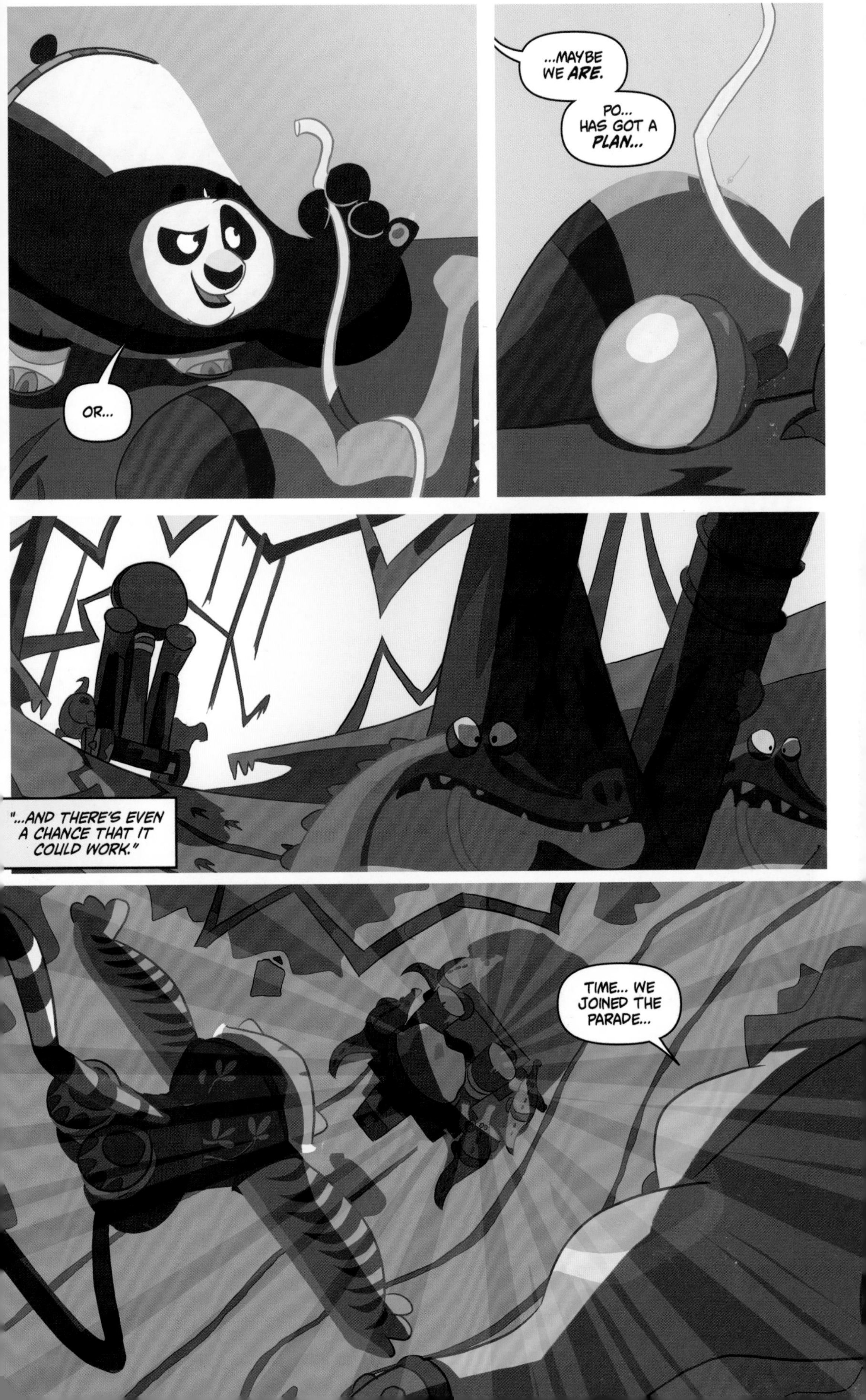
OR...
...MAYBE WE ARE.
PO... HAS GOT A PLAN...
"...AND THERE'S EVEN A CHANCE THAT IT COULD WORK."
TIME... WE JOINED THE PARADE...

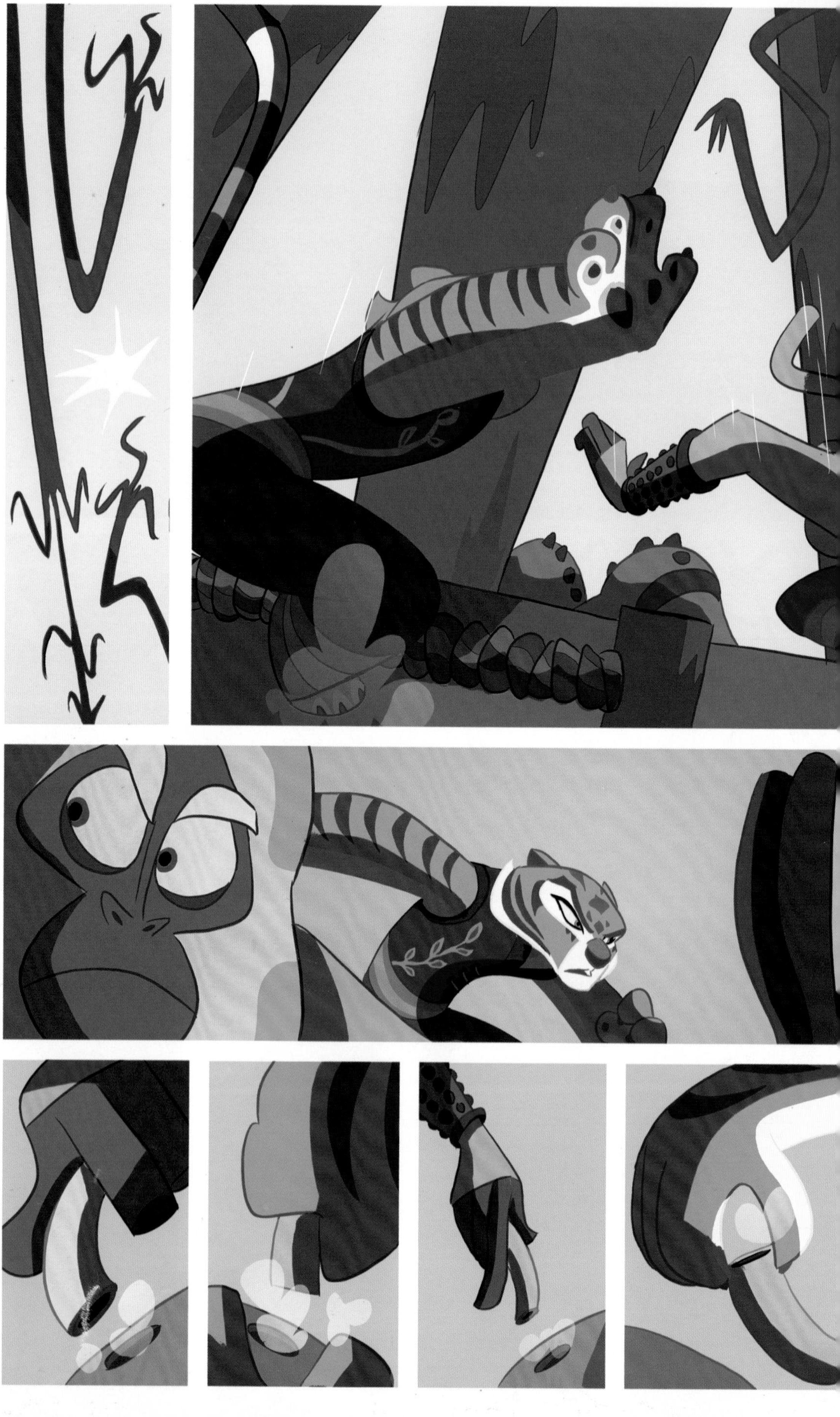

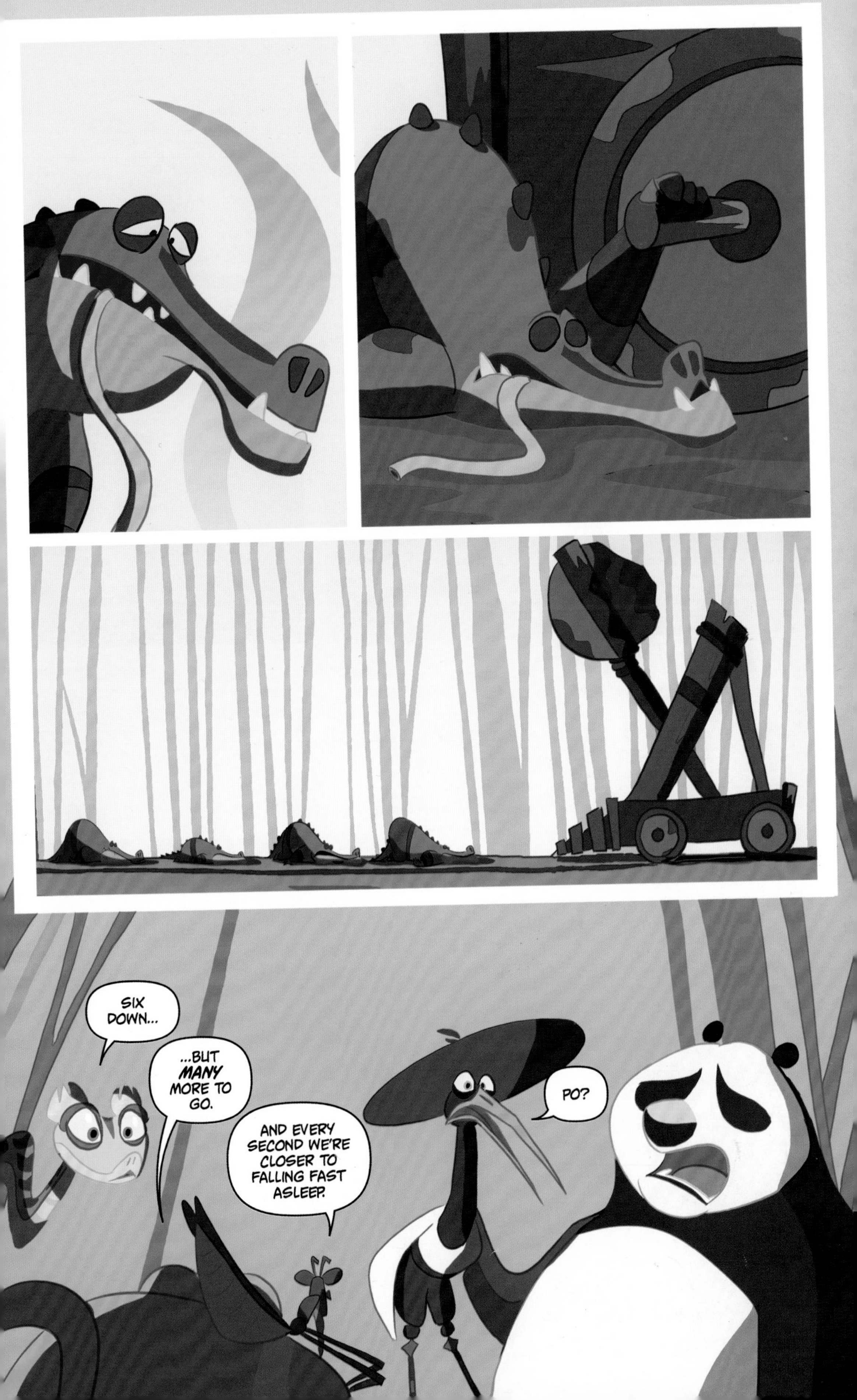
SIX DOWN...
...BUT MANY MORE TO GO.
AND EVERY SECOND WE'RE CLOSER TO FALLING FAST ASLEEP.
PO?

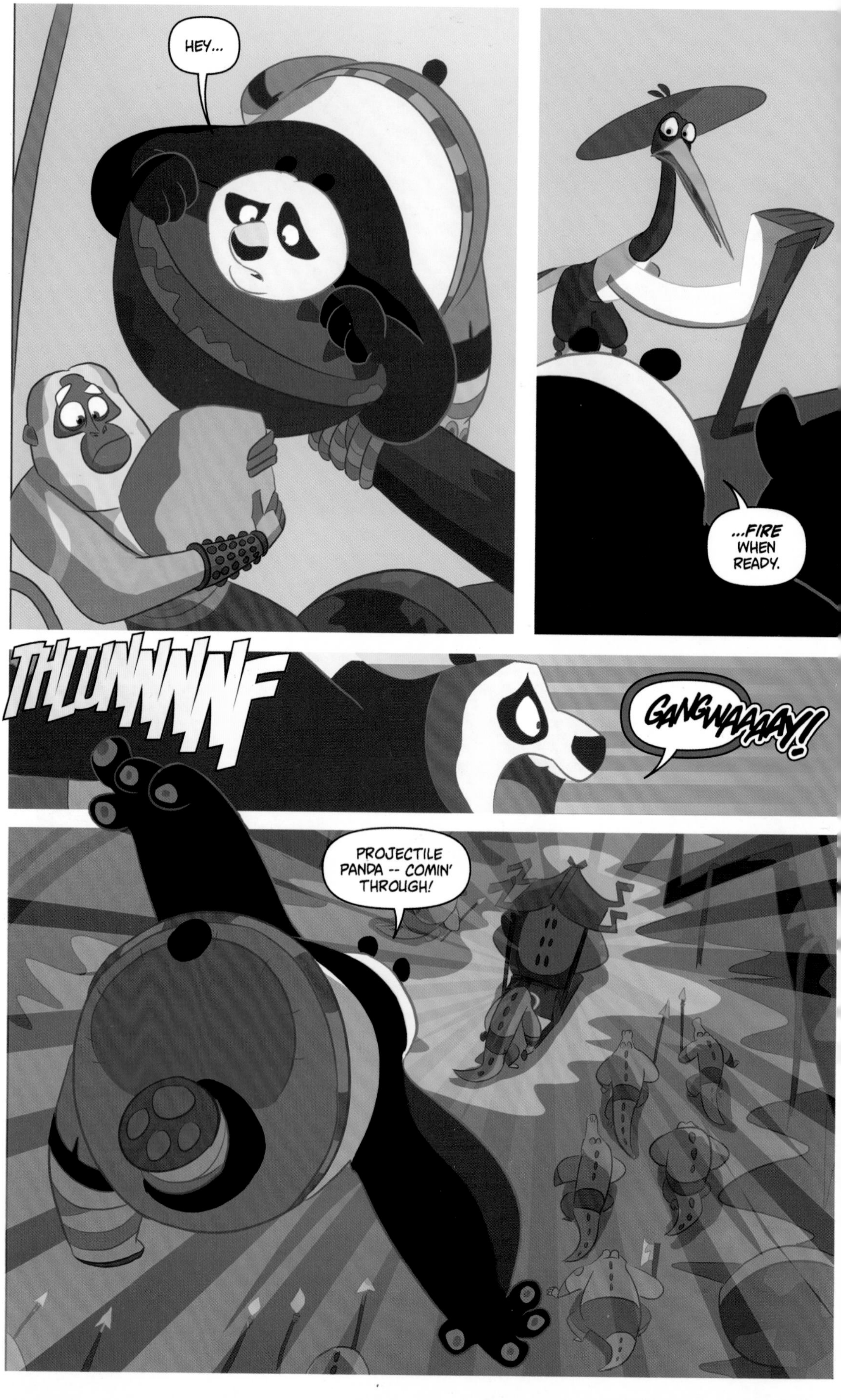
HEY...
...FIRE WHEN READY.
THLUNNNNF
GANGWAAAAY!
PROJECTILE PANDA -- COMIN' THROUGH!

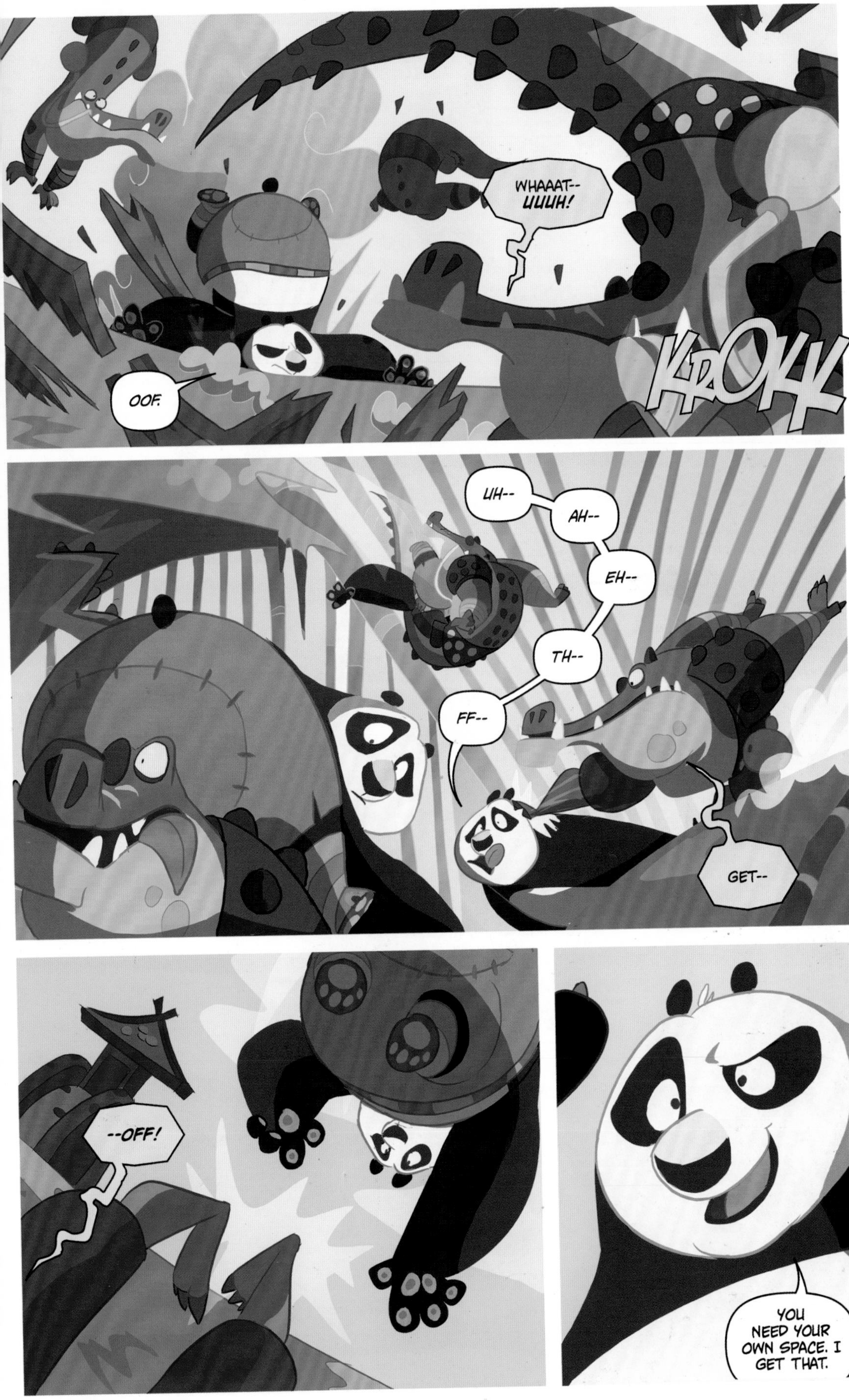
WHAAAT--
UUUH!
OOF.
KROKK
UH--
AH--
EH--
TH--
FF--
GET--
--OFF!
YOU NEED YOUR OWN SPACE. I GET THAT.

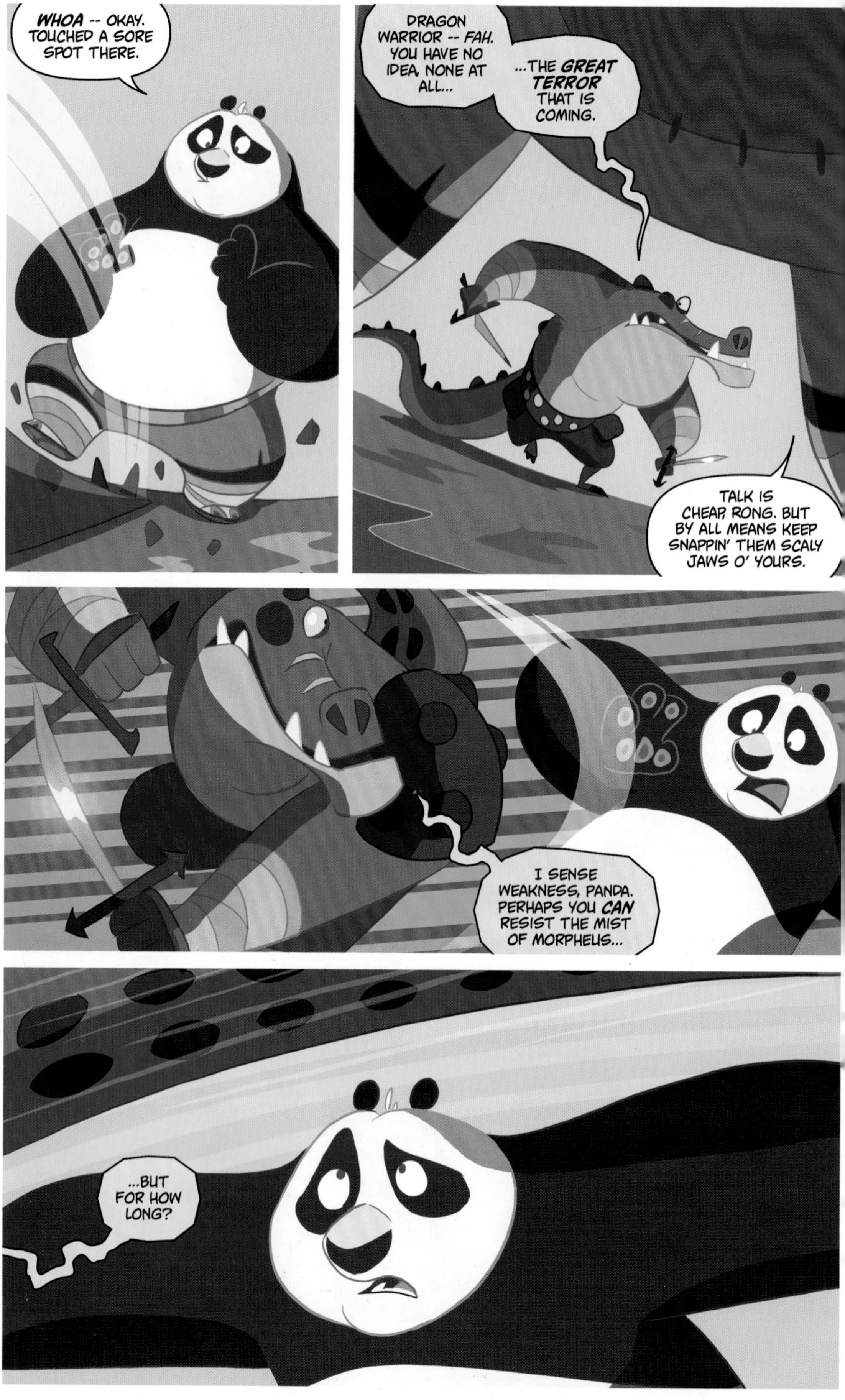
WHOA -- OKAY. TOUCHED A SORE SPOT THERE.
DRAGON WARRIOR -- FAH. YOU HAVE NO IDEA, NONE AT ALL...
...THE GREAT TERROR THAT IS COMING.
TALK IS CHEAP, RONG. BUT BY ALL MEANS KEEP SNAPPIN' THEM SCALY JAWS O' YOURS.
I SENSE WEAKNESS, PANDA. PERHAPS YOU CAN RESIST THE MIST OF MORPHEUS...
...BUT FOR HOW LONG?

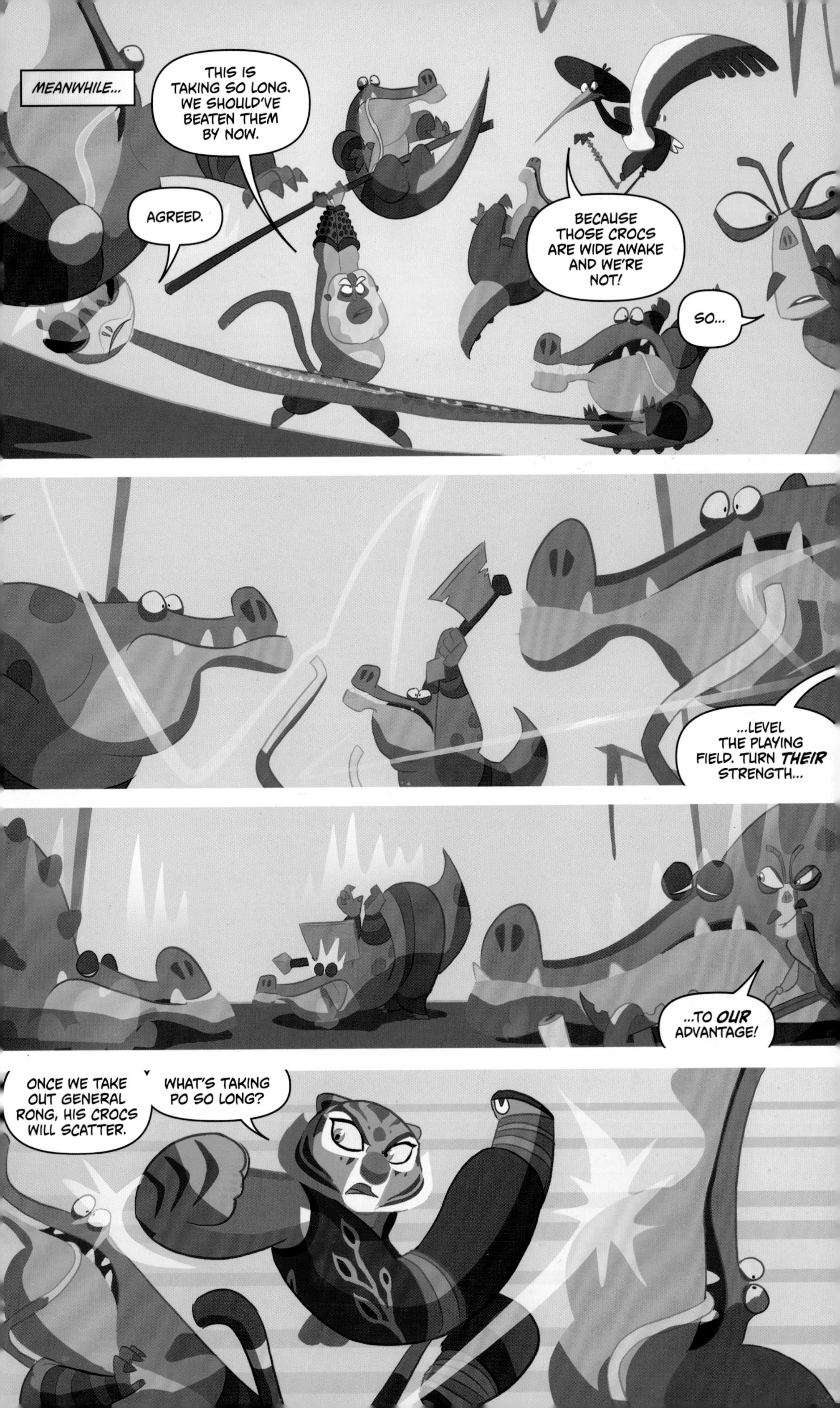
MEANWHILE...
THIS IS TAKING SO LONG. WE SHOULD'VE BEATEN THEM BY NOW.
AGREED.
BECAUSE THOSE CROCS ARE WIDE AWAKE AND WE'RE NOT!
SO...
...LEVEL THE PLAYING FIELD. TURN *THEIR* STRENGTH...
...TO *OUR* ADVANTAGE!
ONCE WE TAKE OUT GENERAL RONG, HIS CROCS WILL SCATTER.
WHAT'S TAKING PO SO LONG?

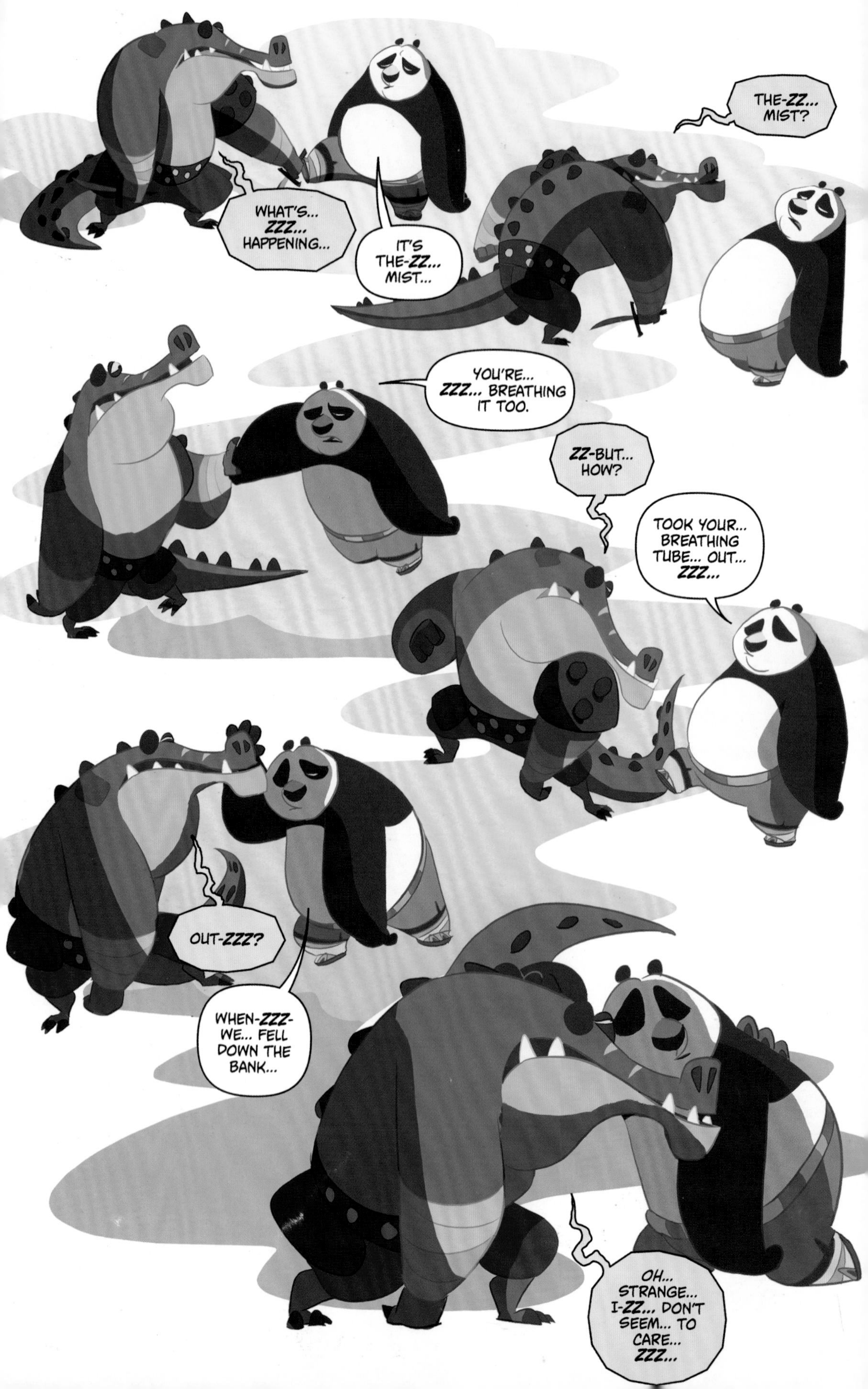
WHAT'S... ZZZ... HAPPENING...
IT'S THE-ZZ... MIST...
THE-ZZ... MIST?
YOU'RE... ZZZ... BREATHING IT TOO.
ZZ-BUT... HOW?
TOOK YOUR... BREATHING TUBE... OUT... ZZZ...
OUT-ZZZ?
WHEN-ZZZ-WE... FELL DOWN THE BANK...
OH... STRANGE... I-ZZ... DON'T SEEM... TO CARE... ZZZ...

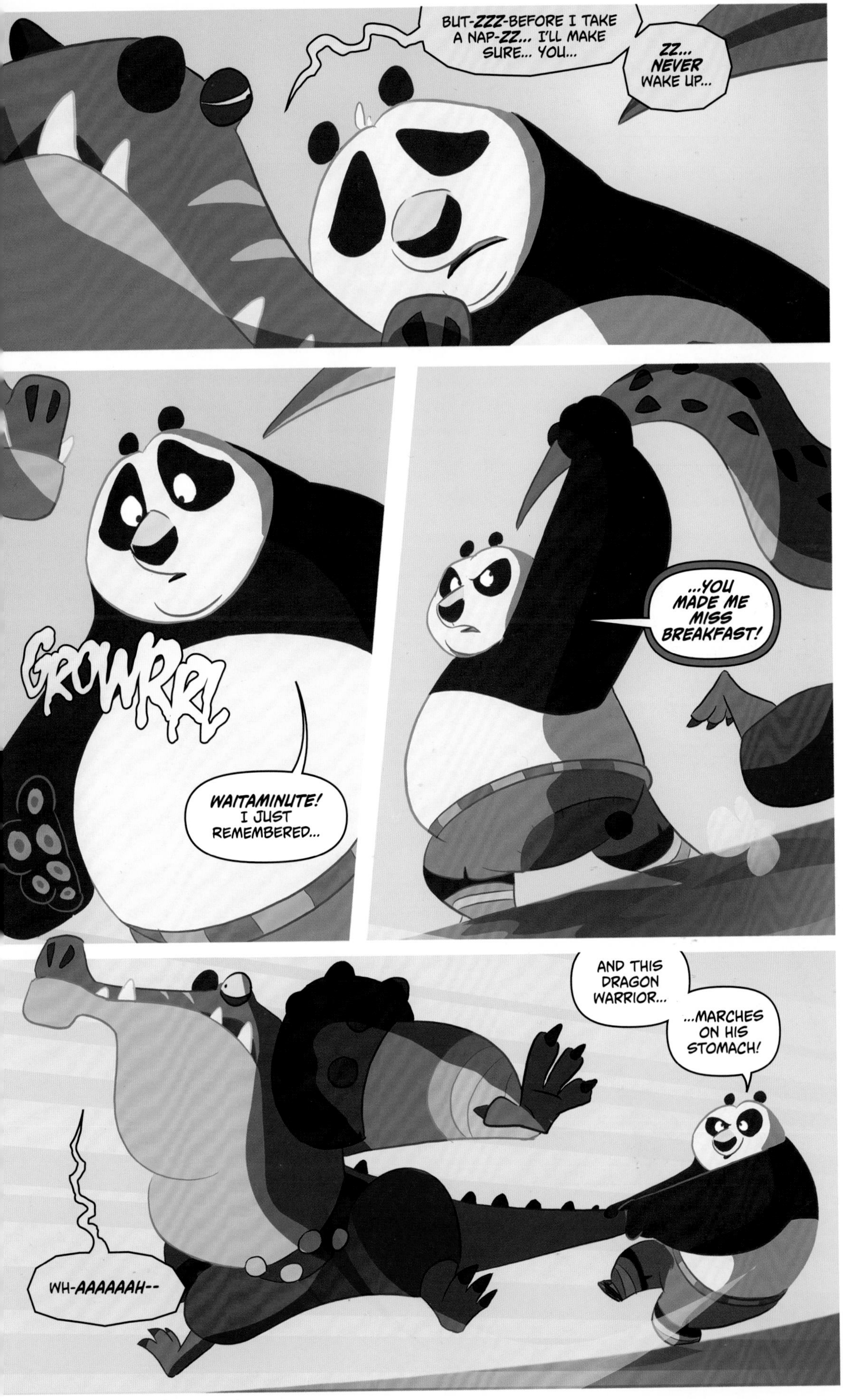

BUT-ZZZ-BEFORE I TAKE A NAP-ZZ... I'LL MAKE SURE... YOU...
ZZ... NEVER WAKE UP...
GROWRRL
WAITAMINUTE! I JUST REMEMBERED...
...YOU MADE ME MISS BREAKFAST!
AND THIS DRAGON WARRIOR...
...MARCHES ON HIS STOMACH!
WH-AAAAAAH--

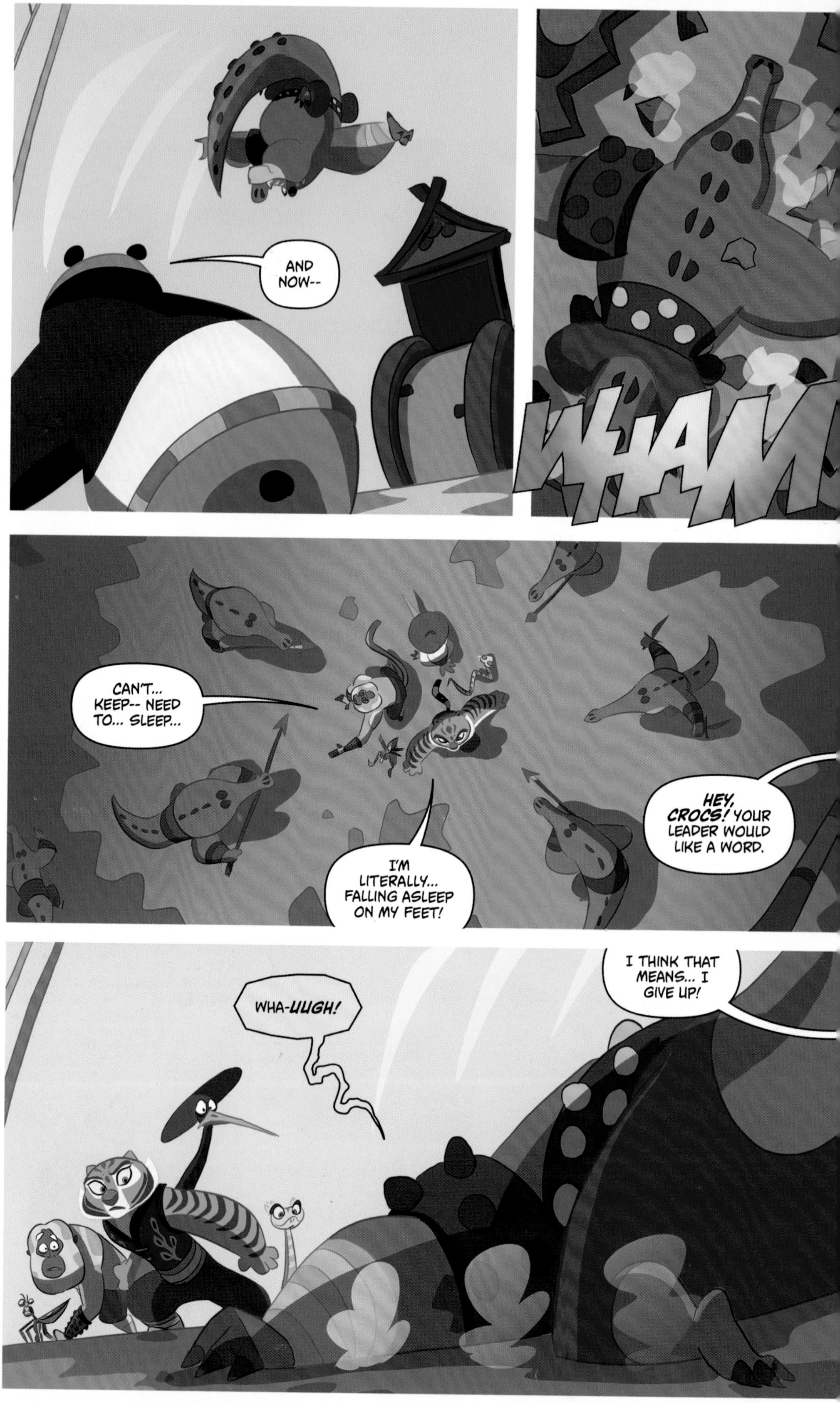
AND NOW--
WHAM
CAN'T... KEEP-- NEED TO... SLEEP...
I'M LITERALLY... FALLING ASLEEP ON MY FEET!
HEY, CROCS! YOUR LEADER WOULD LIKE A WORD.
WHA-UUGH!
I THINK THAT MEANS... I GIVE UP!

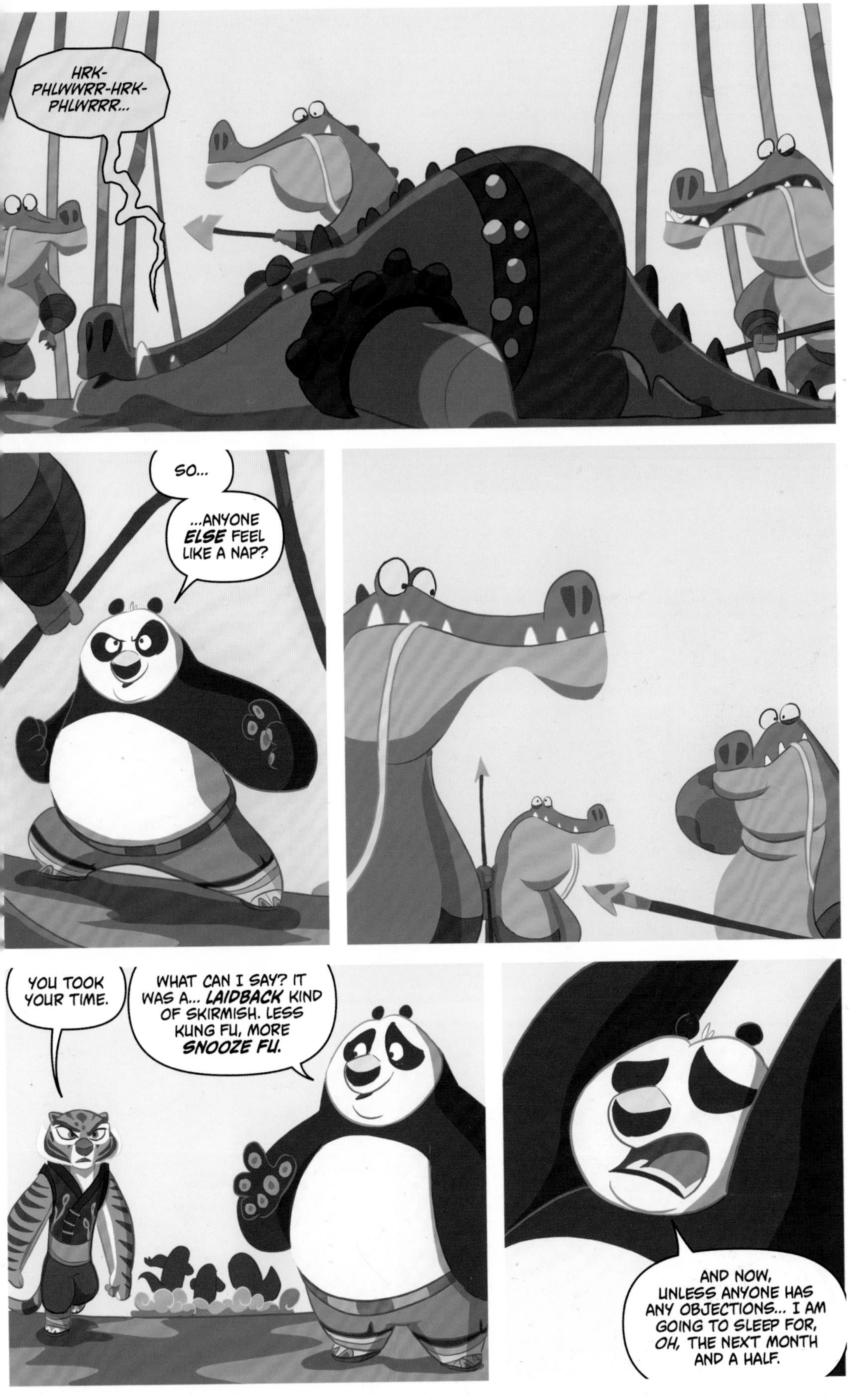
HRK-PHLWWRR-HRK-PHLWRRR...
SO...
...ANYONE ELSE FEEL LIKE A NAP?
YOU TOOK YOUR TIME.
WHAT CAN I SAY? IT WAS A... LAIDBACK KIND OF SKIRMISH. LESS KUNG FU, MORE SNOOZE FU.
AND NOW, UNLESS ANYONE HAS ANY OBJECTIONS... I AM GOING TO SLEEP FOR, OH, THE NEXT MONTH AND A HALF.

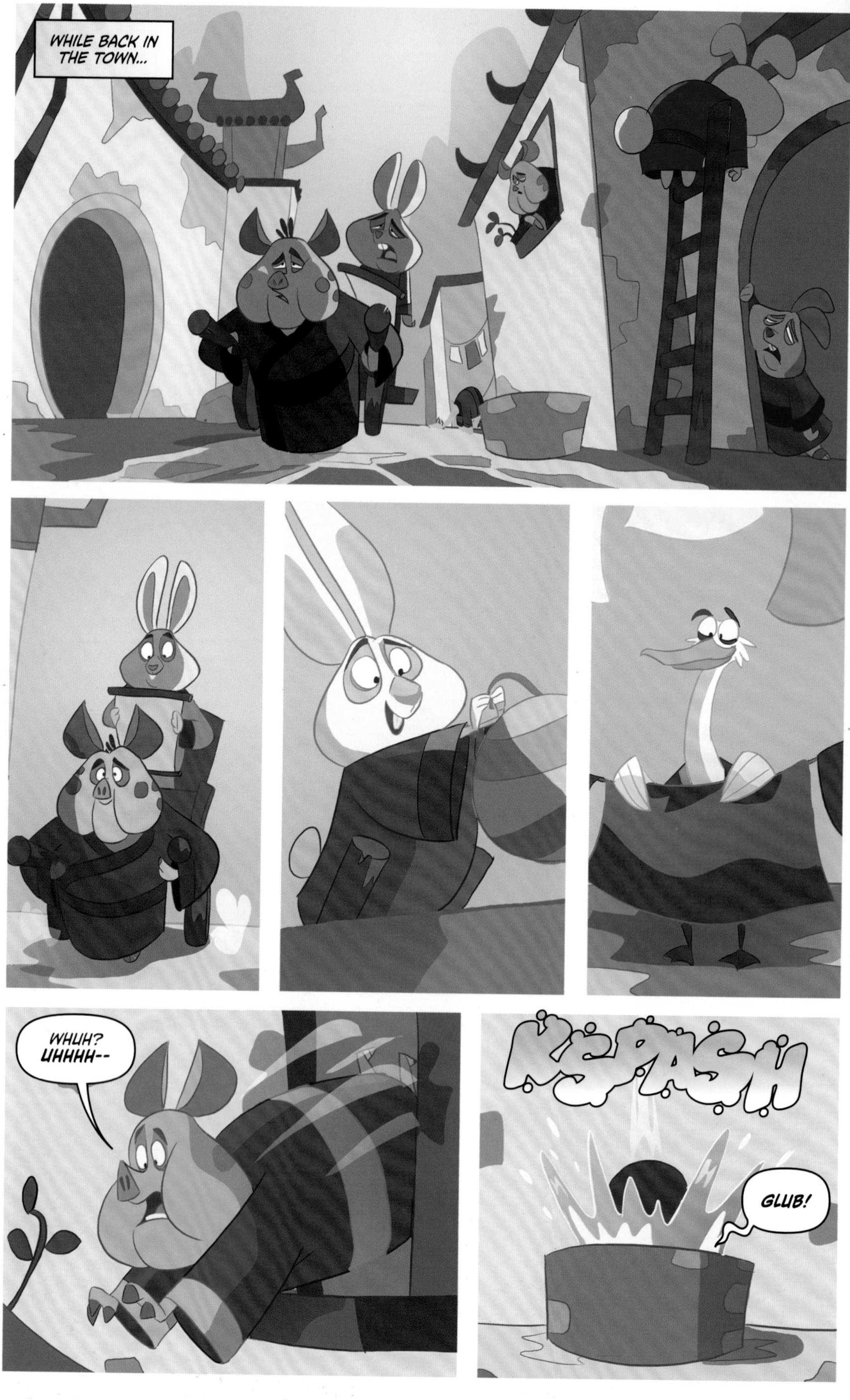
WHILE BACK IN THE TOWN...
WHUH? UHHHH--
KSPASH
GLUB!

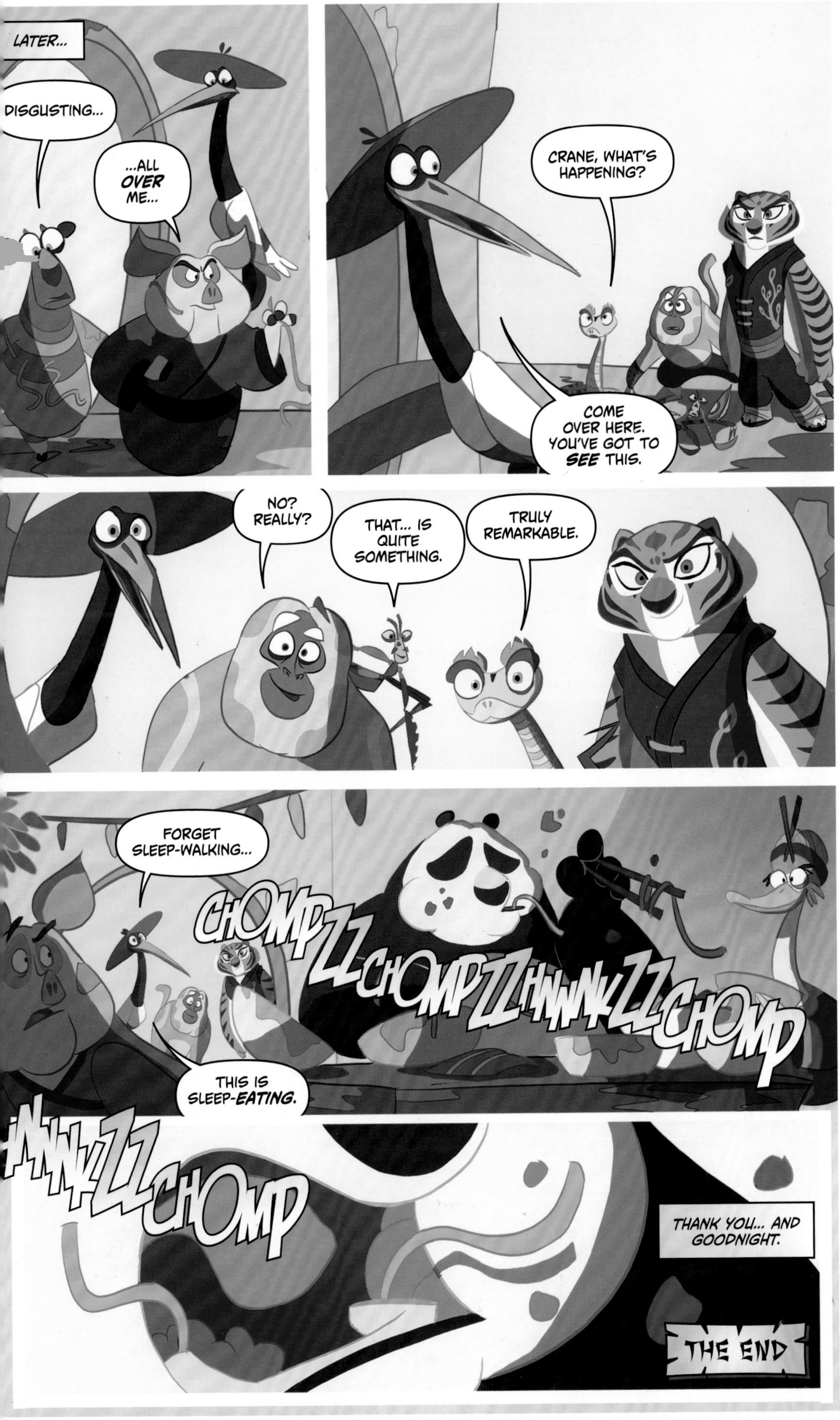
LATER...
DISGUSTING...
...ALL OVER ME...
CRANE, WHAT'S HAPPENING?
COME OVER HERE. YOU'VE GOT TO SEE THIS.
NO? REALLY?
THAT... IS QUITE SOMETHING.
TRULY REMARKABLE.
FORGET SLEEP-WALKING...
CHOMPZZCHOMPZZHNNNKZZCHOMP
THIS IS SLEEP-EATING.
HNNNKZZCHOMP
THANK YOU... AND GOODNIGHT.
THE END

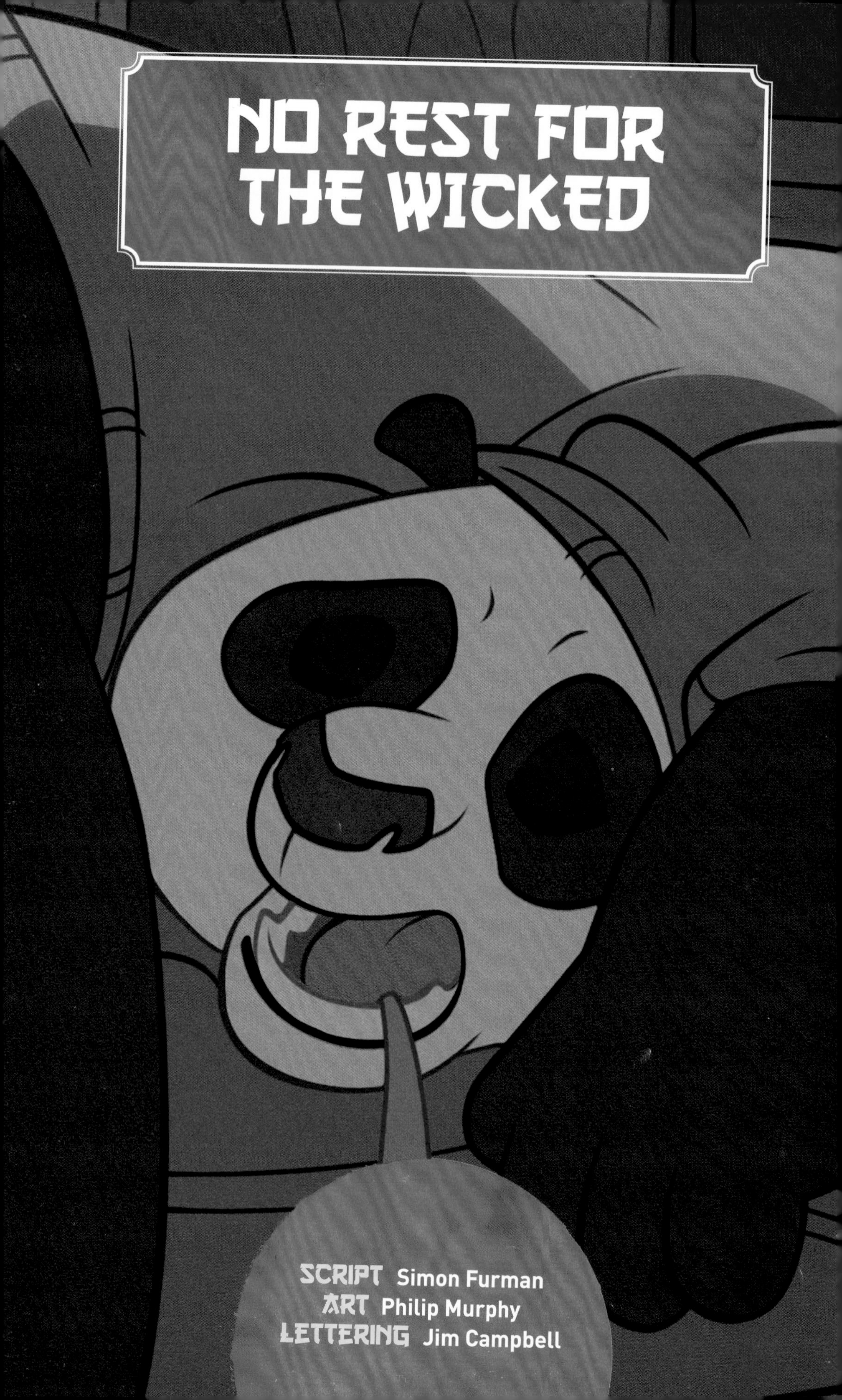
NO REST FOR THE WICKED
SCRIPT Simon Furman
ART Philip Murphy
LETTERING Jim Campbell

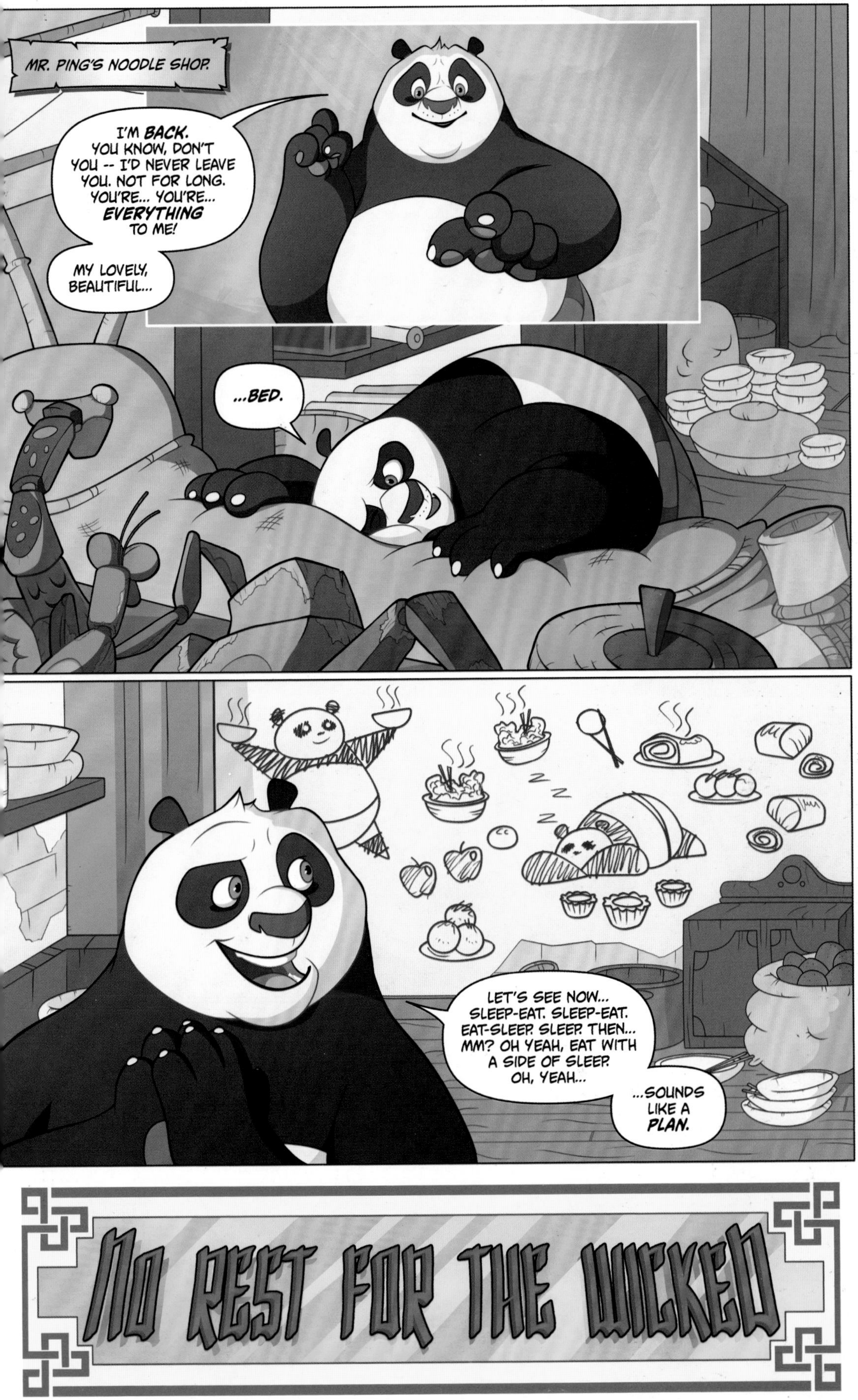
MR. PING'S NOODLE SHOP.
I'M BACK. YOU KNOW, DON'T YOU -- I'D NEVER LEAVE YOU. NOT FOR LONG. YOU'RE... YOU'RE... EVERYTHING TO ME!
MY LOVELY, BEAUTIFUL...
...BED.
LET'S SEE NOW... SLEEP-EAT. SLEEP-EAT. EAT-SLEEP. SLEEP. THEN... MM? OH YEAH, EAT WITH A SIDE OF SLEEP. OH, YEAH...
...SOUNDS LIKE A PLAN.
NO REST FOR THE WICKED

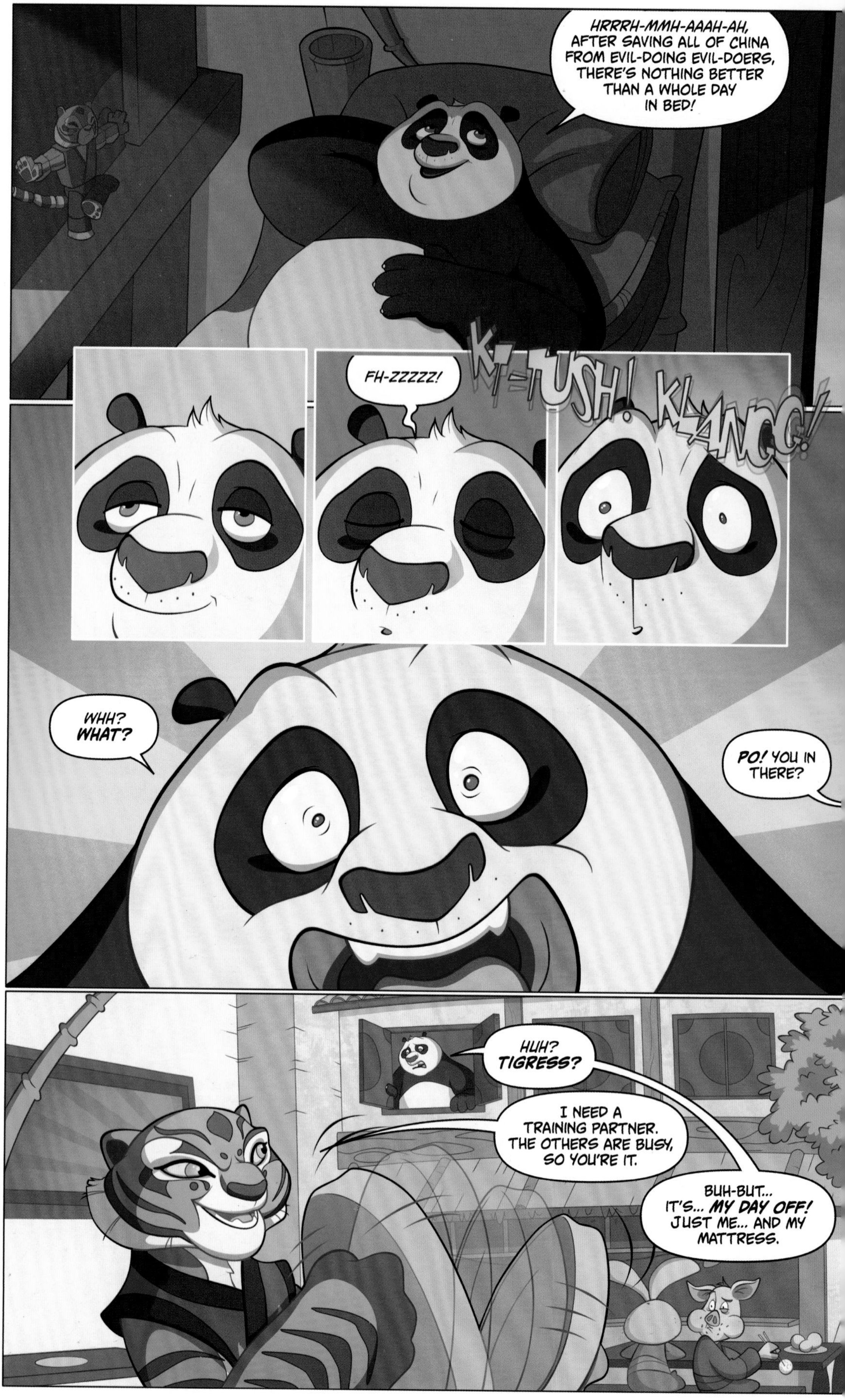
HRRRH-MMH-AAAH-AH, AFTER SAVING ALL OF CHINA FROM EVIL-DOING EVIL-DOERS, THERE'S NOTHING BETTER THAN A WHOLE DAY IN BED!
FH-ZZZZZ!
KI-TUSH! KLANGG!
WHH? WHAT?
PO! YOU IN THERE?
HUH? TIGRESS?
I NEED A TRAINING PARTNER. THE OTHERS ARE BUSY, SO YOU'RE IT.
BUH-BUT... IT'S... MY DAY OFF! JUST ME... AND MY MATTRESS.

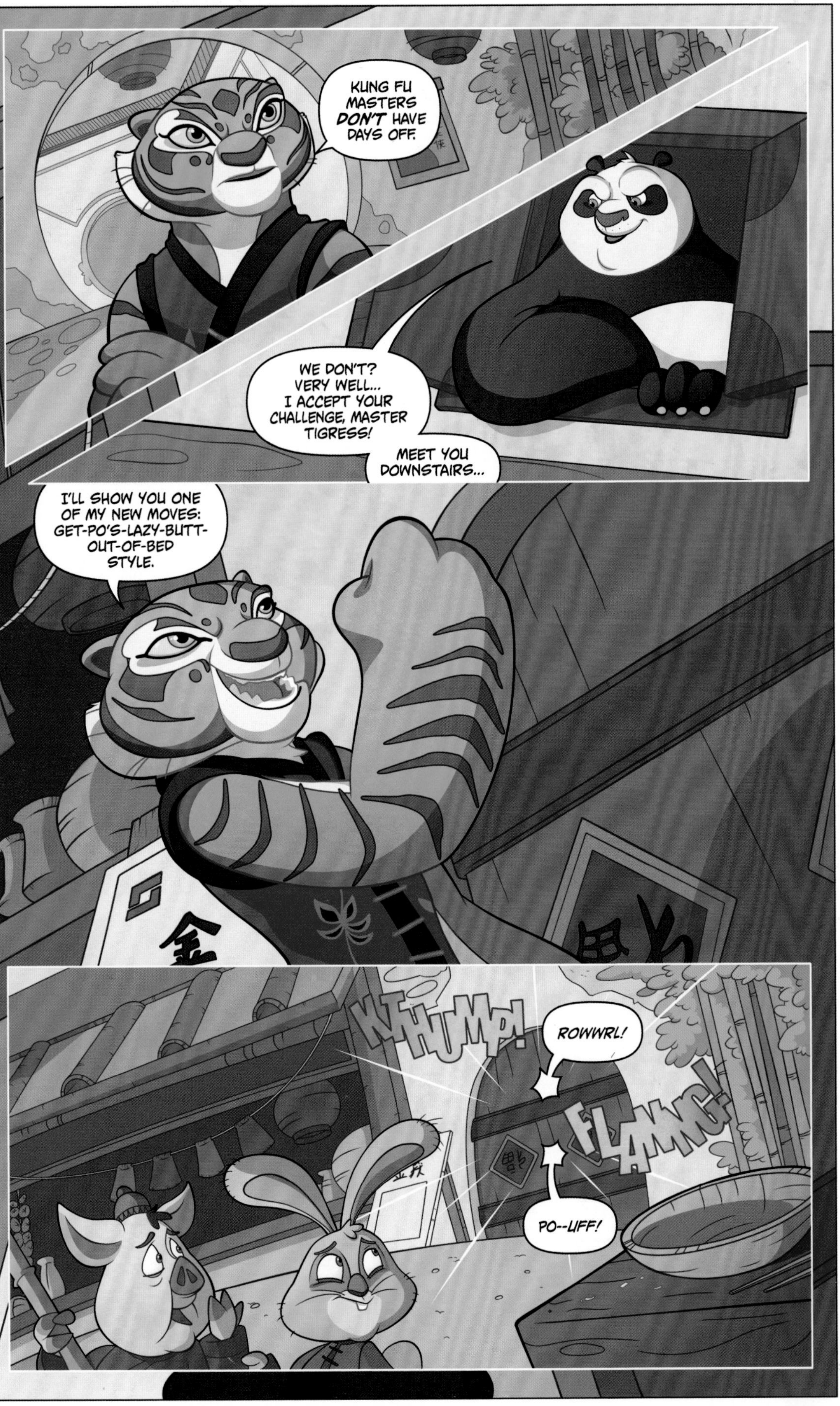

KUNG FU MASTERS DON'T HAVE DAYS OFF.
WE DON'T? VERY WELL... I ACCEPT YOUR CHALLENGE, MASTER TIGRESS!
MEET YOU DOWNSTAIRS...
I'LL SHOW YOU ONE OF MY NEW MOVES: GET-PO'S-LAZY-BUTT-OUT-OF-BED STYLE.
KTHUMP!
ROWWRL!
FLANNG!
PO--UFF!

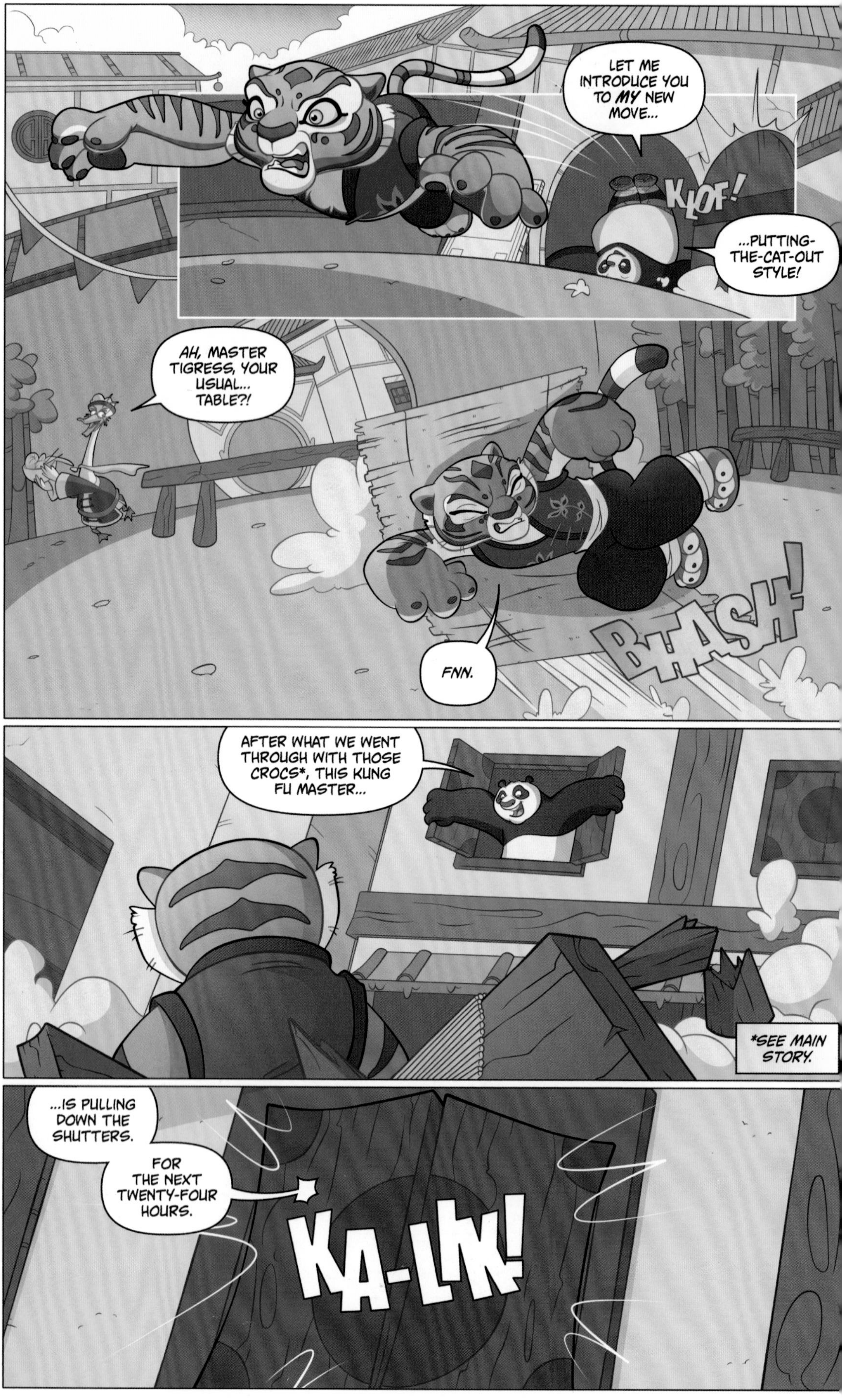

LET ME INTRODUCE YOU TO *MY* NEW MOVE...
KLOF!
...PUTTING-THE-CAT-OUT STYLE!
AH, MASTER TIGRESS, YOUR USUAL... TABLE?!
BLASH!
FNN.
AFTER WHAT WE WENT THROUGH WITH THOSE CROCS*, THIS KUNG FU MASTER...
*SEE MAIN STORY.
...IS PULLING DOWN THE SHUTTERS.
FOR THE NEXT TWENTY-FOUR HOURS.
KA-LIK!

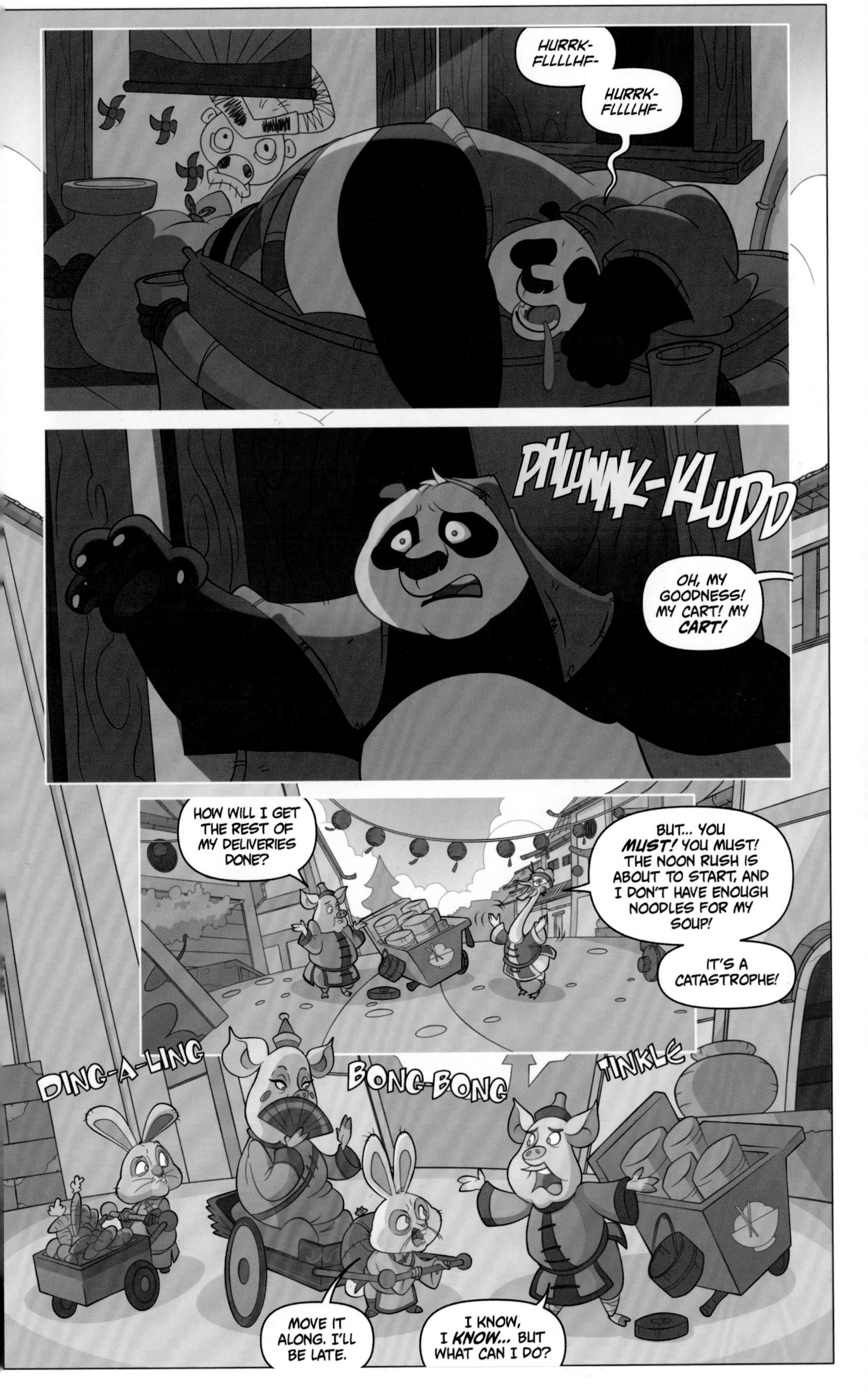
HURRK-
FLLLLHF-
HURRK-
FLLLLHF-
PHLUNNK-KLUDD
OH, MY GOODNESS! MY CART! MY CART!
HOW WILL I GET THE REST OF MY DELIVERIES DONE?
BUT... YOU MUST! YOU MUST! THE NOON RUSH IS ABOUT TO START, AND I DON'T HAVE ENOUGH NOODLES FOR MY SOUP!
IT'S A CATASTROPHE!
DING-A-LING
BONG-BONG
TINKLE
MOVE IT ALONG. I'LL BE LATE.
I KNOW, I KNOW... BUT WHAT CAN I DO?

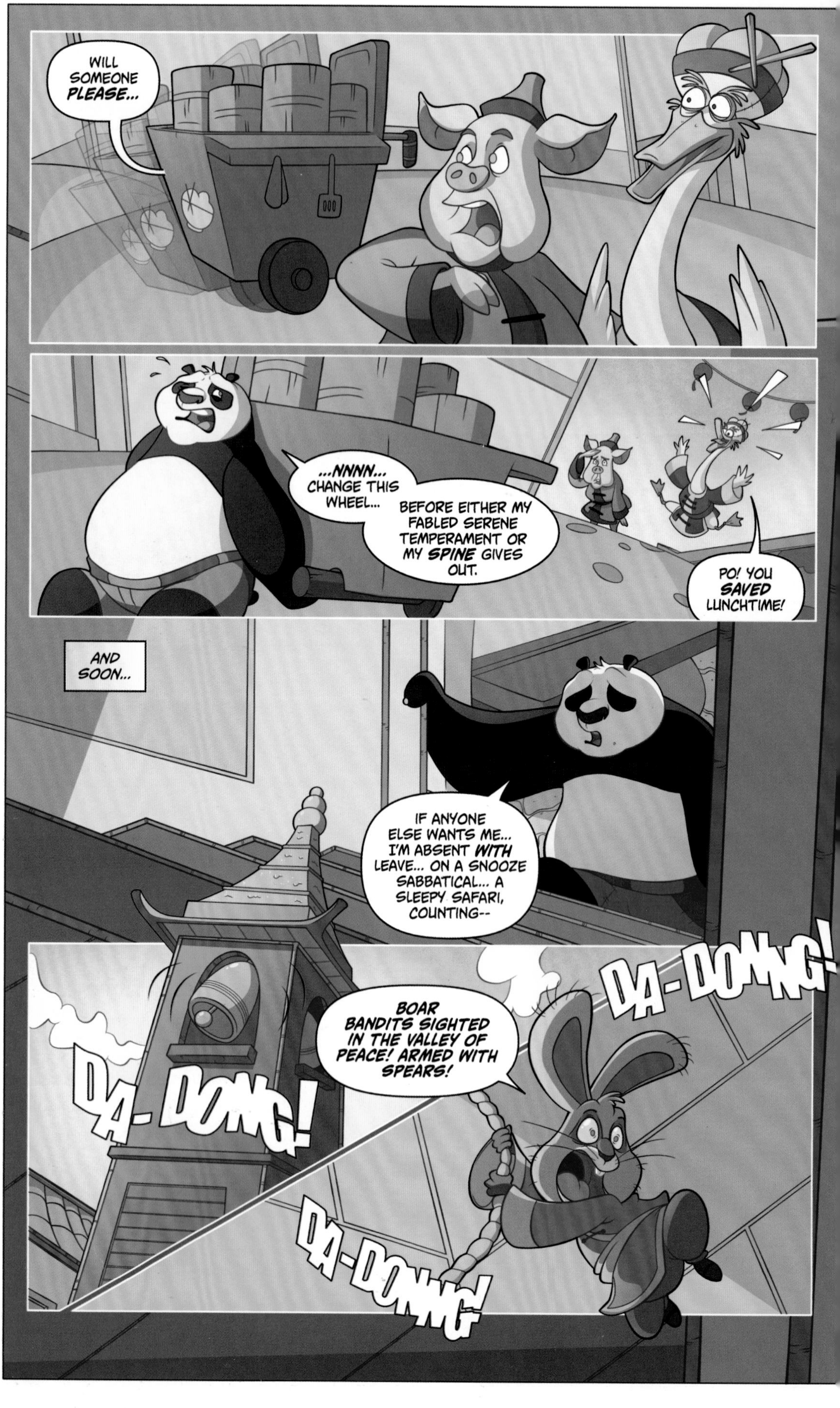
WILL SOMEONE PLEASE...
...NNNN... CHANGE THIS WHEEL...
BEFORE EITHER MY FABLED SERENE TEMPERAMENT OR MY SPINE GIVES OUT.
PO! YOU SAVED LUNCHTIME!
AND SOON...
IF ANYONE ELSE WANTS ME... I'M ABSENT WITH LEAVE... ON A SNOOZE SABBATICAL... A SLEEPY SAFARI, COUNTING--
DA-DONNG!
BOAR BANDITS SIGHTED IN THE VALLEY OF PEACE! ARMED WITH SPEARS!
DA-DONG!
DA-DONNG!

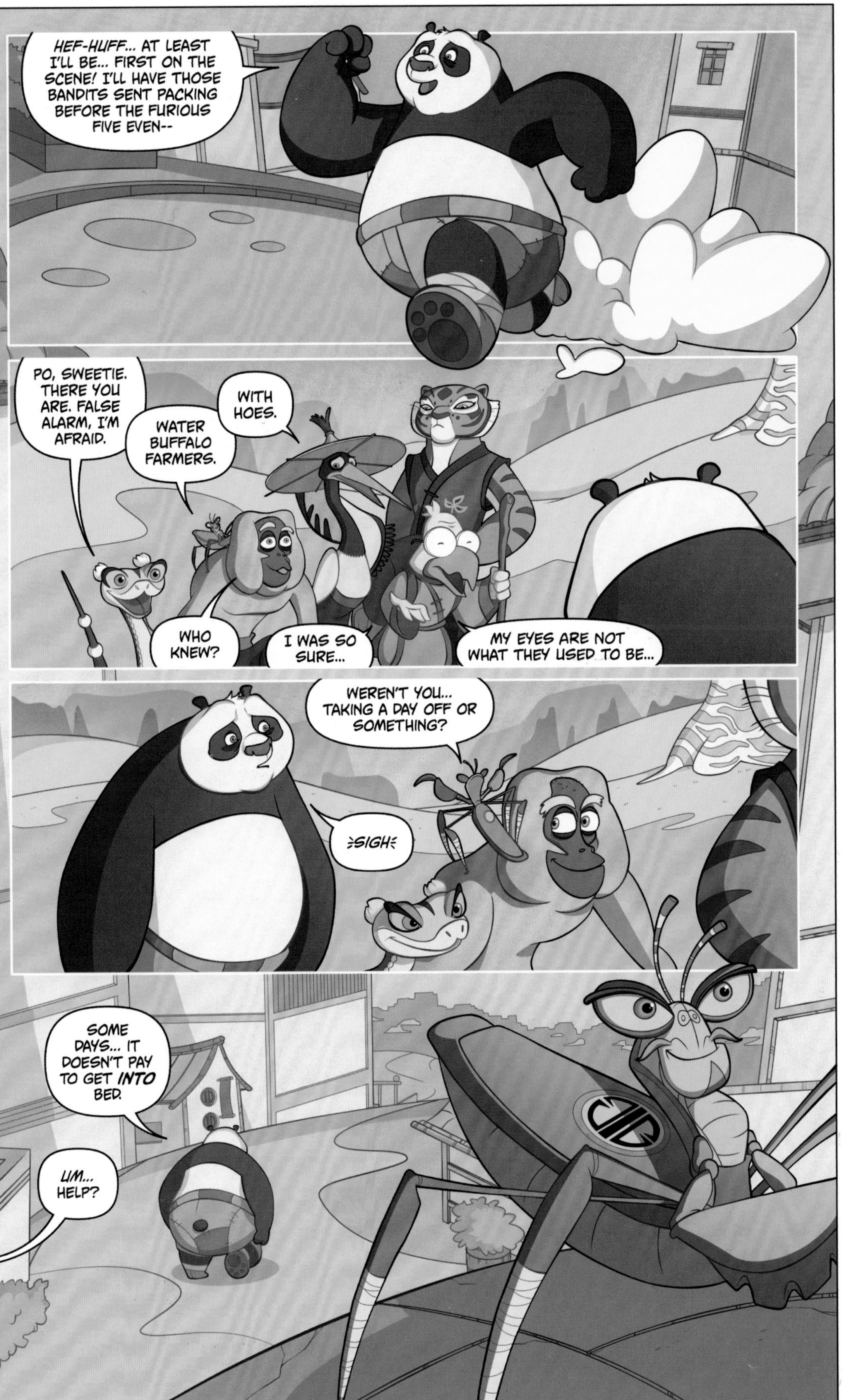
HEF-HUFF... AT LEAST I'LL BE... FIRST ON THE SCENE! I'LL HAVE THOSE BANDITS SENT PACKING BEFORE THE FURIOUS FIVE EVEN--
PO, SWEETIE. THERE YOU ARE. FALSE ALARM, I'M AFRAID.
WATER BUFFALO FARMERS.
WITH HOES.
WHO KNEW?
I WAS SO SURE...
MY EYES ARE NOT WHAT THEY USED TO BE...
WEREN'T YOU... TAKING A DAY OFF OR SOMETHING?
SIGH
SOME DAYS... IT DOESN'T PAY TO GET INTO BED.
UM... HELP?

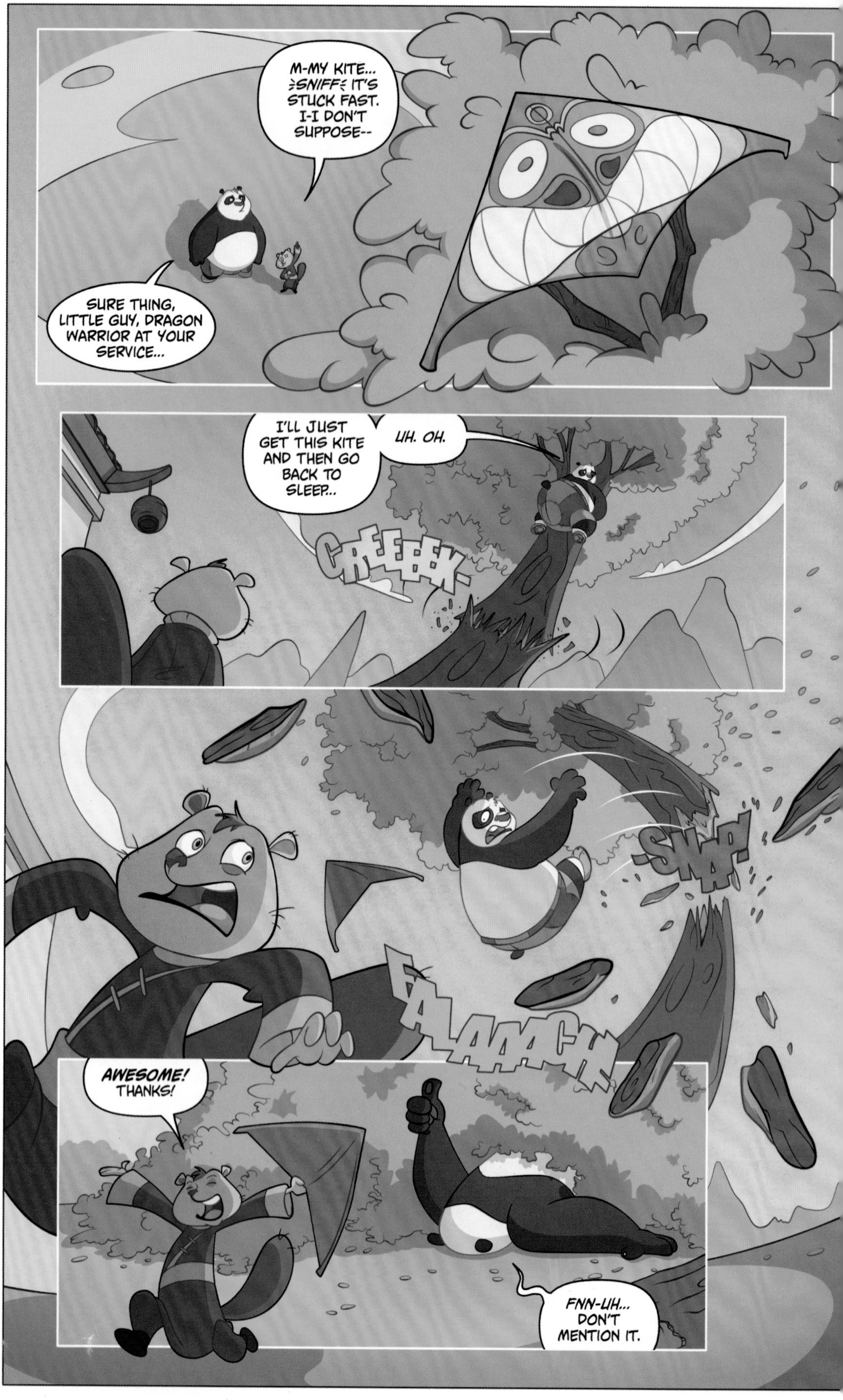

M-MY KITE... ≷SNIFF≶ IT'S STUCK FAST. I-I DON'T SUPPOSE--
SURE THING, LITTLE GUY, DRAGON WARRIOR AT YOUR SERVICE...
I'LL JUST GET THIS KITE AND THEN GO BACK TO SLEEP...
UH. OH.
CREEEEK-
-SNAP!
FAAAAACH
AWESOME! THANKS!
FNN-UH... DON'T MENTION IT.

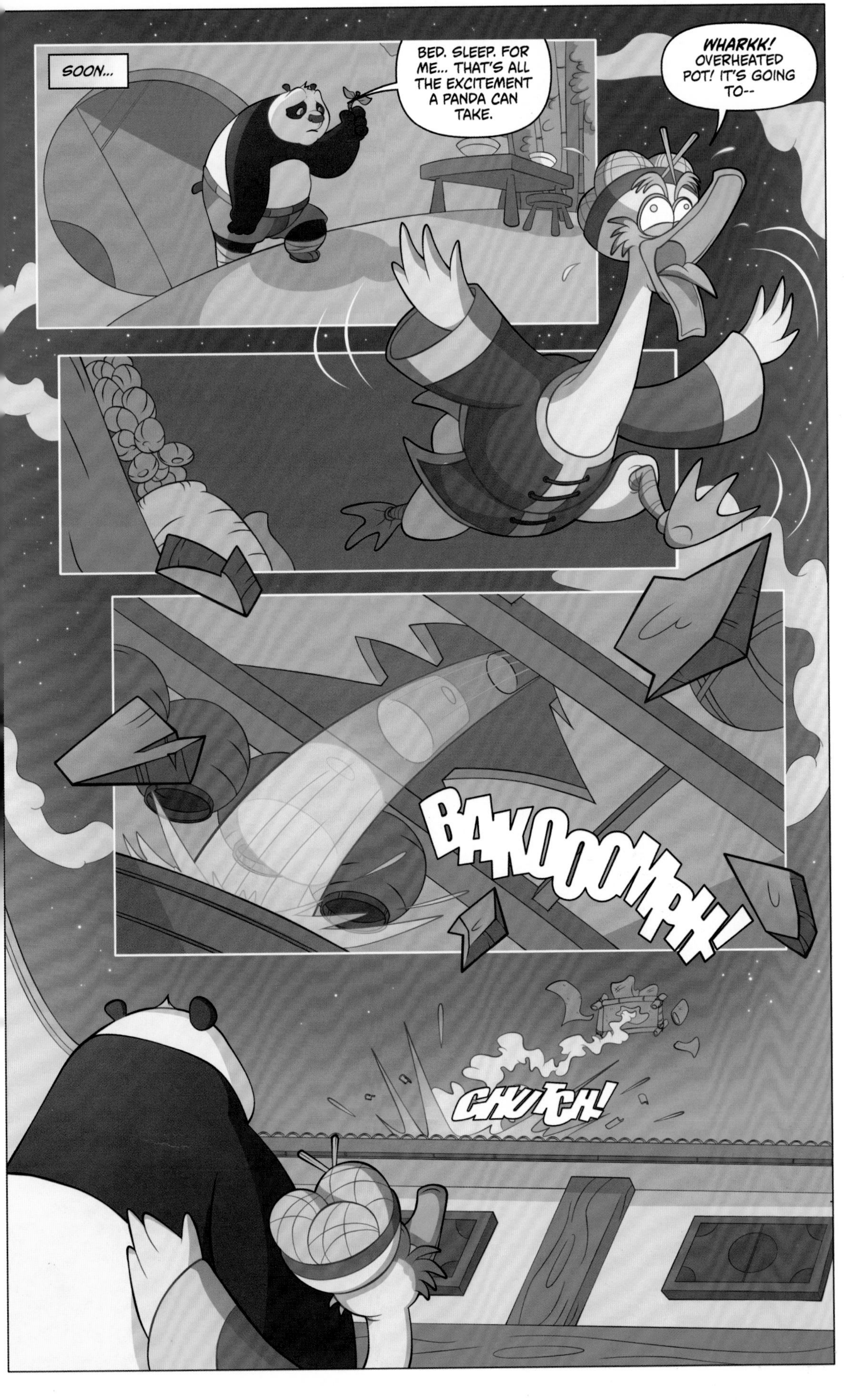

SOON...
BED. SLEEP. FOR ME... THAT'S ALL THE EXCITEMENT A PANDA CAN TAKE.
WHARKK! OVERHEATED POT! IT'S GOING TO--
BAKOOOOMPH!
CHU-TCH!

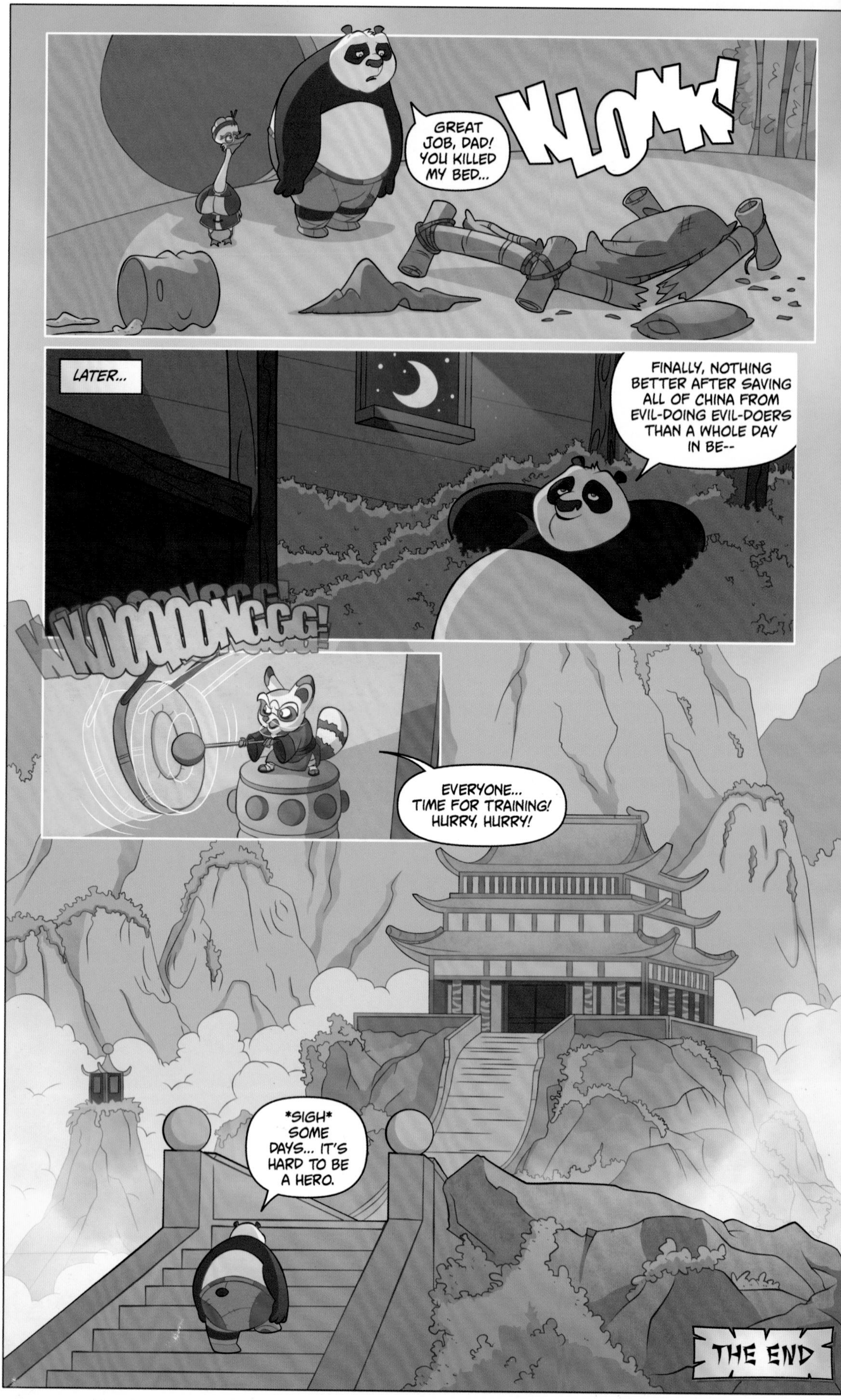
GREAT JOB, DAD! YOU KILLED MY BED...
KLONK!
LATER...
FINALLY, NOTHING BETTER AFTER SAVING ALL OF CHINA FROM EVIL-DOING EVIL-DOERS THAN A WHOLE DAY IN BE--
KKOOOOONGGG!
EVERYONE... TIME FOR TRAINING! HURRY, HURRY!
SIGH SOME DAYS... IT'S HARD TO BE A HERO.
THE END

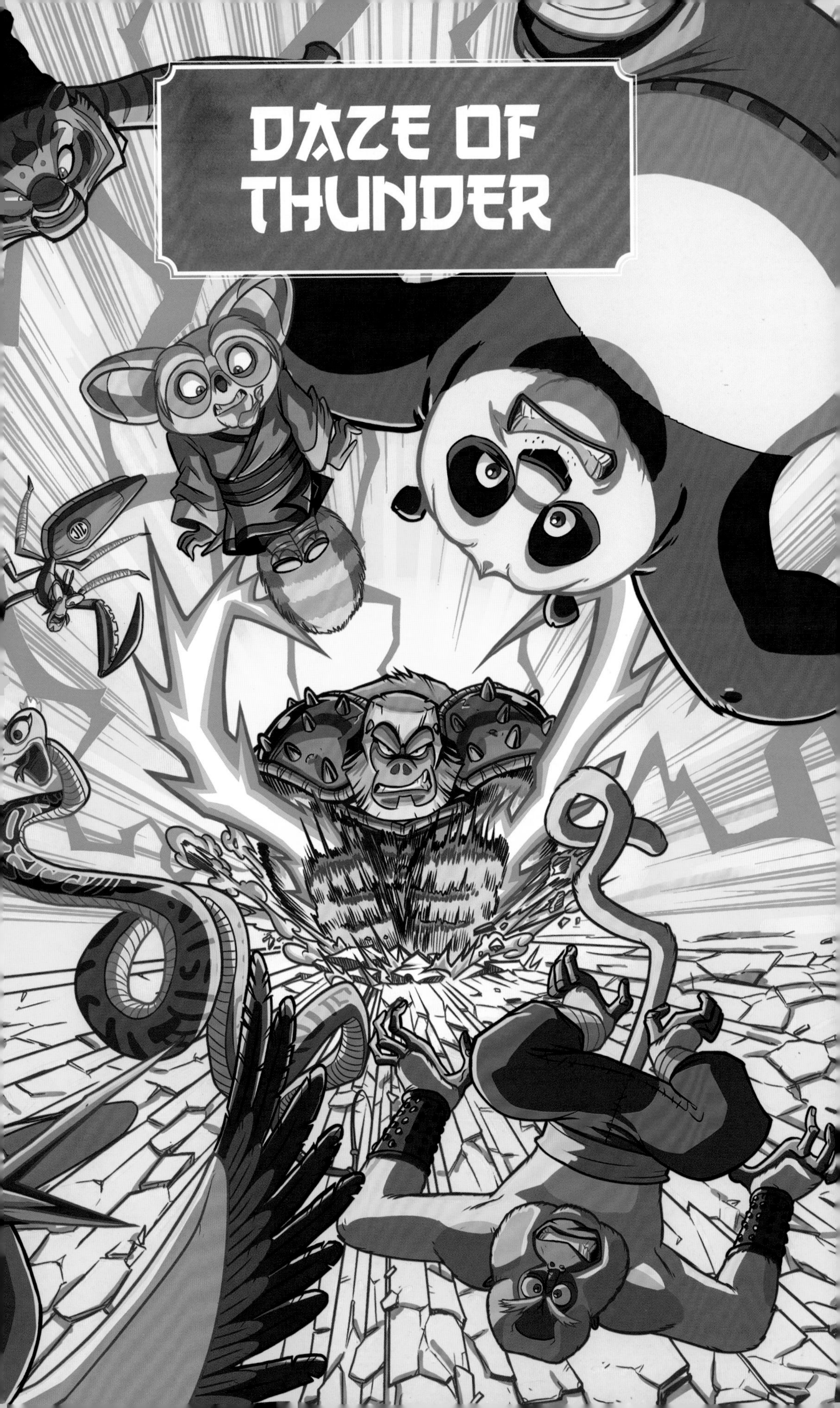
DAZE OF
THUNDER

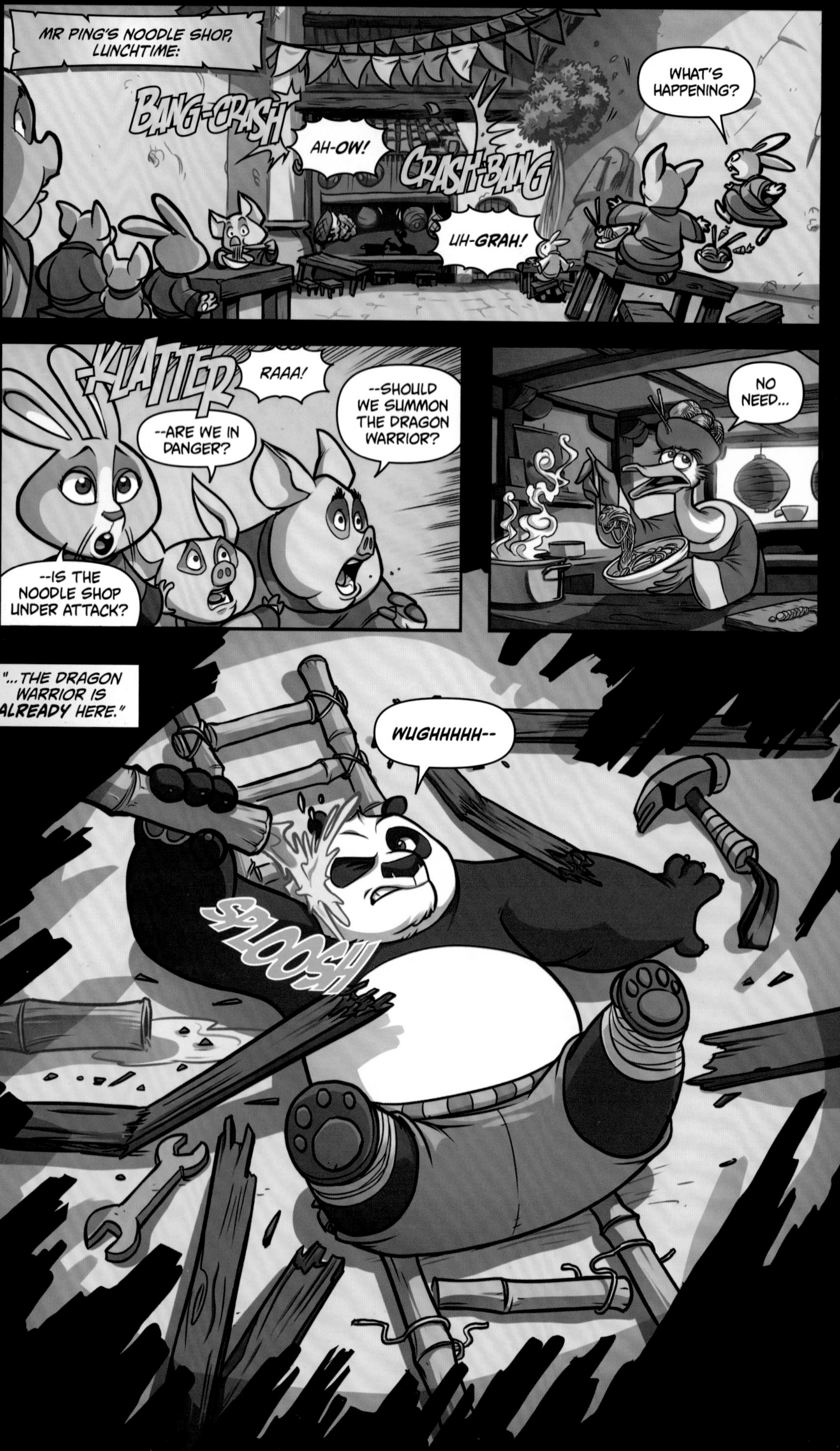
MR PING'S NOODLE SHOP, LUNCHTIME:
BANG-CRASH
AH-OW!
CRASH-BANG
UH-GRAH!
WHAT'S HAPPENING?
KLATTER
RAAA!
--ARE WE IN DANGER?
--SHOULD WE SUMMON THE DRAGON WARRIOR?
--IS THE NOODLE SHOP UNDER ATTACK?
NO NEED...
"...THE DRAGON WARRIOR IS ALREADY HERE."
WUGHHHHH--
SPLOOSH

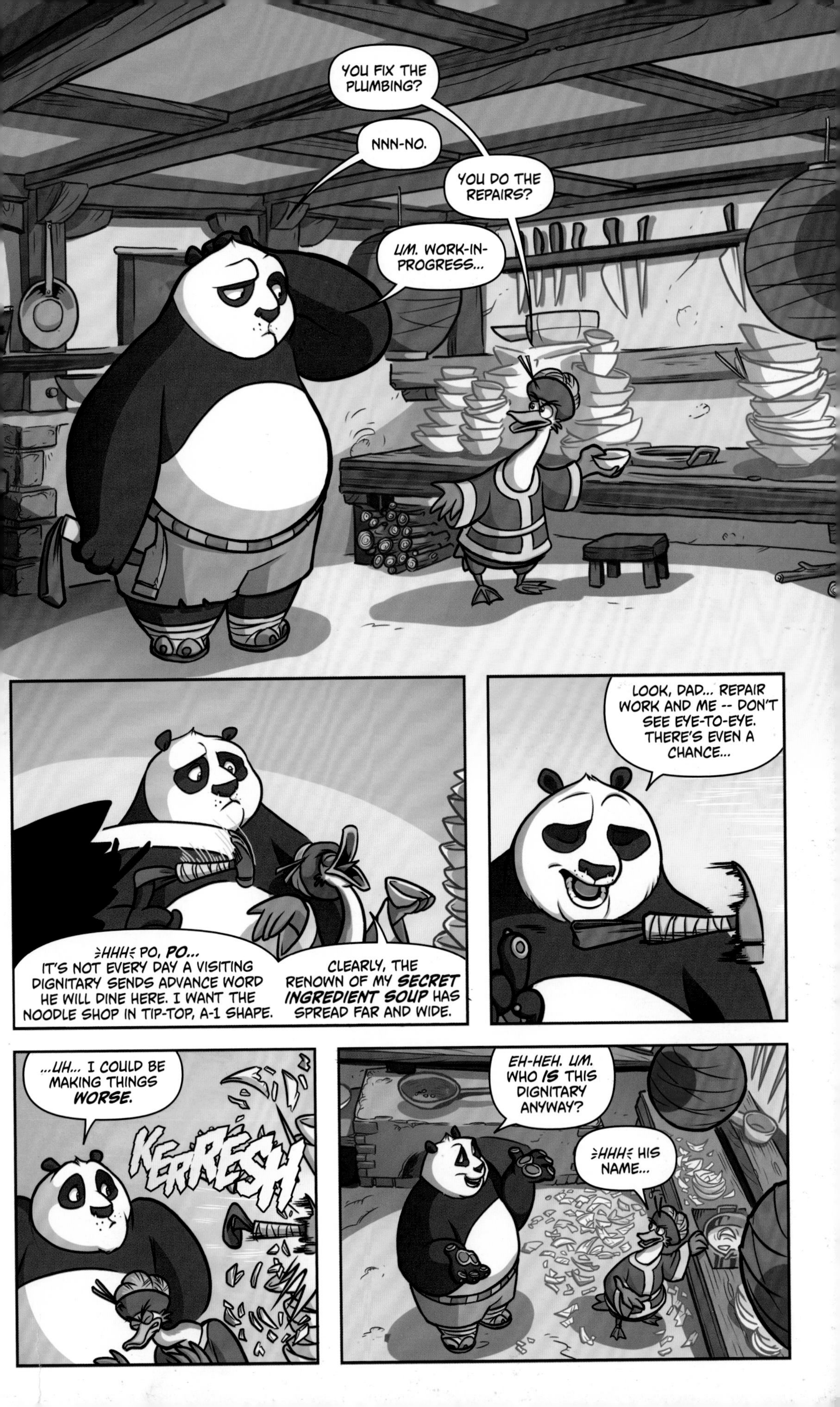
YOU FIX THE PLUMBING?
NNN-NO.
YOU DO THE REPAIRS?
UM. WORK-IN-PROGRESS...
HHH PO, PO... IT'S NOT EVERY DAY A VISITING DIGNITARY SENDS ADVANCE WORD HE WILL DINE HERE. I WANT THE NOODLE SHOP IN TIP-TOP, A-1 SHAPE.
CLEARLY, THE RENOWN OF MY SECRET INGREDIENT SOUP HAS SPREAD FAR AND WIDE.
LOOK, DAD... REPAIR WORK AND ME -- DON'T SEE EYE-TO-EYE. THERE'S EVEN A CHANCE...
...UH... I COULD BE MAKING THINGS WORSE.
KERRESH
EH-HEH. UM. WHO IS THIS DIGNITARY ANYWAY?
HHH HIS NAME...

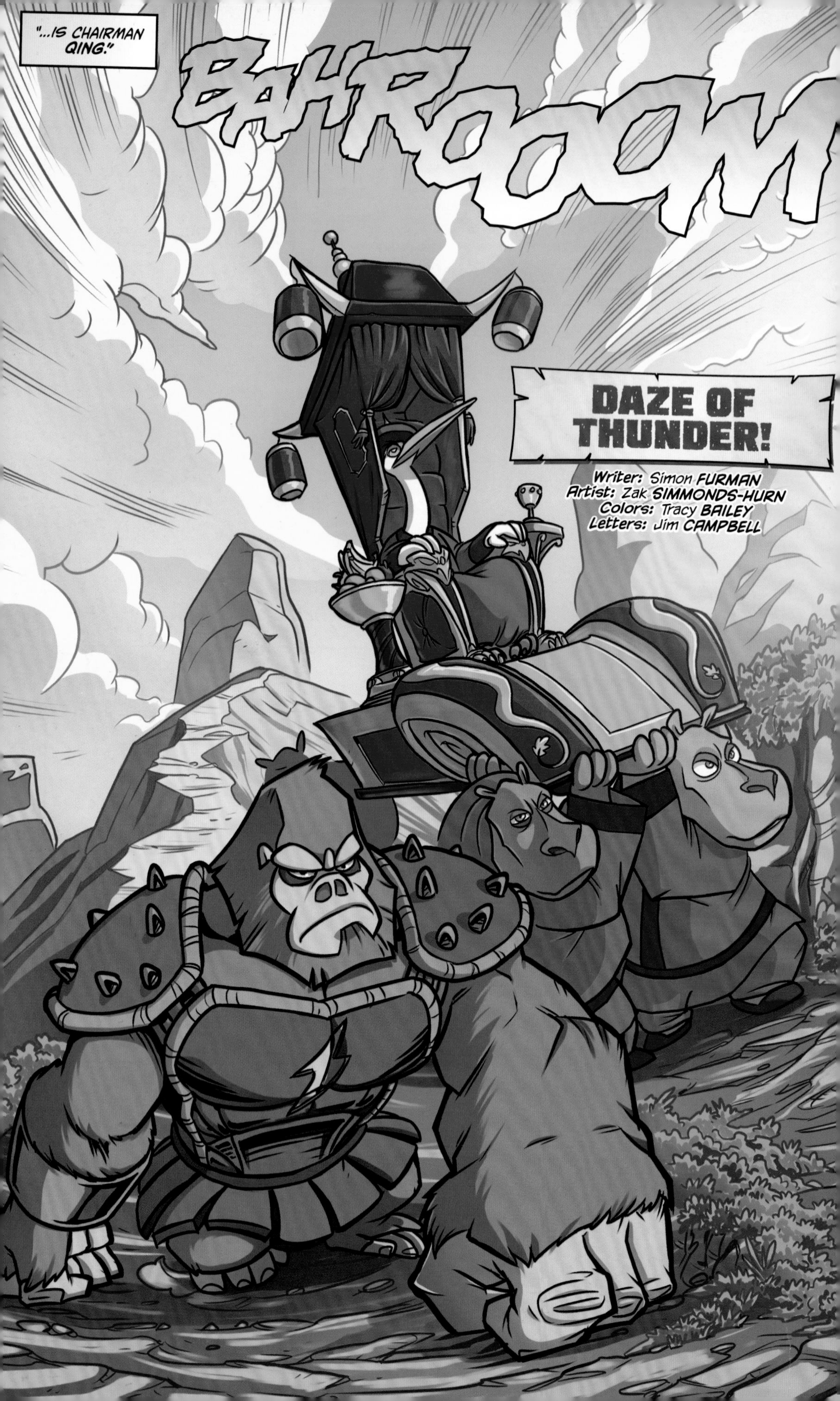
"...IS CHAIRMAN QING."
BAHROOOM
DAZE OF THUNDER!
Writer: Simon FURMAN
Artist: Zak SIMMONDS-HURN
Colors: Tracy BAILEY
Letters: Jim CAMPBELL

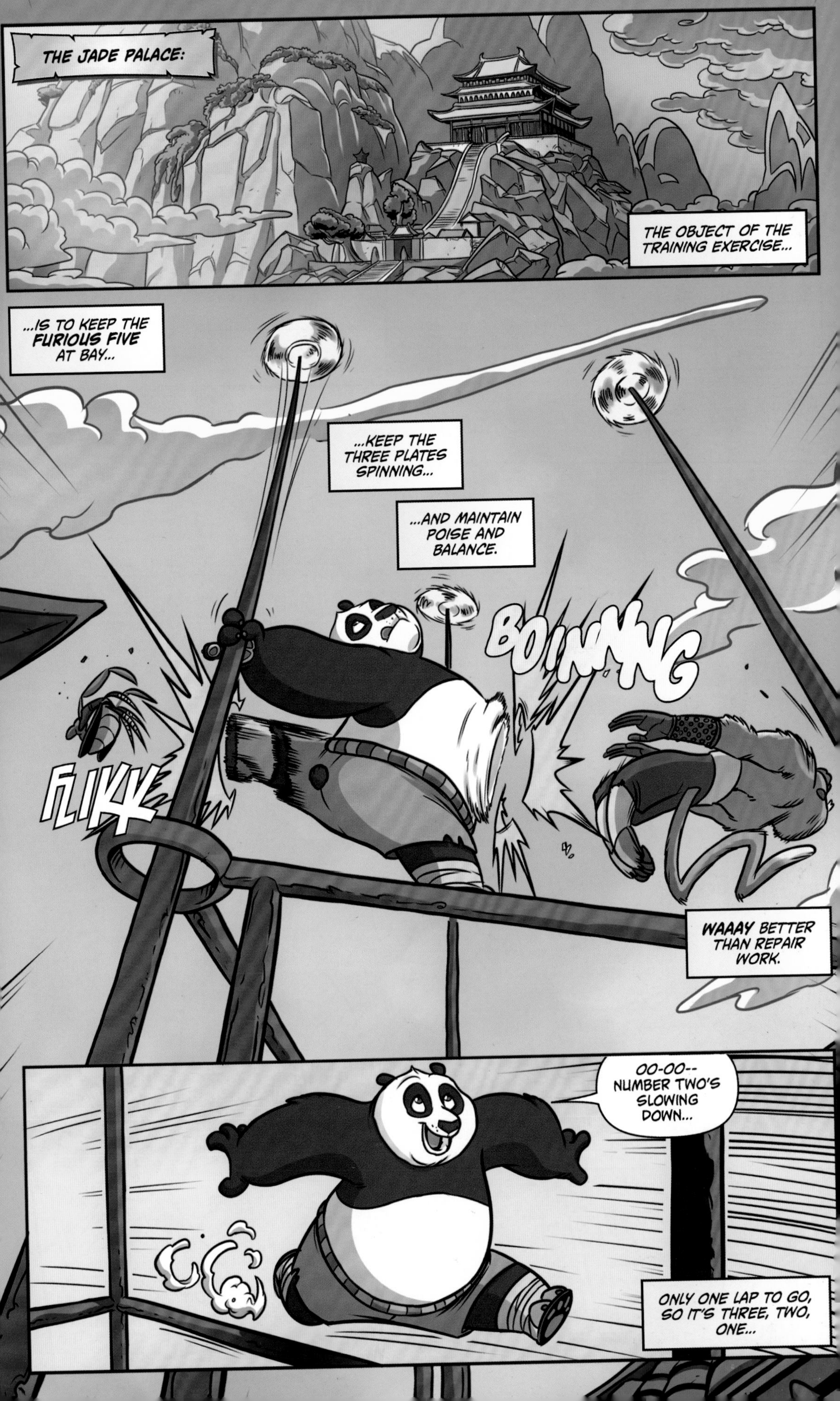

THE JADE PALACE:
THE OBJECT OF THE TRAINING EXERCISE...
...IS TO KEEP THE FURIOUS FIVE AT BAY...
...KEEP THE THREE PLATES SPINNING...
...AND MAINTAIN POISE AND BALANCE.
BOINNNG
FLIKK
WAAAY BETTER THAN REPAIR WORK.
OO-OO-- NUMBER TWO'S SLOWING DOWN...
ONLY ONE LAP TO GO, SO IT'S THREE, TWO, ONE...

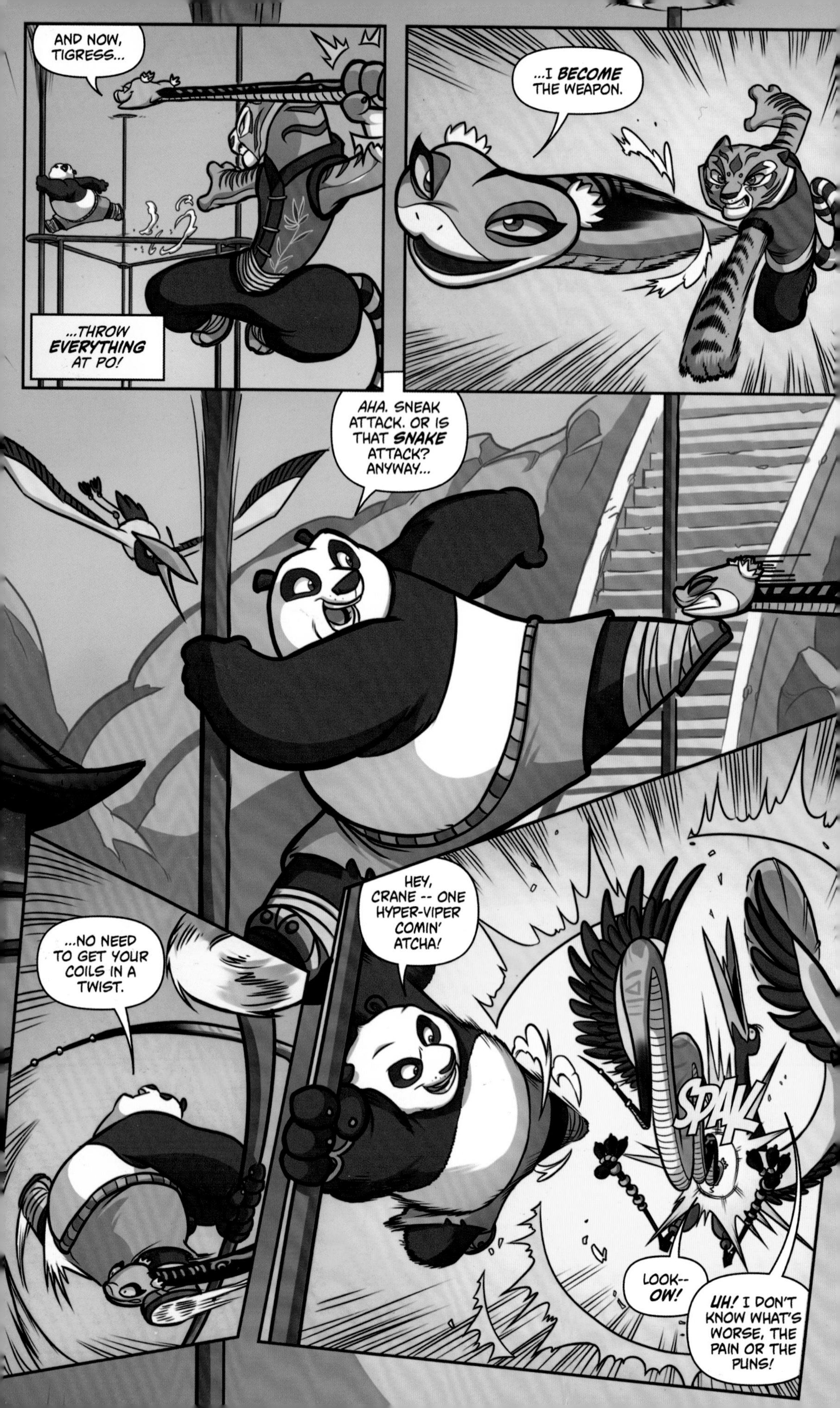
AND NOW, TIGRESS...
...THROW EVERYTHING AT PO!
...I BECOME THE WEAPON.
AHA. SNEAK ATTACK. OR IS THAT SNAKE ATTACK? ANYWAY...
...NO NEED TO GET YOUR COILS IN A TWIST.
HEY, CRANE -- ONE HYPER-VIPER COMIN' ATCHA!
SPAK!
LOOK-- OW!
UH! I DON'T KNOW WHAT'S WORSE, THE PAIN OR THE PUNS!

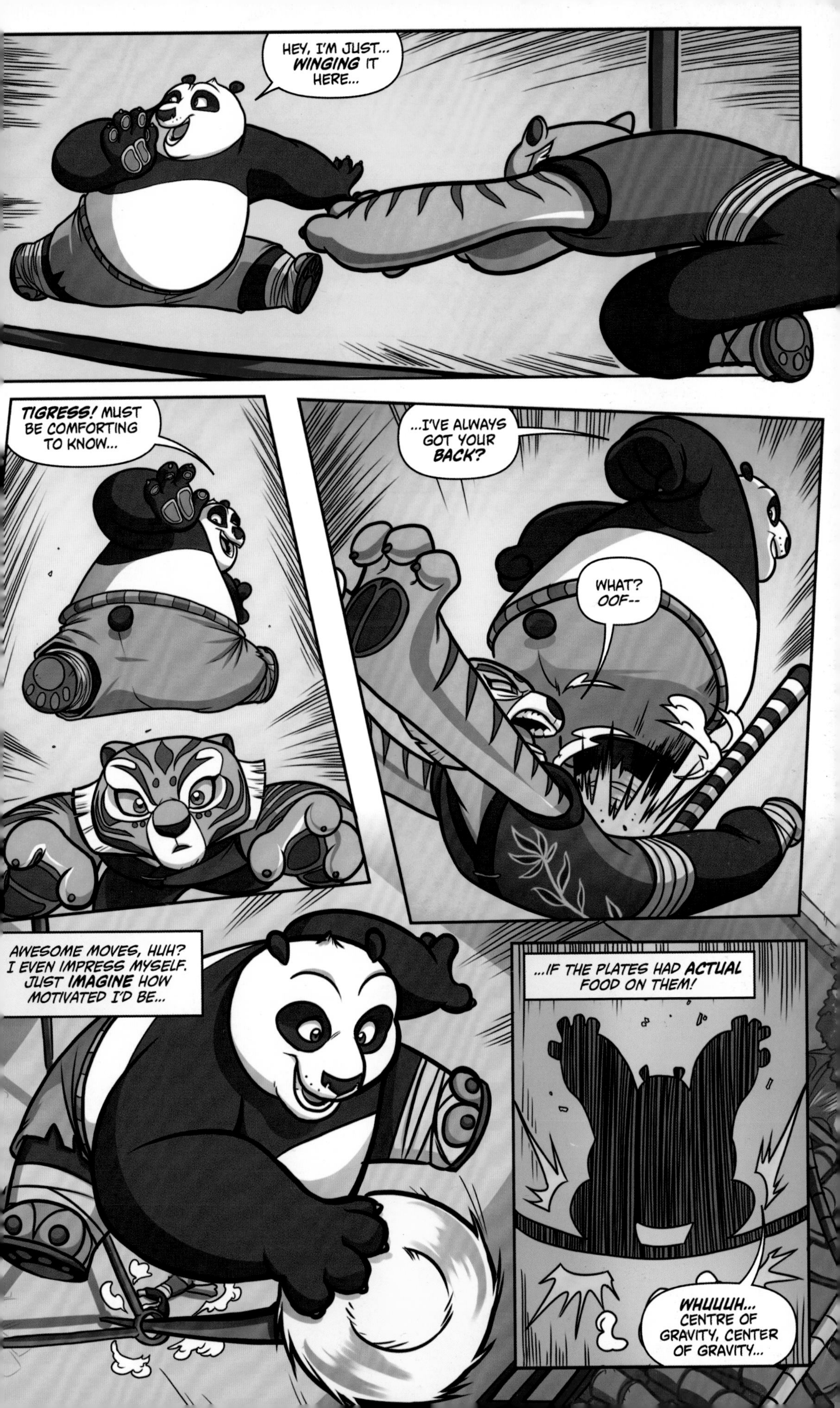

HEY, I'M JUST... WINGING IT HERE...
TIGRESS! MUST BE COMFORTING TO KNOW...
...I'VE ALWAYS GOT YOUR BACK?
WHAT? OOF--
AWESOME MOVES, HUH? I EVEN IMPRESS MYSELF. JUST IMAGINE HOW MOTIVATED I'D BE...
...IF THE PLATES HAD ACTUAL FOOD ON THEM!
WHUUUH... CENTRE OF GRAVITY, CENTER OF GRAVITY...

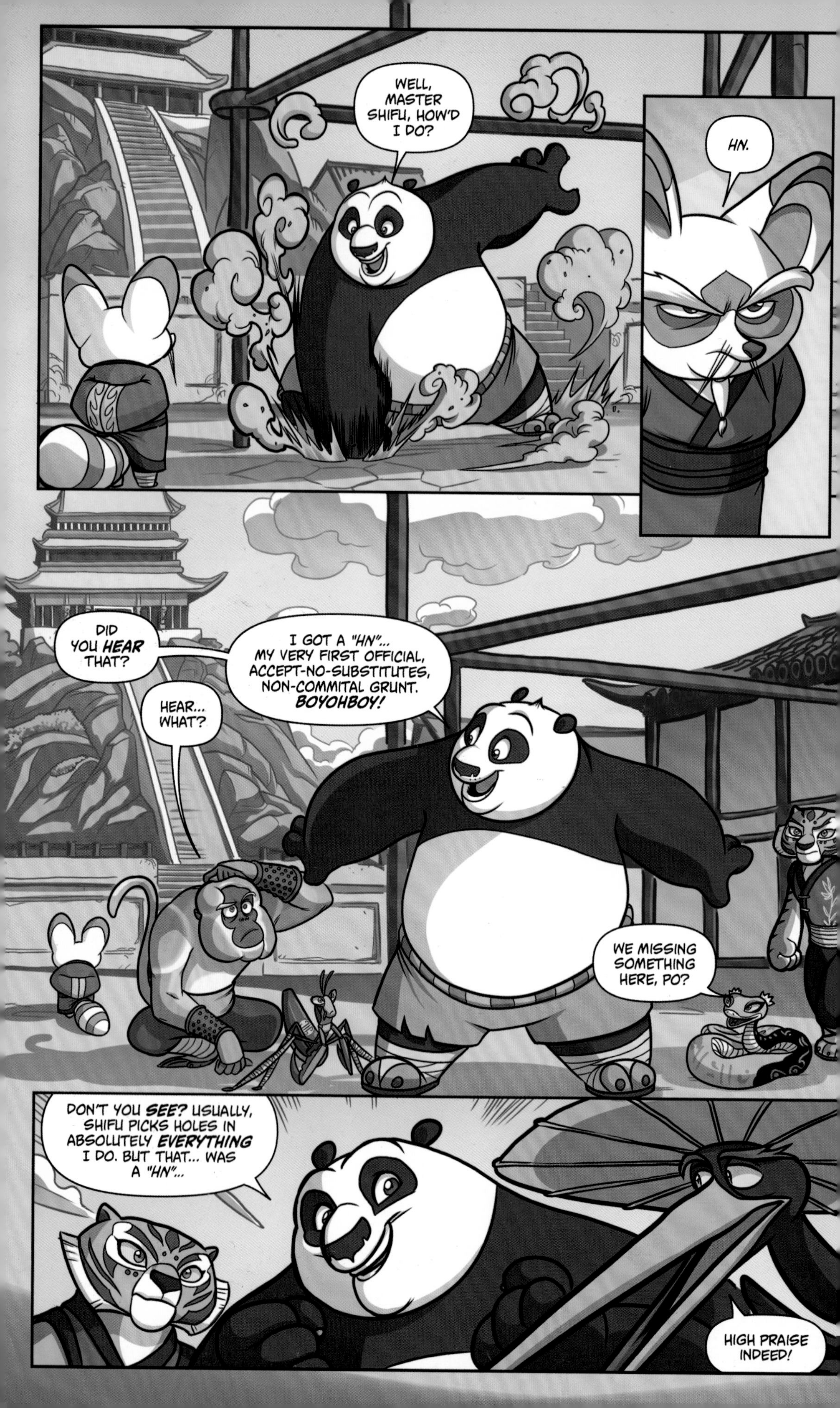

WELL, MASTER SHIFU, HOW'D I DO?
HN.
DID YOU **HEAR** THAT?
I GOT A "HN"... MY VERY FIRST OFFICIAL, ACCEPT-NO-SUBSTITUTES, NON-COMMITAL GRUNT. ***BOYOHBOY!***
HEAR... WHAT?
WE MISSING SOMETHING HERE, PO?
DON'T YOU ***SEE?*** USUALLY, SHIFU PICKS HOLES IN ABSOLUTELY ***EVERYTHING*** I DO. BUT THAT... WAS A "HN"...
HIGH PRAISE INDEED!

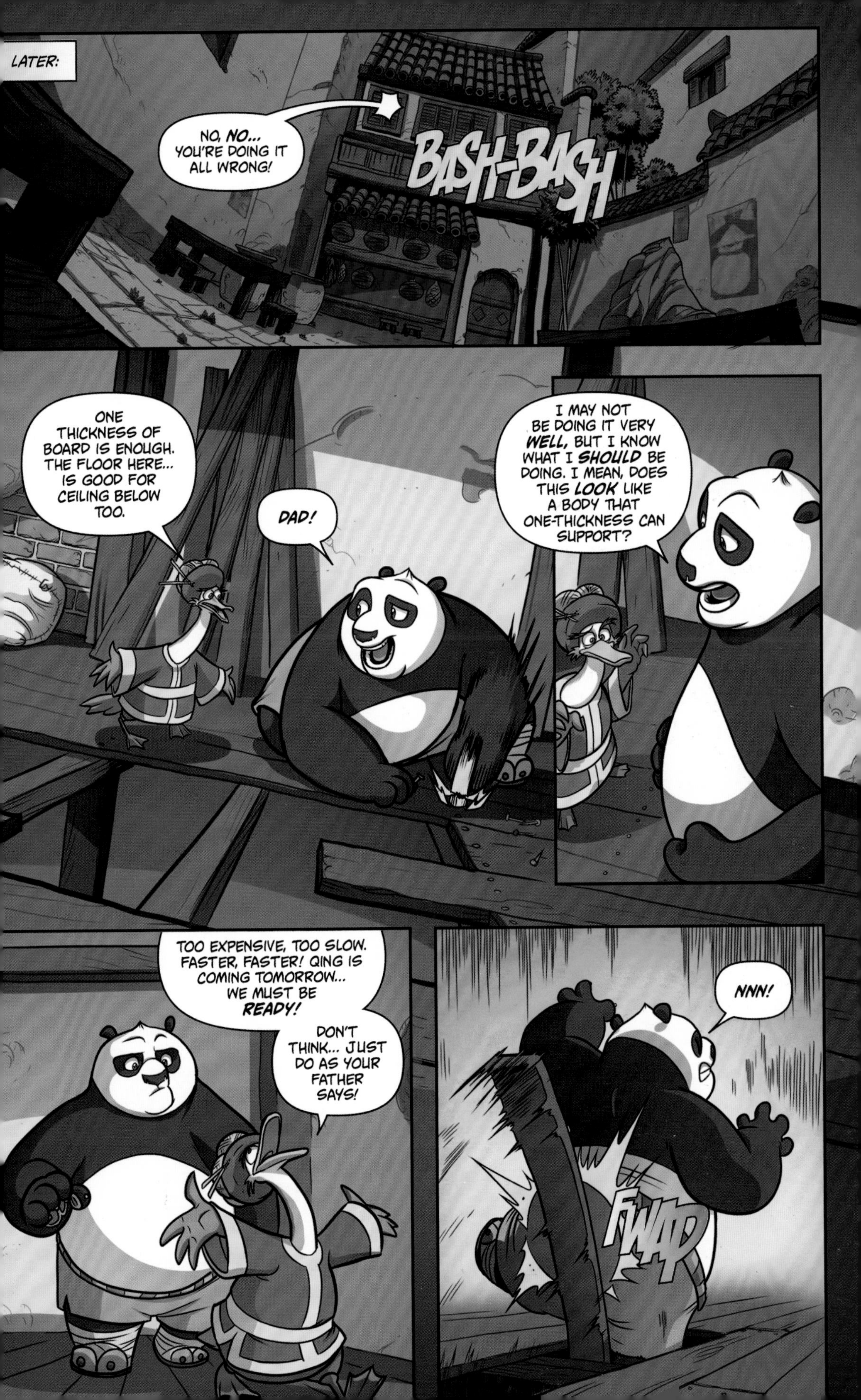
LATER:
NO, NO... YOU'RE DOING IT ALL WRONG!
BASH-BASH
ONE THICKNESS OF BOARD IS ENOUGH. THE FLOOR HERE... IS GOOD FOR CEILING BELOW TOO.
DAD!
I MAY NOT BE DOING IT VERY WELL, BUT I KNOW WHAT I SHOULD BE DOING. I MEAN, DOES THIS LOOK LIKE A BODY THAT ONE-THICKNESS CAN SUPPORT?
TOO EXPENSIVE, TOO SLOW. FASTER, FASTER! QING IS COMING TOMORROW... WE MUST BE READY!
DON'T THINK... JUST DO AS YOUR FATHER SAYS!
NNN!
FWAP

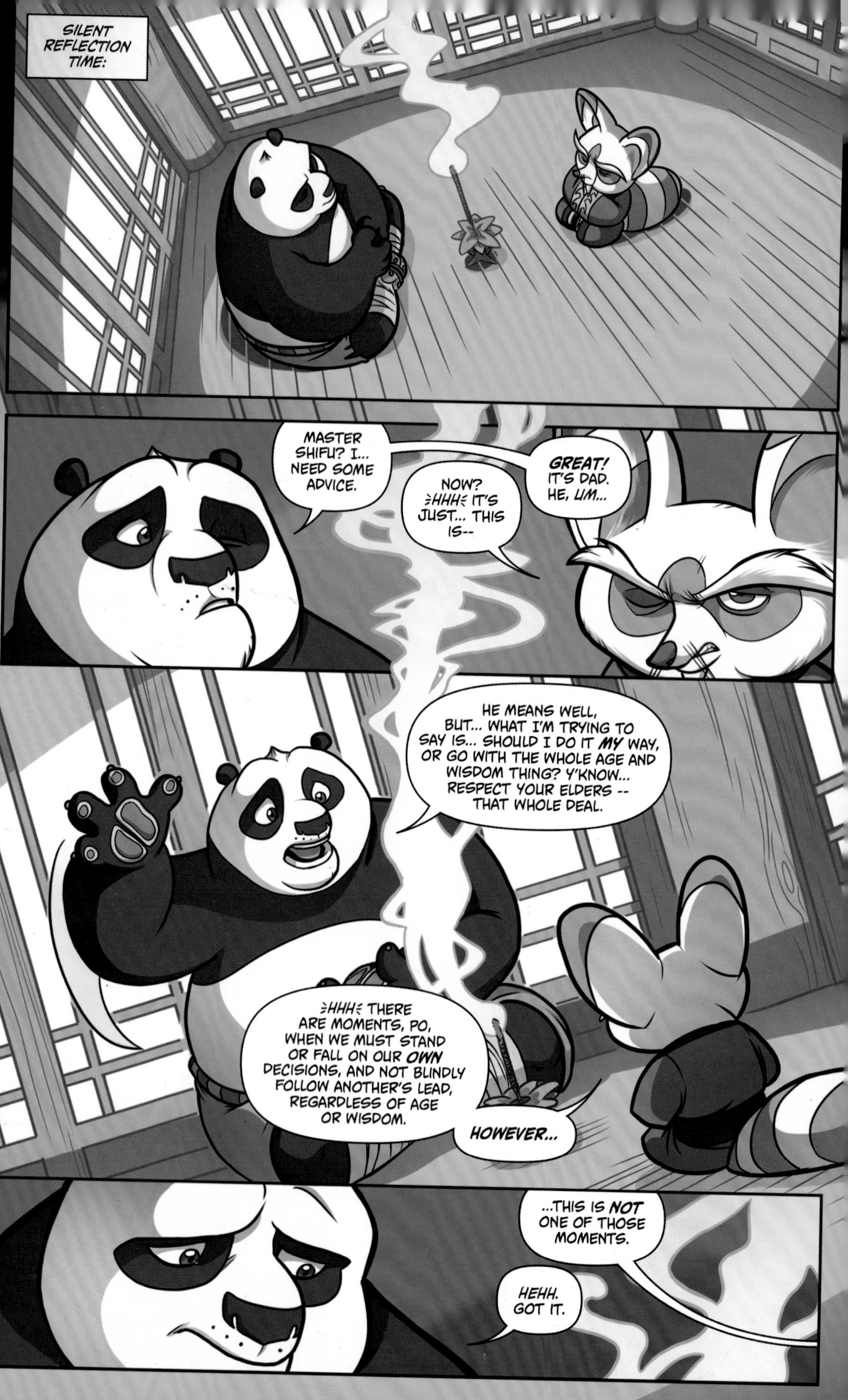
SILENT REFLECTION TIME:
MASTER SHIFU? I... NEED SOME ADVICE.
NOW? HHH IT'S JUST... THIS IS--
GREAT! IT'S DAD. HE, UM...
HE MEANS WELL, BUT... WHAT I'M TRYING TO SAY IS... SHOULD I DO IT MY WAY, OR GO WITH THE WHOLE AGE AND WISDOM THING? Y'KNOW... RESPECT YOUR ELDERS -- THAT WHOLE DEAL.
HHH THERE ARE MOMENTS, PO, WHEN WE MUST STAND OR FALL ON OUR OWN DECISIONS, AND NOT BLINDLY FOLLOW ANOTHER'S LEAD, REGARDLESS OF AGE OR WISDOM.
HOWEVER...
...THIS IS NOT ONE OF THOSE MOMENTS.
HEHH. GOT IT.

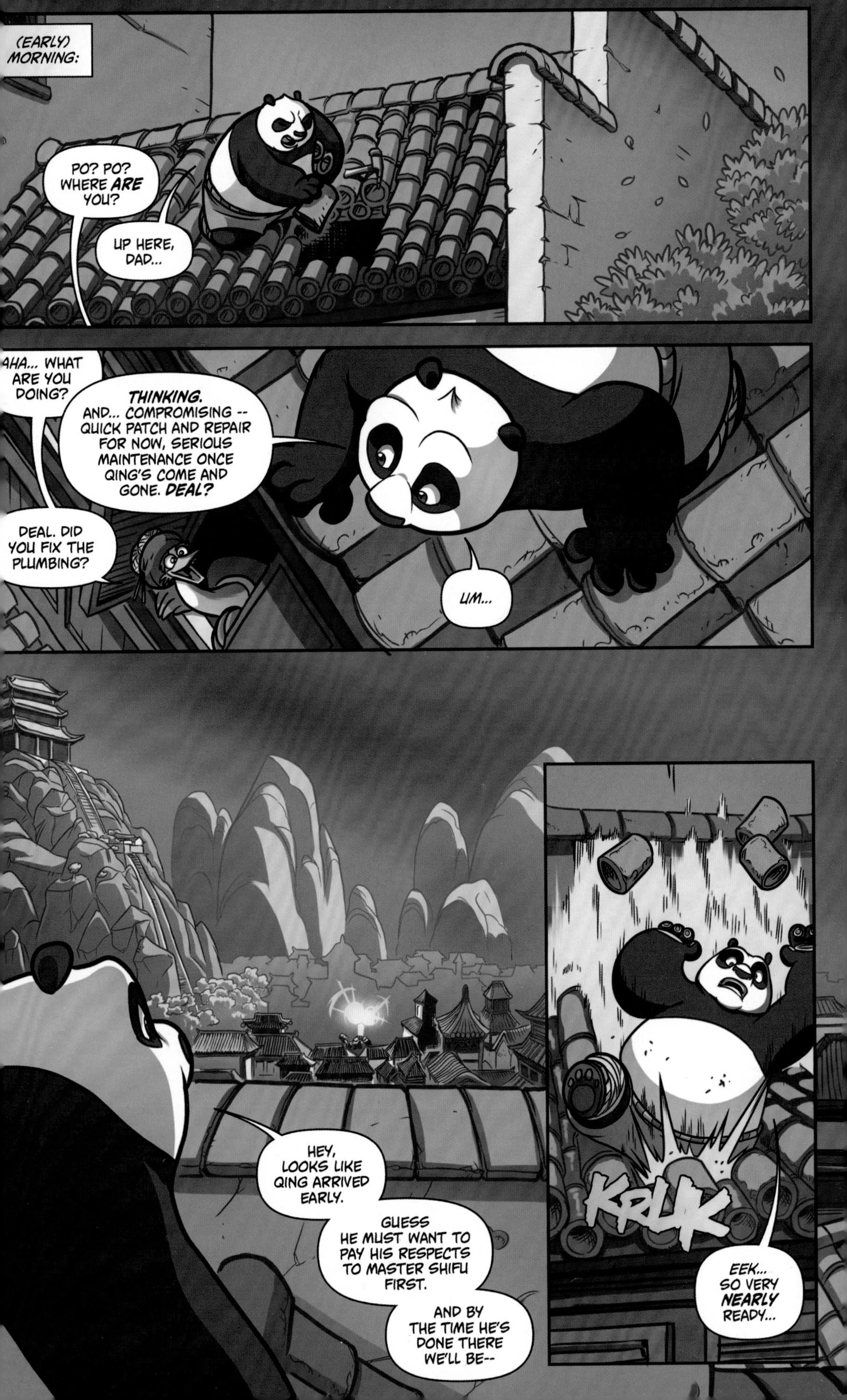

(EARLY) MORNING:
PO? PO? WHERE ARE YOU?
UP HERE, DAD...
AHA... WHAT ARE YOU DOING?
THINKING. AND... COMPROMISING -- QUICK PATCH AND REPAIR FOR NOW, SERIOUS MAINTENANCE ONCE QING'S COME AND GONE. DEAL?
DEAL. DID YOU FIX THE PLUMBING?
UM...
HEY, LOOKS LIKE QING ARRIVED EARLY.
GUESS HE MUST WANT TO PAY HIS RESPECTS TO MASTER SHIFU FIRST.
AND BY THE TIME HE'S DONE THERE WE'LL BE--
KRUK
EEK... SO VERY NEARLY READY...

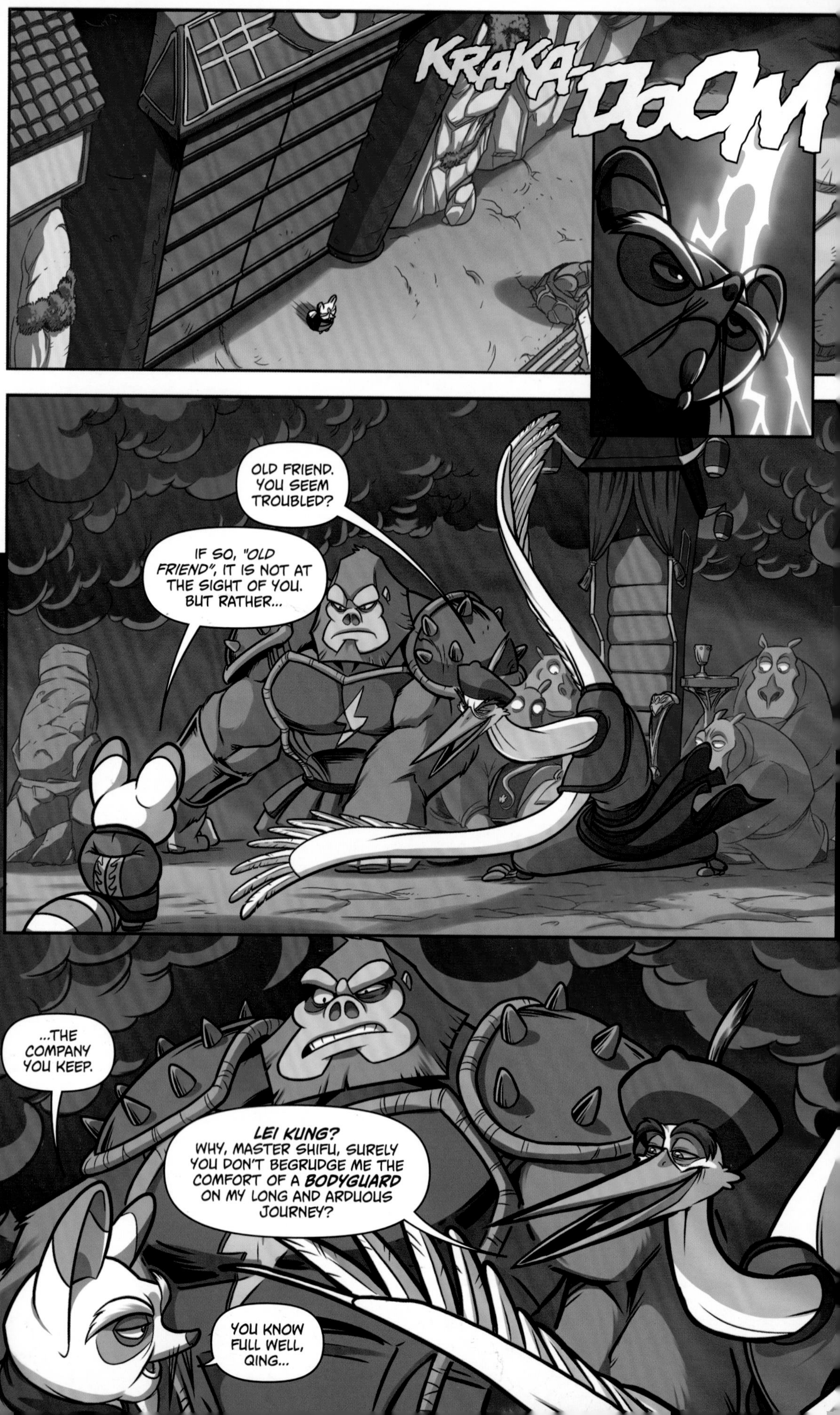
KRAKA-DOOM
OLD FRIEND. YOU SEEM TROUBLED?
IF SO, "OLD FRIEND", IT IS NOT AT THE SIGHT OF YOU. BUT RATHER...
...THE COMPANY YOU KEEP.
LEI KUNG? WHY, MASTER SHIFU, SURELY YOU DON'T BEGRUDGE ME THE COMFORT OF A BODYGUARD ON MY LONG AND ARDUOUS JOURNEY?
YOU KNOW FULL WELL, QING...

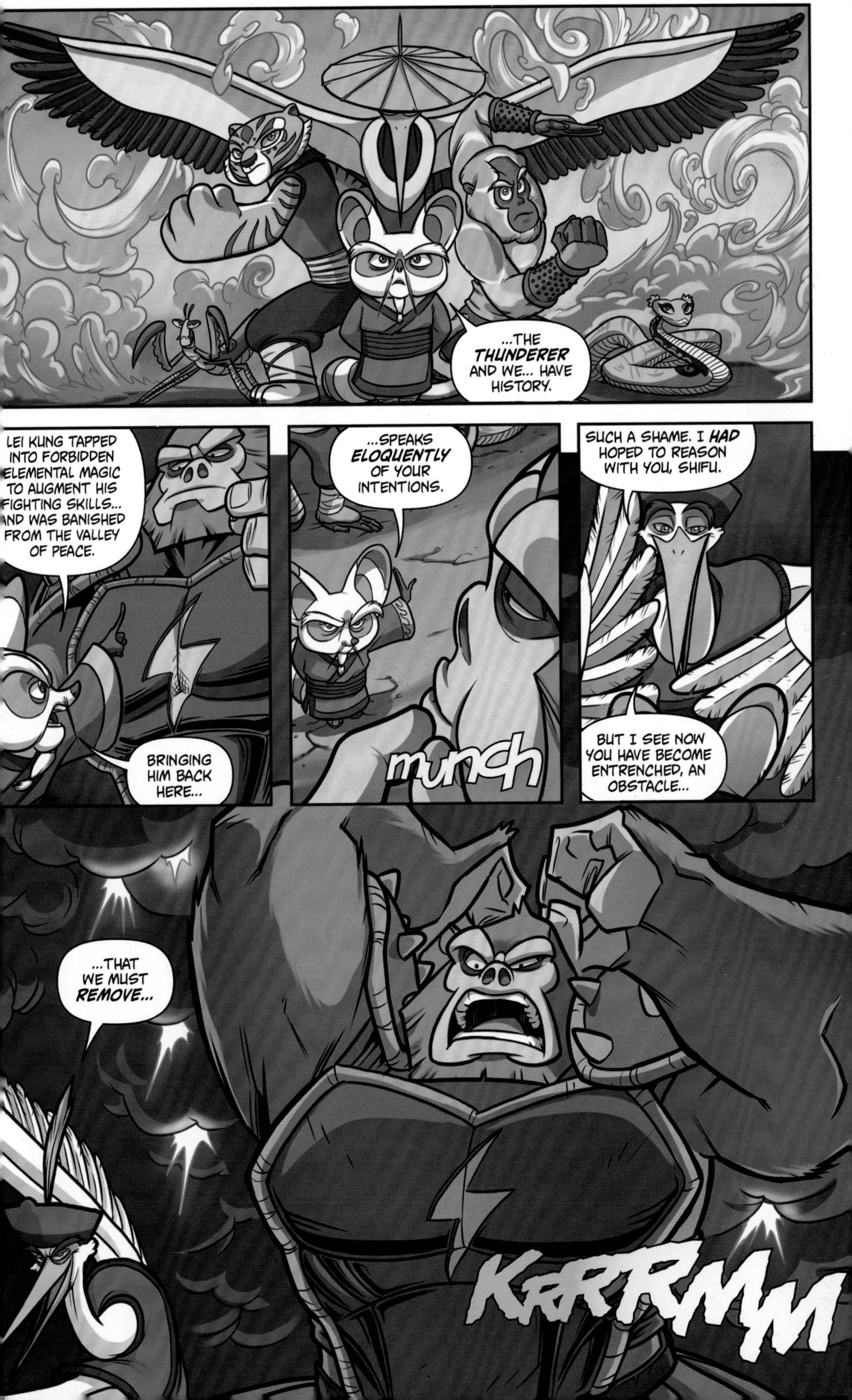

...THE THUNDERER AND WE... HAVE HISTORY.
LEI KUNG TAPPED INTO FORBIDDEN ELEMENTAL MAGIC TO AUGMENT HIS FIGHTING SKILLS... ND WAS BANISHED FROM THE VALLEY OF PEACE.
BRINGING HIM BACK HERE...
...SPEAKS ELOQUENTLY OF YOUR INTENTIONS.
munch
SUCH A SHAME. I HAD HOPED TO REASON WITH YOU, SHIFU.
BUT I SEE NOW YOU HAVE BECOME ENTRENCHED, AN OBSTACLE...
...THAT WE MUST REMOVE...
KRRRMM

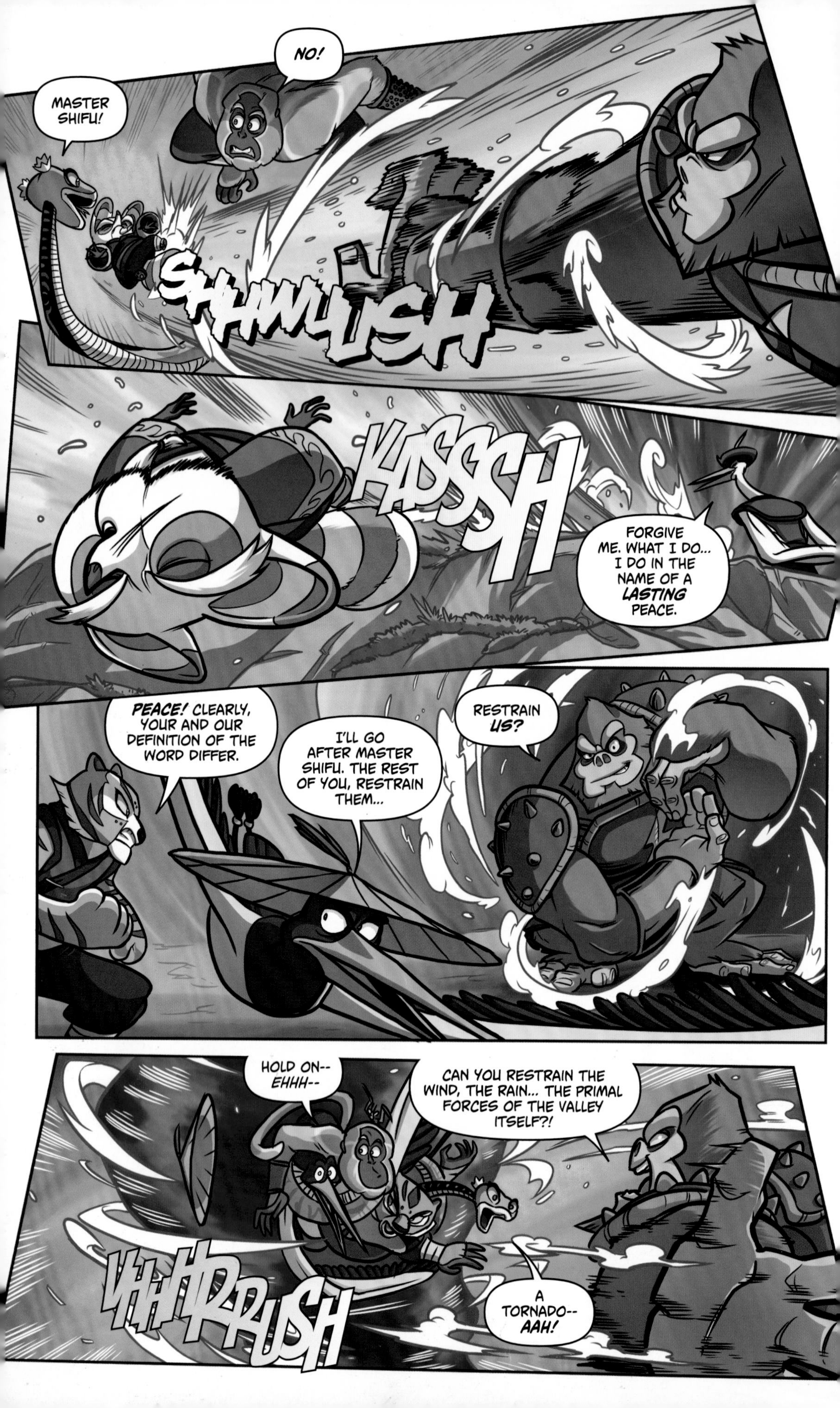
MASTER SHIFU!
NO!
SHHWUSH
KASSSH
FORGIVE ME. WHAT I DO... I DO IN THE NAME OF A LASTING PEACE.
PEACE! CLEARLY, YOUR AND OUR DEFINITION OF THE WORD DIFFER.
I'LL GO AFTER MASTER SHIFU. THE REST OF YOU, RESTRAIN THEM...
RESTRAIN US?
HOLD ON-- EHHH--
CAN YOU RESTRAIN THE WIND, THE RAIN... THE PRIMAL FORCES OF THE VALLEY ITSELF?!
VHHRRUSH
A TORNADO-- AAH!

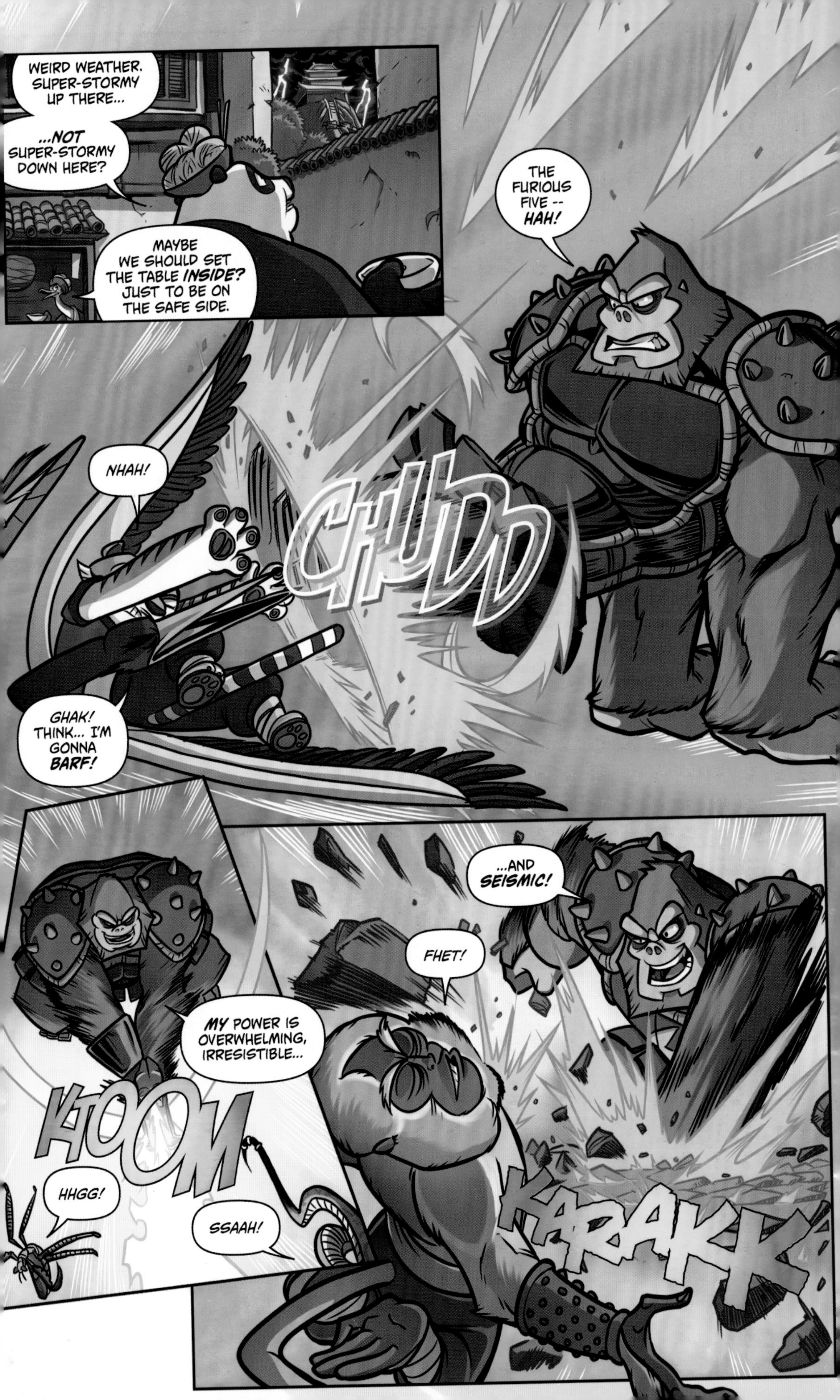

WEIRD WEATHER. SUPER-STORMY UP THERE...
...NOT SUPER-STORMY DOWN HERE?
MAYBE WE SHOULD SET THE TABLE INSIDE? JUST TO BE ON THE SAFE SIDE.
THE FURIOUS FIVE -- HAH!
NHAH!
CHUDD
GHAK! THINK... I'M GONNA BARF!
MY POWER IS OVERWHELMING, IRRESISTIBLE...
KTOOM
HHGG!
SSAAH!
...AND SEISMIC!
FHET!
KARAKK

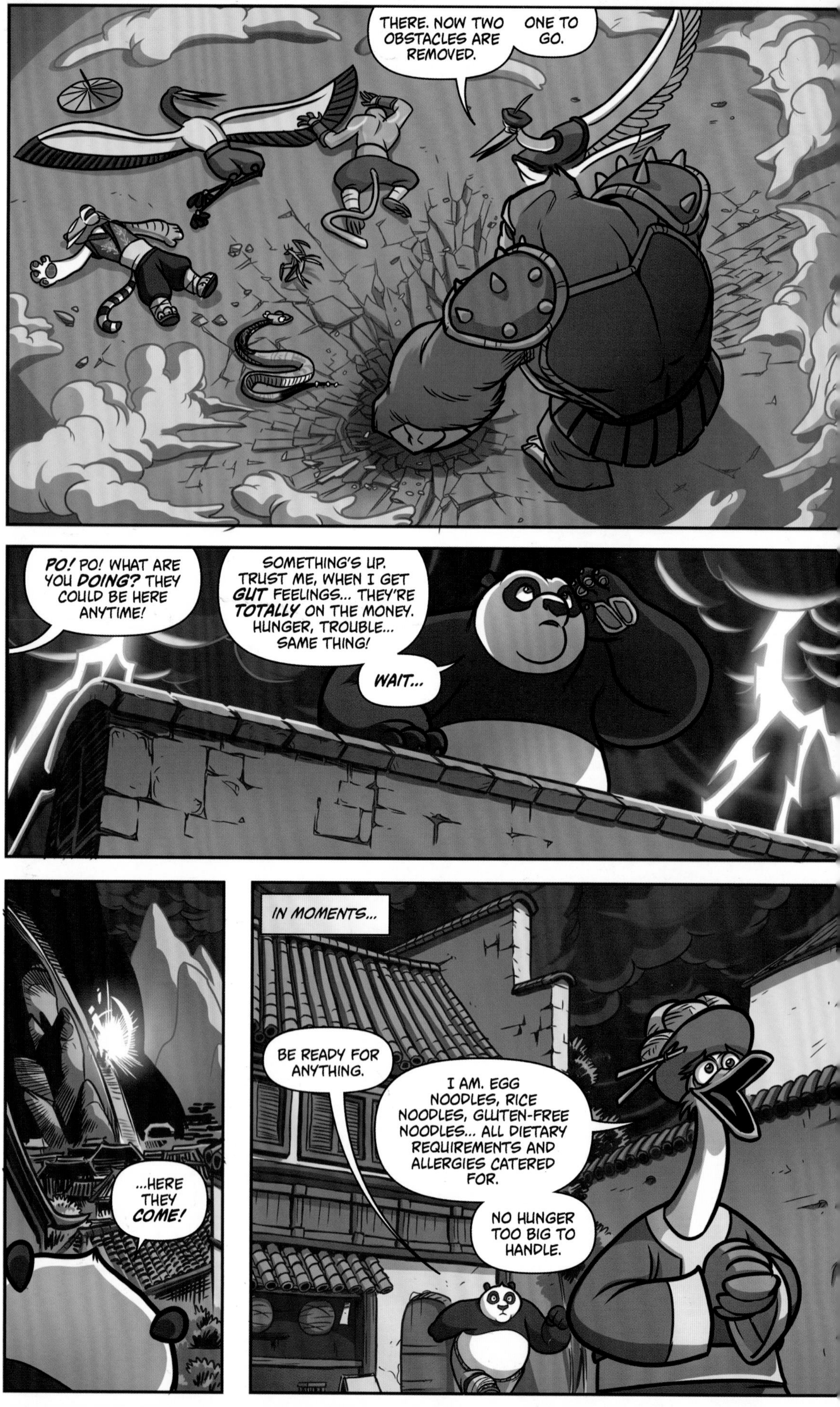
THERE. NOW TWO OBSTACLES ARE REMOVED.
ONE TO GO.
PO! PO! WHAT ARE YOU DOING? THEY COULD BE HERE ANYTIME!
SOMETHING'S UP. TRUST ME, WHEN I GET GUT FEELINGS... THEY'RE TOTALLY ON THE MONEY. HUNGER, TROUBLE... SAME THING!
WAIT...
...HERE THEY COME!
IN MOMENTS...
BE READY FOR ANYTHING.
I AM. EGG NOODLES, RICE NOODLES, GLUTEN-FREE NOODLES... ALL DIETARY REQUIREMENTS AND ALLERGIES CATERED FOR.
NO HUNGER TOO BIG TO HANDLE.

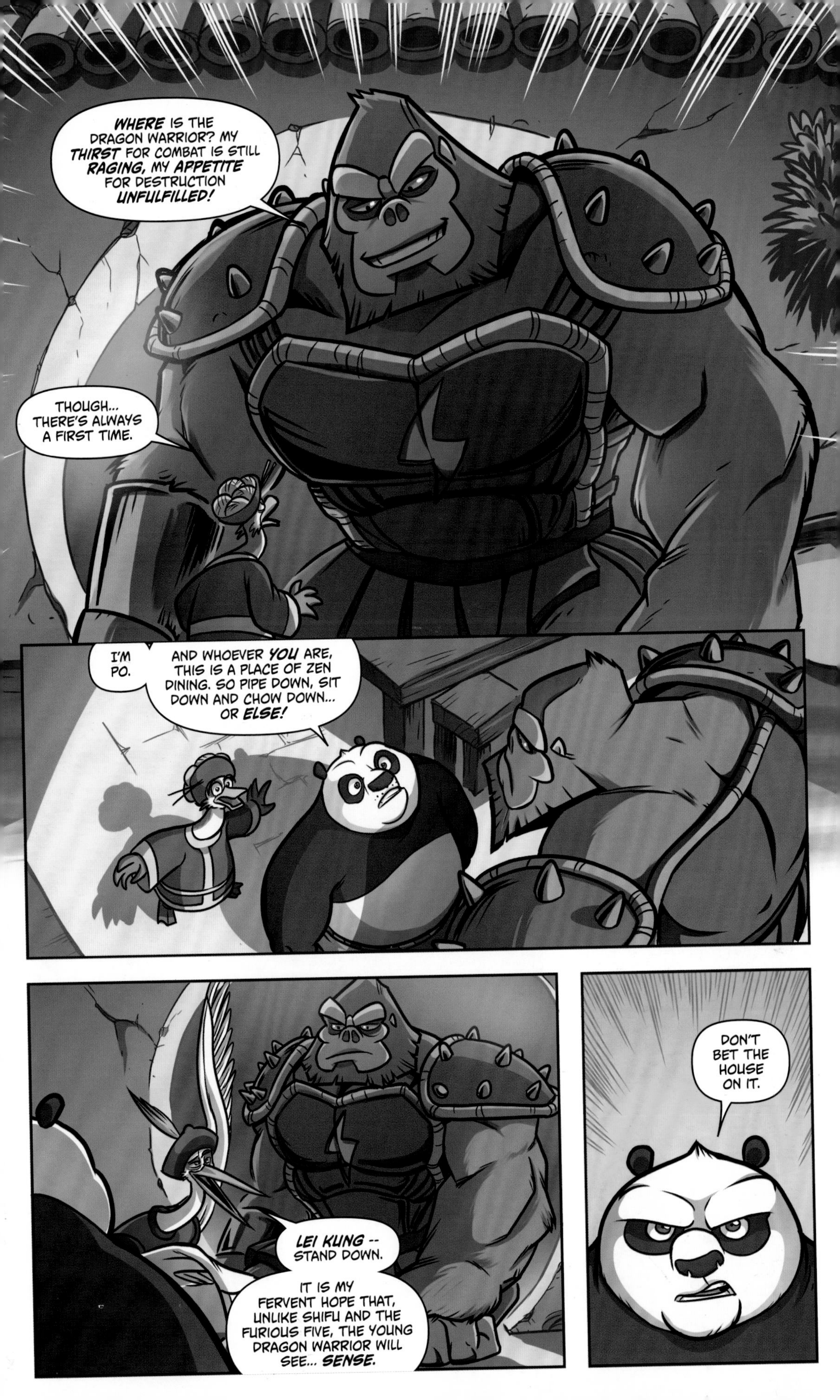

WHERE IS THE DRAGON WARRIOR? MY THIRST FOR COMBAT IS STILL RAGING, MY APPETITE FOR DESTRUCTION UNFULFILLED!
THOUGH... THERE'S ALWAYS A FIRST TIME.
I'M PO.
AND WHOEVER YOU ARE, THIS IS A PLACE OF ZEN DINING. SO PIPE DOWN, SIT DOWN AND CHOW DOWN... OR ELSE!
LEI KUNG -- STAND DOWN.
IT IS MY FERVENT HOPE THAT, UNLIKE SHIFU AND THE FURIOUS FIVE, THE YOUNG DRAGON WARRIOR WILL SEE... SENSE.
DON'T BET THE HOUSE ON IT.

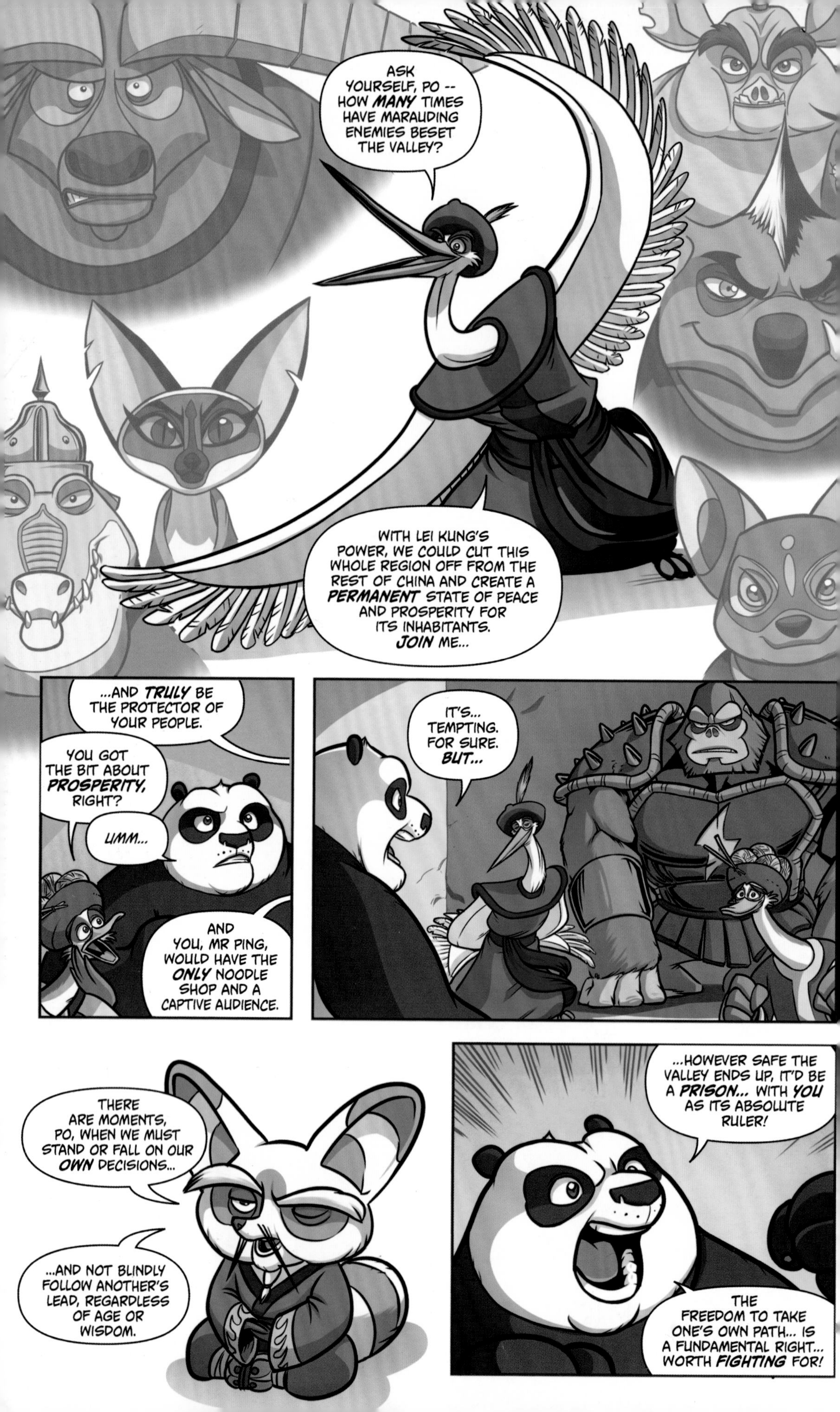

ASK YOURSELF, PO -- HOW MANY TIMES HAVE MARAUDING ENEMIES BESET THE VALLEY?
WITH LEI KUNG'S POWER, WE COULD CUT THIS WHOLE REGION OFF FROM THE REST OF CHINA AND CREATE A PERMANENT STATE OF PEACE AND PROSPERITY FOR ITS INHABITANTS. JOIN ME...
...AND TRULY BE THE PROTECTOR OF YOUR PEOPLE.
YOU GOT THE BIT ABOUT PROSPERITY, RIGHT?
UMM...
AND YOU, MR PING, WOULD HAVE THE ONLY NOODLE SHOP AND A CAPTIVE AUDIENCE.
IT'S... TEMPTING. FOR SURE. BUT...
THERE ARE MOMENTS, PO, WHEN WE MUST STAND OR FALL ON OUR OWN DECISIONS...
...AND NOT BLINDLY FOLLOW ANOTHER'S LEAD, REGARDLESS OF AGE OR WISDOM.
...HOWEVER SAFE THE VALLEY ENDS UP, IT'D BE A PRISON... WITH YOU AS ITS ABSOLUTE RULER!
THE FREEDOM TO TAKE ONE'S OWN PATH... IS A FUNDAMENTAL RIGHT... WORTH FIGHTING FOR!

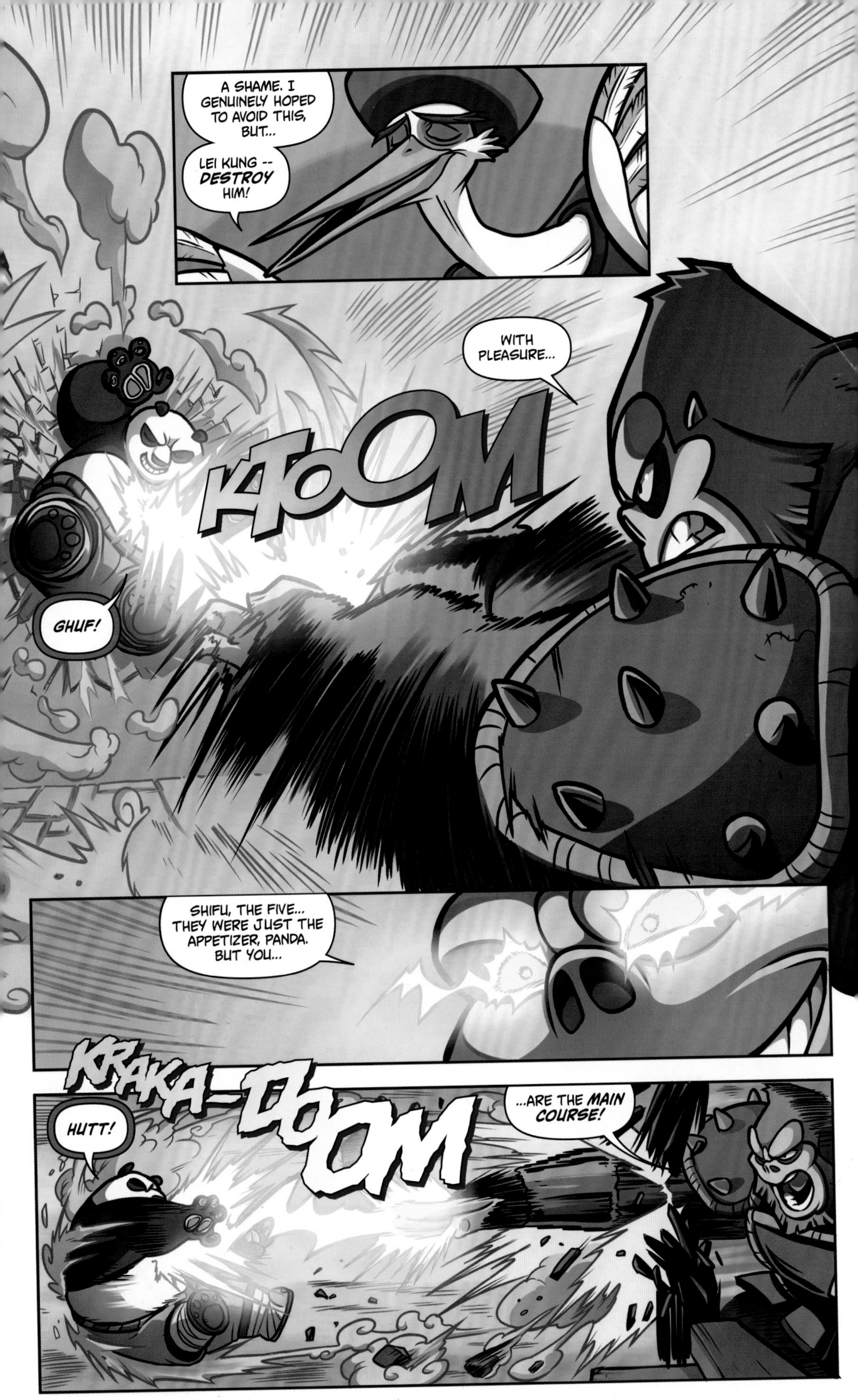

A SHAME. I GENUINELY HOPED TO AVOID THIS, BUT...
LEI KUNG -- DESTROY HIM!
WITH PLEASURE...
KTOOM
GHUF!
SHIFU, THE FIVE... THEY WERE JUST THE APPETIZER, PANDA. BUT YOU...
KRAKA-DOOM
HUTT!
...ARE THE MAIN COURSE!

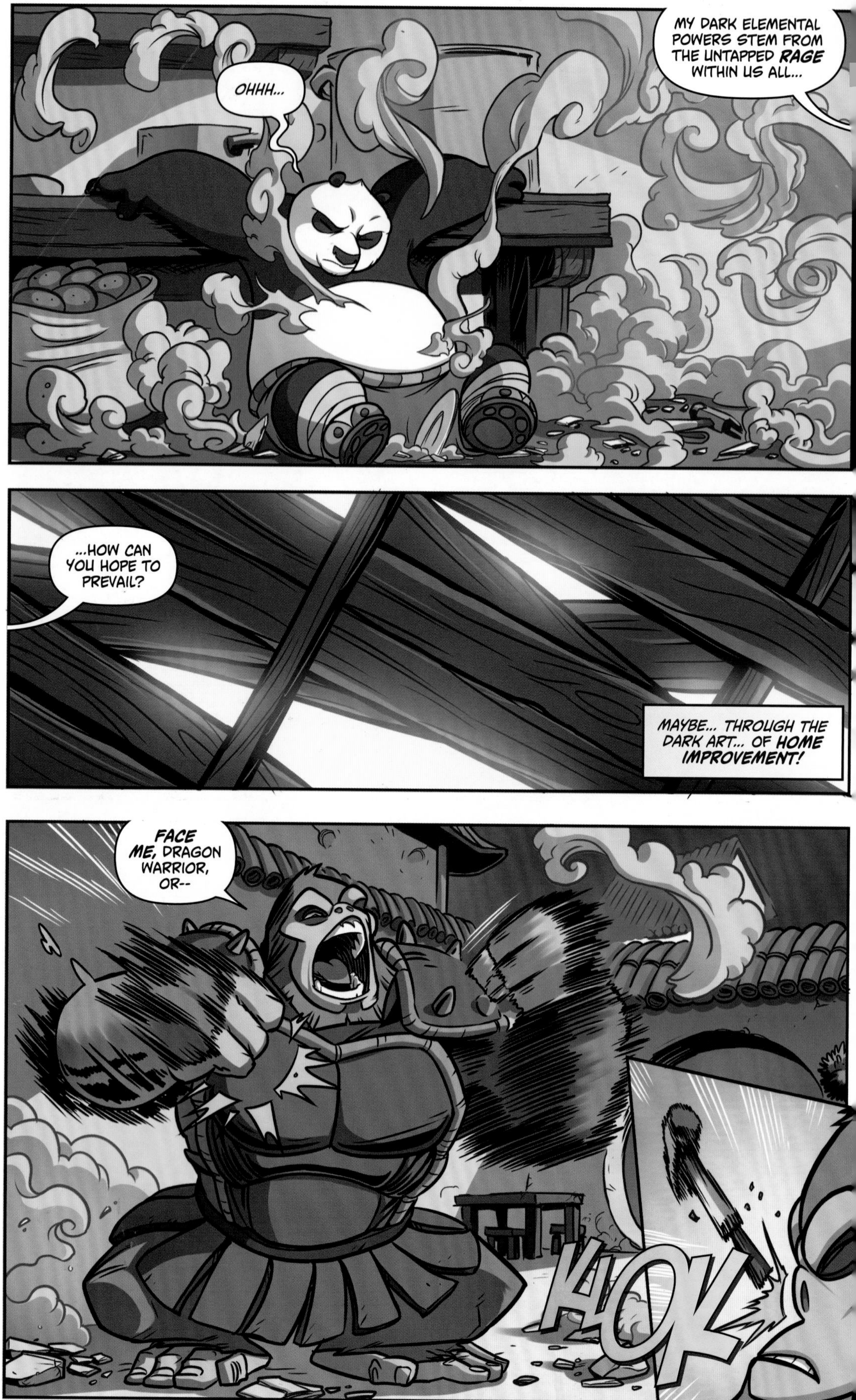
OHHH...
MY DARK ELEMENTAL POWERS STEM FROM THE UNTAPPED RAGE WITHIN US ALL...
...HOW CAN YOU HOPE TO PREVAIL?
MAYBE... THROUGH THE DARK ART... OF HOME IMPROVEMENT!
FACE ME, DRAGON WARRIOR, OR--
KKOK

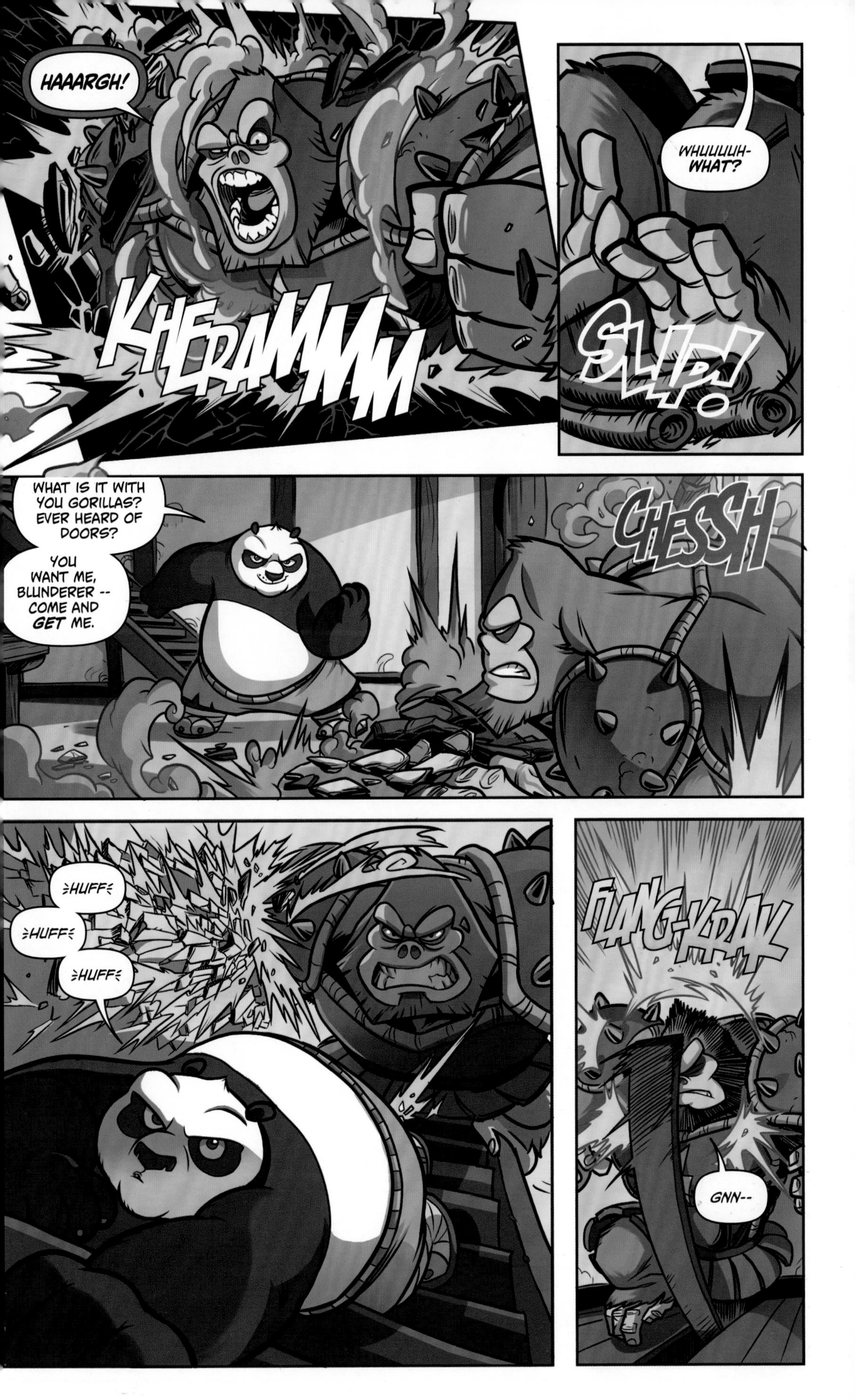
HAAARGH!
KHERAMMMM
WHUUUUH-WHAT?
SLIP!
WHAT IS IT WITH YOU GORILLAS? EVER HEARD OF DOORS?
YOU WANT ME, BLUNDERER -- COME AND GET ME.
CHESSH
HUFF
HUFF
HUFF
FLANG-KRAK
GNN--

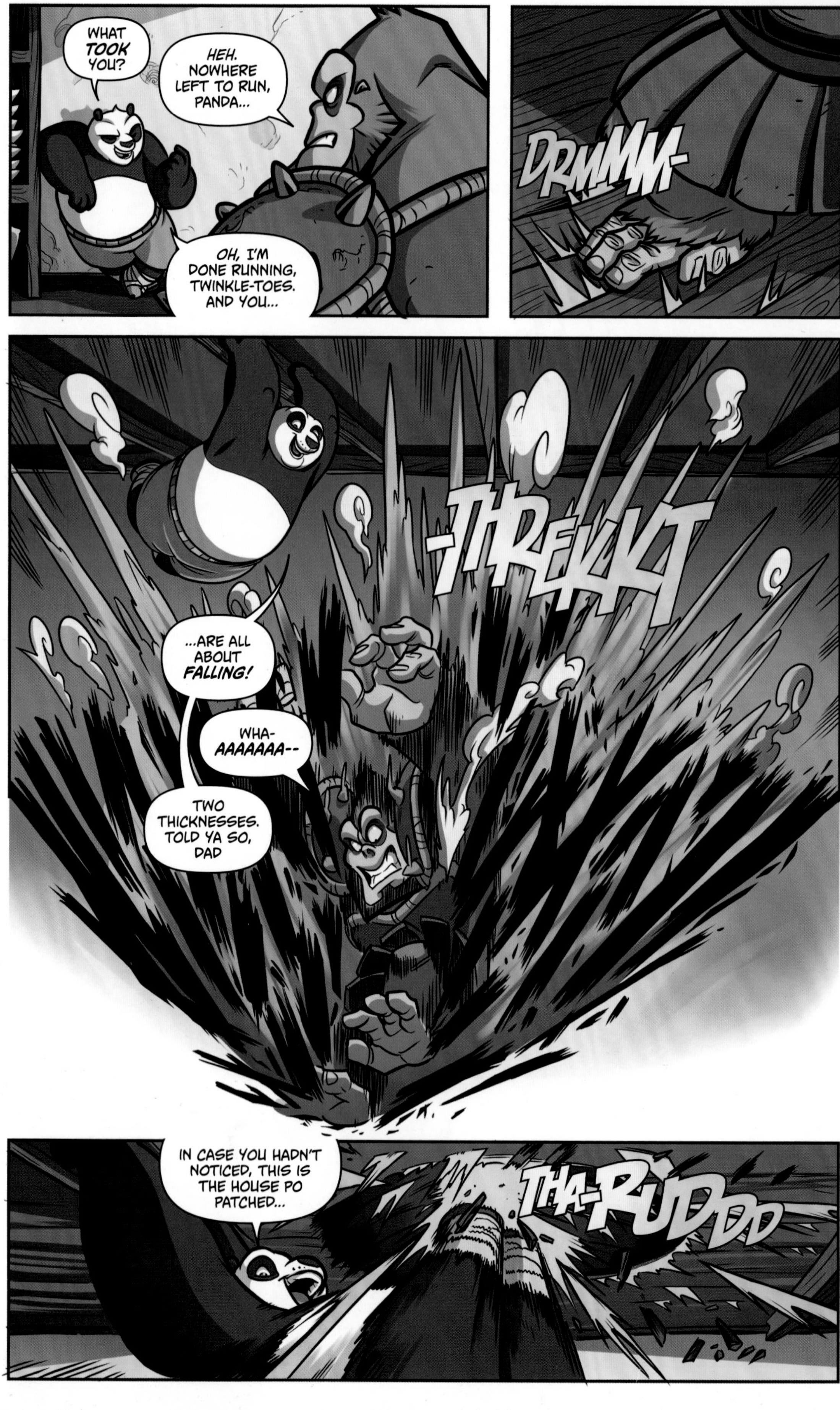
WHAT TOOK YOU?
HEH. NOWHERE LEFT TO RUN, PANDA...
OH, I'M DONE RUNNING, TWINKLE-TOES. AND YOU...
DRMMMM-
-THREKKT
...ARE ALL ABOUT FALLING!
WHA- AAAAAAA--
TWO THICKNESSES. TOLD YA SO, DAD
IN CASE YOU HADN'T NOTICED, THIS IS THE HOUSE PO PATCHED...
THA-RUDDD

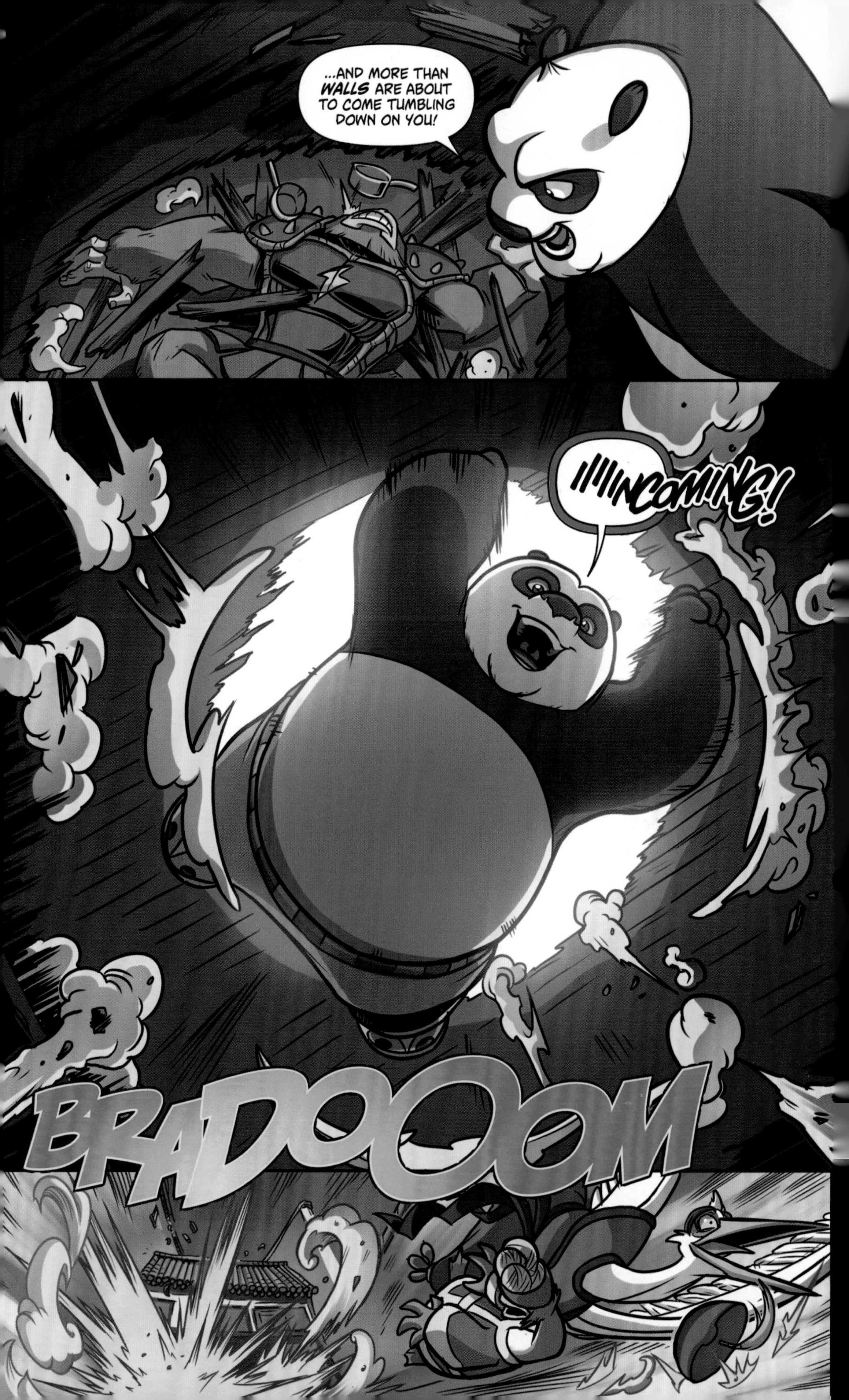
...AND MORE THAN WALLS ARE ABOUT TO COME TUMBLING DOWN ON YOU!
I'IIINCOMING!
BRADOOOM

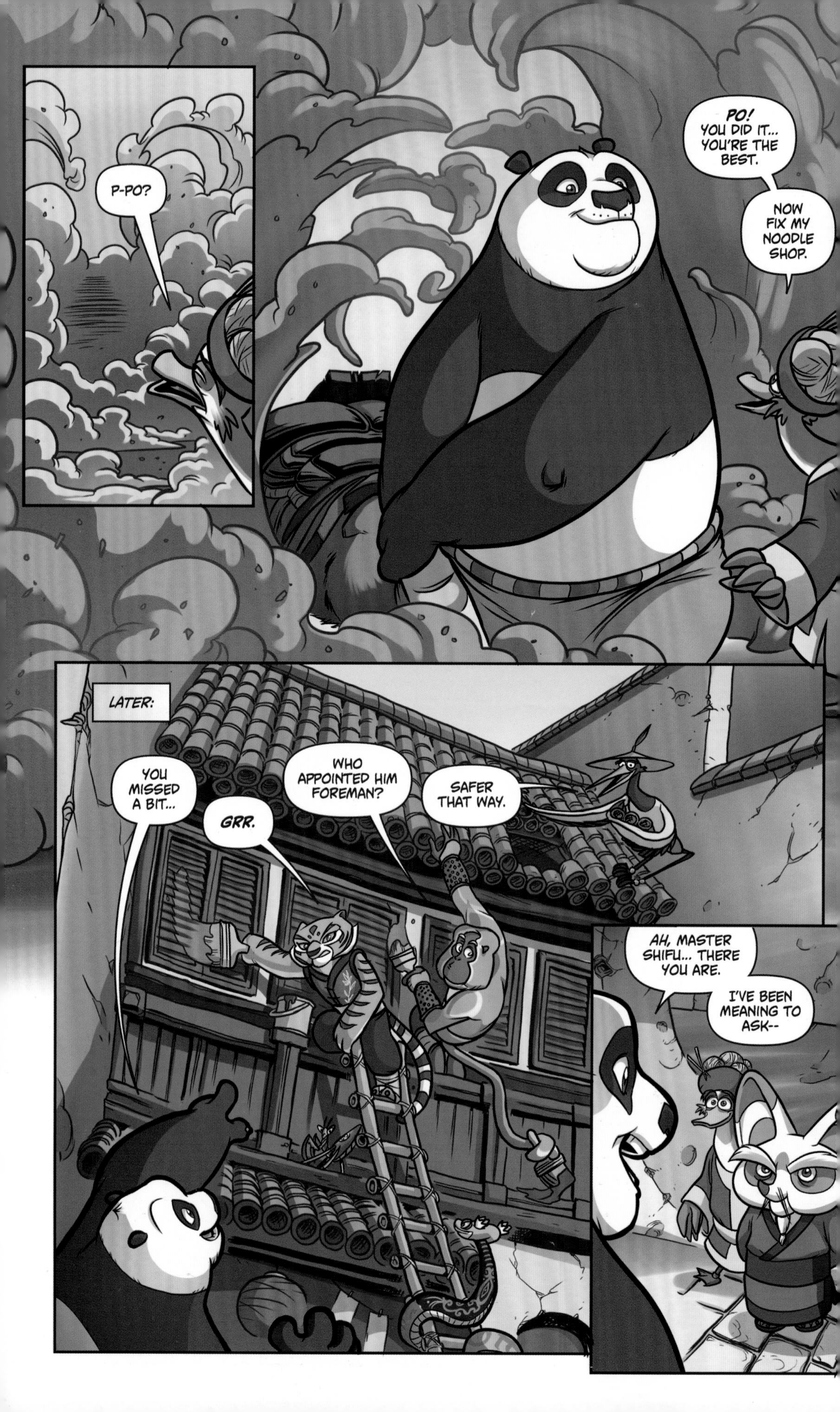
P-PO?
PO! YOU DID IT... YOU'RE THE BEST.
NOW FIX MY NOODLE SHOP.
LATER:
YOU MISSED A BIT...
GRR.
WHO APPOINTED HIM FOREMAN?
SAFER THAT WAY.
AH, MASTER SHIFU... THERE YOU ARE.
I'VE BEEN MEANING TO ASK--

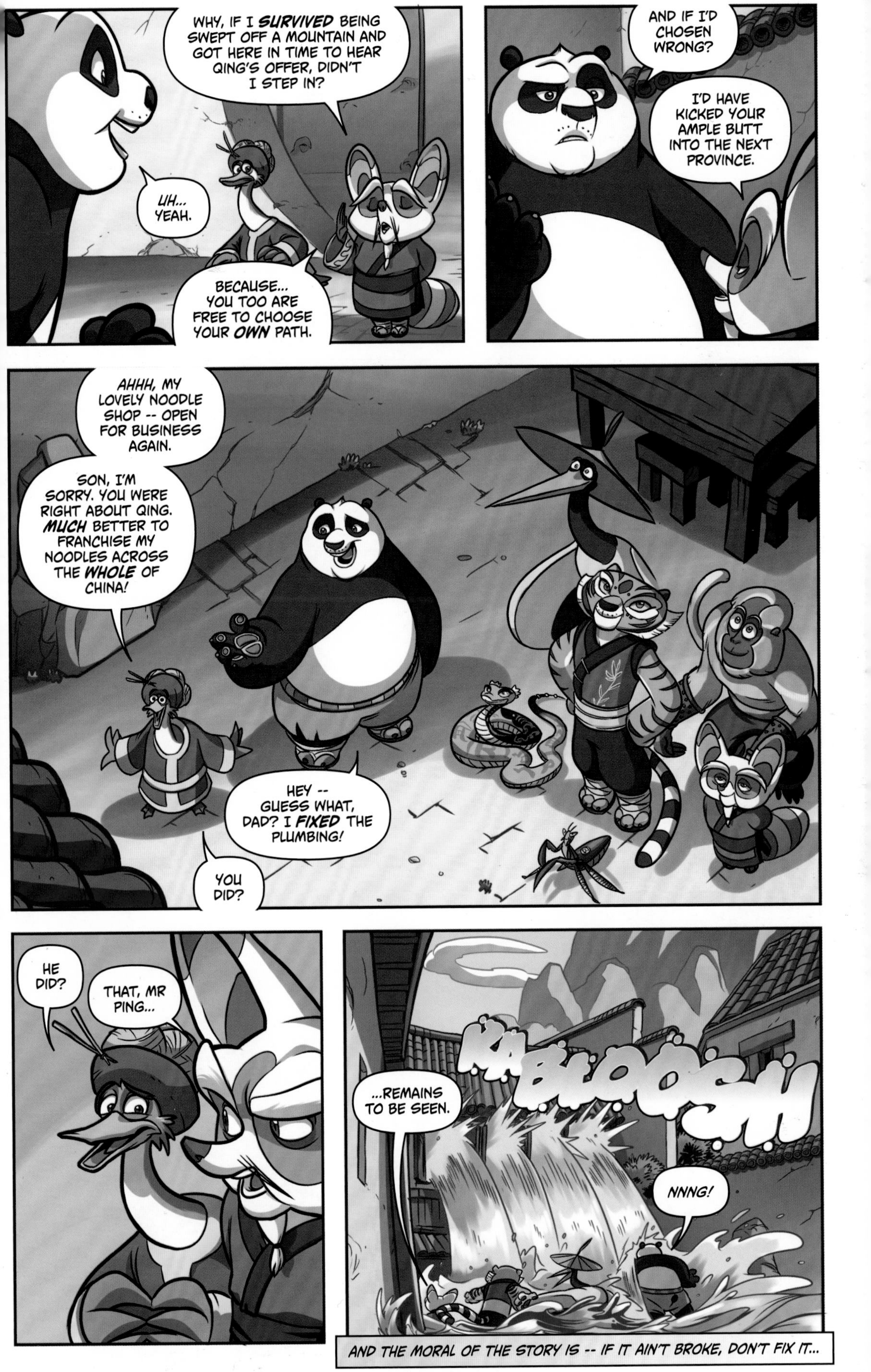
WHY, IF I SURVIVED BEING SWEPT OFF A MOUNTAIN AND GOT HERE IN TIME TO HEAR QING'S OFFER, DIDN'T I STEP IN?
UH... YEAH.
BECAUSE... YOU TOO ARE FREE TO CHOOSE YOUR OWN PATH.
AND IF I'D CHOSEN WRONG?
I'D HAVE KICKED YOUR AMPLE BUTT INTO THE NEXT PROVINCE.
AHHH, MY LOVELY NOODLE SHOP -- OPEN FOR BUSINESS AGAIN.
SON, I'M SORRY. YOU WERE RIGHT ABOUT QING. MUCH BETTER TO FRANCHISE MY NOODLES ACROSS THE WHOLE OF CHINA!
HEY -- GUESS WHAT, DAD? I FIXED THE PLUMBING!
YOU DID?
HE DID?
THAT, MR PING...
KA BLOOSH
...REMAINS TO BE SEEN.
NNNG!
AND THE MORAL OF THE STORY IS -- IF IT AIN'T BROKE, DON'T FIX IT...

DIVIDE & CONQUER

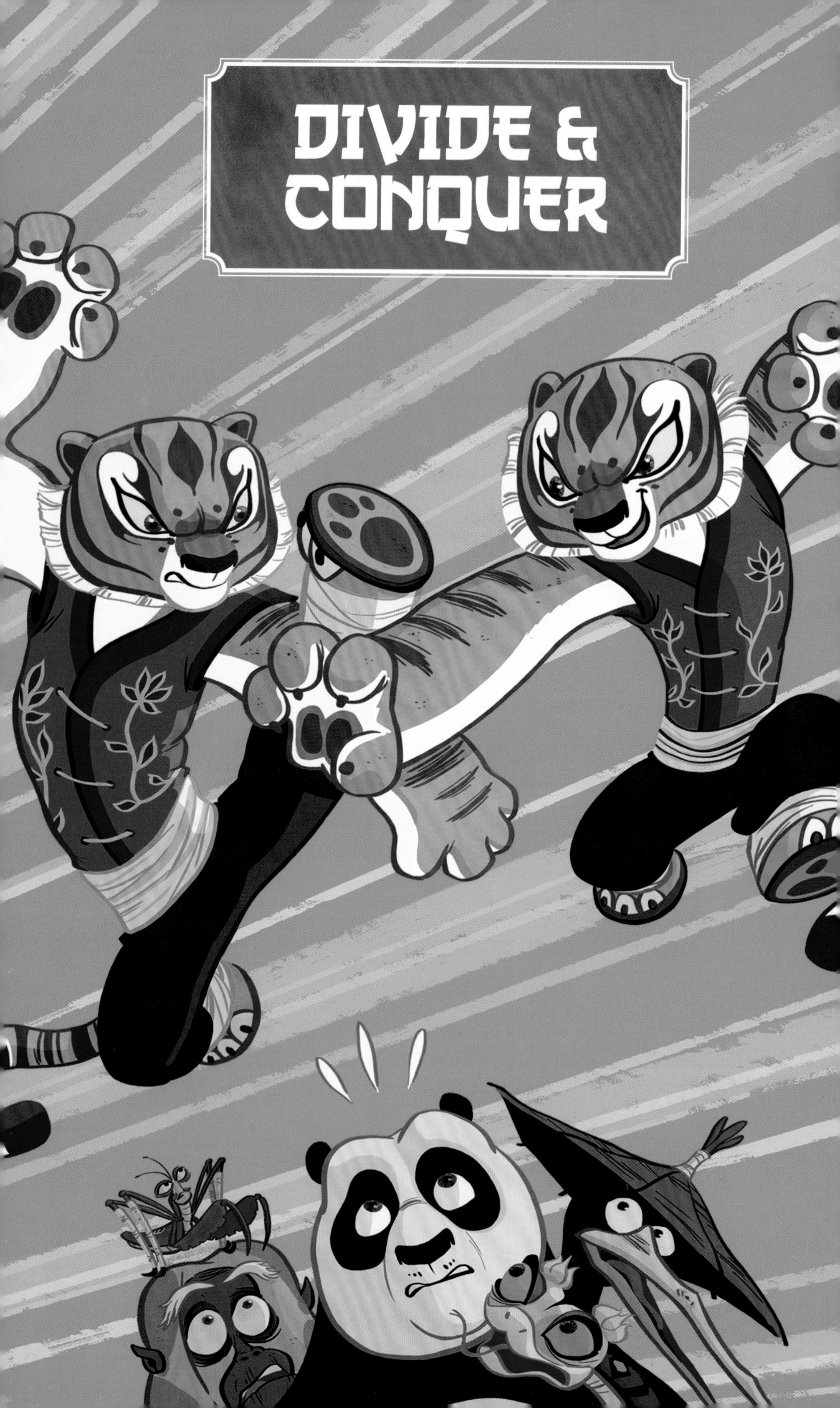

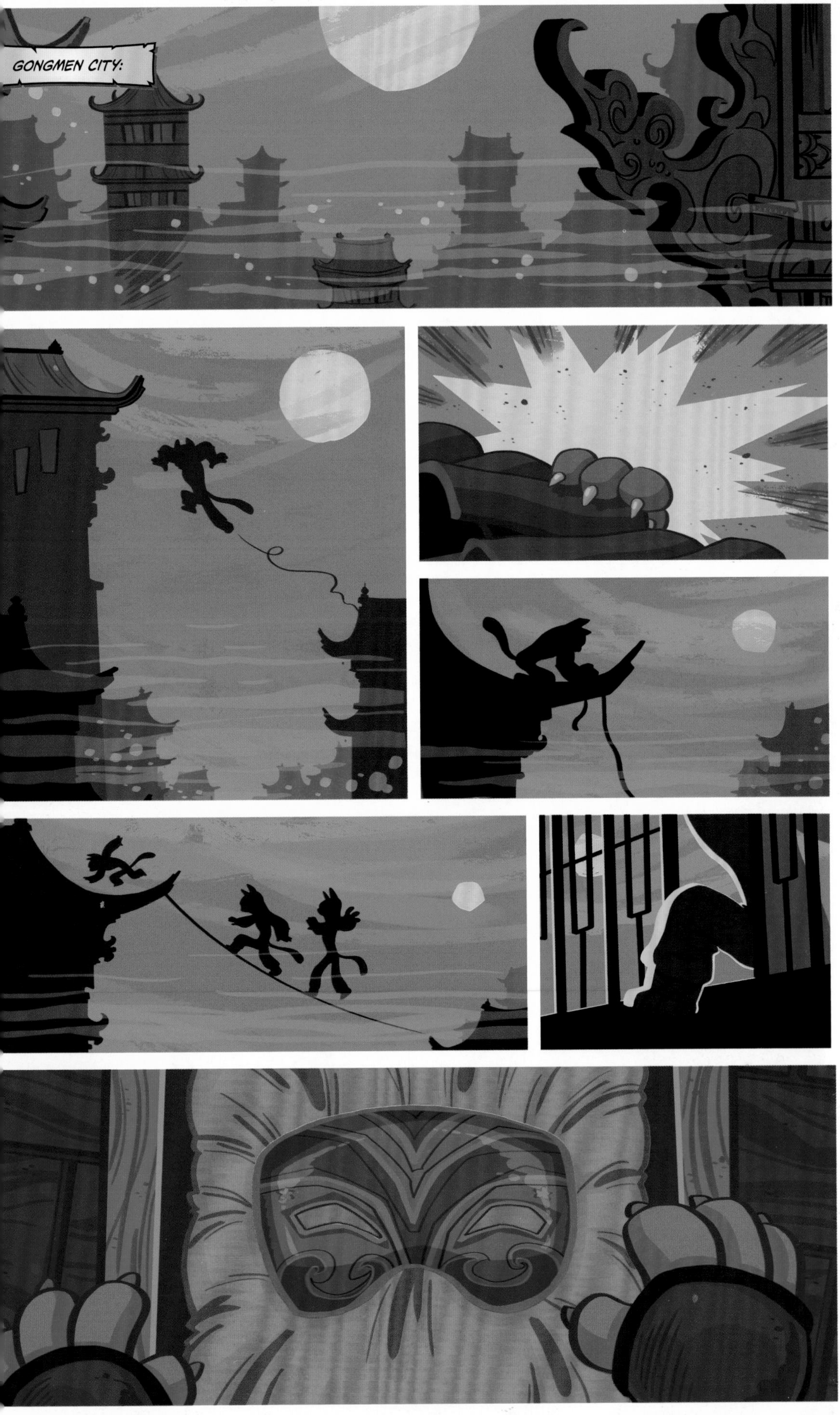
GONGMEN CITY:

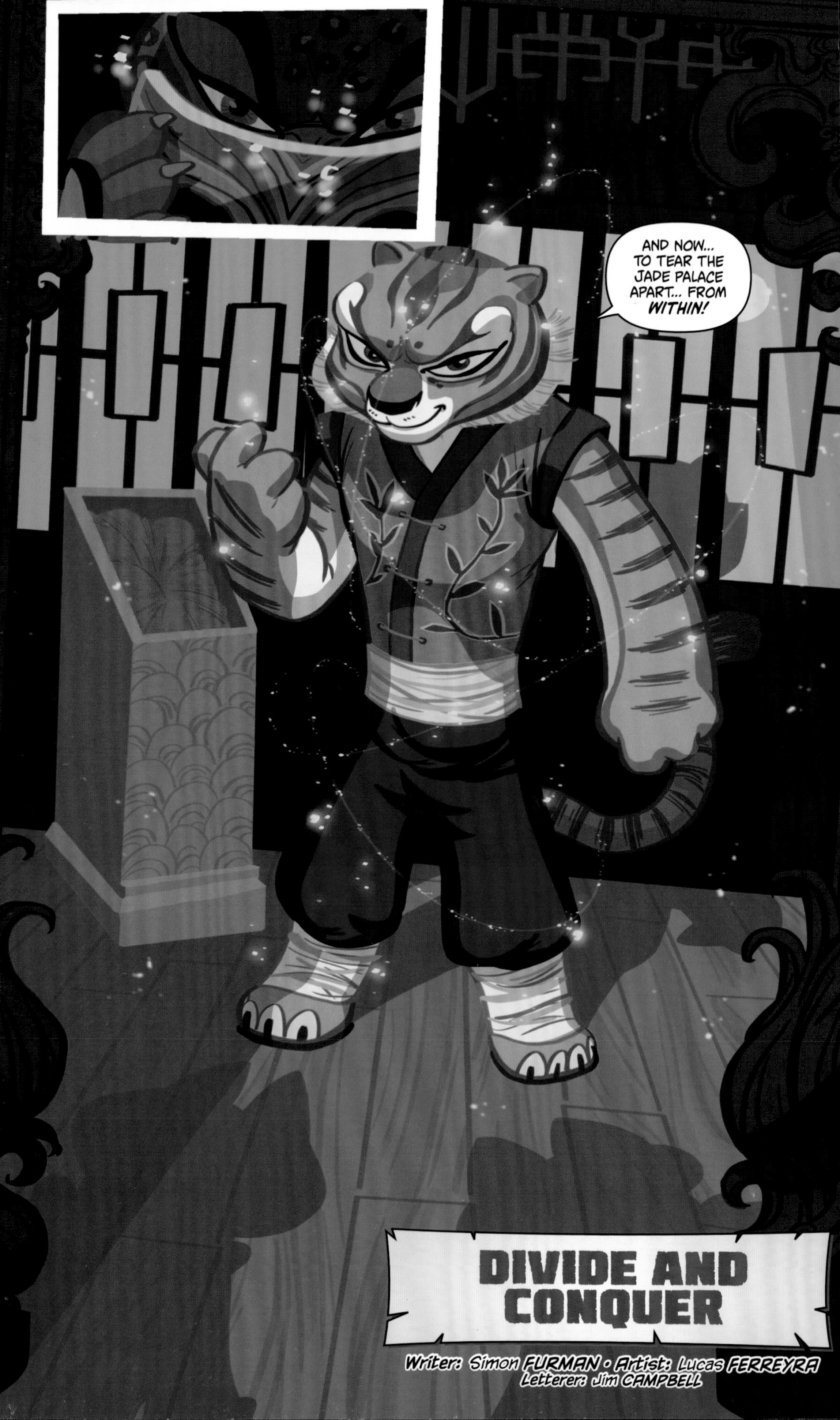
AND NOW... TO TEAR THE JADE PALACE APART... FROM WITHIN!
DIVIDE AND CONQUER
Writer: Simon FURMAN • Artist: Lucas FERREYRA
Letterer: Jim CAMPBELL

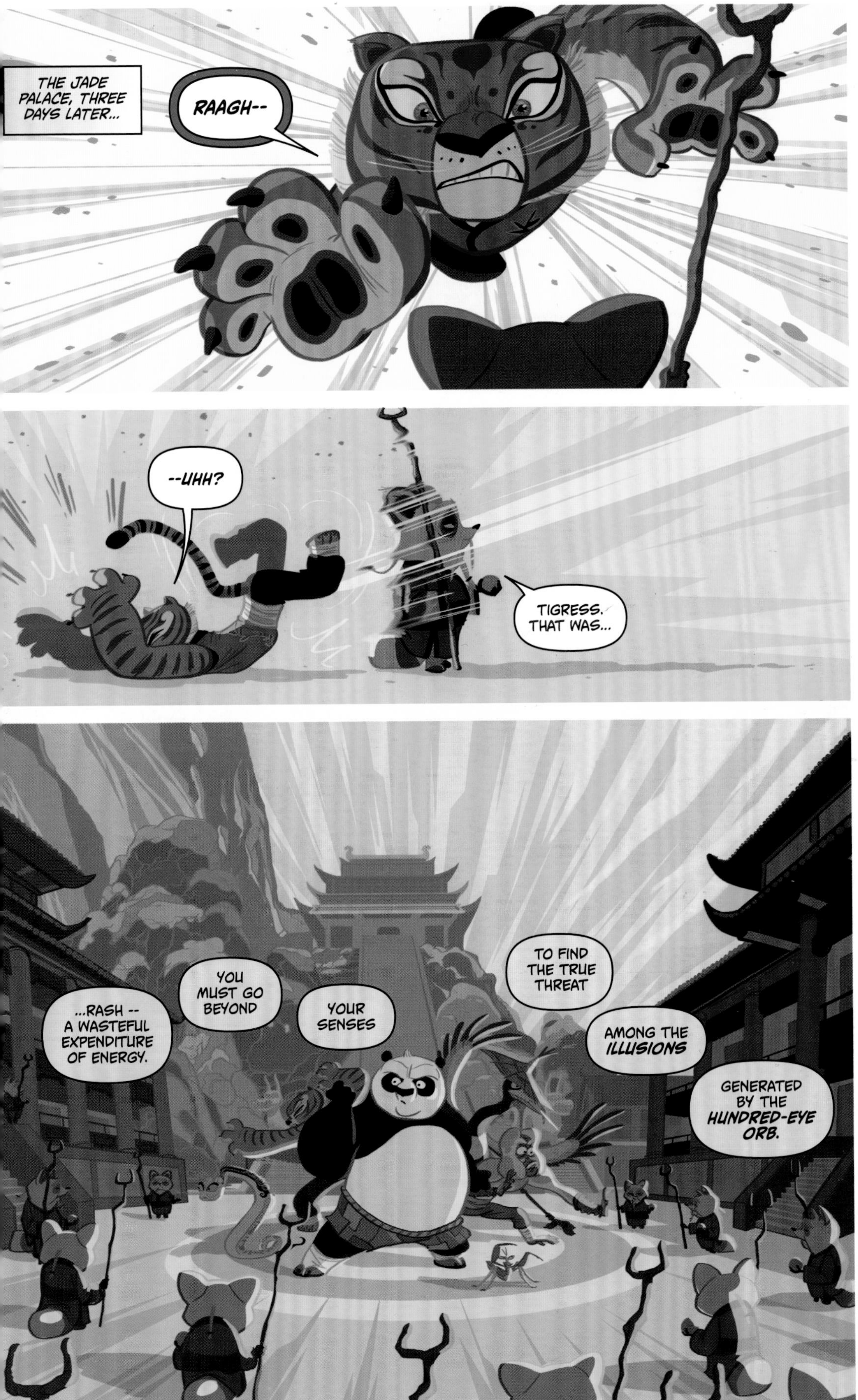
THE JADE PALACE, THREE DAYS LATER...
RAAGH--
--UHH?
TIGRESS. THAT WAS...
...RASH -- A WASTEFUL EXPENDITURE OF ENERGY.
YOU MUST GO BEYOND
YOUR SENSES
TO FIND THE TRUE THREAT
AMONG THE ILLUSIONS
GENERATED BY THE HUNDRED-EYE ORB.

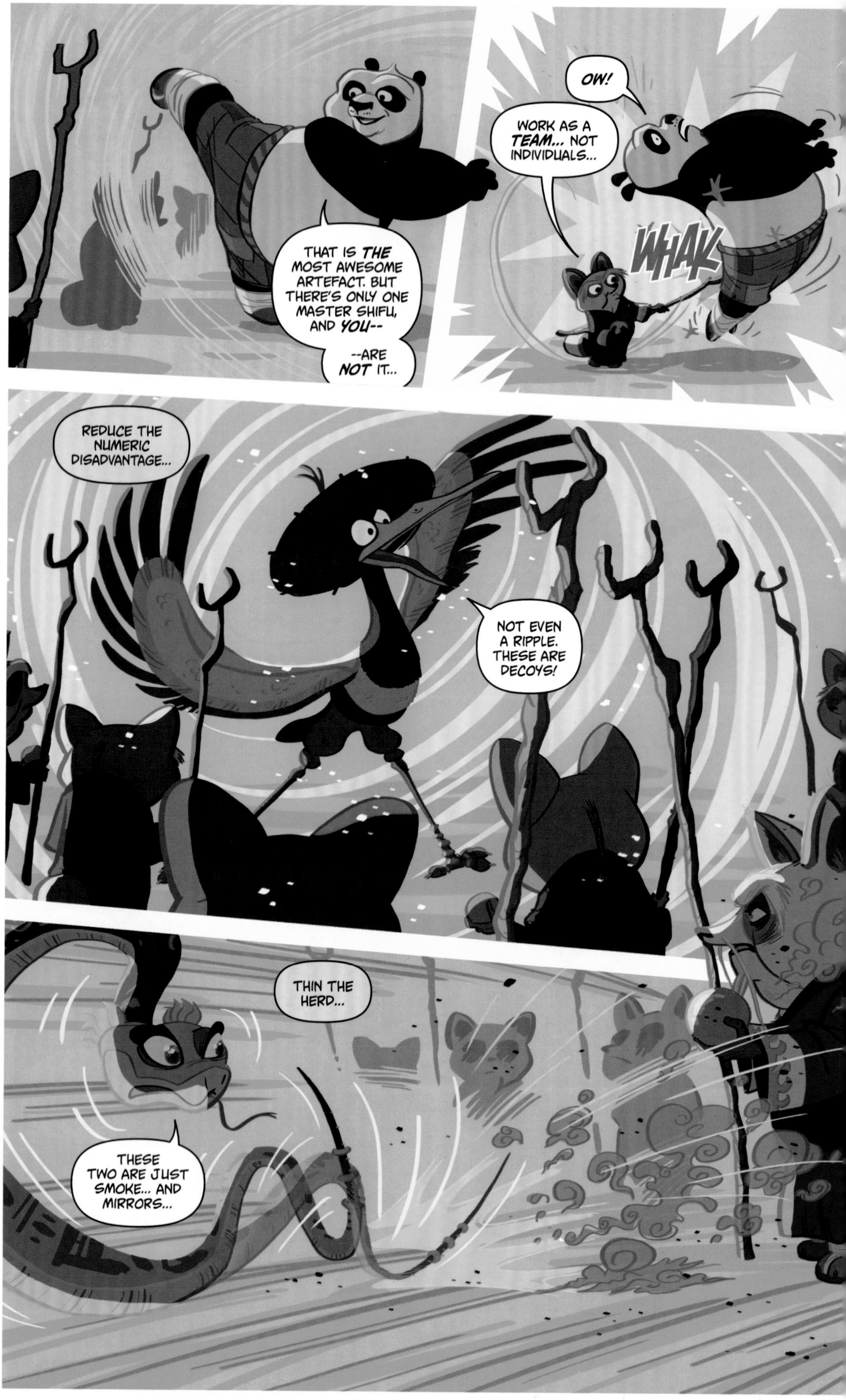
THAT IS THE MOST AWESOME ARTEFACT. BUT THERE'S ONLY ONE MASTER SHIFU, AND YOU--
--ARE NOT IT...
OW!
WORK AS A TEAM... NOT INDIVIDUALS...
WHAK
REDUCE THE NUMERIC DISADVANTAGE...
NOT EVEN A RIPPLE. THESE ARE DECOYS!
THIN THE HERD...
THESE TWO ARE JUST SMOKE... AND MIRRORS...

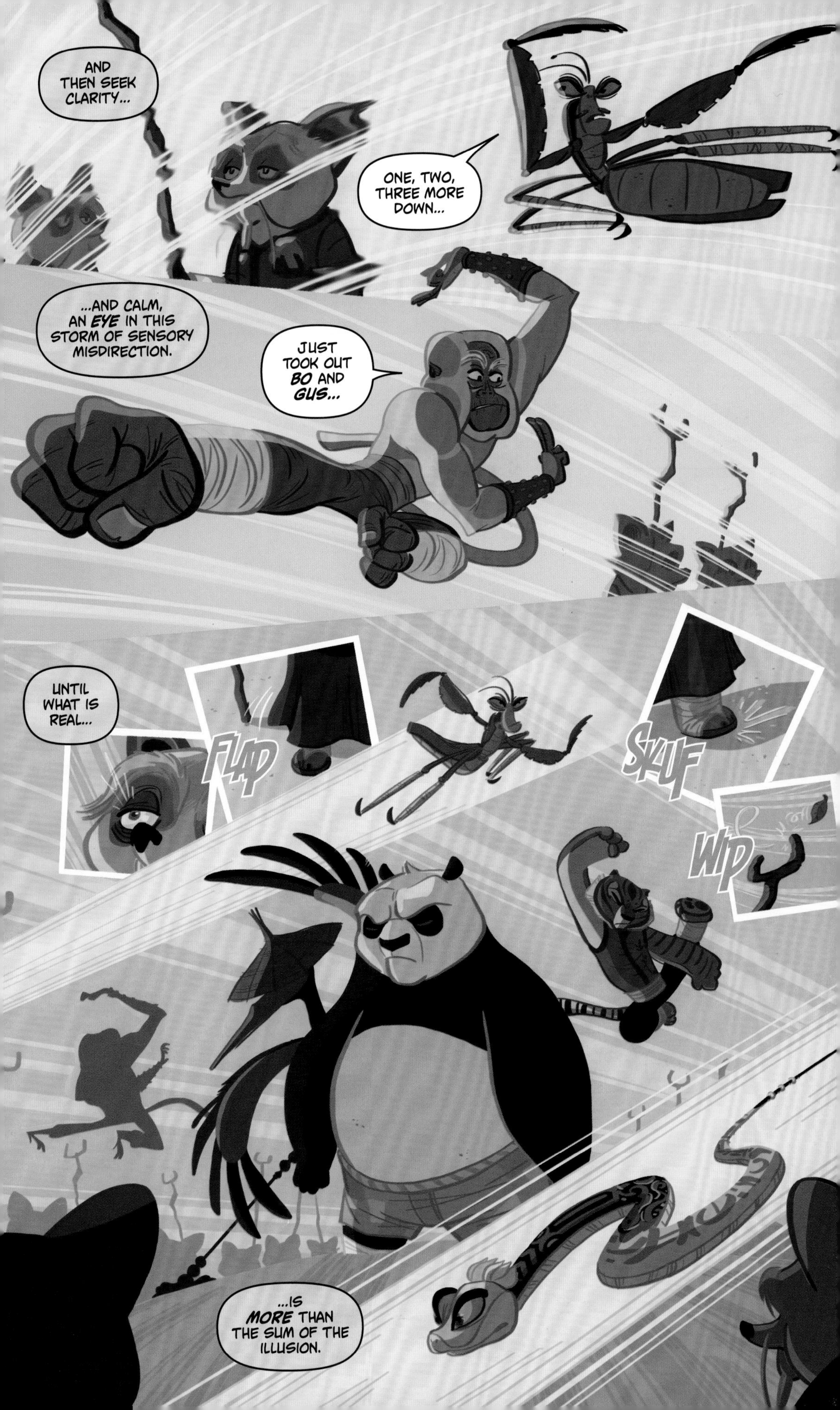
AND THEN SEEK CLARITY...
ONE, TWO, THREE MORE DOWN...
...AND CALM, AN EYE IN THIS STORM OF SENSORY MISDIRECTION.
JUST TOOK OUT BO AND GUS...
UNTIL WHAT IS REAL...
FLAP
SKUF
WIP
...IS MORE THAN THE SUM OF THE ILLUSION.

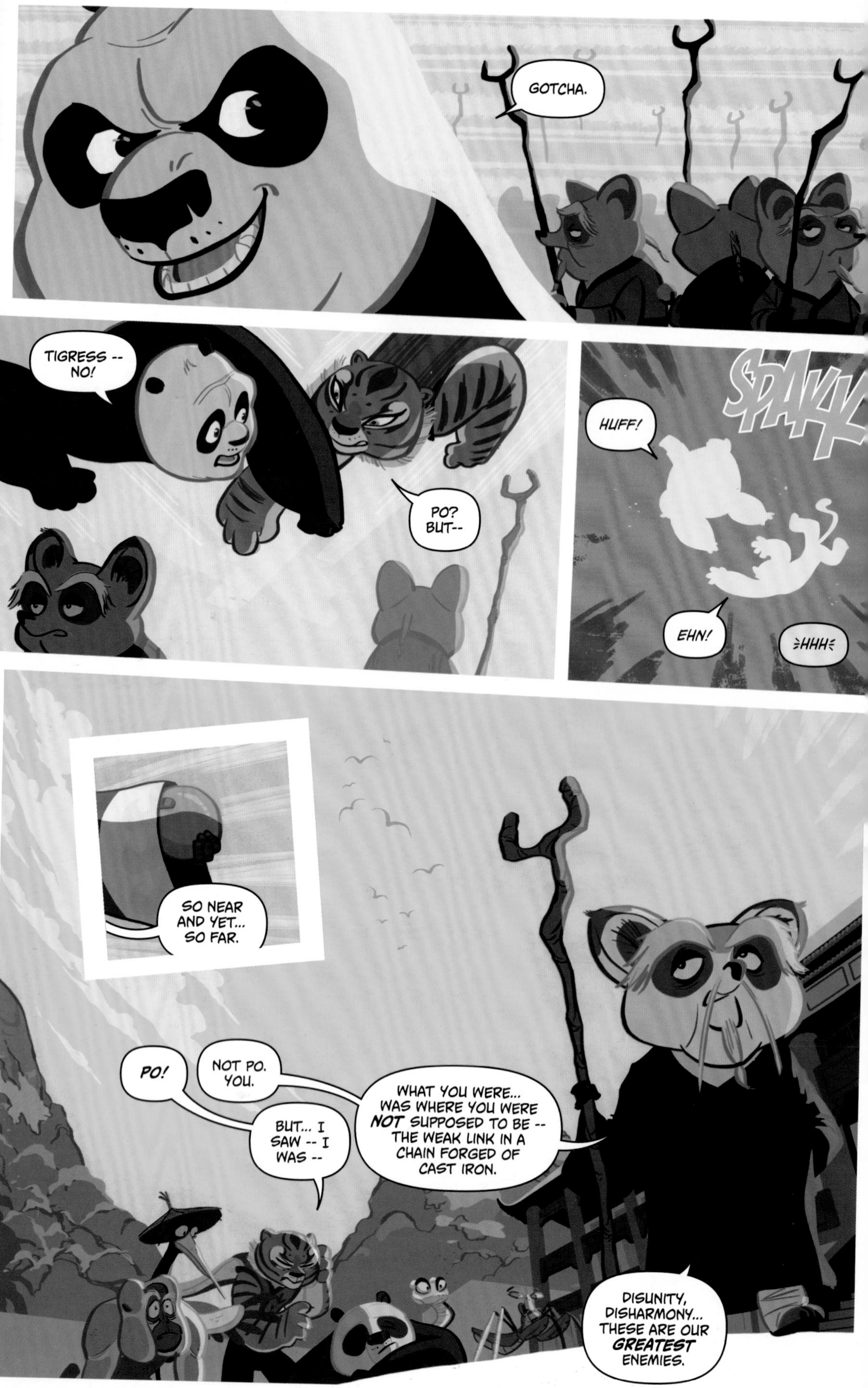

GOTCHA.
TIGRESS -- NO!
PO? BUT--
SPAKK
HUFF!
EHN!
HHH
SO NEAR AND YET... SO FAR.
PO!
NOT PO. YOU.
BUT... I SAW -- I WAS --
WHAT YOU WERE... WAS WHERE YOU WERE NOT SUPPOSED TO BE -- THE WEAK LINK IN A CHAIN FORGED OF CAST IRON.
DISUNITY, DISHARMONY... THESE ARE OUR GREATEST ENEMIES.

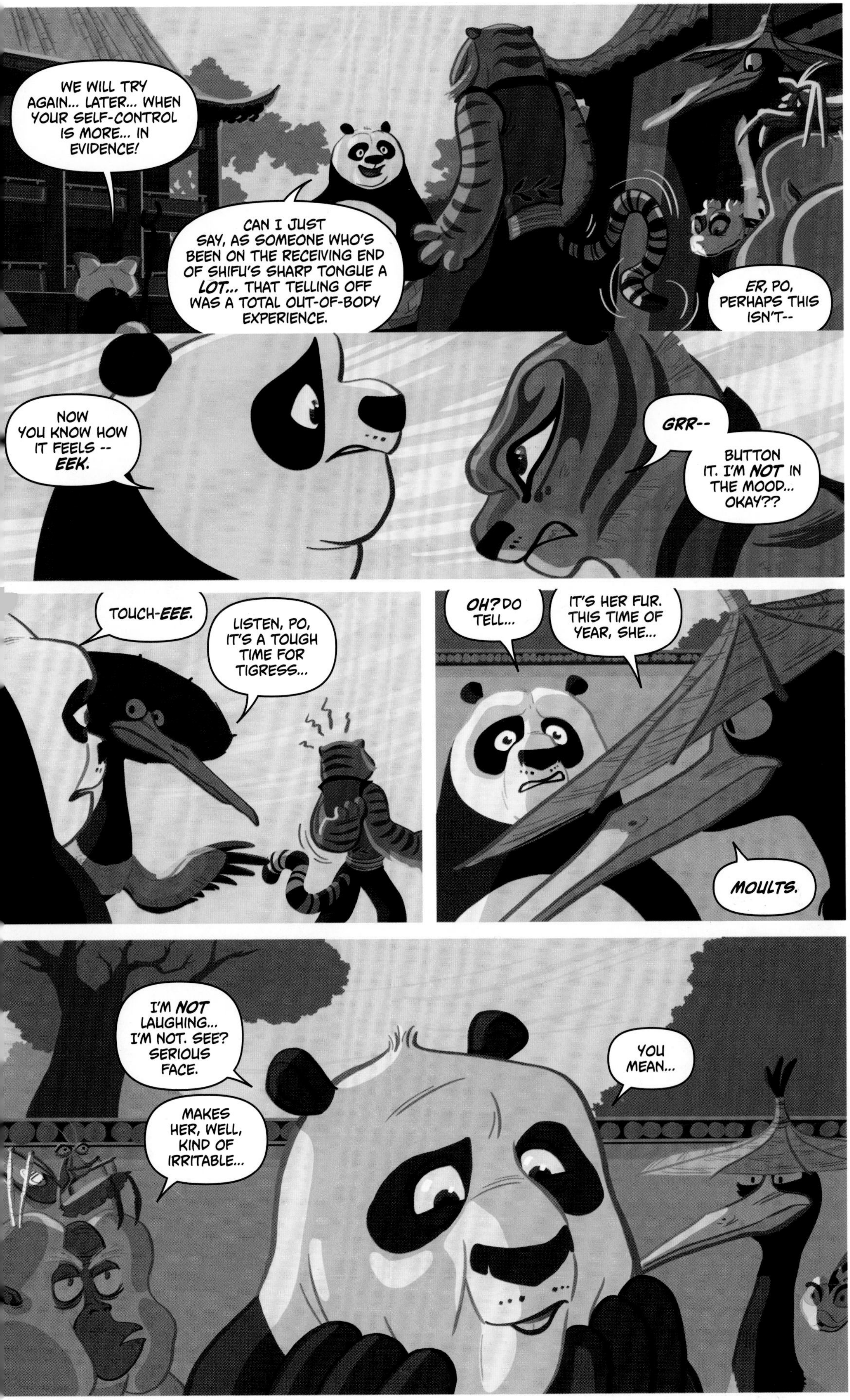
WE WILL TRY AGAIN... LATER... WHEN YOUR SELF-CONTROL IS MORE... IN EVIDENCE!
CAN I JUST SAY, AS SOMEONE WHO'S BEEN ON THE RECEIVING END OF SHIFU'S SHARP TONGUE A LOT... THAT TELLING OFF WAS A TOTAL OUT-OF-BODY EXPERIENCE.
ER, PO, PERHAPS THIS ISN'T--
NOW YOU KNOW HOW IT FEELS -- EEK.
GRR--
BUTTON IT. I'M NOT IN THE MOOD... OKAY??
TOUCH-EEE.
LISTEN, PO, IT'S A TOUGH TIME FOR TIGRESS...
OH? DO TELL...
IT'S HER FUR. THIS TIME OF YEAR, SHE...
MOULTS.
I'M NOT LAUGHING... I'M NOT. SEE? SERIOUS FACE.
MAKES HER, WELL, KIND OF IRRITABLE...
YOU MEAN...

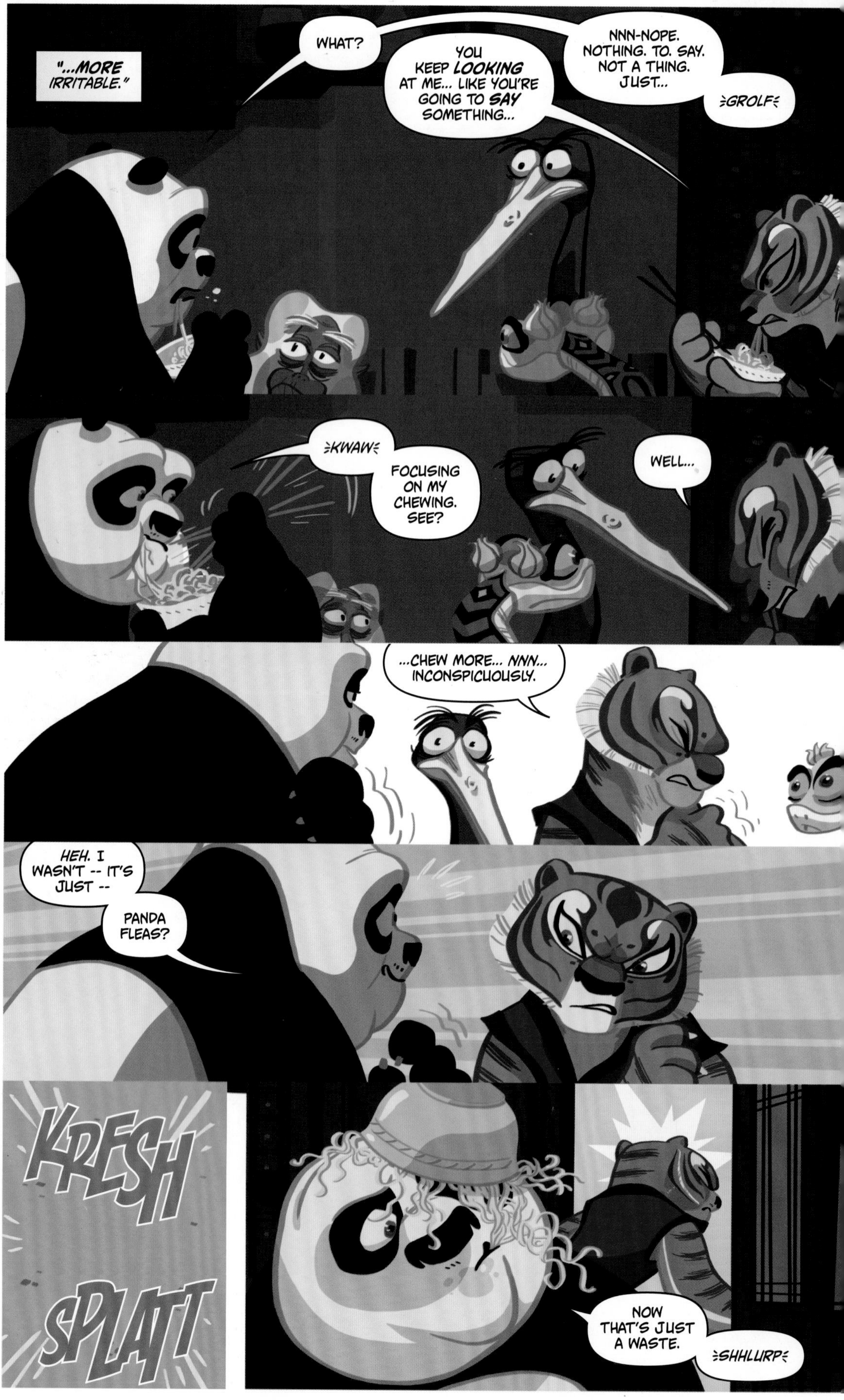
"...MORE IRRITABLE."
WHAT?
YOU KEEP LOOKING AT ME... LIKE YOU'RE GOING TO SAY SOMETHING...
NNN-NOPE. NOTHING. TO. SAY. NOT A THING. JUST...
GROLF
KWAW
FOCUSING ON MY CHEWING. SEE?
WELL...
...CHEW MORE... NNN... INCONSPICUOUSLY.
HEH. I WASN'T -- IT'S JUST --
PANDA FLEAS?
KRESH
SPLATT
NOW THAT'S JUST A WASTE.
SHHLURP

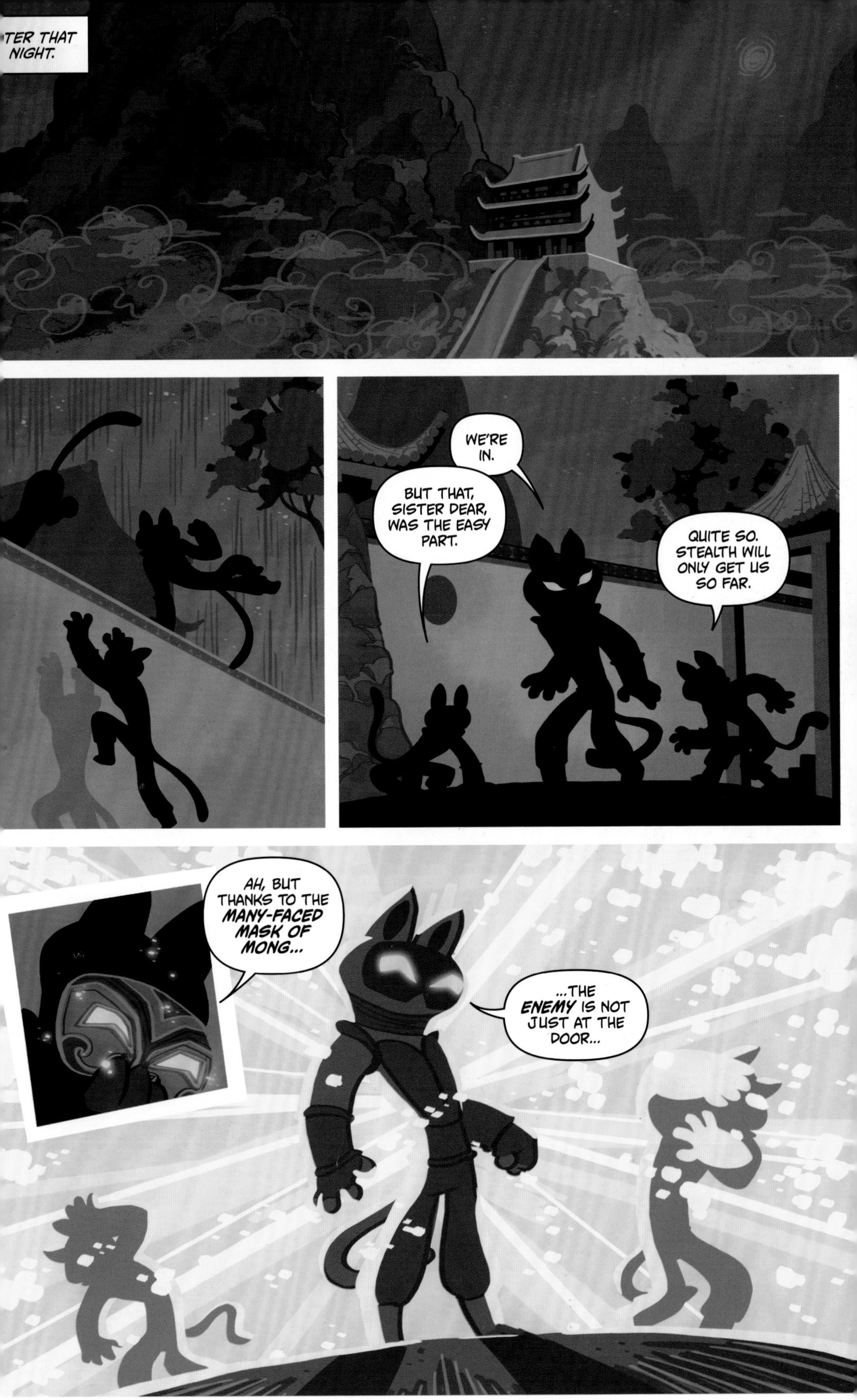
TER THAT NIGHT.
WE'RE IN.
BUT THAT, SISTER DEAR, WAS THE EASY PART.
QUITE SO. STEALTH WILL ONLY GET US SO FAR.
AH, BUT THANKS TO THE *MANY-FACED MASK OF MONG...*
...THE *ENEMY* IS NOT JUST AT THE DOOR...

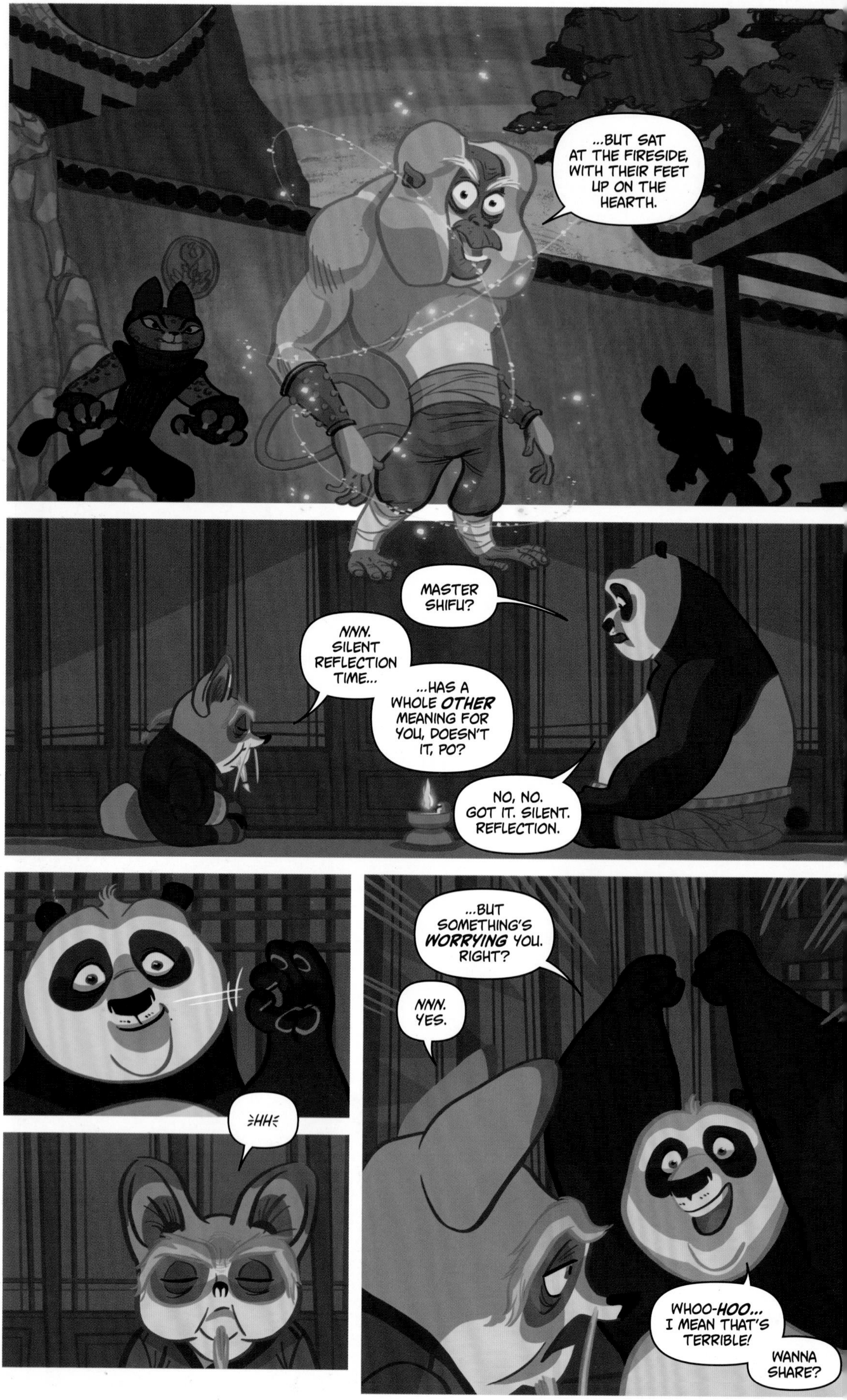
...BUT SAT AT THE FIRESIDE, WITH THEIR FEET UP ON THE HEARTH.
MASTER SHIFU?
NNN. SILENT REFLECTION TIME...
...HAS A WHOLE OTHER MEANING FOR YOU, DOESN'T IT, PO?
NO, NO. GOT IT. SILENT. REFLECTION.
HH
...BUT SOMETHING'S WORRYING YOU. RIGHT?
NNN. YES.
WHOO-HOO... I MEAN THAT'S TERRIBLE!
WANNA SHARE?

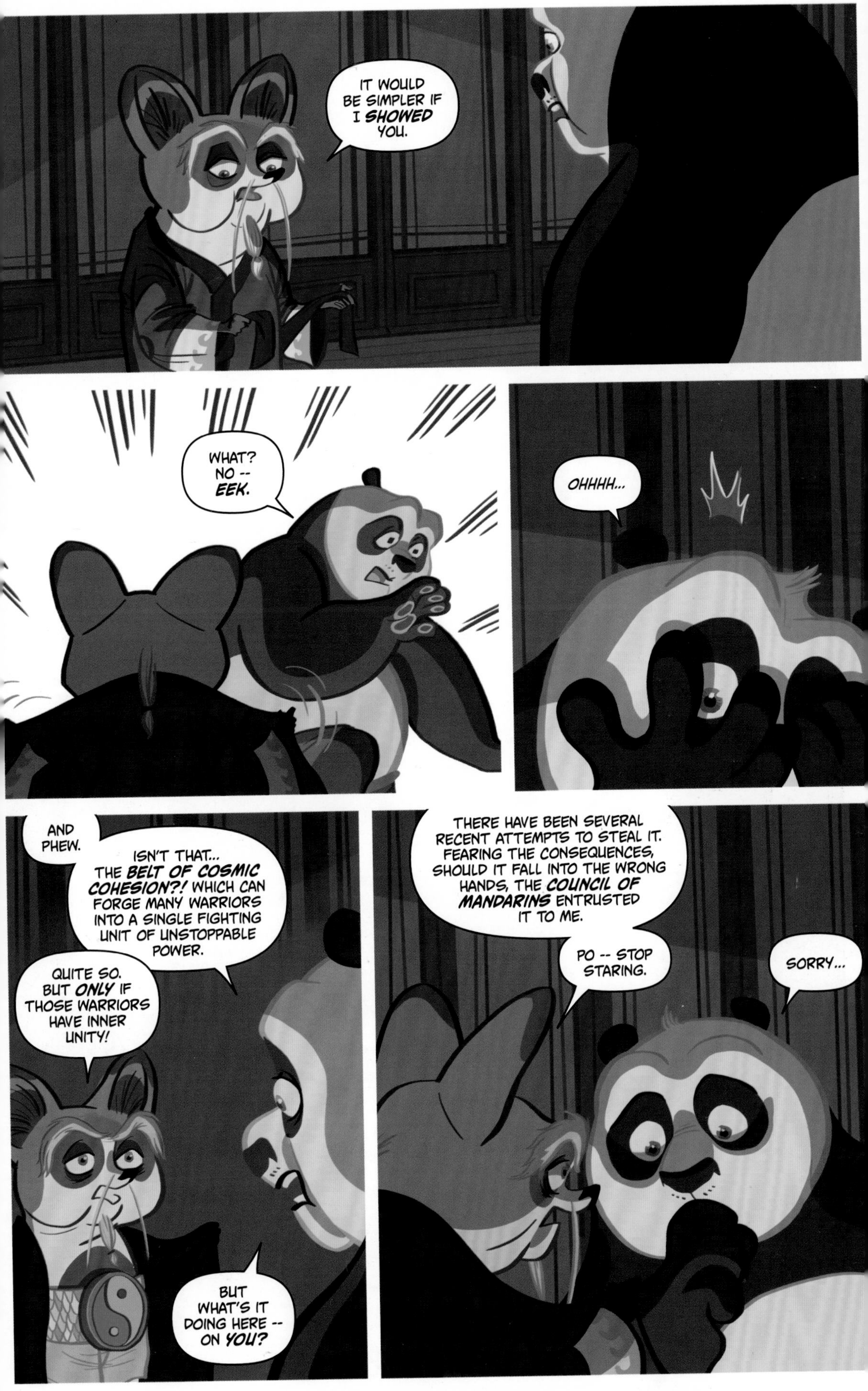
IT WOULD BE SIMPLER IF I SHOWED YOU.
WHAT? NO -- EEK.
OHHHH...
AND PHEW.
ISN'T THAT... THE BELT OF COSMIC COHESION?! WHICH CAN FORGE MANY WARRIORS INTO A SINGLE FIGHTING UNIT OF UNSTOPPABLE POWER.
QUITE SO. BUT ONLY IF THOSE WARRIORS HAVE INNER UNITY!
BUT WHAT'S IT DOING HERE -- ON YOU?
THERE HAVE BEEN SEVERAL RECENT ATTEMPTS TO STEAL IT. FEARING THE CONSEQUENCES, SHOULD IT FALL INTO THE WRONG HANDS, THE COUNCIL OF MANDARINS ENTRUSTED IT TO ME.
PO -- STOP STARING.
SORRY...

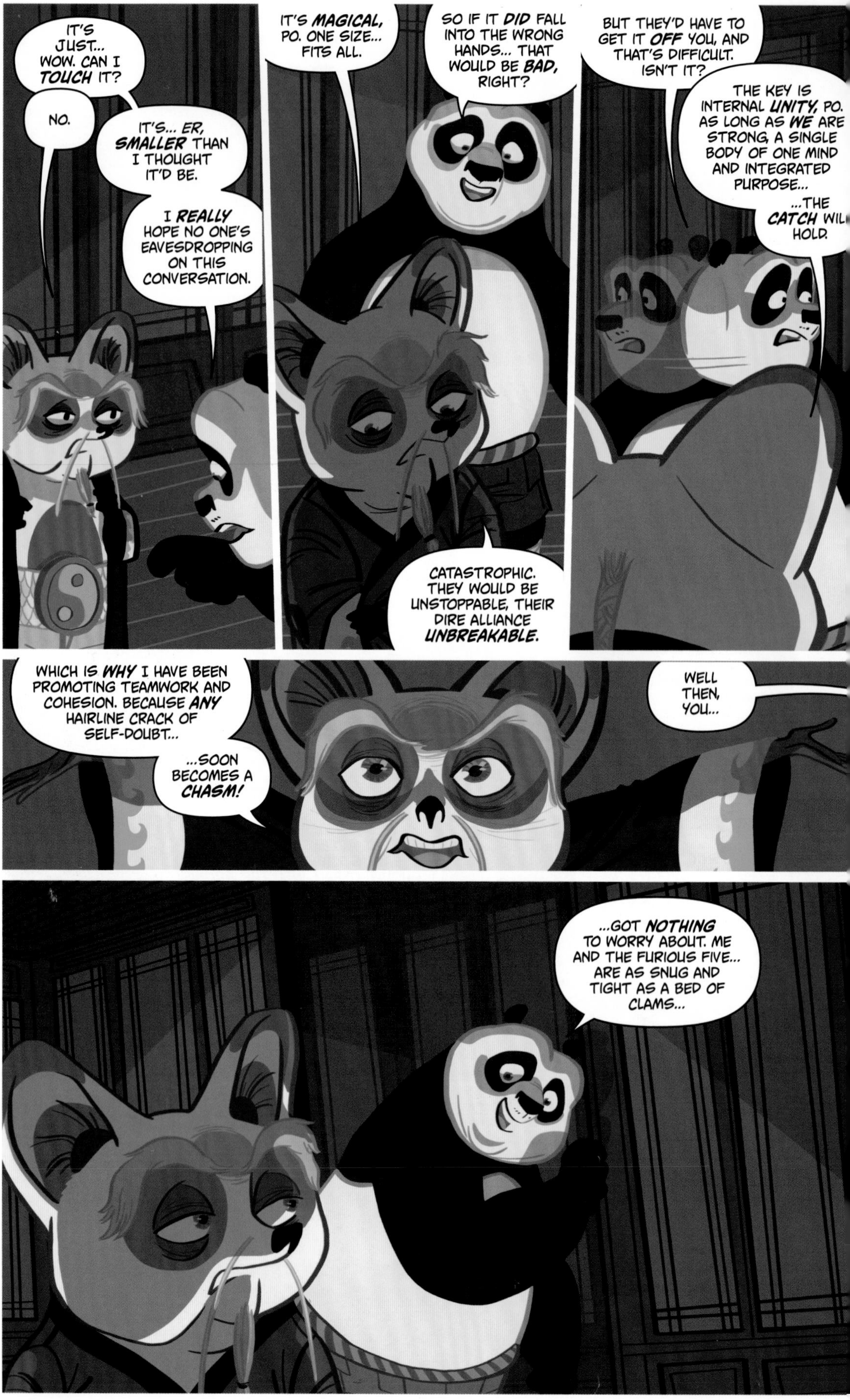
IT'S JUST... WOW. CAN I TOUCH IT?
NO.
IT'S... ER, SMALLER THAN I THOUGHT IT'D BE.
I REALLY HOPE NO ONE'S EAVESDROPPING ON THIS CONVERSATION.
IT'S MAGICAL, PO. ONE SIZE... FITS ALL.
SO IF IT DID FALL INTO THE WRONG HANDS... THAT WOULD BE BAD, RIGHT?
CATASTROPHIC. THEY WOULD BE UNSTOPPABLE, THEIR DIRE ALLIANCE UNBREAKABLE.
BUT THEY'D HAVE TO GET IT OFF YOU, AND THAT'S DIFFICULT. ISN'T IT?
THE KEY IS INTERNAL UNITY, PO. AS LONG AS WE ARE STRONG, A SINGLE BODY OF ONE MIND AND INTEGRATED PURPOSE...
...THE CATCH WIL HOLD.
WHICH IS WHY I HAVE BEEN PROMOTING TEAMWORK AND COHESION. BECAUSE ANY HAIRLINE CRACK OF SELF-DOUBT...
...SOON BECOMES A CHASM!
WELL THEN, YOU...
...GOT NOTHING TO WORRY ABOUT. ME AND THE FURIOUS FIVE... ARE AS SNUG AND TIGHT AS A BED OF CLAMS...

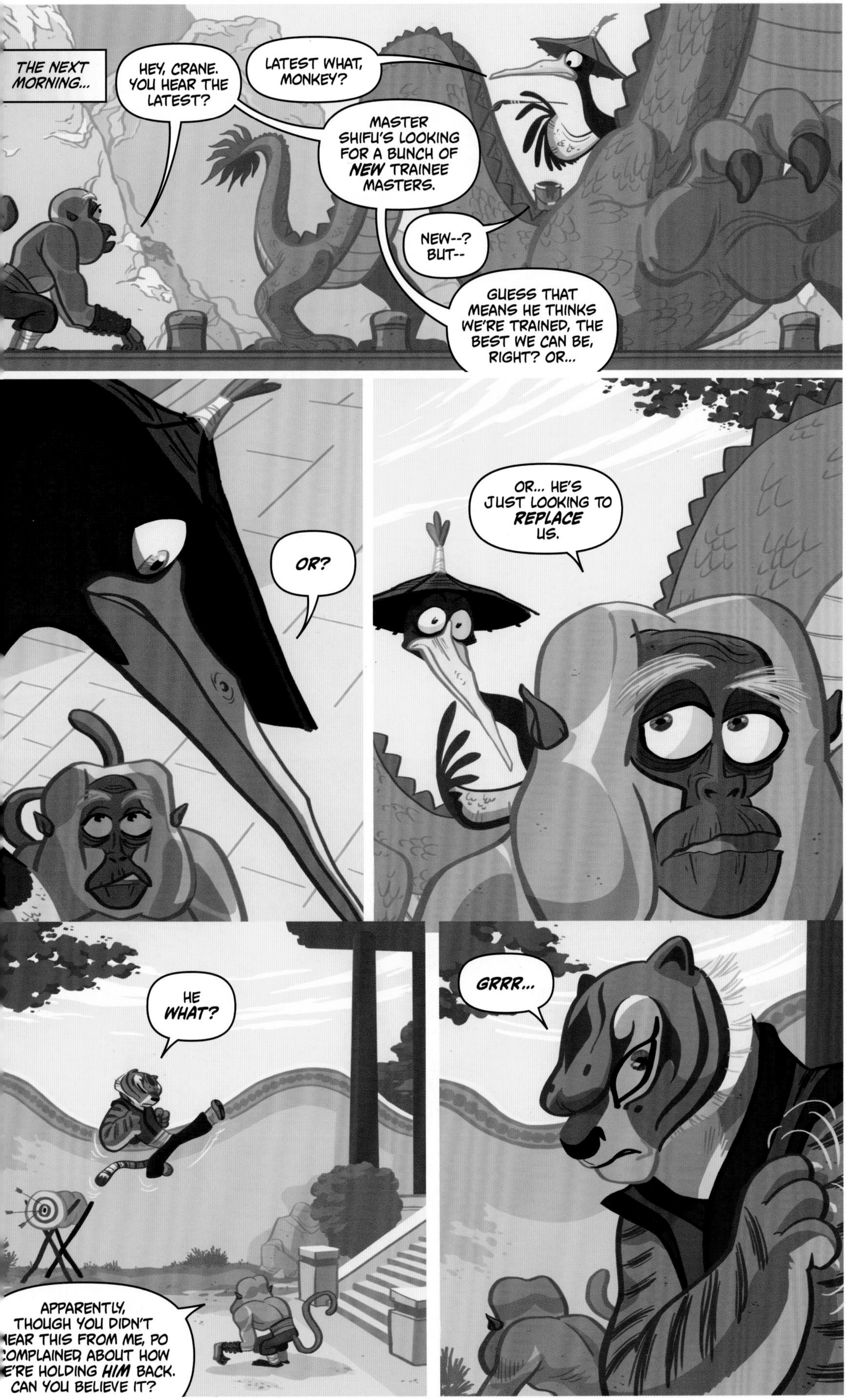

THE NEXT MORNING...
HEY, CRANE. YOU HEAR THE LATEST?
LATEST WHAT, MONKEY?
MASTER SHIFU'S LOOKING FOR A BUNCH OF NEW TRAINEE MASTERS.
NEW--? BUT--
GUESS THAT MEANS HE THINKS WE'RE TRAINED, THE BEST WE CAN BE, RIGHT? OR...
OR?
OR... HE'S JUST LOOKING TO REPLACE US.
HE WHAT?
APPARENTLY, THOUGH YOU DIDN'T HEAR THIS FROM ME, PO COMPLAINED ABOUT HOW WE'RE HOLDING HIM BACK. CAN YOU BELIEVE IT?
GRRR...

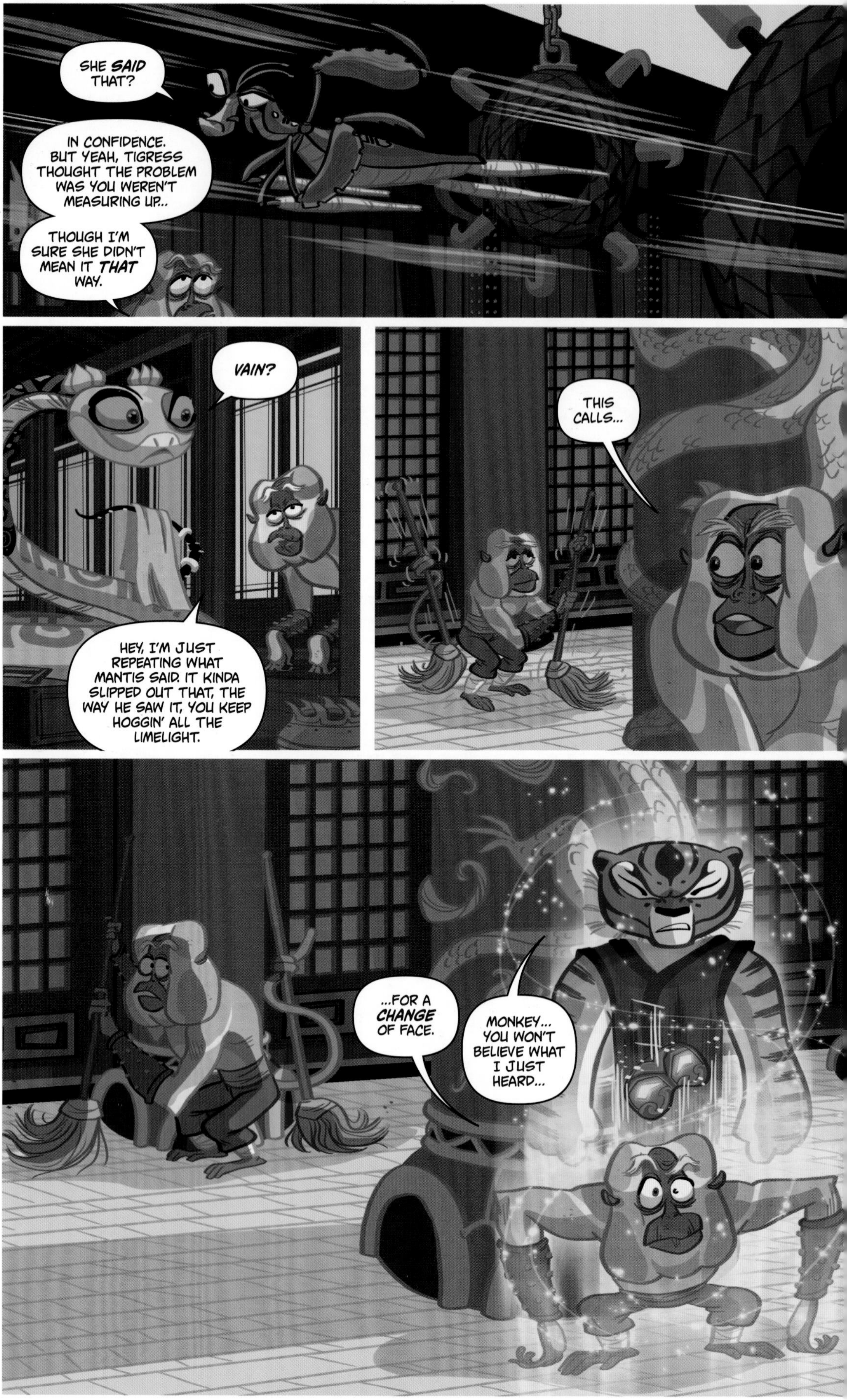
SHE *SAID* THAT?
IN CONFIDENCE. BUT YEAH, TIGRESS THOUGHT THE PROBLEM WAS YOU WEREN'T MEASURING UP...
THOUGH I'M SURE SHE DIDN'T MEAN IT *THAT* WAY.
VAIN?
HEY, I'M JUST REPEATING WHAT MANTIS SAID. IT KINDA SLIPPED OUT THAT, THE WAY HE SAW IT, YOU KEEP HOGGIN' ALL THE LIMELIGHT.
THIS CALLS...
...FOR A *CHANGE* OF FACE.
MONKEY... YOU WON'T BELIEVE WHAT I JUST HEARD...

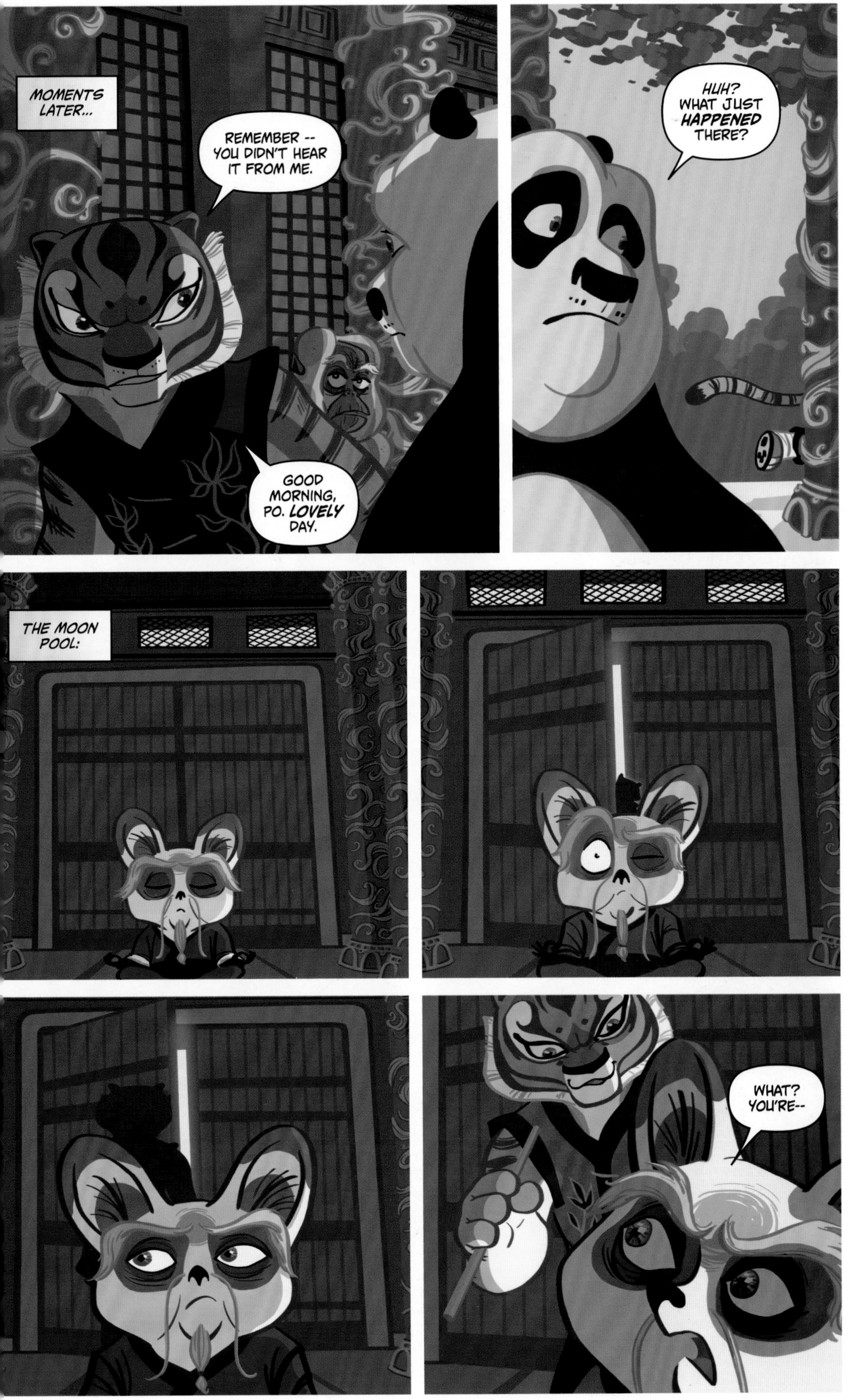
MOMENTS LATER...
REMEMBER -- YOU DIDN'T HEAR IT FROM ME.
GOOD MORNING, PO. LOVELY DAY.
HUH? WHAT JUST HAPPENED THERE?
THE MOON POOL:
WHAT? YOU'RE--

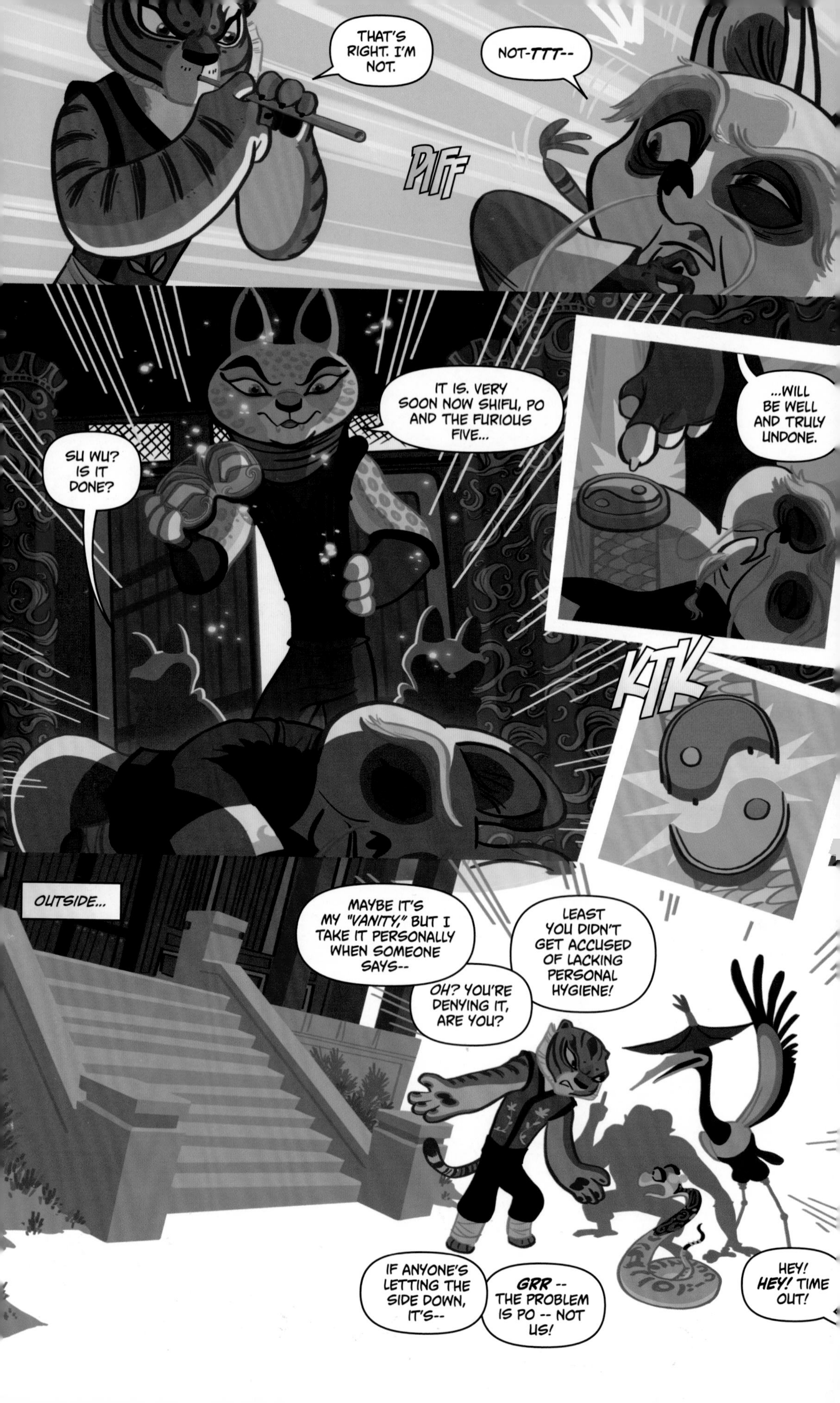
THAT'S RIGHT. I'M NOT.
NOT-TTT--
PIFF
SU WU? IS IT DONE?
IT IS. VERY SOON NOW SHIFU, PO AND THE FURIOUS FIVE...
...WILL BE WELL AND TRULY UNDONE.
KTK
OUTSIDE...
MAYBE IT'S MY "VANITY," BUT I TAKE IT PERSONALLY WHEN SOMEONE SAYS--
OH? YOU'RE DENYING IT, ARE YOU?
LEAST YOU DIDN'T GET ACCUSED OF LACKING PERSONAL HYGIENE!
IF ANYONE'S LETTING THE SIDE DOWN, IT'S--
GRR -- THE PROBLEM IS PO -- NOT US!
HEY! HEY! TIME OUT!

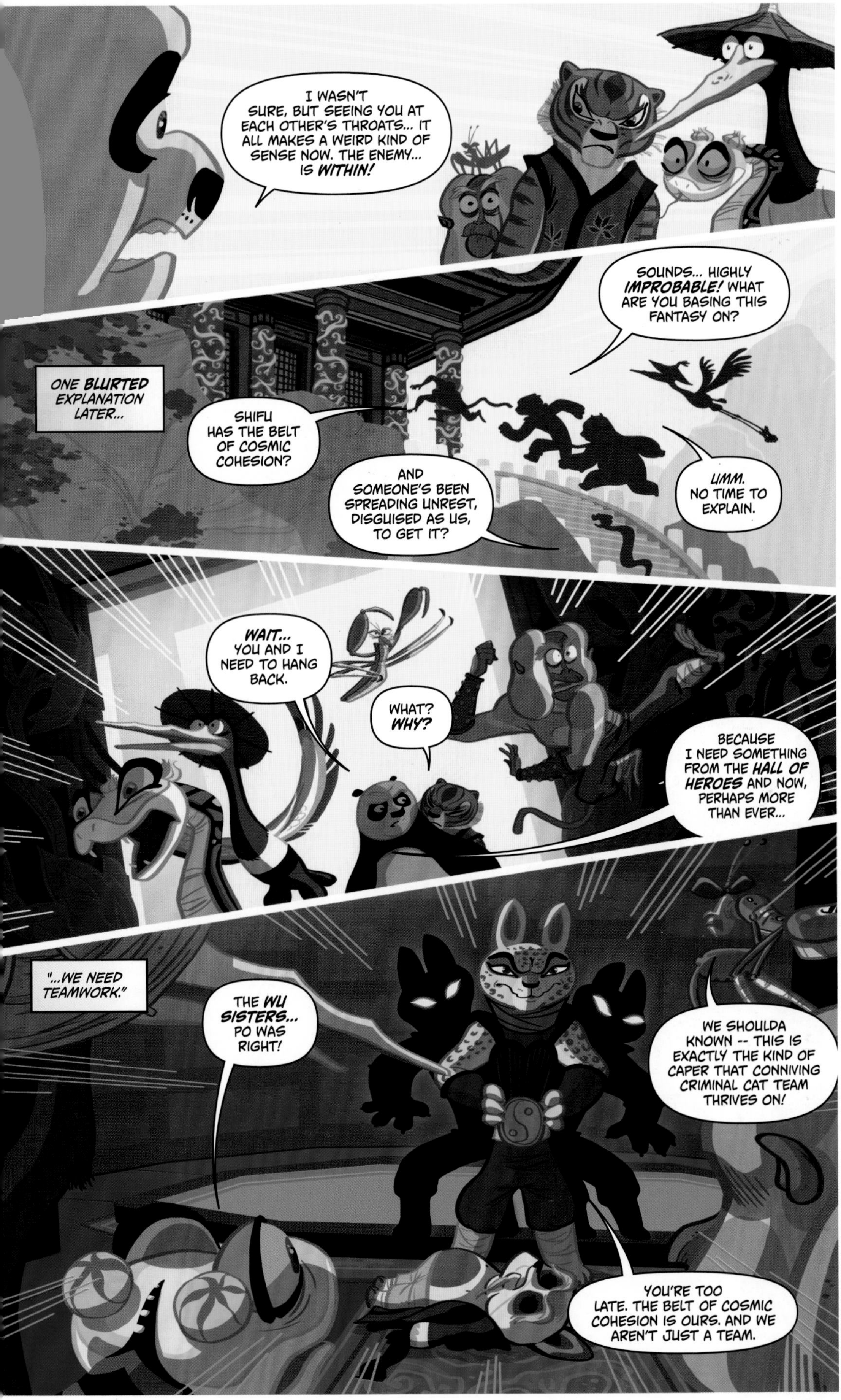

I WASN'T SURE, BUT SEEING YOU AT EACH OTHER'S THROATS... IT ALL MAKES A WEIRD KIND OF SENSE NOW. THE ENEMY... IS *WITHIN!*
SOUNDS... HIGHLY *IMPROBABLE!* WHAT ARE YOU BASING THIS FANTASY ON?
ONE **BLURTED** EXPLANATION LATER...
SHIFU HAS THE BELT OF COSMIC COHESION?
AND SOMEONE'S BEEN SPREADING UNREST, DISGUISED AS US, TO GET IT?
UMM. NO TIME TO EXPLAIN.
WAIT... YOU AND I NEED TO HANG BACK.
WHAT? **WHY?**
BECAUSE I NEED SOMETHING FROM THE **HALL OF HEROES** AND NOW, PERHAPS MORE THAN EVER...
"...WE NEED TEAMWORK."
THE **WU SISTERS...** PO WAS RIGHT!
WE SHOULDA KNOWN -- THIS IS EXACTLY THE KIND OF CAPER THAT CONNIVING CRIMINAL CAT TEAM THRIVES ON!
YOU'RE TOO LATE. THE BELT OF COSMIC COHESION IS OURS. AND WE AREN'T JUST A TEAM.

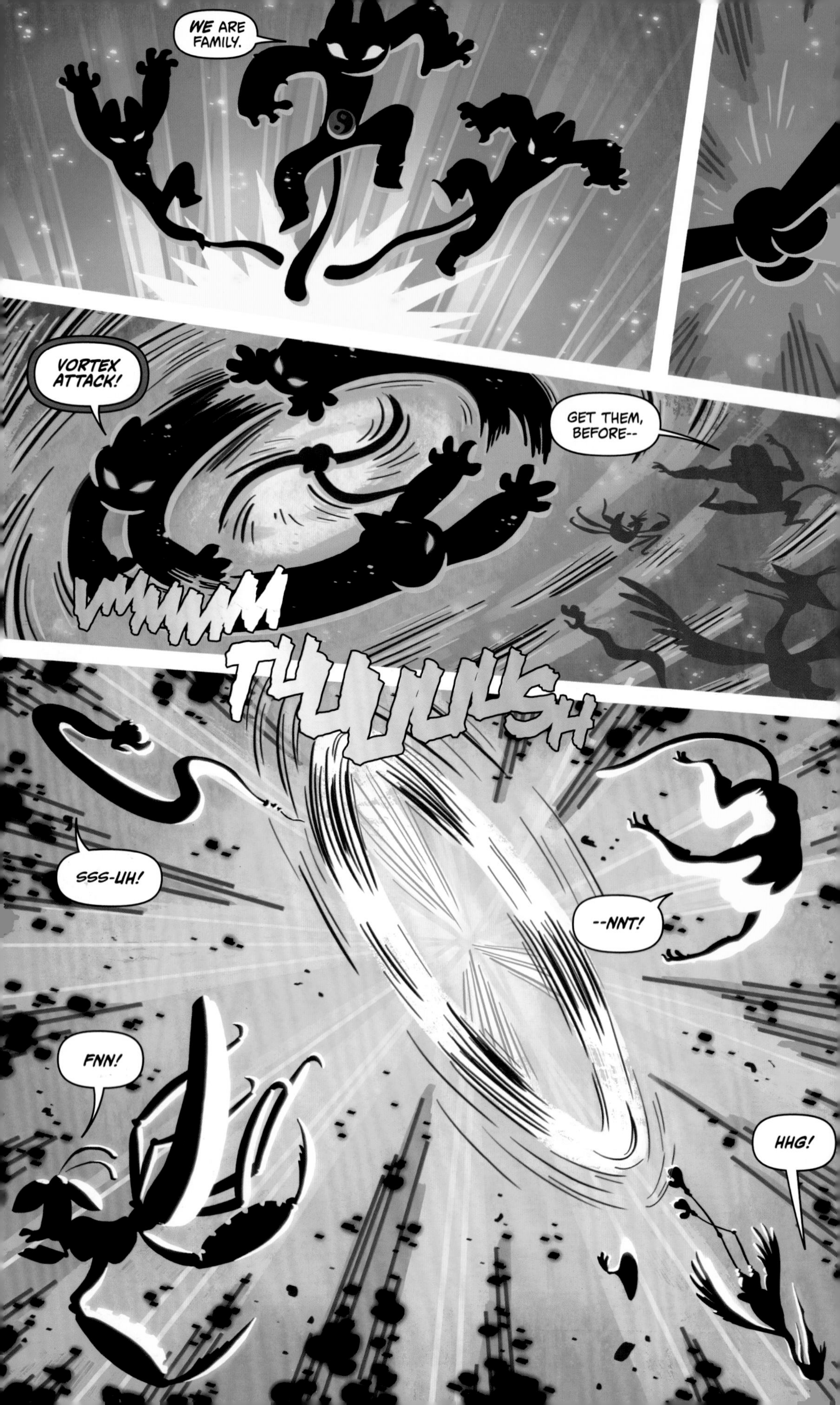
WE ARE FAMILY.
VORTEX ATTACK!
GET THEM, BEFORE--
VMMMM
TUUUUUSH
SSS-UH!
--NNT!
FNN!
HHG!

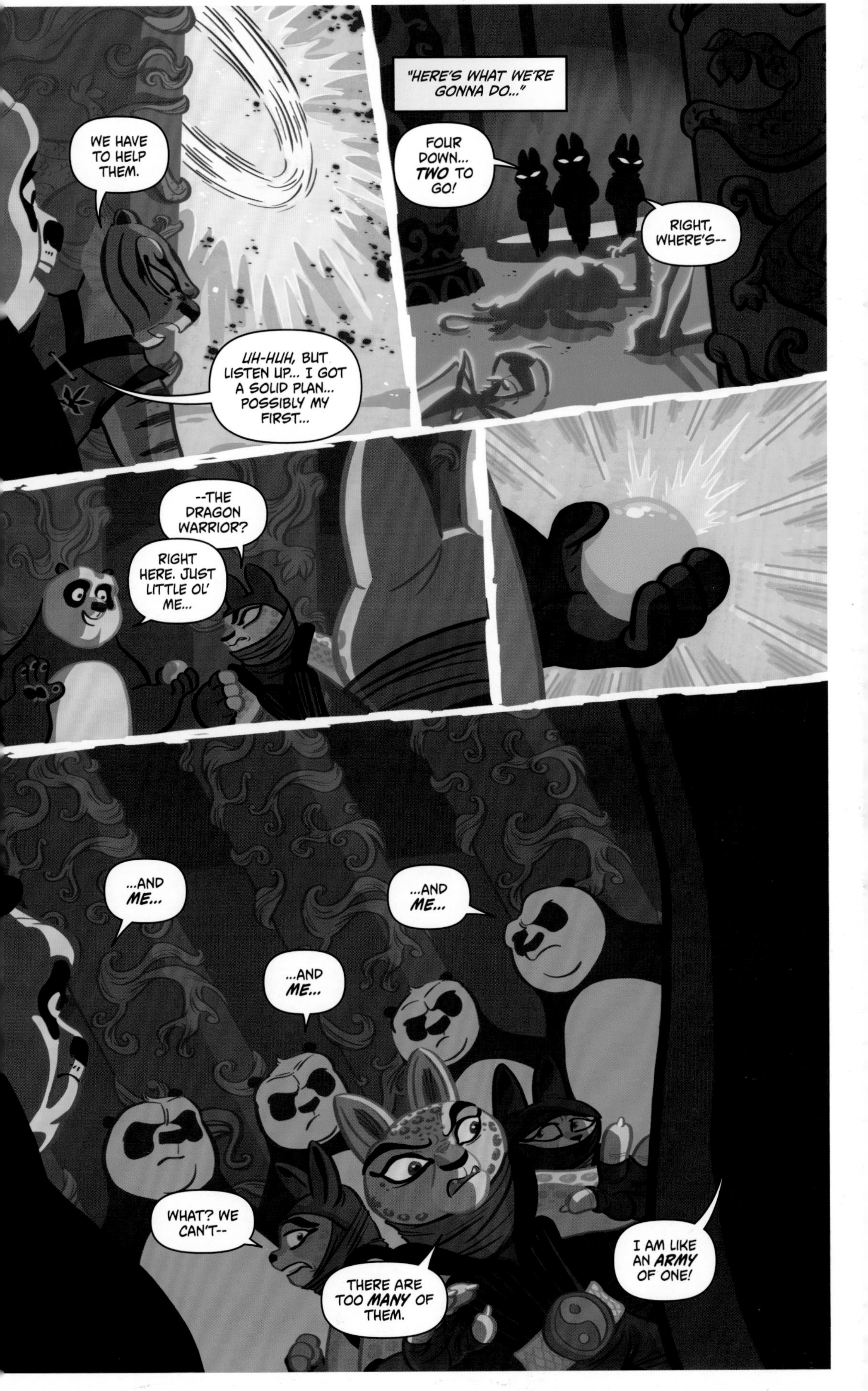
WE HAVE TO HELP THEM.
UH-HUH, BUT LISTEN UP... I GOT A SOLID PLAN... POSSIBLY MY FIRST...
"HERE'S WHAT WE'RE GONNA DO..."
FOUR DOWN... TWO TO GO!
RIGHT, WHERE'S--
--THE DRAGON WARRIOR?
RIGHT HERE. JUST LITTLE OL' ME...
...AND ME...
...AND ME...
...AND ME...
WHAT? WE CAN'T--
THERE ARE TOO MANY OF THEM.
I AM LIKE AN ARMY OF ONE!

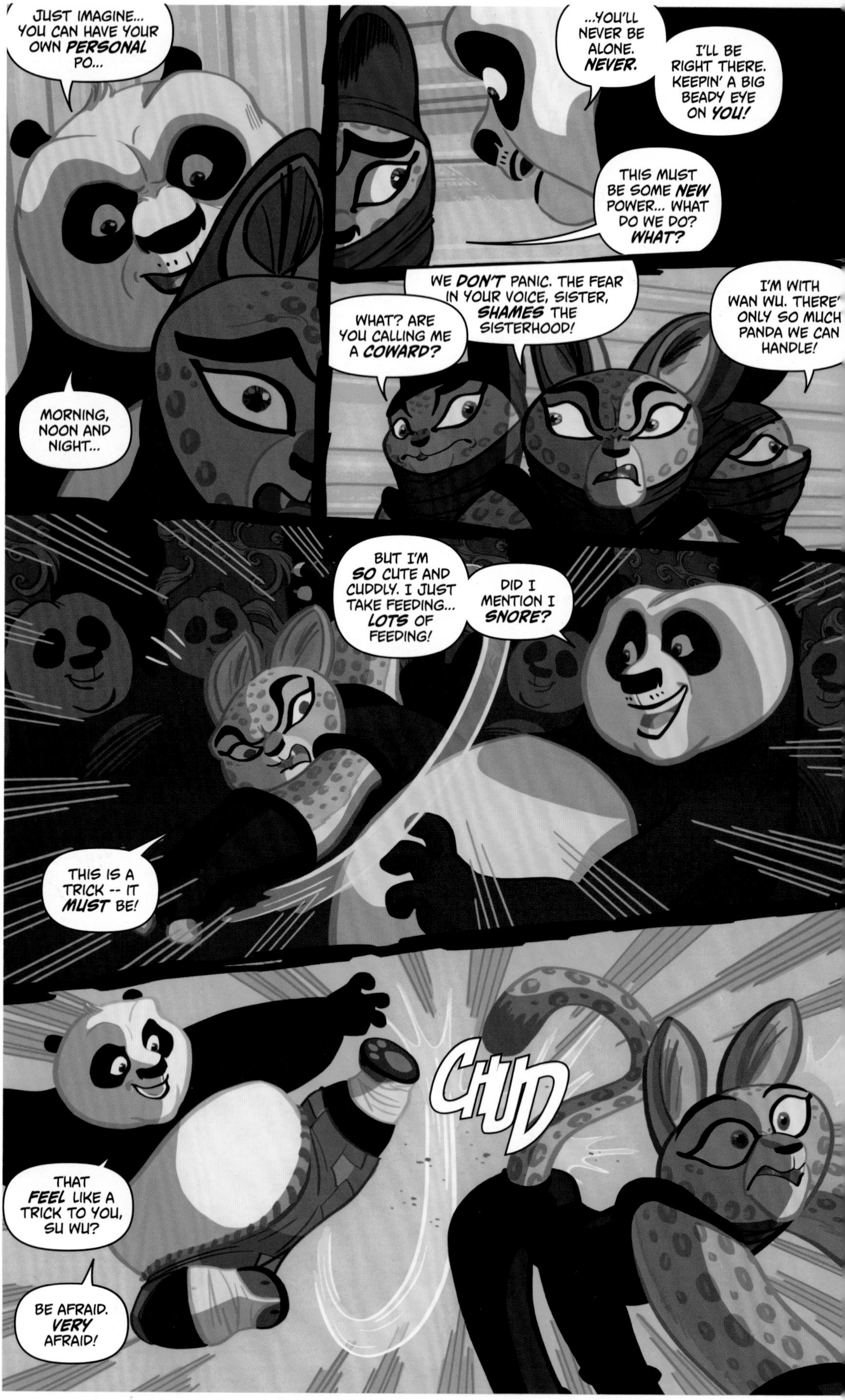

JUST IMAGINE... YOU CAN HAVE YOUR OWN PERSONAL PO...
MORNING, NOON AND NIGHT...
...YOU'LL NEVER BE ALONE. NEVER.
I'LL BE RIGHT THERE. KEEPIN' A BIG BEADY EYE ON YOU!
THIS MUST BE SOME NEW POWER... WHAT DO WE DO? WHAT?
WE DON'T PANIC. THE FEAR IN YOUR VOICE, SISTER, SHAMES THE SISTERHOOD!
WHAT? ARE YOU CALLING ME A COWARD?
I'M WITH WAN WU. THERE' ONLY SO MUCH PANDA WE CAN HANDLE!
BUT I'M SO CUTE AND CUDDLY. I JUST TAKE FEEDING... LOTS OF FEEDING!
DID I MENTION I SNORE?
THIS IS A TRICK -- IT MUST BE!
CHUD
THAT FEEL LIKE A TRICK TO YOU, SU WU?
BE AFRAID. VERY AFRAID!

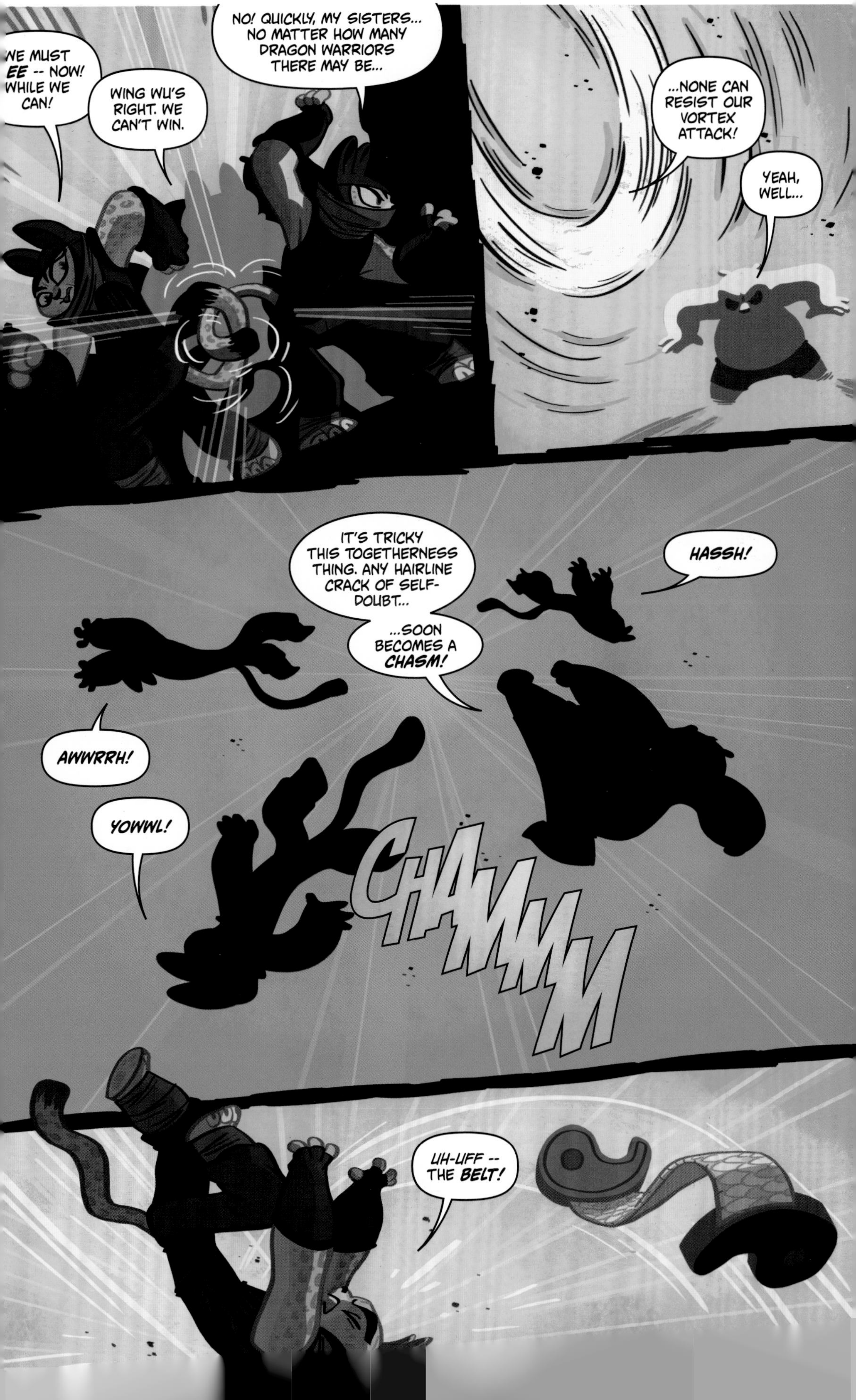

WE MUST EE -- NOW! WHILE WE CAN!
WING WU'S RIGHT. WE CAN'T WIN.
NO! QUICKLY, MY SISTERS... NO MATTER HOW MANY DRAGON WARRIORS THERE MAY BE...
...NONE CAN RESIST OUR VORTEX ATTACK!
YEAH, WELL...
IT'S TRICKY THIS TOGETHERNESS THING. ANY HAIRLINE CRACK OF SELF-DOUBT...
...SOON BECOMES A **CHASM!**
HASSH!
AWWRRH!
YOWWL!
CHAMMMM
UH-UFF -- THE **BELT!**

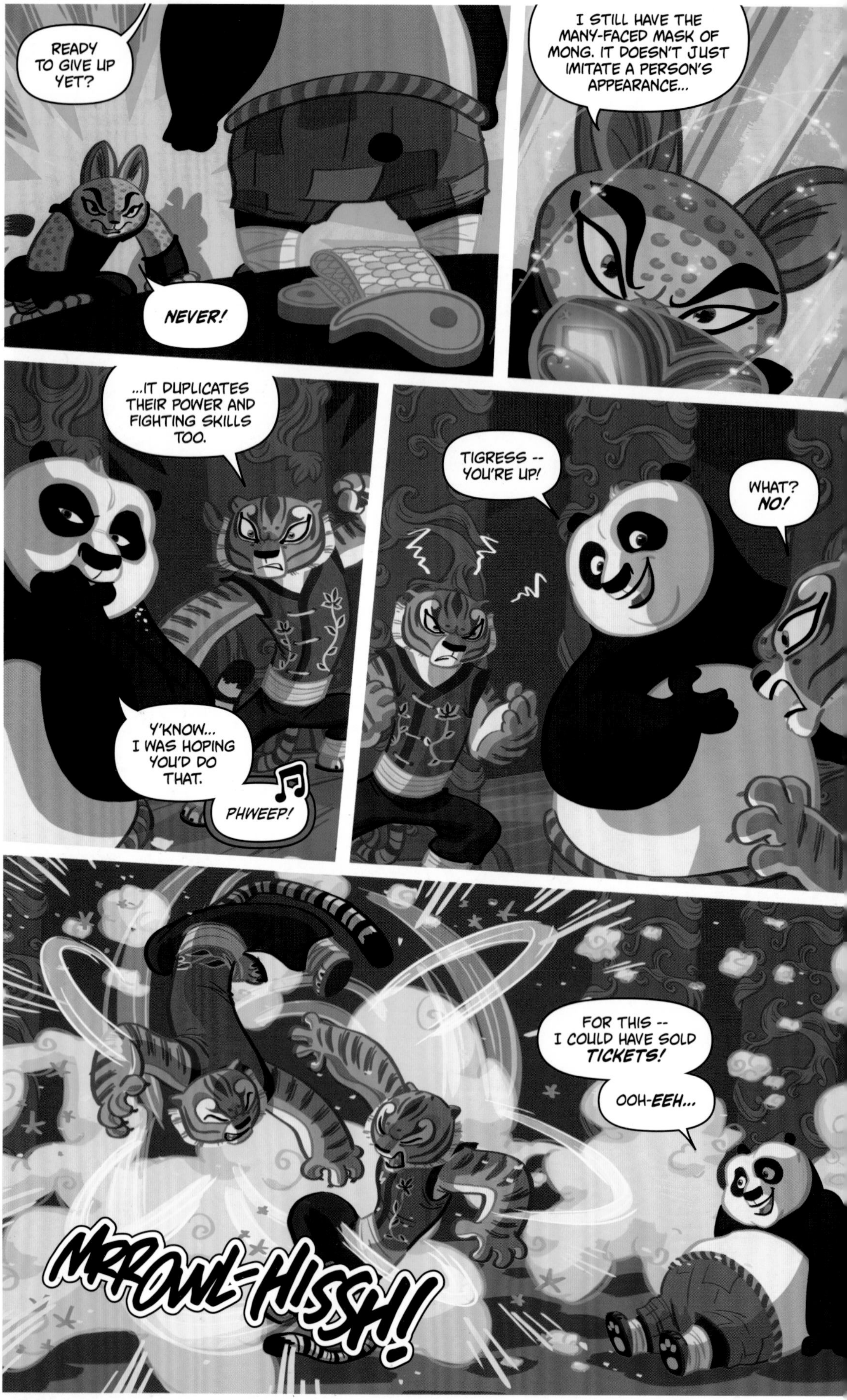
READY TO GIVE UP YET?
NEVER!
I STILL HAVE THE MANY-FACED MASK OF MONG. IT DOESN'T JUST IMITATE A PERSON'S APPEARANCE...
...IT DUPLICATES THEIR POWER AND FIGHTING SKILLS TOO.
Y'KNOW... I WAS HOPING YOU'D DO THAT.
PHWEEP!
TIGRESS -- YOU'RE UP!
WHAT? NO!
FOR THIS -- I COULD HAVE SOLD TICKETS!
OOH-EEH...
MRROWL-HISSH!

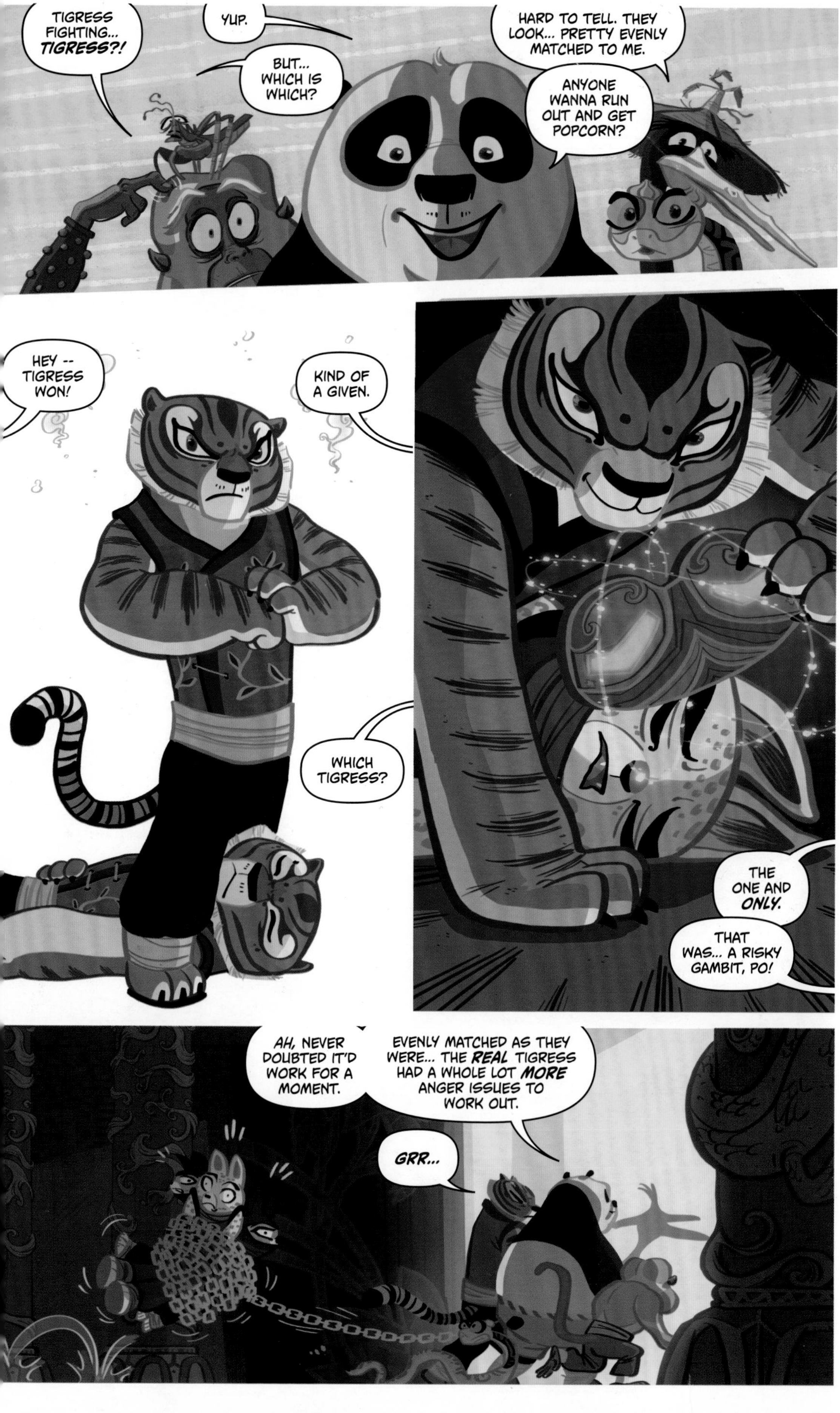
TIGRESS FIGHTING... *TIGRESS?!*
YUP.
BUT... WHICH IS WHICH?
HARD TO TELL. THEY LOOK... PRETTY EVENLY MATCHED TO ME.
ANYONE WANNA RUN OUT AND GET POPCORN?
HEY -- TIGRESS WON!
KIND OF A GIVEN.
WHICH TIGRESS?
THE ONE AND *ONLY.*
THAT WAS... A RISKY GAMBIT, PO!
AH, NEVER DOUBTED IT'D WORK FOR A MOMENT.
EVENLY MATCHED AS THEY WERE... THE *REAL* TIGRESS HAD A WHOLE LOT *MORE* ANGER ISSUES TO WORK OUT.
GRR...

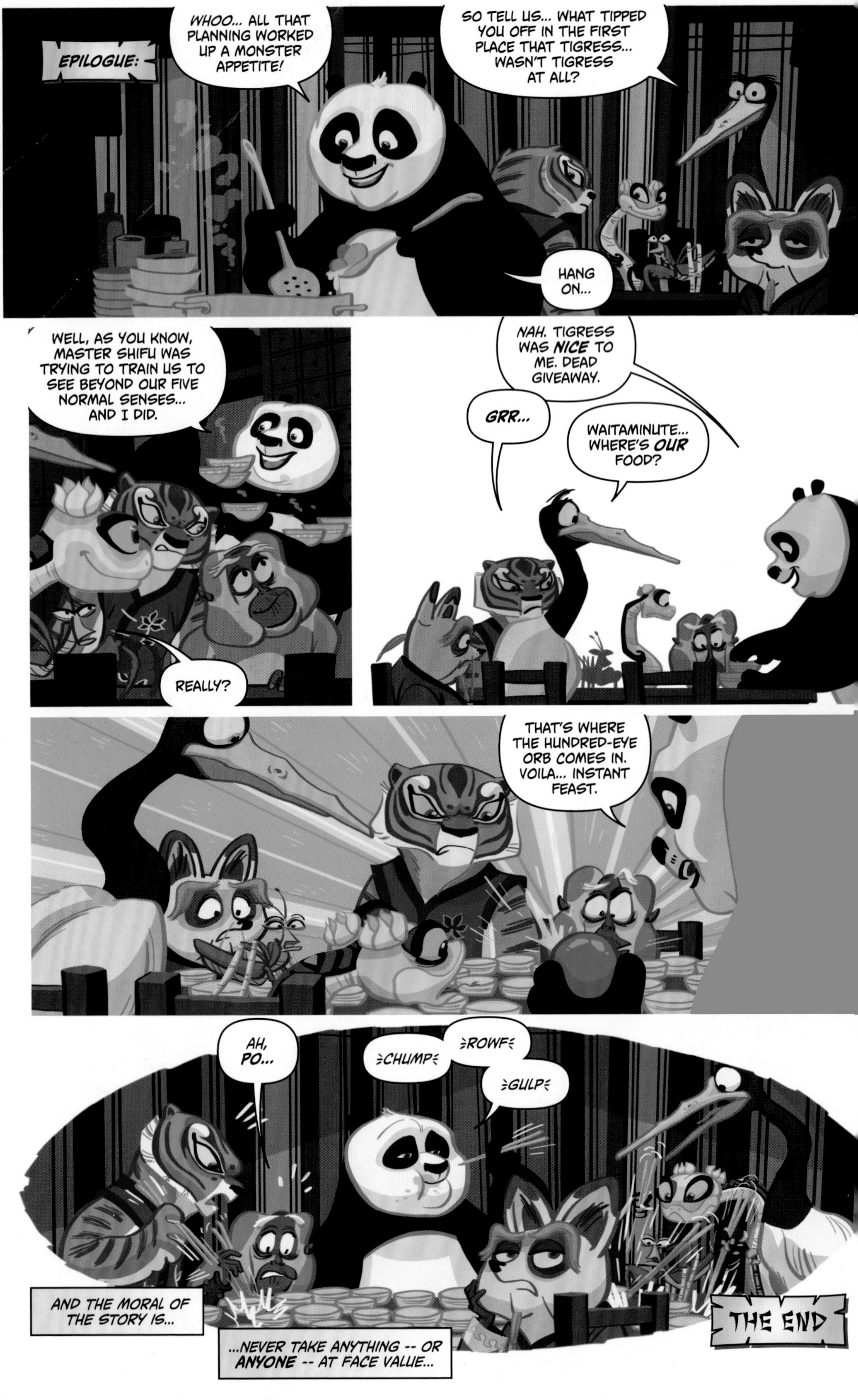
EPILOGUE:
WHOO... ALL THAT PLANNING WORKED UP A MONSTER APPETITE!
SO TELL US... WHAT TIPPED YOU OFF IN THE FIRST PLACE THAT TIGRESS... WASN'T TIGRESS AT ALL?
HANG ON...
WELL, AS YOU KNOW, MASTER SHIFU WAS TRYING TO TRAIN US TO SEE BEYOND OUR FIVE NORMAL SENSES... AND I DID.
REALLY?
NAH. TIGRESS WAS NICE TO ME. DEAD GIVEAWAY.
GRR...
WAITAMINUTE... WHERE'S OUR FOOD?
THAT'S WHERE THE HUNDRED-EYE ORB COMES IN. VOILA... INSTANT FEAST.
AH, PO...
CHUMP
ROWF
GULP
AND THE MORAL OF THE STORY IS...
...NEVER TAKE ANYTHING -- OR ANYONE -- AT FACE VALUE...
THE END

PO

NAME: Po

OTHER KNOWN ALIASES:
The Dragon Warrior

OCCUPATION: Dragon Warrior (and occasional Noodle Chef)

DAD: Mr Ping

KUNG FU TEACHER:
Master Shifu

FRIENDS: Tigress, Viper, Crane, Monkey and Mantis (AKA the Furious Five!)

TEACHER: Master Shifu

COMBAT STYLE: Panda Style

FAMOUS VICTORIES: Tai Lung and Lord Shen

INTERESTS: Kung fu, dumplings, noodles

WARRIOR SELECTION

Initially, many believed Po was mistakenly chosen as the Dragon Warrior. He had an accident with some fireworks and was launched up into the air, landing right in front of the great Master Oogway as he selected the Dragon Warrior. Oogway's finger settled on Po! But Oogway knew it was fate.

BECOMING THE DRAGON WARRIOR

It was no easy task; it meant a lot of hard work, and a lot of bruises! One day, Master Shifu presented Po with the Dragon Scroll, which contained the secret to limitless power, and only the true Dragon Warrior could grasp its meaning. Po proved himself, understanding that the secret was to believe in yourself.

ORIGIN

When Po was just a baby, his village was attacked by a peacock named Lord Shen. Po's mother sacrificed herself to save Po, hiding him in a crate of radishes. Whilst Mr. Ping was surprised to discover Po in his radish order, he happily adopted him.

TITAN COMICS COMIC BOOKS

AVAILABLE MONTHLY NOW!
ALSO AVAILABLE DIGITALLY.
WWW.TITAN-COMICS.COM

TITAN COMICS GRAPHIC NOVELS

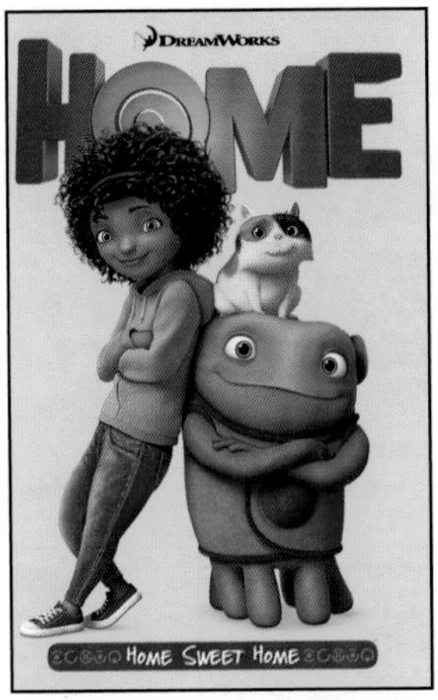
DreamWorks
HOME
HOME SWEET HOME

HOME: HOME SWEET HOME

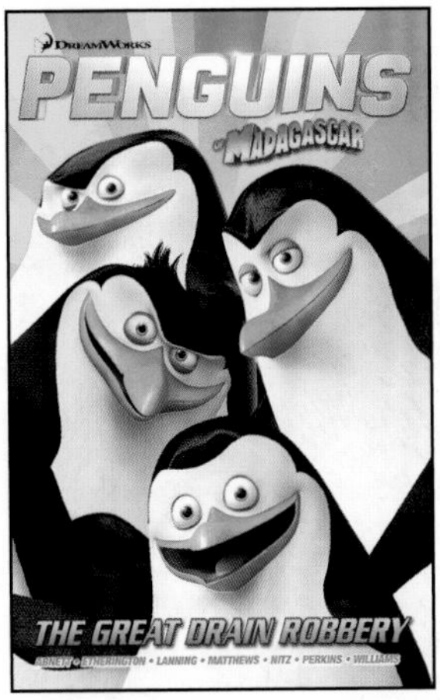
DreamWorks
PENGUINS
of MADAGASCAR
THE GREAT DRAIN ROBBERY

PENGUINS OF MADAGASCAR:
THE GREAT DRAIN ROBBERY

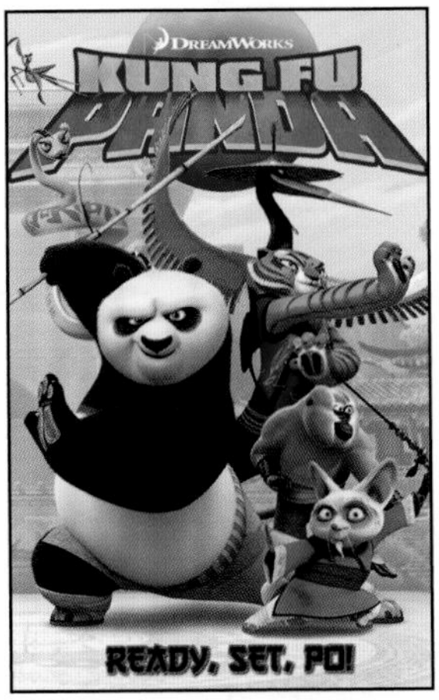
DreamWorks
KUNG FU PANDA
READY, SET, PO!

KUNG FU PANDA –
READY, SET, PO!

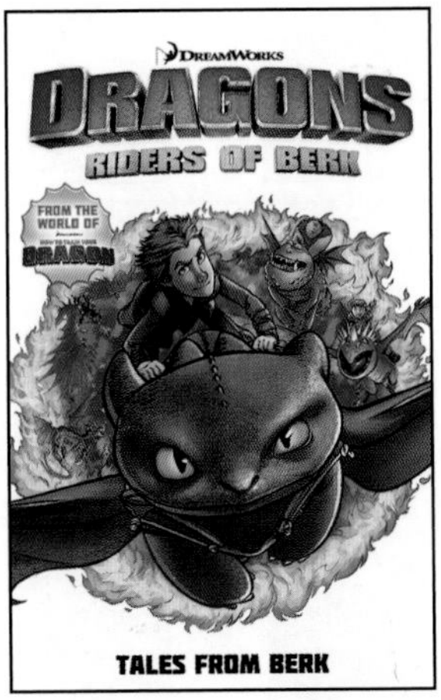
DreamWorks
DRAGONS
RIDERS OF BERK
FROM THE WORLD OF
DRAGON
TALES FROM BERK

DREAMWORKS DRAGONS:
RIDERS OF BERK – TALES FROM BERK

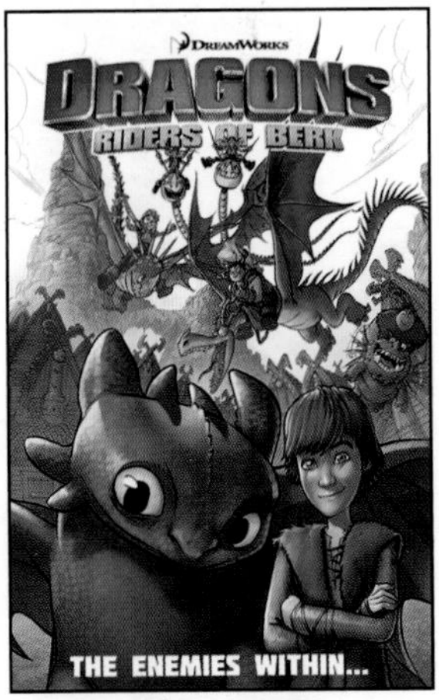
DreamWorks
DRAGONS
RIDERS OF BERK
THE ENEMIES WITHIN...

DREAMWORKS DRAGONS:
RIDERS OF BERK – THE ENEMIES WITHIN

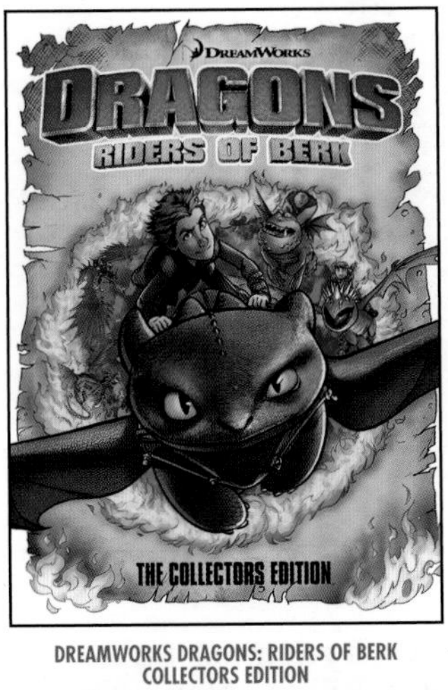
DreamWorks
DRAGONS
RIDERS OF BERK
THE COLLECTORS EDITION

DREAMWORKS DRAGONS: RIDERS OF BERK
COLLECTORS EDITION

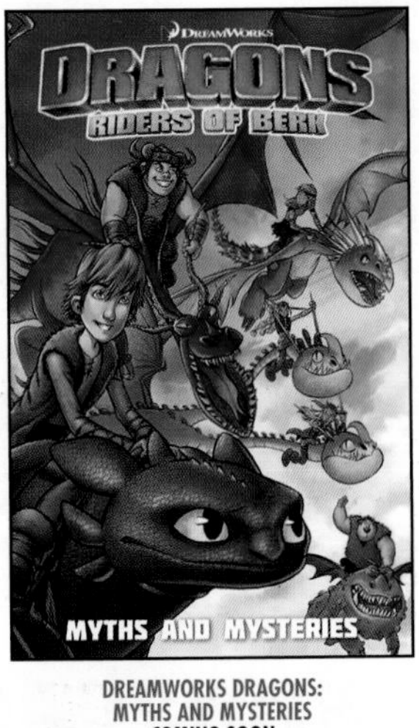
DreamWorks
DRAGONS
RIDERS OF BERK
MYTHS AND MYSTERIES

DREAMWORKS DRAGONS:
MYTHS AND MYSTERIES
COMING SOON

TITAN COMICS

WWW.TITAN-COMICS.COM

DreamWorks Animation SKG

TITAN COMICS DIGESTS

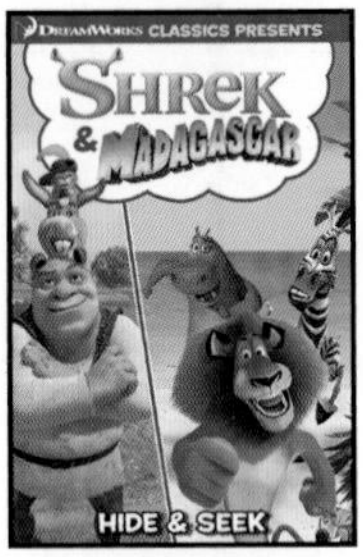
DreamWorks CLASSICS PRESENTS
SHREK
& MADAGASCAR
HIDE & SEEK

Dreamworks Classics
– 'Hide & Seek'

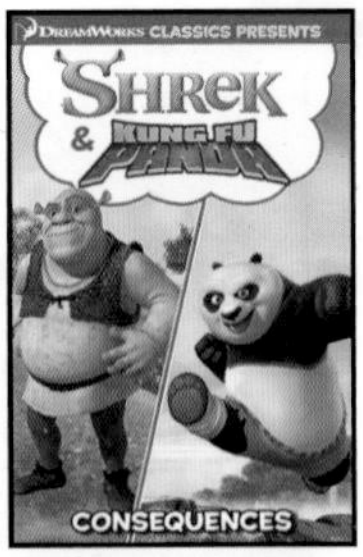
DreamWorks CLASSICS PRESENTS
SHREK
& KUNG FU PANDA
CONSEQUENCES

Dreamworks Classics
– 'Consequences'

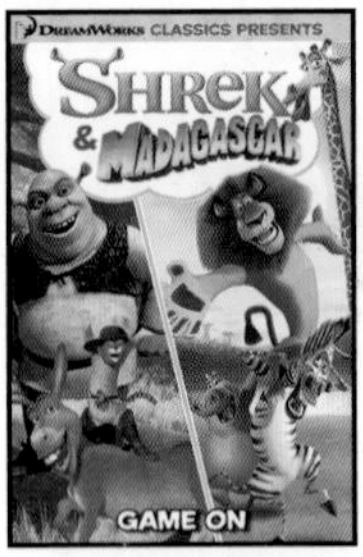
DreamWorks CLASSICS PRESENTS
SHREK
& MADAGASCAR
GAME ON

Dreamworks Classics
– 'Game On'

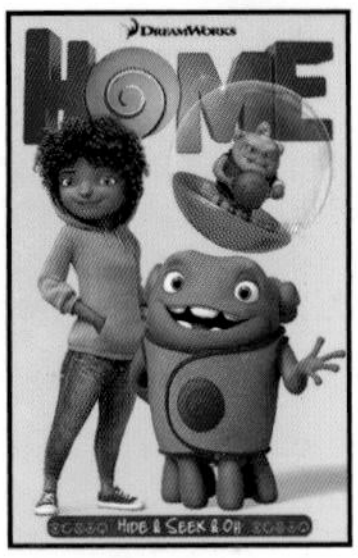
DreamWorks
HOME
HIDE & SEEK & OH

Home –
Hide & Seek & Oh

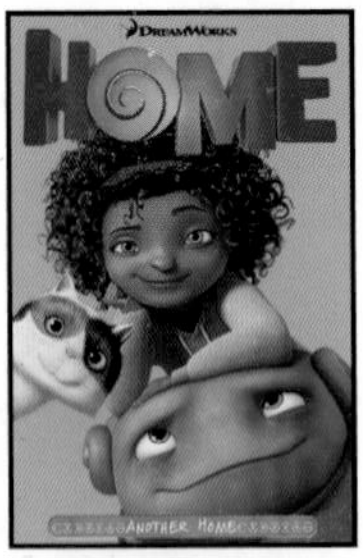
DreamWorks
HOME
ANOTHER HOME

Home –
Another Home

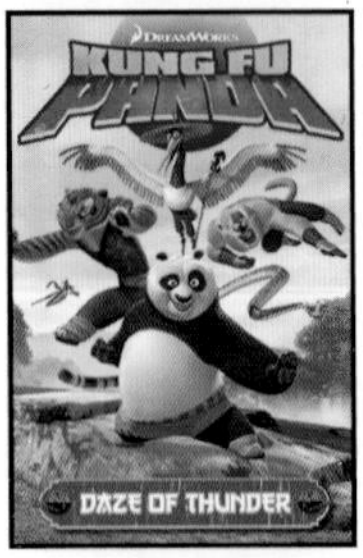
DreamWorks
KUNG FU PANDA
DAZE OF THUNDER

Kung Fu Panda –
Daze of Thunder

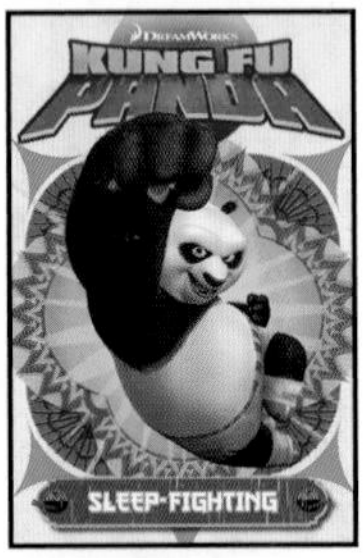
DreamWorks
KUNG FU PANDA
SLEEP-FIGHTING

Kung Fu Panda –
Sleep-Fighting

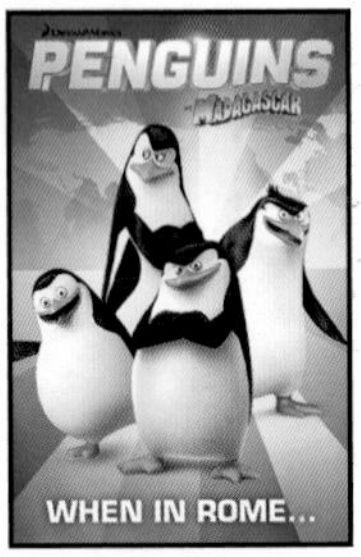
PENGUINS
OF MADAGASCAR
WHEN IN ROME...

Penguins of
Madagascar – When in
Rome...

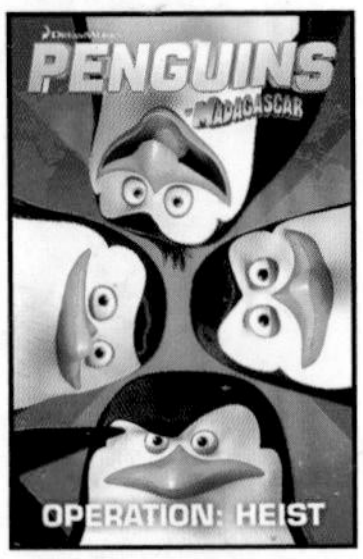
PENGUINS
OF MADAGASCAR
OPERATION: HEIST

Penguins of
Madagascar –
Operation: Heist

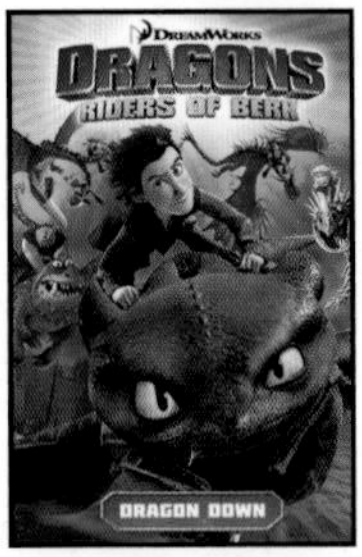
DRAGONS
RIDERS OF BERK
DRAGON DOWN

DreamWorks Dragons:
Riders of Berk –
Dragon Down

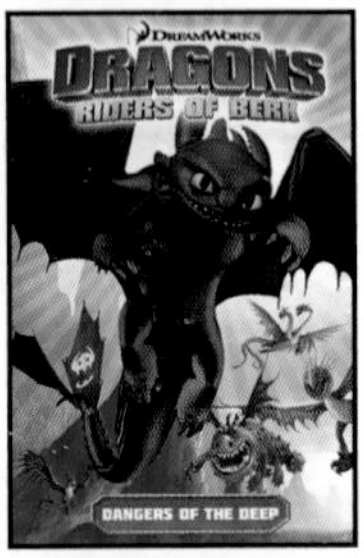
DRAGONS
RIDERS OF BERK
DANGERS OF THE DEEP

DreamWorks Dragons:
Riders of Berk –
Dangers of the Deep

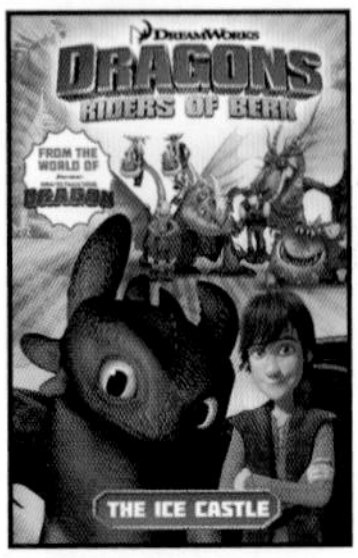
DRAGONS
RIDERS OF BERK
THE ICE CASTLE

DreamWorks Dragons:
Riders of Berk –
The Ice Castle

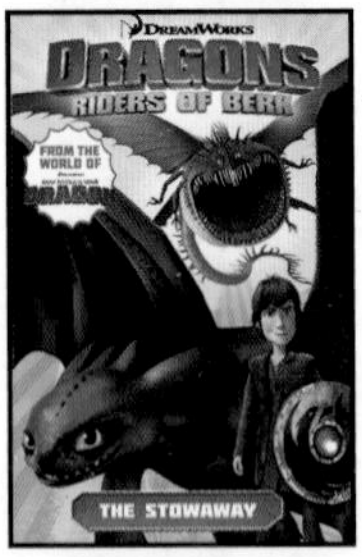
DRAGONS
RIDERS OF BERK
THE STOWAWAY

DreamWorks Dragons:
Riders of Berk –
The Stowaway

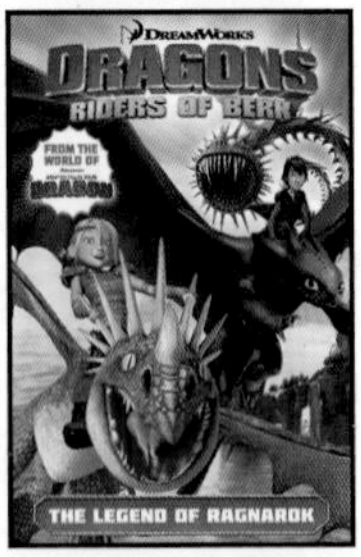
DRAGONS
RIDERS OF BERK
THE LEGEND OF RAGNAROK

DreamWorks Dragons:
Riders of Berk – The
Legend of Ragnarok

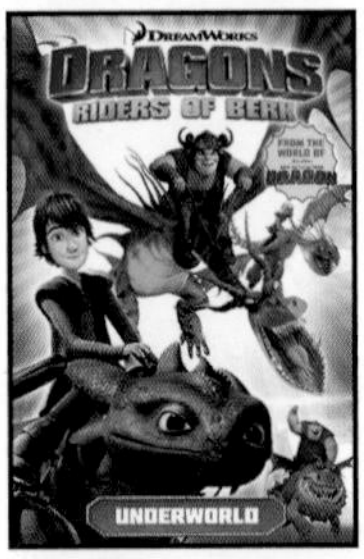
DRAGONS
RIDERS OF BERK
UNDERWORLD

DreamWorks Dragons:
Riders of Berk –
Underworld

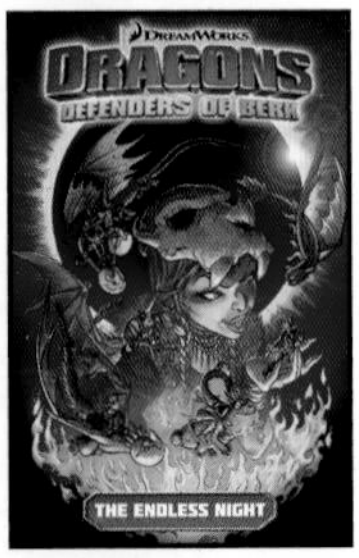
DRAGONS
DEFENDERS OF BERK
THE ENDLESS NIGHT

DreamWorks Dragons:
Defenders of Berk -
The Endless Night

WWW.TITAN-COMICS.COM

ALSO AVAILABLE DIGITALLY

TITAN COMICS

DREAMWORKS ANIMATION SKG